THE
KAMINSKY
CURE

THE KAMINSKY CURE

Christopher New

DELPHINIUM BOOKS

HARRISON, NEW YORK • ENCINO, CALIFORNIA

THE KAMINSKY CURE

First Edition

Cover and interior design by Jonathan Lippincott

Library of Congress Catalogue-in-Publication Data is available on request.

ISBN 978-1-88-328567-8

16   17   18   RRD   10   9   8   7   6   5   4   3   2   1

*I owe a special debt to Evelyn Toynton for her encouragement and to my editor
Joseph Olshan for his perceptive comments and suggestions. Without them this edition
of* The Kaminsky Cure *would not have come about.*

THE
KAMINSKY
CURE

1

Well here I am at five and three-quarters

It's Christmas 1939 in a little Austrian village that's now part of Hitler's Third Reich and I'm just beginning to notice things. Like what my brother and sisters are about and why my parents are often crying and my father usually shouting when he isn't crying. I think it has something to do with the war we're fighting, which according to the wireless is due to The International Jewish Conspiracy, whatever that is. But that's not all. I don't know it yet, but I was born at the wrong time and in the wrong place.

Not that it wasn't quite an achievement getting me born at all. I arrived too early, presented myself the wrong way round (Was I trying to climb back inside? You couldn't blame me), there was no doctor, and the midwife had to yank me out like a cork from a bottle. No wonder I protested. No wonder my mother never had another child, either—both of us had had enough. But anyway there I was, a pint-sized runt, the last of the litter, and that's how I've stayed.

Achievement or not though, you could say my getting born, or conceived for that matter, was really a big mistake. First of all there's the as yet unraised question of my paternity. (Paternity's

3

going to be a favorite topic in my family.) And then there's the undoubted fact, though I don't know that yet either, that my mother Gabi is a Jew (she converted to Christianity in her teens), while my very Aryan father Willibald Brinkmann—if he is my father—is a Lutheran pastor who has a sneaking admiration for Hitler. (Many Lutheran pastors have, and for some of them it isn't sneaking, either—they're openly trying to prove that Jesus wasn't really a Jew.) On top of that they don't like each other anyway.

For all these reasons they each wish they weren't married to who they are. But separation is just about unthinkable. For one thing, marriage is supposed to be a sacred union for Lutheran clergymen. For another, the only thing that can protect my mother and possibly us children is that she's married to an Aryan. And Willibald's admiration for the little corporal doesn't extend so far that he'd actually throw us to the Nazi wolves.

My sister Ilse, the oldest child, is closest to him, insofar as anyone is. She goes in fear of a Jewish curse (that is, our mother's) and wishes she could become a nun. My brother Martin is my mother's favorite. He wants to be a Panzer commander when he grows up, which in a sense he never will. Sara's nearest me in age. Her only wish is to sit next to one of the other girls in the village school (even Leni, just in front of her, who has head lice), instead of being relegated in despised half-Jewish exile to the back of the class alone.

None of these wishes is going to come true.

The village we live in, Heimstatt, is lodged deep in the Alps, squeezed between the cliff-like mountains and a black and glacial lake that holds many bodies and many secrets, with more of both to come. For five months of the year the winter sun never makes it above the surrounding mountain tops, and when the merest sliver of it makes its first brief gleaming reappearance each spring, the villagers all come out of their houses to watch and celebrate. The chief business of this ancient place is its ancient quarry, the chief characteristics of its inhabitants inbreeding and goiters. People were living here in the Stone Age, and some of them still are.

I'm told it was snowing when I was born, and I believe it, because it's always snowing here in Heimstatt in February. Thick silent wodges of it, filling the somber daylight with their muffling presence. The mountains that stand like grim gravediggers round the coffin-shaped valley become invisible, and you can hardly even see the lake, which is frozen solid except for the swath the ferry crunches through the ice as it grinds its way across to the railway station on the other side. Gloomy and cold—it's not an auspicious way to start your life.

Ilse came in to see me in my parents' bed soon after I bawled my indignant birth-announcement out. Giving me the ghost of a tender smile and a bit less for my mother, she returned like a shadow to the cloister of her chilly room. Ilse was made for a quiet life, but a quiet life has not been made for her.

When Martin was allowed, or rather cajoled, in to see me, he took an even more cursory glance. My appearance in the world didn't interest him very much, and my continuation in it doesn't either. Nothing ever does interest him very much, in fact, except himself.

Sara came in last. She peered across the bed to where I lay exhausted beside my mother like a blob of toothpaste that's been squeezed out of a too narrow tube, then put her hand out to stroke—not my face, crumpled and outraged as it was—but my mother's, one side of which is always stiff and set, as though half of her can't smile anymore. Which it can't. Then she went off to sit by the big green tile oven in the kitchen and tell herself another story. Since the real world was disappointing her already, she'd begun building a make-believe one instead, a refuge where she could refashion the days of her life before going back to face them.

The midwife was soon heading for the door, wrapped up to go and deliver the next baby, and if Frau Kogler thought anything about helping Jewish women reproduce, she didn't say so (but then the Nazis hadn't taken over yet). Her lifelong boast is going to be that in all the three villages she was responsible for she never had two babies arrive at the same time, a coincidence she'll put down to a benevolent Providence rather than the essentially casual and unsynchronized character of alpine coupling. Or would she put *that* down to Providence too?

Willibald is given to powerful bursts of emotion, whether of joy or anger, and on the day of my birth, having tearfully thanked God rather than Frau Kogler for a safe delivery, he spent the next few hours in his study composing doggerel about the miracle of life and God's gift of another child. He's over six feet tall (or would be if he unrolled himself and stood up straight), but stooping, hollow-chested and narrow-shouldered. He also wears a cat's pelt, a tabby of no great distinction, next to his skin, which he claims prevents rheumatism. He's never separated from prophylactic Tabby and they even bathe together in the zinc bath once a week, after which Tabby gets dried on the tile oven in the kitchen along with the towel. If my mother had to share the wedding night with Tabby, it's not surprising she soon fell out of love.

Whenever they meet a hard stare, Willibald's large brown eyes slide away like raw eggs slipping off a tilted plate. But he uses them to melting effect in church, where he's a throbbing histrionic preacher and never has to lock eyes with a single soul. In Heimstatt no one understands his sermons, and almost no one comes to hear them. But things have been better in the past and will be so again. His most appreciative audience though will always be himself.

A Protestant pastor in a Catholic country, his congregation consists of about a dozen rigid elders who come to nearly every service, and a couple of hundred flaccid backsliders, who rarely come at all. The Catholic church up the hill by contrast is larger and always full, and at first Willibald, watching the villagers going to midnight mass on Christmas Eve—seven hundred strong and all carrying lighted candles—must have felt like a snake-oil salesman wondering if he isn't marketing the wrong brand. But for a long time now he's had other and more pressing things to worry about, and he will have for a good while still to come.

The other creatures in the Pfarrhaus—parsonage—when I was born were Frau Jäger, who cleans for and filches from us, a Saint Bernard dog called Brutus, several rabbits and a few rats in the cellar. All of them are purebred Austrians with village pedigrees a meter long. But *we* are of different stock, we are not like them at all. No, my parents are German, native Berliners. They speak High German, and however much they try, they can no more get their tonsils round the local yodel than they can fit their limbs inside the local dress—which is one more strike against them in the village, as if there weren't enough already.

I don't know it yet, but we are here only because my father's marriage to his no longer loved or loving Jewish wife cost him his fashionable parish in Germany. No sooner had the Nazis been voted into power there than a trio of brawny Brownshirts turned up on his doorstep and told him to go and find another twig to perch on. He was offered a refuge in England by the Bishop of Chichester, but his patriotism prevented him from going to a country which might one day be at war again with the Fatherland. (Patriotism's going to be another favorite family topic.) So he found a parish in neighboring pre-Nazi Austria, which he should have known was more or less like jumping out of the fire into the frying pan. It didn't take long to feel the heat again. I'd only just had my fourth birthday in fact when our German brothers marched into Austria amid general jubilation to unite us with the Fatherland and rid us of the malignant Jew, whatever that was. (I thought it was something like the rats in the coal cellar.)

I woke to find Heimstatt in a party mood that March day, with swastikas flapping in the breeze over every house but ours. "We've been united with the Fatherland," Willibald said in mingled pride and fear. Then he locked himself in his study and I heard him alternately crying and shouting. Frau Jäger and my mother swiftly closed the windows; I didn't understand why—it wasn't a cold day.

We children weren't allowed out. We never were. Standing on the balcony of the huge rambling Pfarrhaus, we watched the processions like bemused prisoners at a Roman triumph—or in my case like a child that hasn't been invited to the next-door kid's birthday party. When I waved and cheered with the rest of the village, my mother told me to stop that at once; when I started jeering, she told me to stop that too. So what was I supposed to do? Martin told me to just shut up, so I did that.

I concluded the reason why we'd been excluded from the celebration was that we were proper Germans, while the Austrians were not, little knowing that in fact it was the other way round and it was now the Austrians who were proper Germans while were not. Nobody told me what had really happened, what it really meant, knowledge being rightly considered more dangerous in my case than ignorance. Never mind, the false conceit propped up my self-esteem. I came to think we Brinkmanns were a people apart, a Chosen People. As indeed we were. Chosen for what, I fortunately didn't know. But I certainly enjoyed lighting the obligatory candle in my window that night to celebrate the Führer's return to his native land. It almost made up for not being allowed to hang out a swastika during the day.

■

How much apart we were Gabi was naturally the first to realize. The inadequate painter in Berlin had turned his attention back to the land of his birth well before the Union, and a frothy stream of anti-Semitism had begun to flow into the village like shit from a leaking sewer, except that there wasn't a sewer to get leaks in yet. Month after month she'd felt people turning against her. At first her "racial background" was merely like a hump or cast in the eye. It made people uneasy, and she began to feel less welcome as the Pfarrer's wife, the visitor to the sick and comforter of the bereaved. Still she persisted, and no one shut the door on her. Then her race became something vaguely sinister, like a gypsy's curse. That was when some doors were shut and those that weren't were opened grudgingly. Finally, after the Union, it was like a leper's sore, and everyone with any sense avoided her completely.

In the beginning, before she got used to it, she would stop people in the street or lane and ask them why they'd cut her. She was afraid she might have offended them by some chance remark—she knew tact wasn't one of her strong points, although she lacked the worldly wisdom to see that worldly wisdom wasn't either. One laborer's wife with rotting teeth and breath to match gave it to her fair and square: "Because Jewish blood stinks!" she spat out before she turned and stumped off on her grim self-righteous way.

All that had made being a Pfarrer's wife difficult enough, not to speak of her unhappy marriage. But since Union with the Fatherland, the life of a Pfarrer's wife has been as closed to her as the local inn, the park and the public bench (I needn't add the public baths).

Precious few in the village will speak to her now, a precious, precious few who go their stolid independent way and take her as she is. Frau Jäger, an illiterate natural poet and filcher of food. Fraülein Hofer, the seamstress. Frau Kogler, the midwife, who dragged me rightly complaining into this world. And Tante Helga, the blind geography teacher, who doesn't really count because she's an outsider like us, an immigrant from Vienna. Blind as a bat, but you should see her open her atlas, feel the corners of the page, then place her finger unerringly on Moscow, Paris or London. She could teach navigation to Luftwaffe pilots. She knows about flying blind all right.

Of the village men, there are still fewer who will pass the time of day with Gabi now. And even so, one of those few, few men is the Catholic priest, who's really an outsider too, an immigrant like Tante Helga. Besides, he greets everyone anyway, because he's too shortsighted to see who they are. And Dr. Koch, the village doctor, who though he's not allowed to treat her, shyly says "Grüss Gott" when he meets her in the lanes. And Dr. Kraus, who's not a doctor for people, and whose wife wears a wig—he nods at everyone as well, although he never speaks. But they're all outsiders too.

■

Soon after the Union, Frau Jäger was summoned to newly installed Ortsgruppenleiter (District Head) and also innkeeper Franzi Wimmer's office and informed she must immediately stop working in a Jewish household. That was illegal according to The Law For The Protection Of German Blood And German Honor: *No Aryan female under forty-five years of age shall work in a Jewish household.*

But Jägerlein, as we call her, has a mind of her own. "It's not a Jewish household," she said flatly, "it's the Lutheran minister's. And he's much more German than you are."

Which was true, of course, and stung. Some Austrians tend to have this nagging suspicion that other people think they stand to Germany as a light operetta stands to the whole of Wagner; and Franzi Wimmer, although he's never seen an opera, is one of them. Is that why some of the most fervent Nazis, starting with the Führer himself, are Austrians? Are they trying to prove they aren't just bit players in some light operetta, but can sing along with the leads in *Twilight of the Gods?*

"His *wife* is Jewish," Ortsgruppenleiter Franzi rejoined with irritated and ponderous distinctness. He'd known Frau Jäger all his life and, no genius himself, thought she was a bit simple.

"So it's a half-Jewish household, then," Jägerlein answered. "And you can just say I'm working for the Aryan half. Are you going to give me a job if I leave them? And besides," she added as she marched out, "what harm has that woman ever done you? She's only looking after her kids like everyone else. Why don't you just leave her alone?"

Most people wear their wickedness a bit uneasily, like a suit they've bought off the peg. It just doesn't quite fit them. They can throw their shoulders back and puff out their chests and suck their bellies in as much as they like, but still the thing just doesn't hang like one that's tailor-made for them. And Franzi Wimmer's no exception. He never does get really used to it, he never can quite fill it out. The fact is, he's just too small for normal wickedness, never mind outsize. Besides, he'd got nothing against the Pfarrer, so why not do the man a favor if you could? You never knew when it might come in useful.

So far as Jägerlein was concerned, then, Franzi decided to let things go until someone kicked his ass and made him do something about it. After all, if anyone pulled him up, he could always argue like Jägerlein that it wasn't strictly a Jewish household according to the letter of the law. And he's going to be a stickler for the letter of the law all right, although it takes him quite a while to make it out. So Jägerlein is still with us.

So is Brutus the Saint Bernard. Next to Jägerlein, he's my best friend. He pulls me round the garden on a little cart with wonky wheels from a discarded pram. Jägerlein or my mother fits the harness for Brutus and puts him, docile and happy, between the shafts. I clamber onto the cart and off we go. Or if the snow is deep, as it is just now, it's a homemade sledge he pulls round the garden, not the cart. I love that dog and he loves me. I probably love him more than anything else in the world, though I don't know if he reciprocates exactly. He loves his bone to chew on too.

The rabbits are still there in their hutches as well. I don't love them so much. And the rats in the cellar, of course. I don't love them at all.

But my maternal grandfather that I've never seen, and therefore don't love either—he isn't anywhere anymore. He died in Berlin several months ago, before the war started. That wasn't the first time I'd seen Gabi crying, when the letter announcing his death arrived, but it was the first time she told me why. "Your grandfather used to be very well-off," she said, dabbing her eyes on her apron. "But then things changed and—" She told me to go and play outside with Brutus.

I asked Ilse, who was reading the Bible in the garden, whether this grandfather that I'd never known had gone to heaven, but Ilse looked doubtful and said she didn't know. I didn't really care much about heaven anyway, so I went to play with Brutus and forgot about my grandfather. I didn't really care about grandfathers either, or grandmothers or uncles and aunts for that matter, because I'd never seen one, any more than I'd seen heaven. And Martin told me a minute later, as he yanked Brutus away from me, that I probably never would see one, since half of them were dead and the other half were . . . But then Ilse glanced up from her Bible and said "Shh, Martin!" He laughed and said "So what?" as he tugged Brutus away. But he wouldn't tell me any more.

All this was puzzling and I might have asked Sara next, since Sara's closer to me in age and everything else, but Sara wasn't there. And Brutus came bounding back because he liked me better than Martin, so I forgot all about it till that night. Then, as I was going to bed, I asked Sara if my other grandfather was well-off too, and she said he was dead now also, but no, she didn't think so, he'd always been rather poor and that was why he was a Nazi, which made no sense at all to me. Gabi's sister, our aunt Frieda, whom I've also never met, was dead as well, she added dreamily. "She used to be a nurse, but then . . ."

Another uncompleted sentence, but I'm getting used to them. It won't be long before I'll know how to finish them, but in the meantime I've got other things to worry about, and so have Sara, Ilse and Martin. My greatest worry is the outside toilet with its gut-wrenching drop beneath the wooden seat down to a dark and noisome pit that gets emptied only twice a year. It's that dark pit, by the way, not any flag-waving, goose-stepping Nazis, that has so far been the terror of my life. In fact I loved and still love the Nazis' uniforms and their bands and their proud solidity—if only I could follow right behind them whenever they march through the village as the other boys do! But that black pit—that's pure terror, and doubly pure at night! What if I fall through the hole in the worn wooden seat? It's big enough. What if something black and slimy slides smoothly up out of it like a serpent of shit to coil itself lovingly around my shivering naked thighs and pull me down under?

But what's a worry to me is nothing to them. They can trot out there in the middle of the night without a qualm. No, it's education that's on their mind, or rather more on Gabi's. They can't go to the nearest high school in Plinden. Not because they're not allowed to—the authorities see no reason at present why half-Jews shouldn't get a limited education to fit them for their limited half-Jew roles in the Thousand Year Reich. No, the problem is it's too far for them to travel by train every day (three hours each way), and although a provident State has arranged lodgings near the school for pupils from far away, it isn't going to lodge half-Jewish children in real Aryan homes. (Nor is it going to lodge them in half-Jewish homes, let alone full-Jewish ones. All the Jews in Plinden have either left already for one thing, or been rounded up and expelled by the zealous Nazi Bürgermeister. And there aren't any half-Jews there anyway for another— we are a lonely breed.)

Now that's a wobble in the orderly arrangements of the Thousand Year Reich: half-Jewish children can go to school with Aryan bluebloods (well, for a time, anyway), but they can't stay in lodgings with them. What did the Nazis think they'd get up to there? Buggery and fornication with the master race? And who exactly did they fear would be doing what to whom? Never mind, mongrel tykes and purebred hounds just shouldn't mix.

So there's a law that all non-Jewish children must attend school, and that means us, because we're not kosher Jews, even if we're not kosher Germans either. And there's a residential regulation that denies Ilse, Martin and Sara (who's about to start high school) the means of doing so. When Willibald meekly presented this paradox to the authorities, the more lowly functionaries were as usual disinclined to consider it.

"If you must marry a Jew, Herr Pfarrer," one observed, raising an eyebrow disdainfully at the very thought of it, "you must expect to have problems."

But someone at a higher desk, where the file was eventually passed, must have contrived a solution. What are bureaucrats for but to tease out the knots and tangles of their own making? The half-Jewish Brinkmann children of secondary-school age would be allowed to receive private instruction for the present, provided they passed the State Examinations; this permission to be subject to annual review. Normally in the Nazi state, private instruction is allowed only on medical grounds—who knows what subversive ideas might be spread by private teachers? But as in this case private instruction would keep half-Jews out of contact with pedigree Aryans, there were sound racial reasons for waiving that rule.

"How could we possibly find the money for private teachers?" Willibald demanded fretfully, dropping the official letter into his wife's lap. "I'll teach them myself. I can teach as well as any schoolteacher! Why waste money on a private teacher, even if we had it to waste?"

He may have exaggerated his didactic powers, but when it comes to saving money, Willibald has no peer. So Gabi saw the money being saved all right, but she didn't see the education. After a month nothing had happened except further work on Willibald's epic drama *King Saul*. He'd been writing this for several years, but somehow it never seemed to get finished. His locked study door leaked a stream of little chuckles and joyful barks when work was going well, together with the smell of tobacco from his long churchwarden's pipe. When work wasn't going well, he went out to make a parish call, and came back smelling of schnapps and more tobacco. Whenever Gabi asked when he was going to start the children's lessons, all she heard was "Soon, soon," soothing or irritated—

2

According to his mood

So in the end Gabi took things into her own hands. She found a fresh young woman graduate from Vienna University, a Doktor of History, no less, who would be delighted to spend some time in a rural pastor's home teaching his children.

Doktor Helena Saur was engaged to a government official with what her parents thought good prospects. Her fiancé was working in Graz that year, and her father wanted her to do something to fill in the time until she was married. The alternative would have been coaching in Vienna, and Heimstatt sounded far more romantic. The fee she requested was room and board plus a paltry sum of pocket money which even Willibald couldn't gripe at, especially when Gabi raised the amount by selling her dead sister Frieda's fur coat in nearby Plinden— she'd never liked the idea of wearing her sister's clothes anyway, although the day will come when she's less fastidious. So everything was arranged, and Frau Doktor Saur duly appeared in Heimstatt.

Only one point had been neglected: Frau Doktor Saur was an ardent Nazi, and Gabi had omitted to tell her she was herself a Jew. Gabi had learnt she must fend for herself, and now she was learning how to do it. It wasn't until a week had passed that Frau Doktor Saur discovered the bitter truth. But by then— cunning Gabi!—she'd grown attached to the children, even, or rather especially, to Martin, who could certainly exert a certain boyish charm when he chose, and she decided to stay.

"I never realized Jews could be so nice!" she confessed to Gabi in whispered surprise. Whispered because she understood by then the subject was taboo among us. The others didn't speak of it because they were ashamed. And I didn't speak of it because I couldn't—I didn't even know. And here in 1939 I still don't know. As far as I'm concerned, Jews are dirty people somewhere far away who the wireless says are bad. They don't interest me. Not like Brutus does, or my rabbits.

"I thought you were all crooks and swindlers," Frau Doktor Saur whispered to Gabi. "But you're not like that at all!"

What did innkeeper and Ortsgruppenleiter Franzi Wimmer think of that, a pure German—well, Austrian—girl staying in a half-Jewish house? And a Party member too! It put him in a fix, but now that he'd allowed Jägerlein to remain in the Pfarrhaus, how could he keep Frau Doktor Saur out? A bureaucrat must be consistent! He solved the problem and eased his conscience with another fudge, finding a way between the prickly regulations like a busy ant between a hedgehog's quills. It was all right for ordinary Aryans, even Party members like the Frau Doktor, to enter the Pfarrer's house because it was half-Aryan. But it wasn't all right for State officials to do so because it was half-Jewish. Really the man displayed the wisdom of Solomon, though that's not how he'd have chosen to describe it.

He called at the Pfarrhaus the next day, remaining on the second doorstep, to announce this rule to Willibald and to request him to see to its strict adherence. And the following day there stood the primary school principal on the very same step, to explain why it would be impossible for him too as a State official to enter the Pfarrhaus. His voice almost choked when he said the words "State official." He'd sweated blood to get his Aryan certificate, without which he could no more teach Aryan children than join the Party, both of which he did, and he was commensurately proud of the status he'd finally achieved. His pedigree hadn't been unquestionably pure: his great-grandfather had been christened Jakob and had a surname that was decidedly ambivalent as well. Brows had been raised, question marks pencilled in the margin, his file held up for weeks. But in the end they'd let it pass. How delicately the jackboot sometimes treads, with what considerate circumspection!

Those Aryan certificates involve Willibald in a lot of extra work, by the way. Worthy citizens who want to keep their official jobs or join the Party often have to track down their parents' and grandparents' and great-grandparents' baptismal records all over the Reich, and then get the local pastor to authenticate them—all, as Willibald frequently complains, without payment to the pastor. A bitter pill for him to swallow, especially when he thinks of his own children's unsatisfactory ancestors, but it's no fun for the aspiring Aryans either. Imagine how much trailing up and down and across the country that entails for those poor people, from city to city, town to town, village to village! And the fear that they might find a Solomon or a David right at the last godforsaken hamlet when all the rest were spotless! Everyone going back to their father's birthplace and their mother's birthplace and then all *their* parents' birthplaces—it's like a rerun of the census of the Jews when Christ was born, only this time the Slaughter of the Innocents is going to be a far, far bigger do.

Frau Doktor Saur turned out to be a lively teacher, and my siblings liked her, even quiet Ilse, whose own meager store of liveliness was long ago used up. Ilse's developing a kind of religious melancholia. Besides spending hours with the Bible or praying in the gloomy church, she often wanders off into the graveyard to lay flowers on the mounds of all the unacquainted dead—she likes them better than she likes the living. She always wears a gold cross pendant on a chain around her neck. She never plays, she never runs, she scarcely even speaks unless to answer questions. And when she eats, she does so with a slow and inward concentration, as though she's saying grace before each bite. In a life of melancholic austerity, Ilse allows herself just one luxury: she has hair ribbons of different colors—red, blue, yellow, green and black—and wears a different color every day in the braids of her glossy long black hair.

No one's realized it yet, but she is quietly splitting up. Her soul's as divided as my mother's face, although her own face is going to remain smooth and Madonna-like until the day she dies. The trouble is, she believes what Nazis say about the Jews. And what the New Testament says about them too. Didn't the Jews kill Our Lord? It's all there in the Bible. Aren't they degenerate and dangerous? It's there in her schoolbooks, in the papers and on the wireless (no cinema in Heimstatt yet). Hasn't her own mother tried to escape her Jewishness by becoming Christian? But she isn't really Christian at all; Ilse can see she no longer believes it. Of course not—she can't escape the taint in her blood, the taint that's contaminated Ilse's own blood too. Sometimes, when she glances at her mother's, well, yes, disturbingly semi-hooded eye, she shivers. There, she feels, there on her mother's own face, is that cunning and sinister expression which the papers and the posters all depict. Oh yes, Ilse's soul's divided all right. She knows the Jews are evil, but she's half a Jew herself.

And doesn't her father fear her mother too, and sometimes even hate her? How often has Ilse, the oldest child, been the silent secret witness of their sudden fierce sibilant quarrels and grimly muttered reproaches, the hissed embittered accusations of this not done or that done wrongly, the habitually frayed tempers of a soured marriage in a sour time? Ever since that day when the Brownshirts came and told them to leave their comfortable parish in Germany, ever since then the pot has simmered, sometimes boiling over, sometimes merely menacingly seething. Once, through the thin wall which separated her bedroom from theirs, didn't she hear her mother almost shriek out that her father was a weakling and a coward?

Then once—and this is worst of all—her father, the minister of God, didn't he call her mother a fornicator with that pig-Jew Josef? And didn't something break off then and drift up from the ice of frozen memories that lay across Ilse's mind, some vague wallowing slippery recollection of a look or word that passed between Dr. Josef Stern and her mother on one of those visits Gabi used to pay him for the children's health, when they were still living in Germany and Ilse was supposed to be too young to understand?

No wonder they were all being rejected and excluded from school and village, and from life itself. God Himself had rejected them. It was His punishment; they must endure it.

Yes, Ilse's waters are still and quiet all right; but they are deep and they are troubled.

But if Martin's are troubled, it's not by thoughts like Ilse's, of the polluted blood that flows in all our veins, still less by indignation at the malevolent madness of the Third Reich. His waters are stirred only by a particular resentment—resentment at the stupidity of those who can't recognize his worth. Hitler and the Nazis bother Martin only because they bother *him*. He's a moral solipsist, and always will be. He's known he was a genius from the days of his pampered childhood when his parents told him so and spoiled him rotten. He had only to pee in his potty or lisp a new word, for Willibald or Gabi to hold up their hands in astonished admiration. No wonder he admires himself—he's imitating them. All that's missing is the global recognition of his superiority. For the rest of his life he's going to be waiting for his manifest due, or insisting on it, rather.

To young Doktor Helena Saur, this bumptiousness seemed a nobly assertive Aryan trait, and Martin soon became her favorite. (Ilse she described as slow, and that became her label. Ilse was slow, everyone agreed, and nodded their heads. Ilse agreed too, and slowly nodded hers.) Our next tutor, Fraülein von Kaminsky, will form a juster view of Martin's character. Still, the truth is, he was and is no fool. You should see his Panzer designs—he pores over them on the dining-room table in every spare moment, sheet after sheet of armored ingenuity.

And how is Sara doing, who happens to bear a name the Nazis have decreed all Jewish females must be known by? Frau Doktor Saur tells my mother she can't make Sara out. In some things she too is slow, but in others very quick. Sara drifts in and out.

It's not surprising. She's the only one of us who's been to primary school (for her last year) here in Heimstatt—the others were too old already, and I till now have been too young. As a matter of course she was put at the back of the class alone, from where she was summoned to the front only once, during the Headmaster's lesson on the rudiments of racial science. Her head could serve as an example of a degenerate skull, though not quite as degenerate as a fully Jewish one. So there she stood before the giggling, sneering class, out came the calipers and measuring tape, and down the damning measurements went in every little ten-year-old's notebook.

"It's not your fault," the Headmaster consoled Sara, sending her back to sit behind Leni of the head lice. "And you're only half-Jewish." But she was banished from the girls' games in the playground, and often had to run, or rather walk, the gauntlet of their taunts. Even Leni was summoned away from her side as they walked fortuitously together down the same lane home from school one day. "Don't go with her, she's dirty," Leni's mother loudly declared. Leni's mother, who hadn't bathed in the public baths for over a year! (Jägerlein says she knows this for a fact, and if anyone does, she should. She's the one who takes in the money and doles out the soap—she doesn't earn enough from us alone.)

Also, Sara has become my mother's reluctant confidante. No one else will do. Martin's a boy, Ilse's too distant, and I am both a boy and too young. Why, I'm too young even to be told of my Jewish taint. Into Sara's sympathetic if unwilling ear have spilled the sorrows and fears that Gabi can't keep all to herself. Has some secret about Dr. Josef Stern spilled too? Not yet—and yet perhaps not quite not yet. There have been intimations, hints, half-smiles that are at once sad and happy. Her faintly lopsided face wasn't always so, Gabi has told her. There was a broken heart and that brought on this slight paralysis of her cheek. But what broke her heart? Ah, how often has Gabi remarked how closely Sara resembles "Onkel" Josef, whom Sara dimly remembers speaking gently to her mother in some large and grand consulting room in far-off Germany? How often has Willibald told her so himself, holding her chin and moving her face this way and that, and not too gently either, scrutinizing her features with eyes that do not smile as at a coincidental likeness, but are troubled, rather, narrowed with suspicion or glowing with a smothered anger. Come to that, how often has he said the same to me?

Just now, Ilse and Martin know as well as Sara what rejection is (my turn will come), but she knows much more than they do what her mother feels and what her father doesn't. But Sara is too young to carry all this added freight. So she tells herself stories to lighten the load. And when Frau Doktor Helena Saur sees her drifting out of her lessons, it isn't always mental vacancy but another of her stories that she's drifting into. Secret, all secret; she learnt long ago how to dissimulate and hide. But there's an old exercise book in the bottom of her wardrobe where she is slowly, painfully, writing them down.

Sara says she never dreams. And when people talk about their dreams she looks puzzled, as though she doesn't quite understand. But she dreams all right. She dreams when she's awake. Her stories are her dreams. And what she dreams are nightmares.

■

But now World War Two has come and Poland has gone and Frau Doktor Helena Saur has gone as well, to marry her government official. She leaves us with an unsuspecting cheerful smile. She'll always be our friend, she says, as she waves us goodbye at the Pfarrhaus door. And so she will be. Especially Gabi's. But she won't always be so cheerful. She's going to discover her spousely duties include combing the carpet fringes and ironing the morning newspaper and the banknotes in her husband's wallet. And she will be beaten for infringements and made to kneel on firewood.

As for her replacement, Gabi has seen to that. Scouring the Vienna papers, she has learnt that a lady with the highest references is prepared to offer coaching in various subjects to private pupils of good family. Correspondence has revealed that this lady is Fraülein Hertha von Kaminsky, a former governess to some family of a distant branch of the Habsburgs, and Gabi has gone to Vienna (staying illegally with Helena before her marriage) to supplicate her help.

Acutely conscious that hers is not what a von Kaminsky might consider a good family, Gabi has abandoned subterfuge this time. Hoping that this dependent of the royal family will be no friend of the upstart Nazis, she has laid her petition frankly and humbly before Fraülein von Kaminsky, who is about as broad as she is tall, in her comfortable apartment on the Ring.

She has ended with the words "I feel so guilty. It's all my fault that my children are being treated like this." Yes, Gabi like Ilse feels guilty. Guilty for being the victim that makes her children victims, while the Führer and his cronies who have brought her to this pass are proudly pinning medals on each other's chests and dreaming of a new Berlin—Germania, the Jew-free capital of their Jew-free Reich. (Most of them are also kind to dogs.)

Fraülein von Kaminsky is not a connection of the Habsburgs for nothing. She possesses a sense of *noblesse oblige* as well as that aristocratic disdain of the Nazis which Gabi had hoped for. So in the New Year she will be coming to teach the older children. What will Ortsgruppenleiter Wimmer think about that? Fraülein Hertha von Kaminsky is no ordinary Viennese like Frau Doktor Helena Saur, but on the fringes of the Habsburgs; and royalty is royalty, even dethroned and at several removes. Whatever he may think about it, at least Franzi Wimmer has precedents to follow. First there was Jägerlein, then there was Frau Doktor Saur. So Franzi's problem won't be new. But the shortsighted Catholic Pater will have something entirely novel to think about. Fraülein von Kaminsky is an ardent Catholic (no doubt that was a condition of her former royal job) and she's going to give him earful after earful at every confession.

There are lots of things I notice this Christmas that I've never noticed before. When my mother takes me shopping, for instance, which is only between the hours of three and five, there are certain village stores she will go into and certain stores she won't. And the stores she will not enter are usually the smarter ones, the fish shop and the cooperative, for instance, which are near the best inns like Franzi Wimmer's and have glossy portraits of the Führer prominently on show inside, while the shops she does enter are the cheaper ones, even the dirtier ones, like the baker whose bread is often stale and the dairy where the milk is often sour. They have pictures of the Führer on their walls too, of course, but smaller ones and not so often dusted. Some of them even have little specks of fly-shit on his face.

I'm puzzled by my mother's shopping choices. I take it that as we are from Berlin, we must be a cut above the rest, so we should be going to the best shops, not the worst. And why do we go only in the late afternoon? I know that other people like Jägerlein go at any time of the day. My mother doesn't explain these anomalies, and I sense I'm not supposed to know the real reason, although I'm still convinced it has to do with our being proper Germans, while the villagers are not. Nobody tells me where I've gone wrong. Nobody explains that Gabi is a vicious and degenerate Jewess, that the best shops won't serve her, that in any case she's allowed to shop only between the hours of three and five so that decent Aryans shoppers can arrange to avoid the disgusting sight of her altogether.

My parents have always been bickering and crying (I think that's normal—what else do I know?), but they never openly mention this source of their troubles. Imagine, I can't recall ever being called a half-Jew yet, let alone a Yid, and perhaps I never have been. I don't even know what a Yid or half-Jew is. Sara does, of course; she knows all right. And so do the others. But not me. Why should I? I'm never allowed out to play with the village children, so they aren't going to tell me. And neither Jägerlein nor my mother is going to either. As for my brother and sisters—they're certainly not going to tell me what it's like to be called a half-Jew or a dirty Yid. Like rape victims, they never tell because they feel they're guilty.

So I haven't noticed what I am yet. But there's something else I do notice this Christmas, and that's how strange Willibald looks, sitting by the tree. He's all dressed up in funny clothes. No, not German St. Nikolaus's clothes nor even Austrian Krampus's, but the field-grey uniform of the Wehrmacht. It must be admitted it's an ill-fitting uniform, but that's what it is.

Yes, Willibald, all of forty-four, has joined the colors and is on Christmas leave from the Eastern Front! He's a lance corporal like his Führer was, a member of the heroic German army (and, the way he tells it, no small hero himself) that has valiantly crushed the treacherous Polish attack on the Thousand Year Reich and sternly subdued the sullen and insidious Slav.

Frau Doktor Saur, come and gone. Fraülein von Kaminsky coming. And now my father a soldier of the Reich? What's going on? No one tells me anything. Is it any wonder I'm confused?

It's quite simple, really, though I won't understand this till much later. Willibald's Jewish "connection" has been catching up with him, and he's been trying to outrun it. He's running for his livelihood, and maybe for his wife's and children's lives as well. Considering what he feels about his wife at least, that's pretty generous of him. The Education Ministry has ruled that not only non-Aryans, but also persons with non-Aryan "connections," are disqualified from teaching Aryan children. And Willibald certainly has some non-Aryan connections—five to be precise. But part of the Pfarrer's duty is to teach religion to Lutheran children in the schools—that's what he's paid for by the Church. And now the State won't let him do it.

The Church Supervisors in Vienna have been wriggling like hooked fish on the horns of a dilemma. The Lutheran children would have to be taught by someone else, but where was the money coming from? If they took it from Pfarrer Brinkmann, his family would starve physically, and even those of them that were Nazi-sympathizers weren't ready for that. But if they didn't take it from Pfarrer Brinkmann, the schoolchildren would starve spiritually, and they couldn't have that either. Would Pfarrer Brinkmann perhaps consider serving in the armed forces of the Reich, from which his age and calling had so far exempted him? Then he'd get a soldier's wage, his family could stay in the Pfarrhaus, but part of the Pfarrer's salary thereby released could be used to pay for alternative instruction for the children in the schools.

Pfarrer Brinkmann jumps at this opportunity. Partly because there's another advantage he's detected: maybe his service in the army will help towards his long-term aim, the Aryanization of his children. (Considering his paternity doubts about some of them, it's pretty big of him to include them all.) Only his children, mark you; he has a lesser glory in mind for his wife. And yet how curious, that Willibald is not merely willing but actually anxious to don the Wehrmacht uniform and take an oath of loyalty to the Führer, who is so intent on cleansing the Fatherland of vermin like his wife and semi-vermin like his children. The truth is, Willibald is still a patriot and wants Germany to win the war. The thought that final victory would almost certainly be final defeat for us is a thought he chooses not to think. So he glories in his military exploits this Christmas, such as they are or as he makes them out to be, without a qualm or scruple.

And how curious too that the non-Aryan connection that disqualifies him from teaching in the Führer's schools does not disqualify him from serving in the Führer's army. There's something wobbly again here in the tidy rhythms of the Third Reich, and it should have offended the bureaucrats' minds. How can they expect to win the war if they can't straighten little things like that out? They should put Eichmann onto it, except that he's too busy cleaning Jews out of Vienna.

And curious too is that I don't remember Willibald going off to the war a few months ago, and I'll scarcely recall him coming back next year. (He doesn't last long; the military soon realizes that final victory and Willibald Brinkmann just do not go together.) Yes, he'll be gone for more than a year, and yet I'll scarcely seem to notice. Perhaps because even when he is there, it often seems as though he isn't.

What does he do in the war, then? The High Command

in Poland do not see him as a front-line soldier, though he will never tell you that, and he becomes a steward in the Officers' Mess. Keeping the accounts for his betters is what he's good at, and there's always the chance of a few perks coming his way in the form of a drop of schnapps or a pat of butter. His last posting is near an obscure and dreary town, Oswiecim by name, in a flat and wooded plain.

In Oswiecim, which once hosted a Polish army barrack, some nifty construction is going to be hustled forward in the summer of 1940. And Willibald will have time to pose on horseback, surveying Polish prisoners, so he later says, as they labor for the Reich. He will tell us that he was guarding them, a solitary horseman subduing by his mere Teutonic presence a thousand unruly and rebellious Poles. But look more carefully at the photo and you see this can't be true. First of all there aren't any Polish prisoners in sight, rebellious or not. Secondly he can only just maintain his precarious perch on the drooping worn-out nag. Thirdly he has no weapon and could hardly have stopped a single Pole escaping, even if there were any there, except by toppling on them from his saddle. Lastly and most importantly, the place will soon be known by its German name of Auschwitz; and the guards at Auschwitz aren't your common or garden Wehrmacht grunts like Willibald. No, they're all elite SS troops, the right stuff, with high ideals and hearts of steel. Willibald is billeted near Auschwitz all right, but he isn't guarding anything except the salt and pepper in an inglorious reserve regiment's officers' mess. He's a tourist in this scene, the horse is the photographer's and Willibald has paid to have his picture taken on it.

It's perhaps some discomfort about that and whatever else he may have heard or seen during his sojourn near Auschwitz that prompts Willibald to concoct a story, heard only after the war, of how he stopped an officer from executing a recaptured prisoner. According to the most sober version of this tale, the officer had already snapped the safety catch off his Luger and aimed it at the prisoner's head when Lance Corporal Brinkmann interposed himself between them and shouted out (and at this point of the narration he will indeed shout out, regardless of where he is, his eyes glaring fiercely at his audience), "Shoot him, Herr Major, if you will! But you must shoot me first!" In some versions the officer then lowers his trembling arm and with hunched shoulders slinks shamefacedly away, while in others he comes to his senses, thanks the valiant corporal and shakes his manly hand. There will even be a version in which the major becomes a colonel and actually salutes Lance Corporal Willibald the hero and declares in throbbing tones (and how Willibald can throb, too!), "Today you have taught a German officer his duty."

But he's not going to tell us all that till after the war, and we haven't even reached the middle yet. Not that we haven't been getting on with it. Christmas has come and gone, and so has spring. After spring came summer, when, according to the wireless, our glorious German forces, who had only just finished with the Poles, started laying into the French and British. Nearly every week in June we heard the village school celebrating another German victory, nearly every week in July. Probably they'd still be at it now in August if it wasn't the summer holidays. But soon the holidays will be over and they'll be—

3

At it again

France has fallen now, and so has just about everywhere else. Belgium, Holland, Denmark, Norway—all defeated by our triumphant forces. The English are certain to be next, especially if our invincible Wehrmacht decides to build the enormous Panzer Martin's been designing on the dining-room table, which (the Panzer, I mean) looks about as big as a battleship. It's still ripe summer, the war will soon be over and Willibald will be coming home the conquering hero. But just at present he's still away with our valiant occupation army in the East. Is that why, despite everything, we seem to be quite happy? Things aren't so bad for Jewish Gabi just now. Her Aryan husband's serving in the Wehrmacht, which she thinks protects her and her half-breed brood for the moment, Fraülein von Kaminsky's teaching the older children in her chesty and superior voice, and I will start primary school in a couple of weeks. We're poor but we aren't starving, and we're getting along all right, my mother says.

So are the preachers getting along all right, a whole series of them, getting along to hold divine service in Willibald's place and to teach the Lutheran children in the local schools. They're getting along to the Pfarrhaus every Sunday as well, to share our midday and sometimes evening meals. And a lot of unusual ladies are getting along too, coming in a very different and irregular series, to stay for a few days or a few weeks and then depart. Spinsters from Hamburg, widows from Frankfurt, a "von" this from here, a "von" that from there and even a "von und zu" from somewhere else. And there are Frau Professor Hoffmann and Gabi's best friend Maria from Berlin, who are both schoolteachers and have known Gabi since she was a child. When I ask Ilse why all these ladies keep visiting us, she says they come to help with the work and keep our spirits up and they're something to do with the Confessing Church, which gives me a funny picture of a church kneeling at the Catholic Pater's confessional. But as I don't yet realize why our spirits need this elevation and no one tells me, I assume this is something else I'm not supposed to know about. Not only do these ladies share our Sunday dinners, they eat every meal together with us, and sometimes talk in hushed voices, when, again, I know I'm not supposed to understand and do not want to anyway.

And then there's Fraülein von Adler, who smokes a pipe and comes all the way from Graunau just to visit us. Her grandfather was the Lutheran minister here in Heimstatt once, and so was her father. But when she was born in our very Pfarrhaus (she stabbed her pipe stem up towards the marriage bed beyond the ceiling as she spoke), she was such a puling infant she seemed to be at death's door. Her father being in the same way in the hospital himself, her mother called in the Catholic priest to get her baptized, so that she'd at least avoid post-mortem psychic deportation to Limbo or Purgatory or wherever the souls of unbaptized babies were supposed to go. Better a ticket on the wrong train than no ticket at all. As it turned out, though, she recovered (so did her father) and didn't need a ticket so urgently. But she'd certainly got one and later on Fraülein von Adler decided she might as well use it, so she's still a Catholic. At least that's what she told us between puffs on her short-stemmed bubbling pipe, peering at us with narrowed eyes through the bluish smoke that stole unregarded across her mannish face. And Ilse says it's true her father was once the Lutheran minister in Heimstatt.

What is a "von" and why do we suddenly know so many of them, I wonder. And what is a "von und zu," which sounds more like a journey than a title? Martin, to whom I foolishly communicate my puzzlement, tells me not to be so stupid, as though the answer's obvious, and anyway we only know two or three of them. I assume again it must have something to do with our being proper Germans. But whatever it is, all these visitors are endlessly intriguing to me, and I watch them come and go with eager fascination—each one is strange in one way or another.

The visiting preachers, for instance, often don't have much to say to the ladies of the Confessing Church, nor to Fraülein Hertha von Kaminsky, although there is much distant heel clicking and bowing when she's around. They don't have a great deal to say to Fraülein von Adler, either, who tends to cackle and point her moistly glistening pipe stem derisively at them whenever they come into the room, as if they're clowns making their tumbling entrance at the circus. And several of them have nothing whatsoever to say to Gabi, even when she brings them their meals, which they usually elect to eat in solemn solitude in the study rather than with the rest of us in the untidy dining room. One of them, Pfarrer Kretschmann, a long thin man with sharply sloping shoulders like a Gothic steeple, announces he'd prefer Aryan Frau Jäger to cook and serve his dinner, although it's her day off on Sundays, that being, my mother pointedly reminds him, the Christian day of rest.

"A German pastor does not need lessons in religion!" this man of peace snaps back. "Least of all from one of you."

My mother takes a swig from a glass of water, but doesn't swallow it yet; she keeps it in her mouth for nearly a minute. That's a trick she's learnt from Fraülein von Kaminsky, who told her it might prevent her from saying something she might subsequently regret. This practice, Fraülein von Kaminsky assured Gabi, was followed by the Habsburgs too, and whenever I think of the Habsburgs, I imagine a whole royal family going about with crowns on their heads and buckets of unswallowed water in their mouths.

Pfarrer Kretschmann is a German Christian, Gabi tells us later, and that's why he doesn't get on with the Confessing Church ladies. I don't doubt he's a German Christian since he's both German and a Christian, but why that should set him against the ladies of the Confessing Church I don't understand, since they appear to be German and Christian too. Apparently Gabi has something else in mind, which the others have already fathomed but I have not. It will be years before I find out he's one of those Nazi Christians who excise the Old Testament from all their teaching and preaching on the ground that it's just Jewish history, unfit for pure Aryan ears. The New Testament is all right by them, although why that isn't Jewish history too is never properly explained. Perhaps some of them think that if it was God that put the bun in Mary's oven, Jesus must have been only half a Jew, since clearly God Himself must be an Aryan. And then perhaps they treat Jesus as an honorary full Aryan in view of his Church's sporadic attempts down the ages to eliminate the Jews, attempts which it is the Führer's destiny to surpass and complete. Perhaps others go the whole hog, and claim Jesus was the full-blown Aryan thing, no half-breeds for them. Wasn't he the pale Galilean, and doesn't Matthew speak of Galilee of the Gentiles?

I've no idea which of these obscure doctrines Pfarrer Kretschmann may adhere to, since I've no idea of the doctrines yet, and I'm never going to go much on theology in any case. All I know is that the Confessing Church ladies oppose them, and that puts them on the wrong side of the Government too. From my observation, it seems that the Confessing Church ladies are pacific while the German Christians are aggressive. Pfarrer Kretschmann's certainly pretty bellicose anyway. He preached a sermon in Vienna at the outbreak of the war in which he announced to his congregation that God was on the side of the German nation under its great leader Adolf Hitler, and that He (God or Adolf?) would bless the German arms with victory. Pfarrer Kretschmann was so proud of this that he had it printed and distributed to his brothers in Christ, and Willibald got one too with a fraternal dedication. It's on his bookshelf, along with a volume entitled *The Science of Race,* by a German university professor, with pictures of every kind of skull from the most decadent up to the noble Aryan. I don't suppose my mother's read either of these works. She doesn't have much time for that kind of reading. Perhaps she doesn't have much stomach for it, either. As for me, I haven't learnt to read at all yet, I don't even know the alphabet. So all this passes over my head for the present, when it isn't going on behind my back.

■

In the last week of August we're going up the mountain for a few days, to a hut where Heimstatt's only meadows are, clinging to a ledge of cliff two thousand meters high. When we come down, Gabi tells me, I'm going to start school. Sara looks at me, then looks away. That gives me a sinking feeling, but there's the holiday up the mountain first, so I try to ignore it and pretty well succeed.

This week will be our Indian summer as it turns out, though I've no clue yet what an Indian summer is. Fräulein von Kaminsky isn't going with us. It's as much as she can do to haul herself up our stairs; she certainly wouldn't make it up the mountain. Unless, Martin is heard to murmur, we rolled her up. No, she's going to Bad Neusee for a few weeks, to visit that distant branch of the Habsburg family where she was once a governess and whose name—von Haltenstein—is seldom off her lips. Before she leaves, however, she takes Gabi aside and imparts some severe words of wisdom to her.

"I have watched how you let Martin have his way in everything," she says. "And I realize it is because you feel guilty. Though why you should feel guilty I do not know, nor why you should feel more guilty towards him than towards the others, just because he's the oldest son. But mark my words, Frau Pfarrer, you are teaching him never to deny himself anything. At present it is only a piece of chocolate or an impertinent remark"—here Gabi swallows and feels her cheeks glow, knowing full well what that impertinent remark was and that she even had the temerity to smile at it herself—"but later on it will be young women. A boy who cannot say no to a piece of chocolate will not be able to say no to a young woman either. I have not been a governess to the Imperial Family for nothing."

What this reveals about the Imperial Family Gabi can only conjecture, but as far as Martin goes, Fraülein von Kaminsky's warning is prophetic. Gabi will continue in her guilt to let Martin always have whatever extra goody's going in these times of wartime rationing and anti-Semitic hardship, and consequently Martin will indeed never deny himself anything. Especially young women, when he graduates from chocolate to them—you could almost pick a football team from the products of his future philandering. Which will be exclusively conducted, by the way, with simple blonde and blue-eyed Aryan girls.

But anyway, here we are at last, going up the mountain. Each of us has a rucksack (Martin's, of course, not only the largest but the best—or anyway the least bad) and we plod up the path past Dr. Kraus's house, where he keeps his bald wife and a golden-haired lady with her baby. I already know Dr. Kraus is not a people doctor like Dr. Koch, the village doctor we never visit and who never visits us, but now I'm told he's a doctor who specializes in rocks. I know there are animal doctors as well as people doctors, so it's no great surprise to me to learn there are rock doctors too. And for months I cherish a mental picture of Dr. Kraus placing a stethoscope on a rock and sounding its heart. The doctor is also an explorer, Jägerlein told me once, and he's been to many countries. She also said he's got some pickled snakes in his bedroom, though how she knows that she didn't say. And now Martin loudly announces that the golden-haired lady who lives with Dr. and Frau Kraus is the doctor's lady-friend, which, since she's certainly female and if she lives there presumably a friend, would seem to me hardly worth saying, if Gabi didn't look uncomfortable and twinkle her eyes fiercely at Martin before he strides on ahead.

Dr. Kraus's wife glances down at us blankly from an upstairs window as she adjusts her wig for the day, while his lady-friend, in the garden with her child, smiles at us remotely. My mother tries out a shy "Guten Morgen" as we pass, but it's a bit too timorous to be heard and anyway the golden head has already turned away. Possibly it only recognizes "Heil Hitler!" or the Austrian "Grüss Gott."

My interest has been tickled by Gabi's twinkling eyes and I'm about to ask her more about Dr. Kraus's lady-friend when I notice something strange beside me on the rising path. There's another boy here, as well as my overbearing brother and myself. Who could this be? This boy is a year or so older than Martin, wears brown leather shorts, says "Heil Hitler!" to me, and gives a cheery smile. Nobody has ever said "Heil Hitler!" to me before, although I've seen them do it in the village and always wished that I could too, so my attempt to do so now betrays my lack of practice. However, he doesn't seem to mind, and says "Grüss Gott" now, as they often do in the village when they've finished sticking their arms out and saying "Heil Hitler!" The boy nods amiably and slips past me towards Martin, who is—where else?—in front, leading the column.

Ilse tells me as I catch her up that this youth is Heinrich Schmidt and he's the son of a consultant, whatever that is, in the hospital in Plinden. But what's he doing here? "He's a friend for Martin," Ilse says, as though Heinrich was a new toy for him to play with. But my brother and sisters don't have friends. Friends are for the village people and Dr. Kraus, not for proper Germans like us. Nevertheless, Ilse says he's a friend for Martin, and that means he must be, because Ilse cannot lie. She cannot walk very fast either; in fact she's beginning to drag one foot a bit. So I soon go on ahead, hoping to catch up with Martin and Heinrich—this friendship business is something I don't understand. But they're striding upwards like a couple of our Panzers racing across France, and I have to let them go.

At the top there's a wooden hut in a meadow of buttercupped grass, and it's Heinrich who manages to unlock the door when nobody else can. We can't see Heimstatt up here, but we can see the icy glacier sheet which once covered the whole land, and the quarry where the village men all work and the other frowning bony mountains round about, which look just as grimly unattainable from here as they did from the village we left four hours ago.

"Where's the toilet?" is my immediate and anxious question. A little worm of fear is wriggling in my stomach at the thought of a distant pit lost in alpine mists and still deeper than the one at home. What monsters could be lurking there? Whatever happens, I don't think I'll go at night. But my fears turn out to be groundless. The toilet isn't even an outside job, never mind one hanging over a far-off alpine ravine. No, it's in a tiny cubicle in the corner of the hut, with a china basin that drains into a cess-pool outside, which is covered with the most handsomely vivid green turf of the whole meadow. (There's a moral in that some-where, but I'm too young to play at Aesop.) Now I know I'm going to enjoy myself up here.

Heinrich is funny and daring and has all the best ideas for games, and even Gabi has to laugh at him. Which reminds me—I've scarcely ever seen my mother smile, let alone laugh, not even in that crooked way which is all that her divided face can manage. And Martin joins in the general admiration, as though recognizing that here at least he's met his match. Un-able to compete with Heinrich, he seems happy to be his lieu-tenant and seconder. Heinrich leads us along dizzy mountain trails which he alone knows because, he says, he once lived a whole summer up here. He helps Ilse climb over boulders (Martin would have gone ahead muttering about useless girls) and carries me piggyback when I'm tired. In the evenings he tells us stories about the mountains, stories he's heard from his father, who apparently has been a great mountaineer. Two Englishmen once went walking up the highest mountain on earth, he says, and were never seen again. But for all anyone knows they might have reached the top and be lying there still, embalmed in the ice. And there they'll stay forever. I'm not sure I like that story, at least not just then, while we're pretty high up a mountain ourselves. But then Heinrich smiles. "Un-til a German finds them," he adds. I find that reassuring. We're in good hands up here.

"Is Heinrich really Martin's friend?" I ask my mother as I'm lying tired out in bed on the last evening of this careless week. I suppose I think him too good to be Martin's friend. I want him to be mine.

"Well, his father was a doctor in a hospital where I worked in the First War," Gabi replies evasively. "We ran into each other in Plinden a few weeks ago, when I was going to the dentist's. And so . . ."

"Did he know Onkel Josef?" Sara asks from the table where she's setting out the breakfast dishes.

"Er, no, I shouldn't think so," my mother replies carefully in a voice that Sara hears as uneasy, although things like that are not the kind of things I notice yet. "They were rather different . . ." First her voice trails off, then she does too, going to the ladder and calling out to Ilse to bring an extra blanket down from the loft, although we've got extra blankets galore down here already.

"What did you do in the hospital?" I ask Gabi. "Were you a doctor too?"

"No, a nurse. Like your Aunt Frieda was."

"Why did Aunt Frieda die, if she was a nurse?"

This dying business makes me feel queasy. Nurses ought to be able to prevent it.

"Oh, something happened," my mother sighs and shrugs, on her way now to the kitchen.

Sara follows her with her pregnant gaze, as well she might— she knows Aunt Frieda killed herself when the Nazis fired her from her hospital in Berlin. Jewish nurses for Aryan patients? Unthinkable! But I don't know that yet and I'm thinking of the dentist we go to in Plinden. There's a dentist who comes once a week to Heimstatt, but we never go to him, just as we never go to see Dr. Koch in the village, but Dr. Wagner in Plinden. I put that down to the superiority of the dentists and doctors in Plinden; only *they* would be up to the care of our proper German teeth and proper German bodies. After all, Plinden is a real town with streets and cars and buses. Obviously they must have better doctors and dentists there. So I believe it's just better medical advice we're after in Plinden, which indeed it partly is.

Sara knows of course there's another reason too: Plinden's far enough away and big enough for people not to have discovered my mother is a Jew. But Sara doesn't tell me that. She probably thinks I'm going to find out soon enough on my first day in school. In the meantime, while everyone else is sleeping on their straw-filled mattresses, she is scribbling in her notebook by the light of a secret flashlight. When she scribbles like that, her face wears a frown of intense concentration such as Frau Doktor Saur used to long to see on it all last year.

That night the loudest biggest nearest storm I've ever known occurs. We're woken first by low rumbles of thunder and flickerings of lightning which seem twenty distant kilometers away, but that's only the overture and it isn't long before the opera begins in earnest. The sullen rumbles turn into roars and the flickering lightning into dazzling jagged flashes as the storm moves swiftly nearer. Then it decides to put us in the front row, and, huddling by the little window, we all watch it stride and strut upon the stage. Great forks of lightning stab the somber meadow all around us and we hear the air fry as they sizzle through the night. The earthshaking crash of thunder follows almost at once. Soon hailstones the size of golf balls are thumping on the roof as well. As Heinrich isn't scared, I'm not either, even when I notice Ilse fingering her golden cross and murmuring a prayer.

Heinrich tells us the bombs falling on London that night are ten times as noisy, and the whole city will soon be rubble. Gabi says "Ach!" as if she's shocked, but then says nothing more. Martin says he'd like to see a proper air raid and Gabi still says nothing more. In fact she seems to want everyone to say nothing more, because then she says we should all go back to bed, the storm is passing and it'll be a long day going down the mountain tomorrow.

On the way down next day I slip on a moss-covered stone and sprain my ankle. Gabi binds it up and Martin and Heinrich take turns carrying me sitting astride their shoulders. When it's Martin's turn, he keeps telling me to stop wriggling and sit still, but Heinrich jiggles and bounces me, pretending he's a horse. I say I wish Heinrich was my brother, and everyone laughs except Martin.

As soon as we reach the village, Heinrich takes the ferry across the lake to catch the train back to Plinden, and we all wave goodbye from the pier. His blond hair flutters like a banner against his tanned forehead and he pulls a funny face as he leans over the stern, while the ferry bears him slowly away. The evening air is chilly now, which means that summertime will soon be over.

Very soon.

■

When we get home tired and happy, all except Ilse (who's only tired), we find an impressive official-looking envelope in the letterbox. While my mother is tearing it open and reading it, one side of her face twitching slightly as she frowns, I discover three things are missing from the house: Brutus the Saint Bernard from his kennel, the rabbits from their hutch and the wireless from the living room. Jägerlein is in the kitchen, tightening both her headscarf and her lips, and says only "Ask your mother" when I demand to know where the dog and rabbits are (I don't care about the wireless). But my mother's still reading the letter, or rather reading it again, with little gasps of indignant incredulity and despair. Martin is impatiently asking what it says, Sara is watching Gabi as if she knows already, and Ilse is retreating slowly up the stairs into the quiet haven of her room.

"Where's Brutus?" I keep demanding. "Where are the rabbits?" Gabi knows she's got some explaining to do, but just then she's in no state to do it. Perhaps she should take a mouthful of water and wait a minute or two, but she's in no state to do that either. So I have to gather the facts from the shouts of anger she blurts out (Jägerlein has already prudently closed the windows) and the sudden rushes of bitter self-reproachful tears. She shows me the letter, waving it about under my nose, but as I can't tell one word from another yet, that doesn't help. Sara tries to fill in the gaps, and gets shouted at for her pains—apparently she's filling them in wrongly or filling the wrong ones in. At first all I know is that the Ortsgruppenleiter has removed dog, rabbits and wireless, and that they won't be coming back. The letter explains why, but whenever Gabi starts to tell me what it says, she breaks out into tears of rage and shame all over again. It isn't till the end of a long unhappy evening that I understand, and the understanding that I carry to bed with me is so heavy that it seems to crush my head into the pillow. I lie there staring out at the mountains looming darkly up outside the window, and in place of any other thought or feeling there's only a desolated sense of irretrievable loss, a loss not only of Brutus and the rabbits, but of innocence itself. And then a dull and paralyzing numbness seeps slowly through my veins like melted lead.

My mother's one of *those,* the race they're always going on about on the wireless, or were until they took it away, the vermin of Europe, the cunning dirty rapacious Jews. And that means I'm half one too, and so are Sara and Ilse and Martin. That's why the dog and rabbits and the wireless have all been taken away; we can't be trusted with them, we can't be trusted with anything. We might listen to the enemy's subversive lies on the wireless, and we'd certainly ill-treat the animals and let them mess all over the place. When Willibald was here, it was apparently all right; we could be kept in line by his stern Aryan discipline. But now he's away serving the Führer, we've become unruly, as degenerate races will, and the laws regarding fully Jewish households must be rigorously applied to our half-Jewish one as well.

This isn't Franzi Wimmer's doing. He's all for the quiet life and a bit of live-and-let-live. All he really wants is to go on a few parades and throw his chest out to impress the women. No, it's the work of that substitute pastor that Gabi crossed about Jägerlein's day off, slope-shouldered Pfarrer Kretschmann. While we were away up the mountain, he trod in a Brutus turd on the path to the door, and that was the last straw. Well, I must admit Brutus laid some big ones. The outraged pastor complained at once to the Ortsgruppenleiter as well as to the Church authorities in Vienna. The Pfarrhaus was like a Polish-Jewish pigsty, he declared (not that he'd ever seen one, and in view of their dietary restrictions it seems unlikely that any kosher Jew would have a pigsty anyway). It stank of dog and rabbit droppings and unswept filth. Clearly when the Aryan Pfarrer wasn't there, the Jewish racial tendencies bubbled and seethed, and the place had become a disgrace to the village and the Church. It was a wonder, he added personally to the Ortsgruppenleiter, that the local authorities had done nothing about it yet. Some people, he suggested with a meaning look, some people might conclude they weren't very diligent in the performance of their duties.

What could an Ortsgruppenleiter do when he was squeezed like that? Franzi Wimmer did what was needed to keep his nose clean, of course. He didn't find it easy with Jägerlein, who wouldn't let him in until he threatened to have her arrested. But she was only an ignorant peasant woman after all. The animals and wireless were taken away. The rabbits got eaten; I don't know what happened to Brutus, but everyone knows Nazis are kind to pedigree dogs—it fits their ideology. The only animals we've got left now are the rats that I hear occasionally squeaking and rustling in the cellar when I'm sent to get coal in the dark. I could do without them, but apparently we belong together.

■

I'm not sure how much I was looking forward to my first day at school before the revelation of my semi-Jewishness, but I'm certainly not looking forward to it now at all. So I'm not a proper German after all, I keep thinking; that's what the village people are, not me. I'm a mistake, a degenerate half-breed, half one of that tribe that proper Germans despise. That's why we shop where we do and don't shop where we don't. Not because we're proper Germans, but because we're not. I keep wishing we hadn't gone up the mountain when we did, so that Pfarrrer Kretschmann wouldn't have stepped on that Brutus turd and I might at least have been spared the anguish of this knowledge till it was thrust upon me in school. I could have lived out my last days of blissful ignorance in peace. But we did go up the mountain and I've had my first history lesson before I've even learnt any history: the past can't be undone.

Every night now, when I go to bed, I miss Brutus a lot and the bunnies quite a lot. And I hope that somehow I'll wake up in the morning and find out it was all a bad dream, Brutus and the bunnies are back and after all I'm as Aryan as my hero Heinrich Schmidt. But I never do. Brutus and the bunnies stay gone and I stay half-Jewish, and the first day of school arrives and I'm tormented by questions of propriety. In fact I'm tormented more by them than by the shame of my polluted blood—I find I can live with being half-subhuman so long as no one jeers at me. It's being humiliated that really bothers me, not the ground of the humiliation. Where should I sit? How should I behave? Should I say "Heil Hitler!" when the others do, or should I keep silent? Each alternative looks perilous. If I say it when I shouldn't, I'll be jeered at or worse. But if I don't say it when I should, I'll still be jeered at or worse. How is a half-Jew supposed to *behave*? Sara could tell me, but I never think to ask her, and she never thinks to tell. She's so used to keeping Gabi's secrets, it's second nature to keep her own as well. Besides, it isn't only Sara. All of them keep secrets because they're all of them ashamed.

Anyway, there I am in the playground watching the other

kids, and afraid they're watching me. They know who I am all right, but I don't know who they are yet. What am I supposed to do? They're all playing with each other, running about and shouting, and I'm just standing there, trying to look as though I happened to have paused for a moment by the gate to see what's going on and then I'm going to join in the fun. And while I'm putting on this act, I'm avoiding every eye and watching every face. And that's when I realize how different my clothes are from the village kids'. I'm wearing outmoded Berlin clothes, some of them ages-old hand-me-downs from my brother Martin. But the others are all wearing smart new Austrian national dress, except that Austria isn't a nation anymore; the Nazis call it Ostmark, which sounds to me like some new kind of money. No wonder some of them are eyeing me. I'd look stupid in this outfit even if I wasn't one of *those*. I feel a hot flush of resentment at my mother for sending me here in these outlandish togs, which only a short time ago I would have taken to be the outward sign of our Germanic superiority. As if I don't have enough on my plate already, without having to worry about looking like a scarecrow.

We're all waiting our turn to see the village doctor, who's just arrived on his large motorbike and sidecar, and is going to examine us to make sure we aren't infectious, deaf, blind or idiotic. If we aren't, we can go to school; if we are, we can't. I begin to hope Herr Doktor Koch will find something wrong with me, so that I can go home and escape the terror of this school business. And since I'm half one of *those,* he very well might. Or perhaps he'll just turn up his nose and refuse to even look at me. After all, I know the real reason now why we don't go to him or to the dentist here, and of course he must know it too.

But my name is called and in I go. Dr. Koch says "Unbutton your shirt," and listens to my chest. He's sitting on a wooden chair with his leather helmet beside him and his goggles round his neck. His stethoscope hose hangs down between his knees.

I gaze at the freckles on his hands and the bluish veins as thick as knotty cords as he lifts the little metal disc and sounds first one of my half-Jewish lungs and then the other. There are little black hairs growing out of the pores on the back of his hands and when I see how loose and wrinkly his skin is, I think he must be very very old. "Turn round," he says, stirring his finger demonstratively in the air, and now I get the disc on my back. It feels flat and heavy, like those iron weights you put on scales. Now I'm sure he's going to say "I can see you're half-Jewish," and give me a disgusted shove, but no, he merely sighs and holds his big silver pocket watch close to my ear, telling me to say when I can't hear it as he moves it slowly away. Next it's whether I can see the figures on the chart on the wall. Then he pats my shoulder and sends me off.

I'm in, and nobody's said a thing to me yet! Maybe it won't be so bad. But then—

"What're you doing here, Jew-boy?" a voice behind me inquires, and I feel my guts turn over and twist.

Meet Fritzi Wimmer, the Ortsgruppenleiter's son. He's staring at me with an unwinking gaze as cold and pitiless as pale blue marble. I watch the future flash by as though in a trailer for a film, if someone can do that who's never seen a film yet. He's going to push me around, get the rest to gang up on me and exclude me from their games. For all I know, he's going to shove me into the lake, which is freezing cold in summer and frozen stiff at any other time. This little Fritzi is going to make my life hell. And that's what he's seeing too in the trailer that's simultaneously flashing past his unmoving eyes. He's got a very pale face with a sharp pointed chin and thinly cruel lips. At least, that's what they look like to me. If not the perfect example of the Aryan type, he's near enough, and his tiny brain's been being poisoned by the steady drip of anti-Semitic venom since the day he was weaned from his mother's milk. Or before, for all I know. He's not very big, but he's going to make up for that by hunting with the pack, where he will be the undisputed leader.

We both know this at once, and the recognition of it flickers between our eyes. But nothing's going to happen yet, because we've all got to line up and file into the classroom, where a benignly smiling yet vaguely menacing Adolf surveys us from the wall with his magnetic sultry gaze. So this is where I'm going to learn to read and write? But all I want to learn just now is whose side teacher's on.

Teacher is Fraülein Meissner, like the Headmaster a Nazi party member—does she have any choice? Does she want any? But like him pedantically fair. Since I'm half-German and half-Jewish, she adopts a proportionately balanced attitude. Perhaps they discussed this in the teachers' meeting before school started—*Item 3. Correct attitude towards mixed race pupils, first degree.* That's how we're all known, Ilse, Martin, Sara and me— mixed race first degree. If only one of Gabi's parents had been Jewish, we'd be mixed race, second degree (the Nazis have these grades worked out to the last decimal place), which isn't quite as bad. But as it is we're saddled with two Jewish grandparents and a Jewish mother, and there are only two things worse than that: having a Jewish father or being kosher Jews, the full real thing. Anyway Fraülein Meissner isn't going to tyrannize me like young Fritzi and his gang, but she is going to put me by myself in the back row like Sara before me. Unlike Sara, however, I won't have to sit behind someone with head lice. This year there isn't anyone with head lice. You've got to hand it to Adolf, he's really cleaned things up.

Fraülein Meissner has the fairest hair I've ever seen. It's so fair it's anemic. She wears it parted in the middle and pulled back severely into a bun at the nape of her neck. But there's nothing severe about her face or figure, both of which are all curvy maternal—aching, you might say, to bear a son for the Father-land as the Führer expects all true German women to do. Per-haps when her soldier fiancé returns from France she'll go ahead and bear one, because really she's just maternity waiting to hap-pen. But at the moment I'm more interested in her generosity to me. She doesn't call me a half-Jew in class, she doesn't look at me with open or veiled contempt, she asks me questions as often as she asks the others, and I'm even allowed to say "Heil Hitler!" to our mural Adolf and join in the prayer for Führer and Fa-therland at the beginning of school, just like all the rest, just like proper Germans. Yes, even if she is a Nazi (and perhaps she only is one so that she can keep her job?), it seems as though she's just. And who knows, her motherly instincts may even turn out to be stronger than whatever ideological convictions she may have. Anyway, I'm going to work on them (the motherly instincts, I mean—I can't do much about her convictions). Yes, things may turn out all right if only I can get away fast enough after the last lesson and give Fritzi Wimmer the slip.

And that's exactly what I do. Lugging my schoolbag on my back, I bolt for it as soon as school is over. And either little Fritzi has lost interest in me already, or else he's biding his time. What-ever it is, for the present I'm safe.

Next morning he ignores me until I unwisely pass too close on the way to the boys' toilet during break. "Push off, Yid," is his counsel, delivered in a voice as featureless as his cold blue gaze. I take this advice and nothing happens, except I nearly wet my pants. Nobody else says anything to me. They almost all treat me as though I'm invisible, boys and girls alike. That's all right by me, especially as I can answer more of the questions Fraülein Meissner asks than the others can, and she seems to like that. But a sense of caution warns me I'd better not stick out, and I make sure I don't answer all the questions that I can. Perhaps that's something bred into my genes.

And so it goes on. I'm accepted as an outsider, a nonentity, a sort of shadow that anyone can step on but nobody needs to, because I keep silent and out of the way. If my forebodings are right and Fritzi really does have it in for me, I must be quite far down the hit list. Which can't be said for—

4

Some of our relations
Many of whom dropped Gabi when Maria, her best if not her only school friend, persuaded her to become a Christian. When she later married a Lutheran pastor, nearly all the others dropped her too. She'd gone over to the Gentiles, she no longer belonged to them. All except her father and sister Frieda, who being agnostic didn't care what she was, and her mother, who, being already dead, didn't care either. And sloppy good-natured Aunt Hedwig, her mother's sister. Apart from her father and sister, Aunt Hedwig was the only relative to call on her after her marriage, or write little letters to her as the years passed. Naturally Hedwig's letters grew less frequent as the distance in time and space expanded. And once the Nazis got their claws into the Jews of Germany, they nearly dried up altogether. But a trickle still flowed, jerky and erratic like the passage of a single raindrop down a dusty window pane. Congratulations on the birth of each child, for instance. A note of condolence on Frieda's death. And then another on her father's. A letter to announce the funeral of a distant uncle in America, or the marriage of a still more distant cousin. Then

came the war, and Gabi heard nothing more until the end of my first week in school, when this letter arrived, written on flimsy paper with little wood chips in it.

My dear Gabi,

It is such a long time since we have heard from each other, but your Onkel Moritz and I have been so busy with work and we are so tired when we get home that we hardly have the energy to write to any of our relatives now—those that are left—and keep in touch. Moritz has to leave at 5 in the morning and doesn't get back till 8 or 9, and the physical work is hard on him as he isn't used to it. His workplace is a long way off, so he's already tired before he gets there. Mine is not so bad, in a factory quite near here, so I can walk, but still it is from 6 till 6 and the work is hard for someone who isn't used to machines. And then there's the walk home and cooking and cleaning etc. Besides, the nearest shop for our people is nearly two kilometers away.

Here in Berlin so many of our friends have gone that we would be quite lonely if we weren't too tired to see people anyway. Your cousin Lotte and Solomon have had to move. Their apartment was confiscated and now they are living in a single room, in a building for our people only. They were told to go to Prenzlauer Berg (quite near your father's old place) and that's it. Of course if they had more money, it might be different.

We counted up last night. About half or more of our friends or relations have left now, some for places where you need visas, others for places where you don't. We always wonder who will be next. And then the regulations always changing, you just don't know what to expect.

Write when you have time. Your life took a different

path from ours long ago and it must be still more different now than it used to be. But how long for?

PS And now we've just been told we have to move too. To a single room in the same building as Solomon and Lotte. That's all we can have now. At least we'll be together, but where will it all end? Here is the address, in case you have the chance to write . . .

Naive as she is (she's never read a newspaper all through in the whole of her life, and never known anything about the public world except as it affected her private one), Gabi doesn't need much sophistication to grasp what realities lie behind the coy references to "our people" and "the others," and where they have to shop. But the one about the places you don't need visas for—what did Hedwig mean by that?

Martin, nearly fifteen-year-old Martin, who spotted at once that this letter's been opened and resealed, can already read between the lines that Gabi never even sees, and he quickly guesses the truth. But that's too much for her to believe, so she doesn't, or at any rate tries not to. No, she answers at once, it means being sent to work in one of the occupied territories in the East, not what Martin said. *That* she cannot believe. For once she's angry with Martin and shouts at him never to say such a dreadful thing again. But really the anger's self-directed; she's shouting down the rising murmur of her own deep-running tide of fears. However she may shout them down in the crowded daytime, though, she always hears their quiet insistence rising in the lonely night. Yes, then the flooding tide returns and beats remorselessly upon her darkened shore. Sometimes, when she just has to tell someone, she whispers her fears to Sara; Sara listens and keeps quiet. Everything settles in her—there's no one *she* can tell, unless it is her notebooks.

As for Martin and the rest of us, Martin's certain that if what he said is true, it's never going to happen to him. He's half-Aryan, to start with, and what's more, he's going to show them somehow he's really one of them. Ilse? She puts her trust in God, much good that will do her. Sara keeps her own counsel, as well as her mother's. And I? Fritzi Wimmer seems a more clear and present danger to me just now than anything that happens to people I've never met in far-away Berlin.

If Gabi wants corroboration of her daylight optimism, it comes in the sunny letters of Willibald's nephew Erwin, whom I've also never met. Erwin's father Harald, Willibald's older brother, is a middle-ranking Nazi near Lüneburg. He and his dutiful wife haven't seen Gabi for years of course, that stands to reason. But Nazis or not, they do send her birthday and Christmas greetings, and what they really think about the Jewish Question nobody exactly knows. As for Erwin himself, he's one of Germany's gallant Luftwaffe heroes, a true knight of the air, and he sends us postcards and occasional letters from somewhere in occupied France. He's busy bombing English cities like Coventry and London. Gabi doesn't exactly like the idea of that, but still, haven't the English bombed Berlin? And like it or not, it's a far cry from . . . from what Martin suggested. How could you believe anything so monstrously barbaric as *that* is going on in the Reich when people like Erwin serve it? No, things can never be that bad! Look at this note from Erwin, for instance, written only a month after Aunt Hedwig's:

Dear everyone at Heimstatt,

First of all many thanks for the birthday card and parcel. I was really pleased to get them both. I've been kept very busy on a night-flying course. It's very interesting work, and I enjoy it greatly.

In my spare time, which is unfortunately pretty limited,

I have made the acquaintance of a very charming made-moiselle, the daughter of a French air officer. We've been round as much as we can of this part of France (I can't say where) together, and it certainly is almost as pretty as my companion. I'm beginning to improve my French as well. Not that I have forgotten Lerke, of course, who will always have first place in my heart.

I've also had one short leave on which I managed to get home to see my parents—the first time in more than a year. They asked me to send you their greetings.

(Later) I would have liked to finish this yesterday, but we were called out on duty. And I thought I would be able to write more today, but now we are on standby to fly off on some more exercises, so I had better close here, otherwise it may not catch the post for several days.

With all good wishes to you all
Your
Erwin

Obviously only a dutiful courtesy note, even Gabi realizes that. Obviously not very inspired, either. But then knights of the air aren't supposed to be poets. The main thing is, he's a decent person. And Gabi notices how she's still included in the general good wishes, although Erwin's father is a middling Party bigwig. *They asked me to send you their best wishes. Good wishes to you all.* Can she read that and believe people like Erwin and his father are out to kill people like Aunt Hedwig and herself?

Well, perhaps she can, but it's very tempting not to.

But now comes more confusion for Gabi, in the shape of a letter from Heinrich Schmidt's father (Heinrich, my idol), whom she worked with in World War One and recently met in Plinden. Poor Dr. Schmidt never realized back then that Gabi was Jewish. Why should he have? She wore a crucifix and went to church and seemed just like all the other German nurses. Besides, in just those years everyone was too busy cutting off soldiers' limbs or sewing up their bodies to bother with the dormant Jewish Question. And when Gabi ran into him outside the dentist's in Plinden, she certainly wasn't going to tell him then. He was pleased to see her, he would like his wife to meet her and he insisted on taking her back for coffee, where she met plump smiling Aryan Frau Schmidt and young smiling Aryan Heinrich, and was politely asked to call again. She didn't, but then she ran into him a second time, on her way to the station. She mentioned her preparations for going up the mountain as an excuse for her neglect. The mountaineer doctor was delighted and at once suggested his son should join us. How could she refuse? Afterwards she avoided Plinden for several weeks, hoping we would slowly be forgotten. But something Heinrich said on his return set an alarm bell off in his father's cautious brain, and he'd been making inquiries. This letter is the upshot:

Frau Brinkmann,

For reasons that I am sure you will appreciate, I regret that it is impossible for the acquaintance we have recently resumed to continue any further.

While I regret this personally, I must also express my surprise that you did not see fit to inform me of your racial background when we first met in Plinden. If I had not happened to discover this by chance, I might not have found out for months, and the consequences for myself and my family, not to speak of yours, could have been grave. I regard your failure to divulge the truth on this matter as a serious breach of trust.

G. Schmidt

"Heinrich," Martin declares bitterly when Gabi guiltily informs him that young Heinrich will no longer be his friend,

"Heinrich is in the Hitler Youth." He says that in the aggrieved tone of someone God has inexplicably turned his face away from and left a shadow on the land. Gabi is more worried that Heinrich's father will report her to the authorities. But Dr. G. Schmidt isn't spiteful or malicious. He isn't even a Nazi, however much of a Hitler Youth his son might be. He merely wants to make his way in the world, stay out of trouble and back the winner. Unhappily for him, he's going to lose his shirt in the final race.

But what does Gabi make of all this? Her husband's Nazi nephew sends her his good wishes, an acquaintance who isn't a Nazi disowns her, and Aunt Hedwig writes mournfully of people going to places where you don't need visas. Gabi simply doesn't know what to make of it, and couldn't do much about it if she did. Openly she hopes for the best, secretly she fears the worst. And all the time she lives from day to day—what else can she do? As for me, I feel I should have guessed that Heinrich Schmidt wouldn't last. He was too good to be true.

Willibald's been writing letters too, letters from the field. His letters though are about, not to, us. He's been writing to the Deputy Führer Rudolf Hess for permission to teach religion again, and to the State Office for Genealogical Research to reclassify his wife and thus us children. That's right, the State Office for Genealogical Research. The Third Reich takes genealogical research as seriously as Mormons do, only the Third Reich's heaven and hell are both on earth.

It's a frustrating correspondence.

Now that victory in Poland and France have been assured, the army is going to discharge the oldest NCO in the regiment, but Corporal (recently promoted from Lance Corporal) Willibald Brinkmann contemplates his return to civilian life with apprehension. How can he earn his living as a pastor if he still isn't allowed to teach religion in the schools, one of the duties on the performance of which his salary depends?

As victory and release grow ever more certain, Corporal Willibald grows ever less so. He's written to the church authorities, who've written to the education authorities to express the hope that Pfarrer Brinkmann will now be allowed to fulfill the terms of his employment. But they've had no answer and are vague as to what to do if the answer, when it comes, is no. He's spoken to his Hauptmann, who's as anxious as Willibald to see the stooping corporal returned to a field where his talents would be more fittingly employed, and the Hauptmann has promised to put a word in for him. He's also casually suggested that if the corporal would only divorce his wife all his troubles would be over. But when Corporal Willibald respectfully reminds him there are the children to consider, and anyway his church doesn't allow its pastors to divorce, the Hauptmann only shrugs his shoulders as though to say you can't make an omelette without breaking a few eggs. But Willibald isn't up to breaking eggs. However much the idea might appeal to him in theory, in practice he just cannot have his omelette. No, there's nothing for it, he's got to plod along the strait and stony path he's found himself on, and hope to make it a little wider, a little less stony.

He's also written to Ortsgruppenleiter Franzi Wimmer, who's going to put a word in for him too. He's even written to the Upper Danube District Chief, who's far too busy to put in any word, either for or against. But the ultimate decision on this sensitive matter can be made only by the Führer or his Deputy. Yes, the Führer or his Deputy have to decide who's going to teach the Protestant religion in a few schools in a rural district of Ostmark. You've got to give them their due—they certainly are hands-on managers. It's a wonder they've got time to plan their great campaigns. Or is that why the air war over Britain isn't going so well?

So now Corporal Willibald has written to beetle-browed, ape-jawed Rudolf Hess, whose prognathous chin displays five-o'clock shadow at all hours of the day and night, and who's soon going to flip his lid and fly off to England—although it would be big-headed of Corporal Willibald to imagine his letter will have much to do with that.

Herr Rudolf Hess
The Deputy Führer of the German Reich
Berlin.

Sir

I hereby respectfully apply for reinstatement as teacher of religion for Protestant students in the state schools of Heimstatt and neighboring villages in the Upper Danube District of Ostmark.

In 1939 the district school authorities prohibited me from giving religious instruction on the grounds of my wife's non-Aryan descent. Since religious instruction was an essential part of my duties, it thereby became impossible for me to act as Lutheran minister for Heimstatt and neighboring parishes, and as the father of four children who were otherwise unprovided for I had to reckon with the loss of my livelihood. This was only postponed by my volunteering to join the army, from which, on account of my age I am shortly to be discharged.

The ground of this request is RG. B1. I.S. 607, which states: "The Deputy Führer may in exceptional cases permit those who are married to a Jew to remain in service." I therefore earnestly request the Deputy Führer to grant me such an exception. In support of my request, I respectfully draw attention to the following:

I. My military service for the Reich
2. My wife's service as a nurse during the World War

*In addition I would mention that my wife's baptism
in the Christian faith occurred before I met her and caused
many difficulties for her with her relations.*

*Notarized copies of the following supporting docu-
ments are enclosed:*

1. Ancestry Certificate
2. Marriage Certificate
3. Baptismal Certificate
4. Military Service Certificate

*In the hope that my request will be granted, especially
for the sake of my four unprotected children, and with an
assurance that if I am allowed to resume religious instruc-
tion, I will prove worthy of the trust placed in me, I remain
Heil Hitler!*
W. Brinkmann,
Evangelical Minister
Presently Corporal Army no. 13859

It doesn't take Hess long to chew that one over. *Request denied,* the message comes promptly back. And the documents
come back promptly too, neatly stamped and initialled. Come
what may, the Deputy Führer's going to hold the line on racial
purity. But Willibald isn't finished yet. No, he sends a different
and more portentous letter now, this time to the State Office for
Genealogical Research. His ultimate aim is the Aryanization of
us children, but the immediate object is pollution-dilution. He
wants to get us reclassified as quarter-Jews. Quarter-Jews have it
better than half-Jews, and meritorious service to the Fatherland
might even achieve them the status of honorary Aryans. Imagine that! Sara and me, who might well be full-Jews, becoming
proper—well, nearly proper—Aryans! Considering Willibald's

doubts about our legitimacy, this really is pretty magnanimous of him. But to get us reclassified as quarter-Jews, he has to first get Gabi reclassified as a half-Jew, which is at least better than being a full one. And it would certainly make *his* life easier as well as ours. The means he chooses for achieving this reflect his chronic preoccupation with paternity. (But then what other means does he have?) If he can't publicly accuse Gabi of adultery, he can at least officially accuse her mother.

State Office for Genealogical Research
Schiffbauerdamm 26
Berlin N. W. 7
Re.: Clarification of parentage of Gabriella Brinkmann, née Brandt.

I hereby respectfully submit a request for the revision of my wife Gabriella Brinkmann's parentage record.
　　According to the records, she is a full-Jew. But there are good grounds for the belief that she is only a half-Jew. She was born on the 29th August 1896. Thus the date of her conception must be between the beginning of the last week of November and the end of the first week of December 1895. But at that time the supposed father, Friedrich Brandt, a cloth merchant, was away meeting clients in Russia. He cannot therefore be my wife's father. As, according to the supposed father (now deceased), the marriage was an unhappy one, there are strong reasons to suspect that the true father of my wife was Herr Brandt's Swedish business partner, Herr Morning, of Stockholm, who was known to have an intimate relationship with my wife's mother, and was in Berlin at the relevant time. Herr Morning was a Nordic Aryan.
　　This view is further supported by the fact that my wife

*of her own will converted to Christianity before I knew her,
although this was against the wishes of her supposed father.
Moreover, it is a remarkable sign of her moral disposition
that she served the Fatherland as a nurse in the 1914–18
War. Finally, the appearance and character of our four children strongly supports the view that my wife is not a full-
Jew. None of them displays any of the recognized features
of that race.*

*I therefore request a re-examination of my wife's par-
entage which would lead to a reclassification of her as a
half-Jew. I hope that my service in the military will be taken
into account in the consideration of this request.*

Heil Hitler!

Poor Willibald. This tissue of inventions won't get him anywhere either. Whatever else Friedrich Brandt was, he was the
father of Gabi. Did Willibald make up the Swedish Herr Morning as well as his adultery, or was there really a business partner
of that name? Gabi has never heard of him, nor of the branch in
Stockholm, but she plays along. As for Willibald's children displaying none of the recognized features of Jewry—you've only
to apply to the primary school principal in Heimstatt to get the
goods on that. Mark you, the primary school principal himself
might not pass those skull-calibrating tests, and nor might Hitler, Goebbels, Hess or half the Party members for that matter.
But then they don't have to.

You can imagine Willibald's application being handed round
the desks at the State Office for Genealogical Research, the widening ripples of derision ruffling the holy silence in that Temple
of the Aryan Race. When they've had a good chuckle, they send
back their negative answer, and Willibald plunges headfirst into
the slough of despair. That, as usual, generates muffled echoes
of Schiller, the model for all his literary productions. Here, for

instance, is a sentence from one more letter that he writes to the Church authorities:

> *Whatever becomes of me, I shall always have the consolation and pride of this one thought: I was allowed to play my part as a soldier in the greatest victory of my Fatherland's arms.*

Yes, that patriotic heart still thumps inside his narrow chest, even if his spirits are down in the dumps. That greatest victory by the way (which you would hardly expect a clergyman to single out as his consolation and pride) consisted in twenty-ton Panzers rolling over outnumbered lance-wielding cavalry while Stukas bombed undefended Warsaw into smoking heaps of rubble. Not that Willibald got any closer to the action than checking the accounts in the officers' mess of that reserve regiment well in the rear.

But, after all, that is not the end of things. Willibald's children aren't going to starve, his wife isn't going to be dragged off to a concentration camp. Not yet, anyway.

He gets his discharge from the army in the autumn of 1940. He lifts me up in his arms as I come unsuspectingly home from school. Feeling the rough sweaty texture of his uniform against my cheek and smelling the heat of stale schnapps on his breath, I turn my head away from his slobbery kiss.

"Won't you give Papa a kiss?" Willibald asks with accusation flaring in his eyes.

I shake my head.

"He's shy," Gabi says quickly. "Give him time to get used to you again."

But Willibald has already dropped me and turned away, muttering something about unnatural children, as Ilse, who has just entered the room, dutifully offers her chaste cheek for the full wet paternal smacker. At least he has no doubts about who sired *her*. I feel ashamed but relieved at the same time. How could I kiss that uniformed stranger?

Willibald can't teach religion to thoroughbred Aryan school-children, but the church does somehow continue to pay him a diminished salary, and the local Aryan children do somehow continue to get instruction in religion, if not from tainted Willibald. So though we're worse off than we were, it's not the end; the worst is still to come.

However, though things aren't as bad yet as they might and will be, something's happened to Willibald. Whatever stomach he might have had for the fight, it's gone out of him now. He's given up trying to get round the Nazis, and now he's merely going to drift with the current, wherever it takes him. That is, when he isn't railing against his fate and the wife it's brought him. He's still got stomach for that all right. In fact, now that he can't fight on the Eastern Front in the Wehrmacht any longer (not that he ever really did), he's got more energy for fighting on the home front. His first campaign, if we discount the incessant guerrilla warfare of his marriage, is going to be against—

5

Jägerlein, Annchen and the French prisoner of war

Gabi's food coupons are stamped with a *J*. And she gets fewer of them than the rest of us. "The Jew," Goebbels has declared, an abstraction he's much addicted to, "The Jew has battened on the German nation long enough." And she doesn't eat her ration's worth even so. She gives some of it to her children and her husband. But still Willibald isn't satisfied. Something, he feels, is missing from his diet. He's learnt about filching in the Officers' Mess, which is certainly a good school, and his experience there has convinced him: Jägerlein must be filching from us. The margarine ration and the egg and meat rations that go onto the kitchen table just don't all come through onto the dinner plates, and he's sure Jägerlein's the one who's responsible for the deficit. So is Gabi sure, she's been sure of it ever since Jägerlein's been with us, but she takes the indulgent view that people brought up with servants are apt to adopt. "It's part of the household expenses," she keeps telling him. "You just have to accept it."

But this is the philosophy of the Officers' Mess, not of the Officers' Mess steward, and Willibald, who was brought up in the back court of a Berlin tenement, will have none of it. "I want some proper accounting done here," he declares, not quite out of Jägerlein's hearing. "I'm going to search her bag." He slams first his fist on the table, then the door to the study, from where after a short time little barks of satisfaction tell us that *King Saul* is getting back on track after the military year of neglect. But next morning, when he appears as usual on the stairs in a nightshirt about half a meter shorter than modesty requires, his mutterings rise again.

"We have a thief in the house . . . She'd better look out or I'll call the police in . . . A search under the mattress would turn up a bit more than a bad smell . . . If no one supervises them it's no wonder the place is like a Polish-Jewish pigsty . . ." This last is slope-shouldered Pfarrer Kretschmann's phrase, the one he used when Brutus and the bunnies were removed from our contagion. Considering he's married to a Jew, Willibald's use of it— presumably he learnt it in the army—seems less than friendly. But at least it does sound more plausible in his mouth than in Pfarrer Kretschmann's, since Willibald may at least have seen a Polish pigsty, though scarcely a Polish-Jewish one, whereas untravelled Pfarrer Kretschmann can hardly even have seen that.

Jägerlein seems not to notice these rumblings, although my mother augments the drama by following Willibald down one step after another, shushing and clucking like a flustered hen. Perhaps that's because Jägerlein has other things on her mind— two, to be precise: Annchen, the girl she's adopted, and François, the French prisoner of war she's fallen in love with. Not to speak of the poetry she keeps reciting and all the work she has with us children always under her feet. Annchen lives with Jägerlein in the room behind our kitchen. François works on Jägerlein's sister's farm four kilometers away on the other side of the lake.

I like it in the kitchen. So does Sara. It's the only place in the big drafty old house that's really warm in the winter, but it's also the only place that's always cheerful at any time of the year. Sara sometimes scribbles her stories there behind the large green tile stove, and listens to Jägerlein when she stands suddenly stock still, gazes absently into the distance and recites one of the poems she learnt in her four years of schooling, or odes of her own that she composes spontaneously whenever the mood is on her.

Today it's April and the Führer's birthday, but Jägerlein is saluting the cuckoo in the woods, not the cuckoo in Berlin. There's been enough of that going on already in the village, what with the flags and the band and parades of Hitler Youth in their semi-military uniforms and the League of German Girls in theirs, bearing flowers for Führer Adolf. I had that in school this morning too. There's been an extra-special birthday prayer for Führer and Fatherland, and Fritzi Wimmer was chosen to raise the swastika flag in the playground. His chilled blue eyes drilled into mine as he did so, as though to let me know he hasn't forgotten, but I glanced away and Heiled Hitler with the best of them.

"Cuckoo, cuckoo, comes the call from the wood," chants Jägerlein, eyes fixed on the washed blue sky outside the steamed-up window. Then she extemporizes, waving her flour-coated hands about as though to pluck the bird of inspiration from the cuckoo-laden air.

All the time she declaims, Annchen stands gazing at her vacant-eyed and open-mouthed, an unregarded streamlet of snot trickling slowly all the way from her red button nose down her chin and onto her pinafore. It isn't the poetry that's emptied her eyes, but the genes she was born with. Annchen is retarded, like several children in our inbred village, and that's the only reason Jägerlein's been allowed to adopt her, although the adoption is quite unofficial. Jägerlein came across her some months ago, dirty and ill-fed, the last of eleven children, playing outside her parents' house in the damp lower alleys where the snow lies longest in winter and the sun shines shortest in summer. She took the girl home with her (that is, to our home), washed and dressed her; and after a few weeks it became accepted that Annchen was now being brought up by Frau Jäger. She's been in the Pfarrhaus now for almost half a year, since well before Willibald's return from his heroic military duties, but as far as he's concerned, she's got to go back to her family. Why, Jägerlein doesn't even have the girl's ration card, no wonder she's filching from us. That's certainly got to stop. Jägerlein says yes, Annchen's going back. But one day leads to another and somehow she never does make that promised journey back to her parents' house, and scarcely even knows it when she passes it now, holding tight to Jägerlein's apron on the way to the shops.

Jägerlein's soliloquy is interrupted by Willibald, who storms into the kitchen in full voice himself, demanding to know who's taken the pen from his desk. Nobody can tell him, but he fixes an accusatory eye on Annchen, who begins to cry. "And why is this child still in my house anyway? Doesn't she have a home of her own to go to, instead of slinking round other people's houses filching their pens?"

"Ach, Herr Pfarrer," Jägerlein answers placidly, rolling the dough out on the table. "What would Annchen want with a pen when she can't even write? Have you looked in the drawer?"

"Of course I've looked in the drawer!" Willibald shouts. "Someone's deliberately taken it, just to spite me!" He's glaring still harder at Annchen now, who blubbers even more, which only strengthens his conviction of her guilt. "What's she crying for if she hasn't stolen it?"

"She's crying because you're shouting at her, Herr Pfarrer," Jägerlein responds equably as she eases the pastry into the pan. "Just like the Frau Pfarrer does when you shout at her."

"Insolence!" shrieks Willibald, his voice breaking with fury into an unfortunate falsetto. His eyes are popping and his face has turned that mottled red which gives him the look of a scraggy raging turkey. "How dare you speak to me like that in my own house!"

Sara has closed her notebook and now I retreat beside her behind the stove. Willibald might start stamping his feet and throwing things soon. But this time Gabi appears, holding his pen in her hand. "Is this what you were looking for? It was on the carpet by the desk."

"Well, who put it *there*?" Willibald shouts, snatching the pen from his wife. "Which idiot put it *there*?" But it's only bluster now he realizes the idiot is himself. The anger slowly melts away, and soon he does too, muttering his way back to the study.

Jägerlein wipes Annchen's face on her pinafore and lays the pan in the oven. Soon she's gazing out at the mountains, whose peaks are just visible for the first time this year, and reciting again. But I'm gazing at Annchen's pinafore, which has been used a few minutes before to polish the bowls which she and Jägerlein eat from. Jägerlein washes our dishes fiercely with hot water and soda, but she never washes her and Annchen's bowls. They lick them clean instead like a couple of cats, their heads nodding assiduously as they move up and down and round and round the smooth white surfaces. Then Jägerlein gives them a wipe with Annchen's pinny and places them on the dresser ready for the next meal.

Next week Jägerlein takes Annchen and me with her to see her French prisoner of war. Martin wants to come too, but Jägerlein says no. "You'll only say something to upset him," she explains, which is certainly something that upsets Martin. In retaliatory jealousy he says something to upset me. "Do you know why Jägerlein doesn't have a husband?" he asks, with the sort of sneer that implies I ought to know but of course I'm far too dumb. The existence of the marital deficiency has never occurred to me before, let alone an explanation for it, and I shake my head. "He hanged himself from the curtain rail," Martin informs me. "His feet smashed the window. And they've never cut him down. When you're there you'll see him still hanging there, with his tongue popping out like this." I gaze at Martin's mime of a twisted head, bulging eyes and protruding tongue, and imagine Jägerlein's husband smashing the window still with his twitching booted feet. It's a good imitation, but Martin's going to find out one day it's nothing like the real thing.

I don't believe him, but yet I don't quite disbelieve him either, and my own feet begin to drag as we approach the farmhouse in the cramped little valley across the lake that grudgingly yields the only agricultural land around that bottomless pit of dark glacial water. I take a good look at all the windows I can see, but there's no rotting corpse hanging in any of them. What about the windows I can't see? I decide I'm not going into any room by myself.

"So this is the little mixture?" an older version of Jägerlein asks gruffly at the door. She looks me over as though I was a cross-bred calf, then opens the door wider to let me in. "Doesn't look too bad. Are they all like him?"

At the table in the kitchen sits a middle-aged man in an old uniform with worn dirty boots. His shoulders are hunched as if he's expecting a blow, and when he hears us at the door he throws us an anxious glance before getting on with what he's doing, which is shovelling a bowlful of stew noisily into his mouth with a large wooden ladle. The ladle's too big (I know this problem myself), so he's sucking the soup off it with hasty gurgling relish.

Jägerlein pulls out the bench beside him and sits down to watch him eat. "Ach, you're so thin still, François," she murmurs, reaching into her bag. François continues to slurp up the stew while she lays something wrapped in one of our cloths beside him. "Go on, open it," she urges as he pushes the empty bowl away at last. "Open it, go on."

He has long fingers with broken grimy nails, and he picks nervously at the ends of the cloth. The cloth falls away fold by tantalizing fold, and he peels the last corner off to reveal fully a quarter of the cake Jägerlein baked with our flour and margarine rations yesterday. "Donke," he mutters and starts cramming that too into his mouth. Jägerlein places her elbows on the table, rests her chin on her folded hands and watches our cake swiftly disappearing.

"He's nearly finished the upper field," Jägerlein's sister announces from the doorway, but Jägerlein barely moves her head. When François has wolfed the last crumbs down, licking them off his fingers and palm, he nods and says "Donke" again. Jägerlein shakes her head deprecatingly, gazing at him with a fond glow in her eyes that I've never seen before and which makes me feel slightly jealous. But François only stares down at the table, his shoulders still anxiously hunched. "Ja, François," Jägerlein says in the soothing tone she uses to Annchen when she's hurt herself. "Soon the war'll be over and you'll be going home to see your people again, all your family and friends . . ." But instead of seeming pleased for François, she appears suddenly quite sad and sighs.

This is my first lesson in the sorrows of love, but I'm not old enough to understand it now, and won't profit from it later when I am. There are some lessons that teach us nothing till we no longer need them. It's not like that with swimming or math, why must it be so with love? Well, anyway, it is, and now Jägerlein is stroking François's forearm shyly as you would a dog you thought might suddenly growl or snap, while I'm beginning to wonder if Jägerlein's husband might be hanging in the toilet, which my bladder's pressure tells me I must shortly visit.

"He's nearly finished the upper field," Jägerlein's sister says again. "He's a good worker, that one."

"You're just like my Hansi was," Jägerlein tells the Frenchman, ignoring her sister's commendation. "He was always hungry too." Annchen looks from one to the other with her empty gaze and begins sucking her thumb. "Always hungry," Jägerlein repeats, then, without taking her eyes off François, addresses me. "No need to cross your legs. The privy's out in the yard."

The Frenchman gets up suddenly, and Jägerlein's hand starts back as though she's been stung. He goes out into the yard himself and shoulders a long-handled hoe that's leaning against the wall. Annchen follows him, her lips making a soft wet cheeping sound around her comforting thumb. And I follow Annchen.

The privy, I discover, has no window. It's just a lean-to against the wall, so I don't have to worry about seeing a corpse dangling from a curtain rail. And as it's broad daylight and sunny, I'm not worried about a monster coming up out of the depths beneath the wooden plank either, to plant its writhing suckers on me and drag me down.

Being on the farm's as good as being up on the mountain last summer, except there isn't any Heinrich Schmidt. The grass is lush and green, there are two brown-and-white cows and Jägerlein's sister gives us a snack of fresh milk and bread with real butter on it, not margarine. I watch the Frenchman hoe the potatoes in the upper field. The bright blade makes a gritty scraping sound as he thrusts it in between the rows, and there the slaughtered weeds lie afterwards, already wilting in the gentle sun. Annchen runs after a rabbit that breaks from the plants at the bottom of the field, but its white scut soon bobs behind the hedge and vanishes. She stands suddenly still, restored to her habitual inertia by bunny's disappearing trick. When I have a go at pulling the dead weeds together with a rake I've found, the Frenchman pauses to watch me, and seems about to show me how to do it. But then he appears to change his mind and bends silently to his work again as though after all it isn't really worth the effort and anyway he might be accused of collaborating with the enemy.

Towards evening an army truck with regimental signs painted on its mudguards clatters into the yard, and a soldier almost as old as Willibald gets out, strolling across the meadow towards François. The Frenchman sees him coming, and leans on his hoe until the soldier calls out to him, jerking his head towards the waiting vehicle. François trudges obediently back to the farmhouse, places the hoe back against the wall and climbs silently over the tailgate of the truck. Other silent men in drab uniforms are sitting there already, gazing out at us with the look that people have on the buses and trams in Plinden, the absent look of strangers idly watching other strangers while their lives proceed internally behind the peepholes of their eyes.

Jägerlein waves a hesitant goodbye, but the Frenchman doesn't respond, and the truck drives off, bumping and rattling over the stones.

Before we ourselves leave, her sister gives Jägerlein a slab of butter and half a dozen eggs in an old shopping bag, which Jägerlein hangs on Annchen's passive arm. On the way home I ask Jägerlein who Hansi was.

"My husband."

"Why did you say François was like him?"

"Because he is," she reasonably replies.

I know that children will be forgiven a candor that adults will not. Children don't pry. They have no secret motive, they simply want to know. So I ask her "Is your husband dead?" "Yes," she answers absently, apparently still thinking of her François.

"When?"

"When what?"

"When did he die?"

"Hansi?" She glances up at the evening sky and calculates. "Ten, eleven years ago. Long before you were born anyway."

I'm getting interested in death; there seems a lot of it around, and I sense it might even happen to me. But when I ask Jägerlein

what he died of, she only sighs and shrugs, as I remember my
mother did last year when I asked her why Tante Frieda died.
"Oh, people die," she murmurs.

"Was he ill?"

She shrugs again. "Things just got too much for him."

◼

That evening at home I innocently remark that the Frenchman
liked our cake.

"Our *cake*?" repeats Willibald. "*Our cake?!*"

He flushes a deep red again and his voice quivers as he de-
nounces Jägerlein for a thief and traitor, feeding the enemy with
our rations and (shaking his fist) probably whoring with them
too. Gabi's eyes flicker silent warnings about his language, which
he wouldn't be using if Fraülein von Kaminsky was here tonight
instead of visiting her Bad Neusee aristocrats again. Then she
tries to shush him, which only enrages him the more. "You too?"
he shouts. "Yes, you've always been on her side!"

"She brought us back some butter and eggs," I manage to
get in, risking a clip on the ear for justice's sake.

"That's enough from you!" he yells, reaching across to administer the expected clip. "Of course she did! She knows I'm
onto her! She's trying to cover it up!"

He starts from the table and heads towards the door while
Gabi follows with the prescribed mouthful of water, flapping
her hands imploringly and squeaking inarticulate and unregarded pleas. Ilse sits with her hands clasped in her lap in an
attitude of suffering prayer. Sara watches her mother with a face
that says "I'll have to deal with this tonight," and I try to pretend
without any success that this isn't really happening but, if it is,
it isn't really my fault. Martin opportunely cuts himself another
slice of what's left of the cake.

Now Gabi's hanging on to Willibald's jacket, because he's

shouting out he's going to search Jägerlein's room and throw the thieving whore and her baggage out into the street. The brat, he adds, is no better than she is, and he won't have the Pfarrhaus turned into a den of thieves and harlots even if his wife doesn't care. With her background she probably wouldn't mind anyway.

At that Gabi forgets the Kaminsky Cure, gulps the water down and screams herself. "Yes, now you've said it, haven't you? Now you've said what you really think!" But he tears himself free and slams the door against the wall. Ilse judges it time to close the windows while Gabi follows her husband to the kitchen, where Jägerlein already has her coat on and is knotting her headscarf under her chin. A small brown carrier bag stands on the floor between her and Annchen, whose ragged jacket is already buttoned too.

"I'm leaving, Herr Pfarrer," Jägerlein announces, picking up the bag. "Do you want to look in here before I go?"

"Yes!" Willibald yells, then "No!"

"Where are you going?" Gabi moans. "It's late, you can't go."

"To the farm," Jägerlein says. "Come on, Annchen."

Annchen is snivelling quietly, her mouth pulled into a slack-lipped grimace. She clutches a fold of Jägerlein's apron in her grubby fist and follows her out of the house.

Willibald stands there panting stertorously, striking a pose of righteous indignation, but I can see he's repenting already and beginning to deflate. Meanwhile Gabi has herself flown into a rage, and screams that Willibald should have the courage to act as he feels and divorce her, send her and the children packing and save his own skin.

That's just the trigger Willibald needs to set himself off again. "And whose children are they?" he thunders, his throat corded and rigid, his eyes bulging like a hanged man's (they reminded me of Martin's imitation), only, unlike a hanged man's, glinting fire. "Tell me that! Whose are they? *Whose?*"

Now Gabi is in tears, and covers her face with her hands. Willibald declares he's got nothing left to live for, yanks a picture off the wall, not a valuable one—we don't have any—raises it in both hands like Moses with a graven image, and hurls it, also Moses-like, to the floor. Then he strides out of the house, pausing to make some eloquent valediction worthy of Schiller. Unfortunately all he comes up with is "The waters will close over my head. I shall never darken this threshold again." Even I sense that isn't top-shelf Schiller, but he delivers it with magnificent presence and stalks out into the night, heading down towards the lake.

Ilse follows unobtrusively, to grab his coattails if he actually does attempt to plunge into the icy waters. She's already picked up the picture and placed it on the table ready for repair. Gabi sinks onto her chair and sobs and sobs. Sara places a tentative hand on her arm just as Jägerlein placed hers earlier on the Frenchman's, and with no better effect.

In the pantry, I discover, are the slab of butter and the six eggs from the farm.

Later on Martin tries to tell me superciliously what whoring is and harlots are, but I only get still more bewildered. In any case, I don't really care. All I want to know is why Jägerlein has left us. I don't believe it's because of my unwitting betrayal or Willibald's fit—she's put up with enough of those in the past. No, it's because of the Frenchman. She likes the Frenchman better than she likes us. I would think that's the greatest betrayal of my life if I knew the word "betrayal." As I don't, I bleed dumbly instead. It hurts me almost as much as it hurt to learn I was a half-Jew, one of the despised underclass. I go to bed by myself and lie awake staring blankly at the darkening mountains till sleep suddenly ambushes me and carries me captive away.

■

When I wake in the morning I hear the tap-tap of Willibald's hammer as he laboriously reassembles the splintered picture frame he smashed last night. I go downstairs and find him chuckling and talking to himself, bending over the table in his short nightshirt. The smell of schnapps is still warm on his breath. But when I hopefully enter the kitchen, it is cold, even though the stove's alight.

Jägerlein has really gone.

And Fraülein von Kaminsky's the next to go, though not because she likes some Frenchman better than us. No, the official educational wind has changed and Ilse, Martin and Sara don't need her lessons anymore. In fact they're not allowed to have them now. It's back to school for them—

6

Though not for long

Perhaps it was Pfarrer Kretschmann dropping the word in Vienna that our home was a Polish-Jewish pigsty. Or perhaps it was just some new official establishing his authority, settling his no-nonsense ass firmly into his chair. Anyway, the half-breeds' homeschooling has to stop, and it's back to school for them. But the rule that half-Jews can't lodge in pedigree German homes remains intact—some things are sacred. So how are we going to manage?

Willibald says we aren't and bids adieu to Fraülein von Kaminsky at the ferry pier with tears in his eyes. "You suffered the little children to come unto you," he begins in a quavery voice, but she cuts him off with the observation that it was actually the other way round and they were hardly little anyway.

She hasn't been happy here since he returned from the army. Perhaps it's his short nightshirt that makes her uncomfortable, or the occasional glimpse it affords of his cat's pelt dangling round his chest. Or his sporadic chuckling and barking in the study, not to mention his domestic histrionics and the occasional readings from *King Saul* he inflicts on her. The contrast with the Habsburg style must have grown acute. Anyway, she's not sorry to go. But before she does, she whispers to Gabi, brushing her cheek with her own, that she should ask Fraülein von Adler what's really going on in the war, because Fraülein von Adler listens black. Overhearing this, I wonder how it's possible to listen in colors. This is perhaps my first philosophical thought, and like most such thoughts quite irrelevant to what's actually going on.

Then away she steams and Willibald mops his eyes with a large white handkerchief, taking care to ensure his grief will be observed. This doesn't help to advance my siblings' education, but on returning to the Pfarrhaus he declares that's quite impossible now anyway and retreats with loud despairing sighs into his study.

But Gabi has been scrutinizing the railway timetable and she says it can be done if only the children can take the three-hours-each-way journey to school. Now they're older, she decides they can. So up they get at four in the morning, eat a slice of bread and sausage, swallow a milky ersatz coffee, run to the first ferry, wait for the first train, doze in the carriage for two hours and dash the last four hundred meters to their separate schools. (In Ilse's case it isn't a dash but a labored scramble.)

Six hours travelling a day seems a lot to spend on secondary education and I hope the war will be over before I have to go to Plinden. As things are, I get up three hours later and come home three hours earlier than they do. It's worth running the risk of being beaten up by Fritzi Wimmer to get that extra sleep. And so far I haven't been beaten up. I'm still almost insubstantial in the primary school, a mere visiting shadow at the back of the class, and I imagine there can't be much fun in beating up a shadow. I ought to know better, and soon I will.

Ilse's been told she's slow so often that she's decided to prove it and gets slower still as the months go by. Now she has to repeat a whole school year, so she's in the same sixth grade as Martin, though not in the same school; he's in the State High School for boys while, since future mothers of future heroes need domestic science and needlework, not math and Latin, she's in the Plinden Catholic Girls' High School down the road, where Sara has also just started.

Sara doesn't pay much attention to Catholicism. She doesn't pay much attention to anything these days except Gabi's anxieties and the contours of her own interior landscape. But this new arrangement suits Ilse down to the ground. She loves the serene sequestered nuns, she places a crucifix over her bed at home, and she joins in all the Catholic rites except communion, which she achingly wishes she could join too. In Lent she eats even less of our meager rations (Willibald says our plates are full, now that Jäger woman has gone, and maybe his is, but I don't notice any change in mine). And at Easter she wears black and drapes a gauzy black veil over her crucifix. Anything, it seems, to escape the taint of Jewish blood, the millstone of Jewish history. When Willibald says grace, which he does in hushed and throbbing tones before every meal, she secretly crosses herself. I've seen her at it, as I glance surreptitiously up while my head's supposed to be reverently down like the others'. Sara's seen it too; I've caught her covertly observing Ilse as I do with her watchful meditating eyes. But Sara doesn't say so any more than I do; she simply lets it drift down through her burdened mind. Perhaps everyone except Willibald has noticed it—he's usually too busy performing his own piety to observe anyone else's. But whoever sees it, no one says a thing. We all still have our secrets, and each of us keeps the others', the better to preserve his own.

I soon have another secret too, the secret of my encounter with the champions of the master race.

Fraülein Meissner arrives at school one Monday with puffy red-rimmed eyelids and pale cheeks. Her fiancé has become one of the dead heroes of the Reich, brutally murdered by a cowardly French terrorist. (The Frogs have paid for it though—ten randomly chosen villagers for one Aryan; Fritzi Wimmer, who tells us so, also opines that ten for one is not enough. Perhaps that comes straight from his father. Then he imitates a machine-gun cutting down a hundred of the Gallic swine.) Now Fraülein Meissner's ripe fecundity will have to find another inseminator, which might not be so easy if suitable Aryan males keep getting picked off like this first one has been. In the meantime she's so upset she forgets to say "Heil Hitler!" on entering the class—or is it that her loyalty's wavering, and she's having trouble hailing the Führer today? Whatever the reason, I half expect her to take her loss out on me, the shadow creature halfway to that under-class against whose devious machinations her fiancé has fallen so valiantly fighting. But she recovers a brave and melancholy poise and teaches as usual. And she hasn't marked me out for her revenge either. In fact she seems to treat me with uncommon kindness today. Her voice softens when she asks me to come out and perform simple multiplication on the board, and she says "Good!" as though she means it when I get it right. Perhaps she's got an inkling of what Adolf has in store for us, or has her hero's death at a terrorist's hand made her realize what it's like to be a victim?

But that's certainly not Fritzi Wimmer's take on things. It seems the day of Fraülein Meissner's bereavement is the day he's been waiting for, the Day of Atonement. So at break in the playground, though I'm keeping my usual wary and solitary distance (even from little Resi Hofer, whose eyes sometimes half-smile at me, although their owner never speaks), he comes deliberately up to me, popping bullets through me with his chilling stare, and I know at once with a void opening where my heart should have been that this is the scene we rehearsed on our first day at school and now we're going to play it out before the destined audience. As I foresaw, he's not alone. There's Heini Beranek, who's got red hair, and Joachim Kubler, whose hair's as brown as mine but his pedigree's all right, and Fredi Bauer, who's simply nondescript and since he's got no character of his own, tags along with the others just to absorb a bit of theirs.

"Jew-boy," Fritzi says affably, thumping my chest and shoving me against the wall. "Whose side are you on?"

I'm not sure how to answer this, since in my panic I don't realize what the options are. Is he talking about some gang in school that naturally I don't know about? "What?" I mutter faintly, my breath going suddenly unsteady on me.

Then comes another thump, and then a couple from Heini and Joachim to let me know what's what. Then one from Fredi too, when he sees how scared I am. "Whose *side* are you on?" Fritzi repeats, feeling two sizes bigger already with that trio at his back. "Are you a German or a Jew?"

By now a larger group is forming round us with all the ardent anticipation of a pack of dachshunds round a cornered rabbit. I can see the finale of this scene as clearly as the beginning and I wish we'd already reached it, but I sense with dull despair we've got to act it out line by line before we can reach the climax and finish it off. As to Fritzi's conundrum, I'm dazedly conscious no answer will do. If I say I'm German, I'll get beaten up for being a lying Yid; and if I say I'm a Jew, I'll get beaten up for being a truthful one. You have to hand it to Fritzi—he may well be slow at the three Rs, but he's all there when it comes to dilemmas. I try the middle path and say I'm both, but of course that's no good either, because how can a German be a Jew? You might as well say a mongrel tyke can be a purebred Doberman.

So now they've got their excuse and the gleeful battering begins. Little boys have little fists, but in Heimstatt they've got heavy shoes as well and soon I'm cowering against the wall doing all I can to ward off kicks as well as punches. That hurts, but it humiliates more, and to my own amazement I begin to feel a flood of resentment, which builds until I suddenly flail out blindly and hopelessly with my fists and feet instead of merely crouching down and covering my face with my hands. This makes me more vulnerable and the drubbing gets worse, but I do at least have the satisfaction of feeling my fist thunk into some squashy part of Fritzi's startled face.

By that time I'm down on the ground, though. There's a lot of shouting and cheering going on and my star of futile courage has collapsed into itself. So have I. I'm just crouching there covering my head as best I can and waiting to die, and at the same time noticing how far away the shouting seems now, as though it's got nothing to do with what's going on here in the playground, but is happening in some other place and time. There's the salty taste of blood in my mouth and there are jabs and thuds and slaps all over me, but they seem far away too now, as though I've got separated from my body so that nothing really hurts.

But abruptly, like that storm passing on the mountain last summer, the hail of blows dwindles to a drizzle and then ceases altogether. The cheering dwindles away too and there's a moment's utter silence before a voice says, "What's going on here? Stop it at once!" It's Fraülein Meissner's voice and it's a weary voice rather than an angry one. "Get up," she says now. And as no one else is down, I suppose she must mean me. So I do get up, slowly and ashamedly, as if I know I'll get the blame for this and probably deserve it.

"Are you hurt?" she asks, peering into my eyes, and I see her face large and concerned through the blur of my tears. Of course I am, but I look away and shake my head. "Go and wash yourself. And you too, Fritz, your nose is bleeding. Go along, both of you."

And through the silent avenue of intently watching faces we go almost side by side towards the boys' washroom. There's no one else there and we bend over the two basins next to each other, slopping cold water onto our faces. "Jewish blood," Fritzi says, wrinkling his nose and nodding at the stuff dripping off my split lip into the diluting water. But I can tell the drama's over now and this is just the epilogue.

"Half-Jewish," I answer, and realize this is only the third time I've ever said anything to him, and they've all been today. "And half-German."

That tickles his ethnological fancy, and he grins, sniffing his own blood back up his nose in a long gurgling slurp. "No wonder it's so thin," he says quite amiably. "Look at mine." He daubs a bit of his blood on the side of his basin. I daub a bit of mine beside it. They look the same to me, and perhaps they do to him too, because he quickly splashes water over them both till they trickle away together in a little pinkish dribble.

The bell is clanging. He jerks his head and I follow him out. And so we return to the classroom almost together, not quite as enemies, not quite like friends. At the end of school I shoulder my bag and walk off, for the first time not slinking away. And nobody accosts me. When I get home I tell my mother I tripped and fell flat on my face, and that's why I've got a black eye and my lip's all cut and swollen. If she doesn't believe me, she doesn't say so. Luckily it isn't bath night till Friday, and by then my other bruises have all faded.

That little drama has an unexpected denouement. I'm not a shadow anymore, I'm there, I'm substantial, an acknowledged member of the class. Not one that anyone cares about, but still. No one except Resi Hofer anyway, whose lips as well as eyes sometimes half smile at me now, although still she never speaks. And Fritzi actually nods at me as I pass him near the gate. I'm almost respectable. I've got a French terrorist to thank for that.

But I'm not the only one to have an eventful school year. Ilse's having some ups and downs as well, and so, more literally, is Martin. Let's follow chronology and start with Ilse, racial science and the bureaucrats.

■

The teachers in the Catholic Girls School are divided in their attitude towards the Führer.

Some remember him in their prayers, where he's mentioned in second place after the Pope, perhaps with a halo visualized above his head. Others have misgivings. Still others don't care one way or the other. The Sister who's principal of the school belongs to the third group; or perhaps to the second. At any rate not to the first, because when Gabi humbly petitioned her to admit her two daughters who unfortunately were at once Protestant and half-Jewish (how she'd learnt to be meek and submissive!), Sister Aquinas made no more objection than to steeple her pale blue-veined hands, blink behind her small rimless spectacles, which she wears at the tip of her retroussé nose, shake her head and sigh, "Well, we needn't tell their teachers everything."

Not all the teachers are nuns. Biology and history are taught by lay teachers. Perhaps that's Sister Aquinas's deliberate choice. Biology and history are ideologically sensitive subjects and it wouldn't do to have ideological disputes erupting among the nuns. They've got to live together after school after all, while the lay teachers go home to their separate families, friends and lives.

But the biology teacher is not only lay, she's also Nazi. Frau Professor Forster, a German from Bavaria, is a dedicated Party member, and when she marches into the classroom she always clips out "Heil Hitler!" which Sister Aquinas never does. (And Sister Aquinas doesn't march in, either. She sails. She's slight and walks with quick little steps so that her habit floats out behind her and her body glides along without swaying or rocking.) Frau

Professor Forster is buxom and blonde; she has produced two sons for the Fatherland already and shows no signs of stopping, which is just as well for the Fatherland, considering the Russian campaign has started. Her husband is an SS officer of whom she's naturally very proud, although what does she know about what he gets up to in the occupied territory of Poland, where he's been posted for more than a year?

Now there comes a time in the curriculum when the science of race must be taught more fully than it can be dealt with at the primary level. There's a lot to this science that primary school youngsters just can't understand and you've really got to delve into it as a teenager if you aren't going to remain an ethnic ignoramus. The time for that delving comes in Ilse's first year at the school. And no teacher's a keener delver than Frau Professor Forster. In fact she sometimes calls the subject the queen of the sciences, which, since it has become the Nazi theology, has a certain plausibility from Frau Professor Forster's perspective, whatever Sister Aquinas might say about it.

Yes, race is to Frau Professor Forster what sex is to a nymphomaniac—she just can't get enough of it. Someone who loves the subject that much is pretty sure to make a proper job of teaching it, and that's exactly what Frau Professor Forster does. No half measures for her. She gives Ilse's class the whole works—chapters from this and paragraphs from that, descriptions of Eskimos and Nubians, American Indians and New Guinea natives, Scandinavian athletes and Teutonic heroes. But that's only the prelude. Next they're treated to visual aids (what a lot of planning must go into those lessons, what thought and care!). Beautifully colored wall diagrams featuring full frontal and profile pictures of the Nordic Aryan (straight, upstanding, intelligent, beautiful, strong and dominant) and the various lower species ranging from the servile Slav through the various types of Asian and Negroid, down to the ultimate depths of the Pygmy and the pernicious hook-nosed Jew. The expressions on those vivid pictures are made to match the description of their characteristics, and Frau Professor Forster, normally a stickler for discipline, allows and even encourages the "Oohs" and "Aahs" which the repulsive faces of the inferior races naturally elicit from her superior Aryan pupils. The Jew, Frau Professor Forster warns them, is particularly dangerous because he possesses a certain low and vicious cunning, which the Pygmy for instance and the Gypsy lack. They're just primitive, while the Jew is actually depraved. That's why the far-sighted Führer has made such a point of eliminating the Jew from our national life, which he (the Jew, she means, not Adolf) is bent on corrupting and destroying. Then comes a brief but solemn reading from the scripture of *Mein Kampf*, which no one understands, but everyone listens to as reverently as they would to the Book of Revelation, which in Frau Professor Forster's worldview it very probably is.

But all that's merely been the introduction; next come the fundamentals. What could be more scientific? She flips down the charts displaying the naked skulls, the basis of the facial features by which we recognized the different races. Now the groundwork of racial science stands revealed. The Aryan skull, they see, is lofty and broad-browed, the Jewish by contrast narrow and with a rodential backward-sloping forehead. The ears are lower and the eye sockets close-set. Frau Professor Forster's own blue eyes, wide-set in her broad bold Aryan brow, survey the class, searching for a good example, one row after another. It isn't enough to know a science theoretically; you have to see its application to the facts.

"Ilse Brinkmann!" she beckons imperiously with one hand, the other resting on her generous hip, so well designed for the parturition of future members of the master race.

Prepared for martyrdom (except it isn't *her* faith she's going to die for), Ilse slowly rises and stands trembling before the class.

Her hands are clasped in front of her and her head hangs low. The end of the world could not be worse than this. Perhaps it *is* the end of the world?

"Don't droop, Ilse! Stand up straight!"

Frau Professor Forster snaps open a little oblong black box on her desk, and out come shiny calipers and slithery measuring tapes still more scientific than those that bore mute and unquestionable testimony to Sara's half-Jewishness in primary school a few years before. Now it's Ilse's turn to be exposed and condemned. Frau Professor Forster measures the quaking adolescent carefully: diameter of skull, length of nose, width of nostrils, width of brow, distance between the eyes, proportion of chin to top of head, set of jaw and ratio of sinciput to occiput. They don't go into that kind of detail in primary school. That's what the secondary level's all about, getting down to the very foundations.

"Now you see how science works," she concludes triumphantly at last. "All the measurements indicate an Aryan head. If we had an Asian or a Jew here, the results would have been very different. Very different indeed."

For the first time in her life Ilse in her astonished relief is less than honest. She doesn't confess the awful truth to Frau Professor Forster, who would find it as hard to bear in her own way as Ilse does in hers. Perhaps she doesn't even believe it *is* the truth anymore. Perhaps she's beginning to think like Martin that she really could be Aryan, that the Jewish stain has been miraculously expunged. Perhaps she's beginning to dream of joining the League of German Girls on the one hand and taking communion on the other, of belonging at last to those from whom she's been so long a lonely outcast. Perhaps she's even thinking that the reason Sara's skull came out as half-Jewish in her very own primary school test (Ilse only found this out by accident) is that Sara's father wasn't Aryan Willibald but Jewish Josef, as Aryan Willibald has indeed so often hinted. Science is objective after all, the instruments don't lie, and they tell everyone that Ilse's passed the Aryan test while Sara has not. She goes back to her place with a wonderful giddy lightness in her head, a sense of precarious joy. Ilse is glowing, like a girl who's felt at last the first caress of love. Yes, it may be autumn outside the classroom, but inside Ilse it is spring. Can summer be far behind?

Yes, very far.

Back in Vienna the bureaucrats have had their morning coffee. They settle their plump or bony bottoms into their comfortable chairs and open their bulging files. And in the files they discover an irregularity, an infringement of the rules. Laws are changing all the time, mark you. It's a wonder the bureaucrats can keep up with them. Yes, those people really earn their money. But keep up with them they must and do. And the latest law, an amendment to the *Aryan Paragraph,* is that half-Jews are now allowed a high school education only till the end of sixth grade, normally the end of their sixteenth year. No exceptions. Even if they're top of the class, that's where the gravy train will stop for them. They get off there and work in factory or field, leaving the brainier stuff for their betters. Not that they can be sure they'll be left in factory or field for long. Half-Jews are still half-Jews even if they're also half-Aryans. But one problem at a time. Just then in Vienna, it's the problem of schooling they're going to solve.

And there's the anomaly. Poor slow Ilse is seventeen already, although she's still in the sixth grade. A half-Jew getting education, using up valuable resources, when she's past seventeen in the sixth grade? Preposterous! It isn't just the grade that's meant to count—it's the age as well of course! Otherwise some of those wily half-Jews would stay in the sixth grade till they were twenty-five! You can certainly see how that crafty Jewish blood works on their character! The half-Jew Ilse Brinkmann must be expelled at once!

So next week when Ilse arrives at school with her head still full of Aryan dreams, she's summoned to Sister Aquinas's office. It's at the beginning of the first lesson, straight after the morning prayer and Frau Professor Forster's radiant "Heil Hitler!"

A man in a suit stands beside Sister Aquinas's desk, his hair neatly clipped and his glasses stern and trim on the bridge of his nose. Sister Aquinas is steepling her pale hands again, or rather sliding one palm against the other as though the steeple they briefly make as they meet is toppling in an earthquake. Her rimless spectacles are on the tip of her nose as usual, until she takes them off and lays them on the desk, either to see Ilse more clearly or to avoid doing so. And Ilse, waiting with butterflies of disquiet fluttering in her stomach, thinks nevertheless quite detachedly that she's never seen Sister Aquinas without her glasses on before and that her eyes look weak and watery, as though she must be seeing everything through an aqueous blur.

"Unfortunately it has become impossible to keep you in the school," Sister Aquinas announces with a sigh and a glance at the man beside her. "It appears that your age was overlooked when you entered . . ." She lifts her hand and the rustling black sleeve falls like a closing wing. "However that may be, the current regulations do not permit"—she hesitates; apparently she doesn't want to say "half-Jews"—"do not permit students in your racial category to remain in school after their sixteenth year."

Ilse, quiet at the best of times, is quiet at the worst as well. While she's trying to take this news in, hearing the unsteady thumping of her heart and feeling loss falling like a stone plumb through her body, she's also wondering what she's supposed to do now. Say "Heil Hitler!"? Go back to her class? Go home? Does that mean she's got to go to another school? (How she hates being a new girl, and always too old for the class!) Or no school at all?

Then the man standing beside Sister Aquinas settles the

last point for her. "You passed the age limit on your seventeenth birthday," he says curtly. "Don't you realize that? You shouldn't be here. Did you think a half-Jew could stay in the sixth grade forever?"

Ilse's lips quiver as she hears that word "half-Jew" (which was also half spat out) and she feels the blood leaching out of her cheeks, but still she doesn't know what to do. She waits with her suddenly tear-filled eyes on Sister Aquinas's already watery ones. But Sister Aquinas is looking down as though now she certainly doesn't want to meet Ilse's appealing glance.

"You can collect your books and personal property now and go home," Sister Aquinas says quietly, like a judge resignedly sentencing a prisoner he privately does not believe is guilty. "Give this note to Frau Professor Forster." She seems to want to say something more, but instead she places her glasses back on the tip of her upturned nose, nudges her notepad to the center of her desk and writes three lines in a fine small hand. Ilse watches the lines crawling across the paper, watches the words *half-Jew* appearing like a wriggling worm upside down on the page, watches Sister Aquinas's soft white blue-veined hands fold and seal the note, watches her reach out with it across the desk. Their hands touch briefly as Ilse takes it. Sister Aquinas's hand is colder than hers. Sister Aquinas seems about to speak again, but again she doesn't. Instead she gives a wan thin smile of farewell. The man beside her watches Ilse leave. His lips are pursed and he is making satisfied hand-wiping motions like a surgeon washing up after the neat excision of a malignant tumor.

Almost worse than leaving school and all its illusory hopes is going back to Frau Professor Forster and asking permission to collect her things. Frau Professor Forster is discoursing on the superior power of the Aryan brain today and the noble skull is on display once more. She frowns impatiently when she has to interrupt her flow to read Sister Aquinas's note.

"*What?*" she exclaims incredulously under her breath. She glances up at Ilse as though she can't believe her eyes, and glances down to read the note again. Her wide Aryan brow frowns. There is a subdued rustle in the class, the rustle of paper gently pushed away, of yawns stifled and whispers not.

When Frau Professor Forster looks up again, it is with a glare of indignation and hurt, the resentful glare of one who's been betrayed. "Take your things and go," she says coldly, and waits in silence, tapping the edge of the folded note against her palm. "Hurry up, will you? You're holding up the lesson!" The other girls watch Ilse with mystified fascination as she closes the lid of her desk and walks like a convicted criminal out of the room. Probably half of them think she's pregnant—they're at that age. After she's closed the door behind her, she hears Frau Professor Forster's voice resume, uncertainly at first, as though she's forgotten what she wanted to say, or even lost confidence in its truth, but then with returning strength and authority.

I will never come here again, Ilse thinks as she walks down the familiar empty corridor, listening to the different muffled voices and varied murmurs as she passes one classroom door after another. The weight of her loss makes her walk even more slowly than usual. *I shouldn't be here. I'm a half-Jew. I shouldn't be here.*

Then there's the lonely walk to the station, the endless hour's wait for the next train, the long slow grinding journey, the trip across the lake on the ferry—everyone staring at her, she's sure, everyone divining her shame—and the fearful dawdling along the lane to the Pfarrhaus. Frau Kogler the midwife glances at her in surprise as she cycles to her next delivery. Dr. Kraus's golden-haired Aryan mistress, airing her golden-haired Aryan baby in a squeaking but Aryan pram, regards her with a knowing look.

That's bad enough, but worst of all will be explaining to

her mother. Ilse knows she'll have to tell her every detail over and over, live through her shame again and again. The shame of her Jewish blood that after all could not be expunged. How could she have dared to hope she'd escape the contagion? It's in her body, an inherited disease like original sin. No, it *is* original sin. She keeps seeing the posters on the walls of Plinden, the cartoons in the newspapers, she keeps hearing the slogans on the wireless we're no longer allowed to listen to, but which she remembers vividly and thinks she hears muttered behind her wherever she goes. Her father knows it and her mother knows it—that's what they quarrel about at night when they think no one can hear them. How could she ever have supposed she'd not been tainted by her mother's blood?

Gabi is elbow-deep in the washtub, which is how she spends much of her time now that Jägerlein is gone, when Ilse appears with her silent hangdog expression. "What, you already!" she exclaims irritably, glancing round at the clock. "Why so early?" Ilse walks silently up to her room and empties her satchel onto her desk. She sits on the edge of the bed and waits, hands clasped in lap, for the storm to break. After a time, when no storm breaks, she unties the red ribbons in her twin dark braids and puts her books away in the bottom of her wardrobe, thinking, correctly, she will never need them again. I will find them there years and years later—Frau Professor Forster's workbook, *The Aryan Race,* obviously a labor of love, and Ilse's own neat notes and answers, what a credit to her teacher, her faded ribbons pressed inside the covers.

It isn't till the washing's done that Gabi thinks to ask Ilse again what brought her home so early. That isn't indifference, but distraction. She's just had her own little brush with authority, as a result of which she's been seeing stars.

■

Little yellow ones in fact, and though they're only made of cloth, they were weighing on her mind like lumps of iron. Authority in her case took the portly shape of Ortsgruppenleiter and innkeeper Franzi Wimmer, who, standing at the proper distance on the second step from the front door (which did at least have the advantage that Gabi didn't have to smell the beer on his breath), informed her that Jewish persons were henceforth legally obliged to wear a yellow star with the word "JEW" on it, in crooked black Hebrew-like letters, whenever they left their homes. Naturally, those stars must not deface Austrian national dress—which Gabi had in any case long ago given up trying to fit into—but were to be clearly visible on the left breast of such nondescript clothes as Gabi was now permitted to wear. And he gave her four yellow stars (admittedly of poor-quality cloth, but after all there was a war on), which she should please sew on forthwith. Not gave, sold. With an official receipt as well. Ten pfennigs each. Making, he carefully and correctly calculated, forty pfennigs in all.

"What about the children?" Gabi asked him woodenly, feeling the rough-napped cloth between her fingers. "Shouldn't they get half a star?"

The Ortsgruppenleiter, who was fond of children, and even didn't really mind us half-Jews (and nor did his son, now that we'd played out our little scene), protested stiffly that he didn't make the laws, it was only his duty to see them carried out. The authorities had not yet made a ruling on half-Jews, but when they did, she could be sure he'd inform her. And as a matter of fact, he went on huffily, if she wanted to know (she didn't, but what choice did she have?), he'd been to some trouble to get those stars for her. He wasn't supposed to carry stuff like that around, it was meant to be supplied by the local Jewish Welfare Office. But as there wasn't one in the village (of course not, there weren't any other local Jews), he'd personally had the stars sent all the way from Linz. The trouble he'd given himself on her account! She could at least be grateful. "Heil Hitler!"

He remembered too late that he should never have said "Heil Hitler!" to a Jew; it degraded the national salute. But saying it had become as automatic by now as opening his fly before he peed. He tried desperately to think of some way of recalling the gesture, but, lacking the resources, merely turned haughtily away.

Gabi, conscious both of the undeserved honor and the prohibition against reciprocating, nodded as the painstaking Ortsgruppenleiter marched unsteadily off, no doubt muttering about ungrateful Yids beneath his beery breath.

Well, that had kept Gabi's head down among the washing all right, and all day she'd felt a little hand-sized star burning against her breast although all four of them were actually stuffed away out of sight in her worn and shapeless apron pocket. It took some energy to turn herself on at last and ask Ilse again what brought her home so early. She imagined a teacher was sick, or there'd been some function of the Catholic Church from which Ilse as a Protestant would naturally have been excluded, but when she hears Ilse reluctantly murmur the actual reason, she gasps and slumps suddenly down. "This is the end!" she shouts. (But there she's wrong.) Then, suddenly shrieking with the sword-thrust of her first gallbladder attack, she slides off her chair down onto the floor.

Ilse thinks *that's* the end. Her mother's dying and she'll be bound to get the blame, and even get a Jewish curse as well. It makes her still more silent, which in turn makes Gabi think she doesn't care about either her mother or being thrown out of school. Which does indeed make her blame Ilse in her raging agony. Ilse waits trembling for the Jewish curse, but, thank God, at least that doesn't come.

Nor do I. Well, not too near. I hear Gabi's groans when I

return home from primary school; and then my father's tragi-comic weeping in the study (he's only just come in and found out what's up himself). Gabi shouts at me to keep out of the way, so I creep behind the kitchen stove and for the hundredth time wish Jägerlein was there again. It's Sara of course who eventually applies hot poultices to Gabi's stomach when she and Martin come home from school, scalding her hands on the steaming flannels. Martin, getting on at once with his latest Panzer design, complains about the basin of hot water and damp towel left standing on the dining-room table. He cannot stand untidiness.

Later that night I wake to hear my mother shouting downstairs. "I will not wear it! I tell you I will not wear it! Even if I never leave this house again, I'll never wear it! Never!" Then there is the sound of Willibald's voice, in an unfamiliar low and pleading tone I scarcely recognize. What he says is drowned in the splashing of water as Sara refills the basin on the dining-room table.

Next day a yellow star has been sewn on the left breast of Gabi's worn black coat. I think it looks smart, but when I try to tell her so, she snaps back, "What do you know about it? Just stop staring like that, will you?"

And the day after that the star is off again. Yes, it's been taken back by poor Franzi Wimmer, who's discovered he'd misread the rules, and Gabi doesn't have to wear it after all. Before she's even had a chance to go out, there he is again, self-important but crestfallen, standing nice and early on that second step below the front door. He's dropped a clanger, he says (or rather doesn't say, but his body language says it for him). He's read the rulebook again, and it seems that Gabi's "privileged" because she's married to an Aryan man, and privileged Jews are not required to wear the Jewish badge of shame. Indeed, and that's why he's come so early, they're not *allowed* to! She'd better give those stars back at once.

What a mess! What a loss of face and time for the ill-informed but earnest Nazi! No wonder his breath is steaming on the bright but cold September air.

"I had no idea I was privileged," Gabi remarks in a rare attempt at irony. Rare and ineffectual; it bounces off Ortsgruppenleiter Wimmer's solid skull like marbles off a granite slab. "*You* may not know it," he declares impressively, his chest swelling with the pride of one acquainted with the regulations, as indeed at last he is—he ought to be, he's spent half the night poring over them. "*You* may not know it, but *I* do. You may be interested to learn that if you were married to an Aryan *woman,* you wouldn't be privileged."

Gabi doesn't think she'd be privileged being married to an Aryan woman either, since she's not that way inclined. But that's not what's in Ortsgruppenleiter Franzi's dogged mind. He means if she'd been a Jewish *man* married to an Aryan woman. Neglecting to say so, he leaves Gabi mystified as to the drift of Nazi race and marriage laws. The mystery continues as Franzi does, going still deeper into the finer points. "But if you were married to an Aryan of either sex and had children who were baptized Christians," he declares, "you'd also be privileged. Unless the children were living abroad." What an expositor the man is, he really ought to have been a lawyer.

"But I *am* married to an Aryan of either sex with children who are baptized Christians!" (What does Gabi mean by "either sex" here? Has she begun to entertain doubts about Willibald's gender? You couldn't blame her—he isn't very virile.)

"Exactly!" Franzi declares triumphantly. "You're doubly privileged! There are two reasons why you can't wear those stars. Return them at once. "Please," he adds, not having lost his sense that she's still the Frau Pfarrer even if she is a Yid, and is therefore still entitled to those few grains of respect.

Gabi does as she's requested and asks for her money back

when she's handed the badges over. Franzi Wimmer considers the top star lying in his hand, to see if its sojourn on Gabi's tainted breast (or rather the coat that would have covered her tainted breast) has damaged or polluted it, then repays her forty pfennigs, for which he in his turn requests and obtains a receipt on the official form he's thoughtfully brought with him. No one would ever find fault with his accounts. This time he remembers not to give Gabi the "Heil Hitler!" salute and mutters a sloppy Austrian "Wiederschau'n" instead, to which she returns a frosty German "Auf Wiedersehen!" which cracks like ice on the autumn morning and indistinctly reminds the poor man he's just a country bumpkin after all who gets the regulations muddled and speaks a dialect that proper Germans ridicule.

So now the stars are gone. But so is Ilse's schooling. And Martin's will be next. Then—

7

One by one the others'

The following week Gabi has a long talk with Willibald in his study.

To begin with her voice sounds calm and reasonable. Then it becomes wheedling, then angry, then alarmed. Willibald's voice starts quiet, becomes curt, changes to angry and ends shrieking hysterically, if a wombless creature can be hysterical. Books are thrown against the door and feet stamped on the floor.

My parents are discussing their children's education.

The shock of Ilse's expulsion has concentrated Gabi's mind. Martin will be expelled at the end of the school year too, when he completes the sixth grade. Then it will be Sara's turn, and eventually mine. Out of school and into the underclass. We can be hewers of wood and drawers of water for the Third Reich, but shakers and movers we certainly cannot. Ilse seems to have accepted her destiny with her customary resignation. She's sure she was born to suffer, and so far history's been on her side. Martin hasn't confronted this idea yet, but it's out there waiting for him, as are one or two other things he doesn't know about yet. As for Sara and me—it's still too far away for us to think about.

Willibald accepts our fate as well, now that Aryanization's out, but Gabi's still full of fight. If the two older children can't go to school, school will have to come to them. Fraülein von Kaminsky must be recalled. Or Frau Doktor Saur-that-was, who isn't enjoying married life as much as she expected. And Gabi's old and best friend Maria Müllendorf in Berlin could be asked to come, or her second-oldest friend Frau Professor Hoffmann. Or some other ladies from the Confessing Church. (*They* haven't been showing up recently, by the way. Not since Willibald's return from the war, in fact. Could it be he doesn't welcome them?) But one way or another, the children's thwarted education must be carried forward.

■

"Education for what?" Willibald asks theatrically. "To work in some factory or sweeping up manure on a farm? Because that's the only job they'll ever get. They won't need any more schooling for that." Then comes a graver objection. "It's bound to be illegal. D'you think our children are being thrown out of school so that they can get a private education by themselves? It's not long since the Authorities stopped them from having private instruction and made them *go* to school." (Whenever he invokes authority, it's with an audible capital *A*.)

"Well, now it's the other way round," Gabi reasonably responds. But then comes Willibald's clincher. "Besides, we can't afford it!"

Gabi certainly has her work cut out this time. But she goes straight to the heart of the matter, and says they can sell things— some of the furniture that came as her dowry, the jewelry and embroidered tablecloths, even the spare bed linen that came from her dead sister Frieda. Frieda meant it for Ilse's dowry, but who knows if or when she'll ever get married?

And that's where the acrimony really starts. Willibald can't bear to part from his possessions, even if they're actually his wife's or daughter's. He'd rather submit to the divine or Adolf's will and let Ilse and Martin get along without any futile further education. If that's what life's got in store for them, so be it, they'll just have to get used to it. It is their lot that God in His unfathomable wisdom has chosen them to suffer. Here the tears flow for the stunted lives they'll have to lead, and perhaps in hope of the rewards in heaven that may await them. But no selling of the family jewels! Is it his fault his children have been denied an education? Now the tears flow for himself, who he imagines will soon be living pitiably in a drafty house if his wife has her way, bereft of tables, chairs, beds and bedsheets.

And in fact Gabi *has* been selling damask tablecloths and linen bedsheets in Plinden and Bad Neusee already, to pay the bills she's run up at the grocery and dairy, the doctor and the dentist. When Willibald learns this, the books and pictures begin to fly, which only depreciates their value for the future sales Gabi has in mind for them. No wonder she's started having gallbladder attacks, and she has one opportunely now.

It's at this point in their discussion that Willibald displaces his anger at his wife and starts shouting curses instead at Deputy Führer Hess, who first of all didn't permit him to teach religion in the schools, then secondly ("That damned traitor!") went off his head and flew to Britain in search of some Scottish duke or other a few months ago; and at the State Office for Genealogical Research for not acknowledging his wife's mother was a dissolute adulteress.

Ilse might be slow in school, but she's no sloth when it comes to scenes like this, and she's already quietly closed whichever windows were still open. Martin maintains an aloof indifference. He's been reading a booklet about the heroes of the SS Panzer regiments, one of whom, a Major Schultz, had chalked up so many kills that the enemy armor he's destroyed in one theater or another apparently weighs as much as all the factories of Coventry put together, which our brave bombers, including gallant cousin Erwin, have recently reduced to ruins. I believe Coventry had quite a lot of factories, so that sounds pretty impressive. Martin will have his work cut out designing a Panzer to beat that, especially if he isn't going to be in school next year. But that doesn't seem to worry Martin. He's sure he can do it; he's got a thing or two up his sleeve. (Incidentally, Major Schultz has just been killed in his Panzer by what obviously can only have been a sneaky shot from an English anti-tank gun in the North African desert. Martin had better stick to the designing side and leave operations to someone else.)

Soon Willibald emerges from his study weeping copiously for all to see, and makes for the front door, followed by Gabi clutching her side. But as he doesn't threaten suicide this time, Ilse does not follow to prevent him. He'll only make a few parish calls. It's nearly four in the afternoon, a good time for coffee, and some of his parishioners still have the real thing. With a bit of luck he might even get a slice of cake and a nip of schnapps as well. After that it will be back to *King Saul* (soon it will be *King David*. The Bible's scope seems boundless), and refuge from the world he simply can't confront.

Gabi, however, has things to do in that world. With a hot-water bottle pressed against her side she sits down at the dining table and writes to Maria Müllendorf in Berlin and to Fraülein von Kaminsky and Frau Doktor Helena Saur-that-was in Vienna. But before she can get any answer she must first endure the vicissitudes of Martin's mountaineering with the Hitler Youth.

And so must he.

Martin has taken matters into his own hands. Matters of

the Hitler Youth, that is. He's never been asked to join the noble band. How could he be? He's a half-Jew. But his inordinate self-esteem has encouraged him to think the omission must be just an administrative oversight—after all, he's half-Aryan too. So he's written a letter to the area headquarters in Plinden, applying to join the sacred brotherhood. He hasn't mentioned the maternal half of his parentage, but he has stressed the paternal half's recent military service and his own devotion to the Fatherland—he's even mentioned his Panzer interests. He always did have difficulty adjusting to reality. None of us know about his temerity until a letter with the official Hitler Youth heading arrives addressed to him. The letter requires him to appear at the next meeting of the Plinden Group, bringing food and clothing for three days, all to be packed in a weatherproof rucksack. Particular attention is to be paid to warm clothes, rain cape and boots suitable for mountain trekking.

Willibald, who usually escapes reality by ignoring it, is as pleased by this as Martin is, whose equally unfortunate attitude is to expect that reality will mold itself to his desires. "They're learning sense at last!" he declares. "Soon all the children will be recognized as true Germans. Mark my words, they'll be going back to school soon, after all. I knew this would happen in the end. Someone higher up must have made a decision." If Gabi's skeptical about that, and if she has mixed feelings about her son joining the Nazi counterpart of the Boy Scouts, she doesn't show it. Any port in a storm. She tries to help Martin pack his rucksack but is soon sent packing herself by the assured young aspirant to Hitler Youthdom.

The glorious morning dawns and not much later we accompany Martin down to the ferry. Martin's in his smartest shorts and shirt, as close as he can get them to the Hitler Youth uniform. "Off to join the Hitler Youth," Willibald announces proudly to a few sparrows snatching up breadcrumbs, to the

Catholic priest, who peers at him mildly astonished, and to Dr. Kraus's wife, who's holding her wig down against the freshening wind and doesn't seem to hear. They are the only other passengers on the ferry, and Martin ignores them, as they ignore each other. Dr. Kraus is an agnostic and his wife's supposed to be one as well, although no one's ever asked her—no one ever asks her anything much. As to the mistress, presumably she's an agnostic too, since she's no more seen in church than the others are. The agnosticism of the ménage à trois in their out-of-the-way house inhibits the Catholic priest's ordinary affability (though the ménage à trois itself does not—he can deal with that), and consequently he ignores Frau Dr. Kraus as much as Martin does. He peers out in silent discomfort instead at the receding bank, which for a time, and after a confusing turn about deck, his myopia induces him to think is the approaching one.

Martin stands at the stern in masterful solitude, one foot placed on the rail, his brown hair fluttering against his forehead. Where have I seen that pose before? I know I've seen it somewhere, but where? Of course! It's Heinrich Schmidt's air of careless command, the nonchalant superiority of the Aryan male. That's how he stood on the ferry that far-off evening after our Indian summer up the mountain. Martin remembers too, I can see he does from the self-conscious look in his eyes. He's imitating Heinrich, the only friend he's ever had, his model Hitler Youth.

Martin takes the train to Plinden, as does the Catholic priest, but although Frau Dr. Kraus buys a ticket, she waits at the station until the train has gone, as though she's forgotten what she's there for or had a sudden change of mind. Then, when the ticket office closes, she starts walking along beside the tracks as though she hopes to catch it up. We see her from across the lake, a small, dark figure receding into the woods, her hand occasionally clutching at her wind-raised wig.

Willibald decides we should celebrate this turn for the better and splurges money and ration coupons on some Apfelstrudel at the best baker in the village, who will not serve his wife. (Gabi waits like a dog submissively outside.) The baker's surly even to Willibald, but Willibald's been swallowing insults and ridicule most of his life and today is no different as he burbles on about Martin joining the Hitler Youth as though the incredulously contemptuous look on the baker's face is a congratulatory grin.

■

Meanwhile Martin has joined a number of other candidates for the junior heroes' brigade. They're told by a ramrod-stiff adult Leader to tag along behind the initiated as they stride up the mountain singing "We're Marching Against England" and "The Banner High." And surely—Yes! That's Heinrich Schmidt up at the front, leading the singing and leading the march! Heinrich Schmidt! He feels his heart is going to burst.

It's a long way up the mountain, further than he's ever been before, and sometimes they pass through shreds of clammy mist that veil them from each other. They pause for lunch, pulling out their sandwiches of cheese and wurst, and Heinrich's laughing and joking with everyone, even the stiff adult leader whose name Martin hasn't yet learnt. Well, nearly everyone. Not the recruits; they're treated with a certain lordly disdain. But it would be too much to expect Heinrich to stoop to them just yet. Wait till they've been enrolled.

Then it's up and on, and before long they're approaching the snow line. And there, nestling just below the snow, is a hut exactly like the one above Heimstatt, except that a swastika is flapping proudly from a tall white pole in front of it.

The initiates dump their rucksacks inside the hut shouting and laughing, while the candidates, shivering slightly (the sun is setting), wait outside in anxious expectation. This is the solemn moment before their rite of passage. In a few minutes, one of them informs Martin, the ceremony will begin. Their names will be called. One by one they will take the oath and be admitted to the brotherhood. "It's like being confirmed," he remarks in awed tones. "Only this is real." And he ought to know—his brother was admitted last year. Martin tries an assured Heinrich Schmidt pose, resting one foot on his rucksack and gazing off towards the distant peaks, but the rucksack sags and topples, and he has to pretend he was merely giving it a casual kick.

Now, at last, as the sun goes down behind the western mountain rim, the sacred ceremonies commence. The Hitler Youths form three sides of a square round the flagpole while the uncertain tyros stand self-consciously by their rucksacks along the other, lowest side. A bugle has appeared and it's Heinrich Schmidt—who else?—who raises it to his pursed lips. Out the noble haunting call rings across the twilit peaks, echoing and re-echoing ever more faintly till it fades away among the rocks and snow. The three rows of Hitler Youths stand with their right arms unwaveringly raised. The fading light shines like torchlight on noble Aryan eye and resolute brow. And then the torches do come out, smoky and resinous pine torches, which burn like beacons in the cold mountain air. And the arms that hold them aloft no more waver now than they did when they hailed the Führer at the going down of the sun.

The ramrod adult's voice now summons the recruits to take the oath of fealty to their Great Leader, Adolf Hitler. One by one they come forward as their names are called and stand with outstretched arm beside the flag, repeating the sacred words in proud and solemn tones. Some even have tears pricking their eyes; they know they'll never live another day like this. They are like monks taking their vows—no, they *are* monks taking their vows: the new Teutonic Knights, monks of race and war. One by one they pass from the flagpole where the oath is administered to take their place in the ranks of their initiated comrades.

When does doubt begin to gnaw at Martin's innards? When he realizes that, while the names are being called in alphabetical order, the Bs have all gone but he has not? Or when he sees Heinrich Schmidt glancing at him with an amused ironic smile in his torch-lit eyes? Certainly, by the time he's the last one standing there beside his sagging rucksack, his stomach's beginning to quake with the suspicion that something isn't going as it should be here.

Then his name is called after all, but not in the same tone as the other names were called. There is something cold in that voice now, something cruel, not the proud and welcoming tone that summoned the others. Martin steps uneasily to the flagpole.

"Martin Brinkmann, what race is your mother?"

Martin Brinkmann swallows. He licks his lips. But he doesn't speak. Perhaps he cannot speak just then. In any case, he feels as though his insides have been suddenly scooped out.

"Martin Brinkmann!" the voice demands again, even more harshly. "What race is your mother? Answer!"

But Martin Brinkmann doesn't answer, because it's true, he cannot speak. Something's quivering in his cheek, but his tongue is paralyzed. He looks helplessly at his tormentor, then drops his eyes. The leader's face is all edges and flint. There's no hope there.

"Is your mother, or is she not, a Jew? Well?"

Martin hangs his head, then slowly nods.

"Yes, your mother is a Jew! Her name is Gabriella Sara Brandt! Your father is the kind of German that marries a Jew! And you are the product, a filthy half-Jew!" Each time he utters the word "Jew" the Leader's lips twist as he injects a little more venom into his voice, a slightly colder sneer. "And now you're trying to creep into the Hitler Youth? Did you think you could hide here of all places? What insolence! Did you think we didn't know? Did you think we don't have records of all your sort?

And even if we didn't, did you imagine we wouldn't smell you out a mile off! Go! Get out of here! Vanish! You're poisoning our air! Go back to the sty where you belong!"

Martin stands a moment unbelieving, then finds he does believe it after all. God has turned his face from him again! He feels suddenly heavy and tired, as though the whole mountain is resting on his shoulders. Then, in a silence as deep as the Heimstatt lake he bends down trembling to pick up his rucksack. He feels he's going to crumple in tears on the ground before them all. But no, he doesn't crumple and he doesn't cry. He's got to go on. He straightens slowly up and slings the rucksack over his back. One of the straps is tangled somehow and he can't get his arm through it. He has to wriggle his shoulder frantically to get the rucksack properly on, and that brief clumsy violent and ridiculous struggle elicits a suppressed snigger from the ranks of the pure disciplined Hitler Youths—such an indignity of course would never happen to them. At last with a final shrug the rucksack is on and he slinks miserably away—away from the torchlight, away from the flag, away from Heinrich Schmidt, away from every hope of happiness, stumbling over the pitiless rocks in the pitiless dark.

Soon, he thinks, soon he'll feel the pain, he'll know how deep the knife has gone. But just now there's only the numbed shock of the wound. The pain won't come till later. Before he passes below the brow of the hill, he glances back and sees Heinrich Schmidt's face smiling broadly now, about to break out into amused laughter. And then the laughter does break out from all of them, the kind of laughter you'd expect to hear in a restaurant if a monkey came in and tried to order a meal.

Martin doesn't know the path. It's dark and misty. He falls several times and several times has to retrace his steps. And for a long time he hears the words of another song echoing faintly at his back. *When Jewish blood sprays from our knives* . . . Then, when he reaches the tree-line at last, the gloomy pines soughing in the rising wind make even his half-Aryan heart uneasy. It's as though ghosts of the old Teutonic heroes so beloved of the Führer and his pebble-eyed henchman Himmler are striding through the somber woods and will any minute appear before him, immense and menacing, the vengeful guardians of the purity of the race. What if he died here, lost among these cold dense pines? For the first but not the last time, he wonders whether dying there and then wouldn't be better than going on living, but nevertheless he does go on living, plodding grimly through the darkened threatening woods.

When at last he reaches the town, the last train has left hours ago. He spends the night huddled by the station and takes the first train in the morning. The ticket clerk, an elderly veteran of the last war, assesses him bleakly and asks why he isn't still up the mountain with the Hitler Youth. Hunching his shoulders, Martin mutters something about being ill, which the clerk neither fully hears nor fully believes, and doesn't care much anyway.

On the train he finds an empty compartment and slouches in the corner by the window. He closes his eyes and sways with weariness, but cannot fall asleep. Heinrich Schmidt is laughing at him behind his sore and weary eyelids, and dozens of Hitler Youths are charging towards him brandishing daggers and chanting *When Jewish blood sprays from our knives . . .*

The train dawdles everywhere along the winding track, but especially as it nears Heimstatt. Then its brakes grind unexpectedly, it shudders to an abrupt unscheduled halt and Martin looks out on reality again. In the trees where the gleaming line curves sharply round the lakeshore, he sees the remains of Frau Dr. Kraus being shovelled into a body bag. She has spread herself across the track and lost, among other parts, her head, which in turn has lost its wig.

■

When he learns of Martin's humiliation, Willibald is secretly relieved the village gossip is so full of Frau Dr. Kraus's self-decapitation that there's scarcely room left in it for Martin's humiliation and his own. Nevertheless, behind the swiftly closed windows he loudly threatens lawsuits, police reports and even personal confrontation with the unknown Hitler Youth Leader, who must have acted like that merely out of personal spite for him (himself, he means, not Martin). Then he subsides at last into the sobbing mode and locks himself into his study. *King David*, he announces later when hunger gets the better of his grief, has been christened with his tears. Yes, that's the day *King David* springs off the blocks, if an advance of three lines in two hours can be described so athletically. An inauspicious start. No wonder its lines are limp and halting.

And Martin's pillow has been christened with his tears as well. I know, because when I pass the door I hear him sobbing quietly to himself, but not the less bitterly for that. He never mentions this episode of the mountain-climbing Hitler Youths again. But he hasn't given up. Someday he knows he'll be recognized and accepted. He has to be. He's Martin.

■

Gabi thinks so too, and she's been doing all she can to bring it about. There are answers from Fraülein von Kaminsky and Frau Doktor Saur-that-was; there's been a hurried, furtive trip to Vienna, where Gabi stayed illegally in Frau Doktor Saur-that-was's apartment while her tyrannical husband was away in Klagenfurt. Helena Saur-that-was is still a Nazi, but calls herself a thinking one—she's got a taste for oxymorons. Still, they say that every Jew has an Aryan angel, and Frau Doktor Saur-that-was is Gabi's. Lucky for Gabi that her privileged status allows her to travel without the Jews' yellow star. Even her angel would never have dared meet an obvious Jew at the railway station and take her into her home. It's still a risky business all the same, and Willibald delivers scared finger-wagging admonitions when Gabi leaves for Vienna. "Six weeks in prison if you're caught in an Aryan house!" he declares. "A hundred and fifty Reichsmarks fine!" And that's the minimum. If it's the Gestapo that gets her, not the ordinary police, she could be in real trouble, and so could he.

Helena Saur-that-was is running risks as well. She'll be in for a fine or prison too if she's caught, not to speak of expulsion from the Party and whatever punishment her husband might impose on her for breaking the law. But she blithely ignores all that. A thinking Nazi, Gabi's Aryan angel.

But only Gabi's Adolf Eichmann, as much a stickler for detail in his own way as Helena Saur-that-was's husband is in his, has been getting down to work in the city, and there are hardly any Jews left there for her to protect by then, even if she's got a mind to. Just the odd one or two who like Gabi are privileged for the time being by their marriage to an Aryan. Just for the time being. It's only logical that if the Aryan dies, the Jew loses that protection and gets snapped up and deported, sometimes at the cemetery gates before they've even had a chance to put their handkerchiefs away. No point in hanging about, after all. The wheels must keep on rolling for final victory, Dr. Goebbels is fond of declaring, and Obersturmbannführer Eichmann is certainly doing his bit to keep them rolling out of Vienna.

■

After some time a couple of letters arrive from Maria in Berlin. Then there are several scenes in Willibald's study, expanding through the whole house as the study runs out of books to throw and pictures to tear down and trample. Next there are several days in which Gabi mainly lies supine and groaning while Sara silently applies steaming towels to her tormented side and Ilse prays in her room. (Martin and I do whatever we usually do, he knowing he's far above all this commotion, I that I am far beneath it.)

And then suddenly a sullen peace descends. Meals get cooked again, dishes get washed. For all I know, *King David* might have moved forward an inch or two. Christmas has come and we even have a tiny tree cut from the mountain and some cheap presents on Christmas Eve. But Christmas isn't the reason for this change of mood, goodwill season though it may be. No, the reason is that Gabi's irresistible force has overcome Willibald's immovable objections, and her latest educational plan is about to be implemented. Two days after Christmas she announces the news to Martin and me.

■

We're going to spend a semester in Berlin.

Yes, just when German troops have torn Russia's heartland open (well, nearly) and shoved the British out of North Africa (well, almost), and the ranter at his cockiest is approving the final plans for the grandiose rebuilding of Jew-free Berlin as Germania, capital of the Thousand Year Reich—just then's the time that Gabi chooses to send Martin and me to that very capital to further our half-Jewish, or in my case possibly full-Jewish, education right under the Führer's snotty nose. You've got to admit she's got a lot of chutzpah—or is she so damned naive she simply can't appreciate the enormity of what she's up to?

Why are they always springing surprises on me? (They aren't *always,* but this one's so big it feels as though they are.) Do they think I'm a rubber ball to be bounced off any old wall? I might not like having to face Fritzi Wimmer every day in the playground, but I'd rather face him any day than start at a new school in Berlin, where something tells me Ortsgruppenleiters' sons will be twice as many and three times as nasty as Fritzi—

who as a matter of fact I'm getting on all right with now, since our little encounter in the playground. No, Martin may think this scheme is fine, but I don't like it one little bit.

But then I realize something: Willibald doesn't like it either. He's scared he'll end up still deeper in the shit, though that's not how he phrases it, and he's certainly in deep enough as it is with his Jewish wife and half- (full-?) Jewish kids. Yet strangely enough, his dislike of it has the opposite effect on me, and I begin to warm to the idea after all. A new principle is slowly taking shape in my brain, a principle I must have gleaned from experience: if Willibald doesn't like it, it's probably all right.

"What about all the air raids?" he demands as Gabi packs my case. He's accepted the decision at last, but that doesn't mean he won't try to sabotage it. "The British are destroying our cities! That brutal Churchill wants to raze them to the ground!" Willibald hasn't got the wireless back, but you can tell he still reads the papers and is a patriot at heart.

Gabi swallows the mouthful of water that, following the Kaminsky principle, she's been holding in her mouth for several minutes or so. "Maria said they haven't had a raid for months," she answers, straining at the lid to see how much more she can cram in. Is that what she believes, or only what she wants to believe?

"And when the barbaric Russians come . . . ?" Now Willibald's voice is near to tears, and his voice chokes in a sob. He really can turn the tap on at a moment's notice. The Russians are in disarray a thousand kilometers east of us, but Willibald's as convinced of the imminent Bolshie danger as any Nazi ideologue. Well, as I said, he reads the papers. He buys one in the village every day. They won't deliver it to us because we've got the Jewish taint. Jews aren't allowed to read healthy Aryan papers, and healthy Aryan papers would get contaminated if they entered our house. Perhaps they aren't so healthy after all.

"Berlin is further away from the Russian front than we are," Gabi says, pushing in an extra pair of socks. I peep at my school atlas later that night and am relieved to discover her political geography at least is right, though only just.

I still don't know what's really going on, except that Martin and I are being sent to Berlin, where, it now occurs to me, we all really belong. But why us two and not the others? No use asking Willibald—he's too deep in sentimental and self-advertising grief. And Martin only looks exasperatedly up to heaven whenever I ask him anything. So my mother is the only source. But she's gone suddenly taciturn and gruff and I see her wiping her eye with the corner of her apron when she thinks no one's looking. (Sara sees it too, as she sees everything, and buries it inside her.) It isn't till weeks later that I piece it all together—Gabi's strategy against the Nazi policy on half-breeds' education.

Frau Doktor Helena Saur-that-was thinks she has spied a loophole in the new regulations, a loophole which Martin might be able to scramble through into the castle of German higher secondary education. As from this year, half-Jews completing the sixth grade will have reached the finishing line. But if they're already in the *seventh* grade, they can continue. Not as far as university, of course—who do they think they are?—but anyway until the end of school.

"The Nazis are just, you see," Frau Doktor Saur-that-was tells Gabi. "They may be hard, but they don't make regulations retroactive." Now that's a bureaucracy which even her manically tidy husband can be proud of. (Her manically tidy husband, by the way, has recently been punishing her more severely for uncombed carpet fringes and carelessly folded newspapers, and she has shown Gabi her knees, sore and scabby from kneeling on the firewood. Gabi has recommended calamine lotion. Frau Doktor Saur-that-was will apply this soothing ointment to her bum as well, though Gabi doesn't know yet that her husband's punishments have extended to that region too. No wonder he sports a duelling scar. Perhaps he thinks the one on *his* cheek should be complemented by one on hers.)

So if Martin can complete both this year's and next year's curriculum in six months, perhaps he could go into the eighth grade next year, just as if he'd been in the seventh grade this year. And then—who knows?—perhaps the regulations will have changed. This anti-Semitism won't last, Frau Doktor Saur-that-was is sure of that. (Has she read *Mein Kampf*? Has anyone? *Can* anyone?) The Führer's far too intelligent not to see what a mistake it is. It's the Reds who are the real enemy. Her eyes glisten when she mentions the Führer, as a nun's would when mentioning the Pope while discussing some questionable doctrine brought in without the seal of papal infallibility and sure to be rescinded. She's an incurable optimist—she has to be, living with a husband like hers. How could she face tomorrow unless she believed things couldn't be worse then than they are today?

Of course she can't teach Martin herself, much as she'd like to—she still remembers what she thinks of as his Aryan charm. Her manically tidy husband certainly wouldn't allow irregularities like that. But perhaps someone else could? There's no doubt Martin's got the brains for it all right. If only he can get a teacher. Pity about Ilse, but there you are, she's just too slow.

Gabi turns first to Fraülein von Kaminsky, but for all her aristocratic contempt of the Nazis, Fraülein von Kaminsky has no desire to risk her hide for either Martin or Willibald, for both of whom she feels an almost equal scorn. And so it's Gabi's oldest friend Maria that's been willingly enlisted. As a teenager, when she helped convert Gabi, Maria wanted to become a missionary and dreamt of martyrdom among the heathen in Africa, and though her dominating father soon put a stop to that, she now yearns for martyrdom through some act of defiance against the heathen at home. A prudent man, although himself no friend of the Nazis, her father would put a stop to that too if he could, but he's grown frail and his dominance over her has weakened. The indifference of age has drifted over him like ash from a dying volcano, and congealed into a dull grey crust. He's past caring about anything much anymore, except his creature comforts. That's Maria's chance, and she's grabbed it with four hands—her own and Gabi's second-oldest friend, Frau Professor Hoffmann's. Not only will Martin go to Berlin and be taught by them, but I'll go as well, and be enrolled in a Berlin primary school, which they have no doubt is far better than the Heimstatt yokels' academy I'm currently attending.

But what about Ilse and Sara? Don't they get a look-in too? Well, if there's anything Willibald and Gabi still agree on, it's that they've given up on Ilse. Frau Doktor Saur-that-was was right; Ilse is just too slow. Perhaps she'll go into a Protestant nuns order, or even a Catholic one if they'll have her, since she seems so popishly inclined, or else just stay at home until something happens—the Nazis pass away, or she does, or she even finds someone to marry her, or . . . well, something or other. After all, the future's just a fog—it's no good peering into it. So's the present, come to that. Only the past, the fairly distant past of pre-Nazi Germany, offers a view worth looking at.

Yes, my parents have given up on Ilse, and so it seems has Ilse. Since her expulsion from school, her clock has been running even slower, and no amount of Gabi's frantic winding can make it gain a second. "*Say* something, Ilse!" her mother sometimes demands. "Why don't you *say* something?" Ilse considers this, then slowly murmurs "What shall I say?" She never was a talker, but now she doesn't speak at all unless she's forced to. And that's the kind of thing she says. Besides, she usually answers so slowly that people stop listening before she's finished, which she consequently rarely does. The problem is, she doesn't think she's got anything to say, except perhaps to God, who appears to have stopped listening too. She's resigned herself to being a half-Jewish leftover, an object of contempt and disgust to everyone including herself. (Or by the Jewish rules, she's fully Jewish, since her mother is. That makes her even worse. She tries not to think of that.) As if to emphasize her unworthiness, she walks still more slowly than before and drags her left foot all the time as though it was shackled to an iron ball. She eats more slowly too, and when we've finished our scanty wartime rations she's still chewing hers with a vacant look in her eyes, as if she was a sad cow ruminating. Yes, everyone has given up on Ilse, but all the same her race is not yet run. Ilse still has miles to go before she sleeps. Miles and miles.

What about Sara, though? She's going to be kicked out of school herself next. In another three years, unless the Nazis change the laws and make it sooner—which they very likely will, the way they're beavering away at the details of their ethnic cleansing. What's to be done about her? Well, Sara's all right where she is just now. Say what you like about Catholic nuns, and Willibald often says quite a lot when he's in his High Lutheran mood, but they are giving Sara a good education. Besides, she *is* only a girl, after all, and, well, education isn't such a big deal for them, is it? But most important of all, someone has to be there for Gabi to confide in, and she certainly isn't going to confide in Willibald or Ilse. That leaves Sara stuck in her by now accustomed role. So —

8

Here we are at Salzburg Station

A couple of half-Jews, if not worse, headed for the sacred citadel of the master race. We don't know it yet, but we've chosen to go to Berlin on the eve of the very day that SS Obergruppen-führer "Bubi" Heydrich is going to open a meeting there which will work out the logistics of the liquidation of my mother's and possibly my race. As our train draws in to the Berlin station, Government, Party and SS officials will be stepping out of their limousines at a charming villa on Lake Wannsee, along whose shore Willibald and Gabi often used to stroll before they were married. And they'll be getting down to business before we've even started our breakfast.

Gabi couldn't have chosen a better, or a worse, date, if only she knew. But luckily she doesn't know, and there we are pacing up and down in blissful ignorance outside the Salzburg Station Restaurant, which all of us can enter except my mother (at least I think we can—this half-Jew business isn't clear), so we all stay out. Not that Willibald isn't tempted to go in by himself and snatch a sizzling wurst, but there are several SS men at one table, and SS men always give Willibald the jitters. All the more so at that moment of brazen racial audacity when Gabi is vicariously bearding the lion in his den. Besides, it's too expensive anyway. So he contents himself with window-eating, giving the menu displayed behind the glass a famished critical once-over. We stand like an ill-assorted flock of hungry sheep around his bony figure, which is as thin as a shepherd's crook, and just about as curved at the top. He pushes his glasses up onto his forehead, cranes his neck to read, shakes his head and chuckles aloud at the effrontery of the prices, worrying inwardly all the time what will happen to him if Gabi's scheme is discovered by the Nazis. It's lucky she's pushed her scheme through now, by the way. She wouldn't be able to see us off in a poignant platform farewell in a few months' time. Railway stations as well as restaurants, not to speak of buses and streetcars, are going to be out of bounds even to "privileged" Jews then. Except if they've got more than five kilometers to go to their forced labor, in which case they can travel standing on the platform at the back.

I have a little brown suitcase and a little brown rucksack. Martin has a large black suitcase and a giant green rucksack. Recently he's been trying to straighten his hair, to give himself a more Aryan look. It's a wonder he hasn't tried dyeing it blond as well. But all that brushing and crimping and gluing has only strengthened the kinky tendency, so at last he's given up. There have to be some curly-haired Aryan heroes, and he's looking about him at the soldiers and policemen, hoping to spot one now. Failing to do so, he throws back his shoulders anyway and struts up and down by himself, trying to look the part of a Hitler Youth Leader which only ill luck and his unlucky genes have so far denied him.

"Make sure you get out at Berlin Anhalter Station, not Berlin Zoo," Gabi anxiously interrupts his promenade. What would we get out at the zoo for, I wonder, though the idea does appeal to me. I think of elephants and lions wandering past the carriage windows. But apparently Gabi means the station, not the menagerie itself, and Martin looks long-sufferingly up at the heavens, or rather where the heavens would be if the station roof didn't block his view, and continues his almost manly progress.

"And keep hold of your brother's hand," she calls out after him.

Will she never learn?

"For God's sake!" Martin explodes theatrically, glancing round to assess the effect of his Führer-like impatience on the watching masses. But the masses don't seem to be watching. Only Gabi. She looks crestfallen and blinks her non-drooping eyelid. I suspect Martin will want to take that out on me when we're safely on the train. Not for the first time I feel I'm not going to enjoy travelling to Berlin with Martin, and I'm pretty sure he feels the same about travelling there with me.

I turn my eyes back to the restaurant again. A large wurst and potato salad stands on top of the glass case on the counter, and on the wall behind it hangs an even larger picture of Adolf, looking resolutely confident. (Well, it's only just 1942 and the bad news has barely started trickling in yet.) For some reason that juxtaposition in my visual field sticks in my mind, and whenever I think of the Führer again, I'm always going to see him presiding over a creamy potato salad on which a fat brown glistening wurst nestles snugly like a fresh Saint Bernard's turd (I haven't forgotten Brutus).

The train leaves on time (what else are Führers for?) and I sit by the window facing forward until Martin, who's been doing the departing-hero act, standing at the window and nonchalantly waving goodbye, turns and pitches me out of it. Now I'm facing backward in the middle seat, between a fat woman who doesn't smile at me, and an SS trooper who's just come in and does. Three featureless middle-aged men who might be anything or nothing sit opposite me in featureless clothes.

"How old are you, laddie?" the SS trooper asks, and drops his cap over my head. Only my ears prevent it from covering my eyes, and everyone except Martin gives some sort of grin. Even the fat woman's tightened lips twitch into an indulgent smile, unless it's a hastily suppressed belch. Martin on the other hand merely scowls resolutely out of the window in an imitation of the Adolf portrait that decorated the Station Restaurant wall.

I can see he's a bit uneasy about this SS trooper. They're supposed to be the elite, the stern and purposeful defenders of the Reich, guardians of its honor, purity, glory and the knives and forks—so what's this one doing, playing games with an insignificant little runt like me? And a not quite pure runt too, I can see Martin inconveniently thinking. His glance strays over the man's uniform, he notes there's no decoration on his tunic yet and I see him concluding this is just a young recruit, lacking the august dignity that Martin would have in his place. Martin gazes sternly away again, the perfect exemplar of Aryan determination and discipline.

Meanwhile the SS man disconcertingly removes his cap from my unworthy head, flings it with a casual flick of his wrist onto the baggage rack (where it flops like a dead crow onto the fat lady's case), loosens his collar, huddles in his corner seat and closes his eyes to snooze.

The light is dimmed, the blackout blinds are drawn, and I sit in the artificial gloaming watching Martin's Aryan stare and the others' shadowed faces. Something's bothering me, but I don't quite know what yet. Something that I'm waiting for, and it's keeping me awake. Maybe it's what's keeping Martin awake too, not just his vigilant Aryan urge. The fat lady nods and bulges beside me, the SS trooper sleeps the sleep of the brave, and the three nondescripts opposite fold their arms, lean back and doze, their heads lolling and jerking like broken puppets. Only Martin and I are awake, as if we're restless with some fever. I'm not sure what the trouble is—and yet of course something in me knows all along—until the ticket inspector slides the door open.

Then I realize. It isn't him, though. It's the voice I hear behind him in the corridor. "Identity cards please!" Now I see Martin's eyes glance back that way too, then meet mine with a wary and complicit look. *That's* what we've both been waiting for and dreading—the moment when they inspect our all-revealing papers, and our racial taint's officially exposed. After the ticket collector's gone, two soldiers appear at the open door, flashing their flashlights over the passengers' faces. And while one inspects their identity cards, the other peers over his shoulder, to make sure there isn't any monkey business.

I watch Martin take both our cards out of his pocket and see my own anxiety upon his face. Are we going to be booted out into the corridor or the luggage van, thrown off the train at the next station—or even right away—or merely sneered at as half-Jews? What will the genial SS trooper, whose Aryan leg is now pressing obliviously against mine, think when he finds out what I am? I move my own leg stealthily away in deference to his coming change of heart. Out go the others' cards, one after the other, in outreached but unworried hands. The fat lady stretches her lips over her teeth and regards them in the dully illuminated mirror, testing her faint but definite lipstick. She leaves her hand out negligently for the return of her papers, which with a muttered thank-you duly occurs. The three nondescripts opposite are not so casual. They turn their faces politely towards the flashlight as the policemen check them against their photos, and murmur thank-yous themselves as they are given back their cards and briefly thanked. The SS trooper doesn't even wake, and the policemen shrug and leave the hero sleeping.

Now they take Martin's and my papers. They play their flashlights thoughtfully over them and us, frown, glance at each other and briefly confer. One of them's older and has a pinched tired face, as if he's sucking his cheeks in or has left his false teeth out. He's the one who peers over the other's shoulder, sniffing out the monkey business, and I sense it's he who's going to decide. I try to look at him pleadingly, and, when that has no effect, try to look away all unconcerned instead. Eventually he shrugs again, as he did for the SS trooper, though certainly not on the same grounds, and nods. They give us each a hard look as they hand the papers back, but the only mark of disapproval is that there's no thank-you for us as they slide the door shut behind them.

I see Martin's face relax as mine must have done when Fritzi Wimmer didn't taunt me but just left me alone. He takes out one of the sandwiches Gabi made that morning and begins to munch it slowly, his lower lip pushed out like Mussolini's. I get one too, after nodding meaningly and tapping his knee. He regards me with the faintest suggestion of a smile, something I don't recall him ever offering me before. He must be feeling as if he's been accepted into the Hitler Youth after all. I even get my proper share of the sandwiches. Maybe Berlin won't be so bad, I think before I drift off to sleep. My leg touches the SS man's again, and I feel contentedly that now I can let it be. Even when my head occasionally lolls against his broad Aryan shoulder, I do not flinch. Who knows? I might actually be going to enjoy being in the heart of the heart of the Nazis.

■

And Tante Maria and Frau Professor Hoffmann, as I've been advised to call them, seem to think so too. Tante Maria is plump and undulating with unfulfilled matronly curves, Frau Professor Hoffmann thin and straight from the feet up, with two prominences at her head, one a beaky nose, the other a large bun of spinsterly grey hair resting on the nape of her neck. The rest of her's as smooth and straight as a weathered beanpole. While Martin starts his private tuition straight away with Tante Maria,

Frau Professor Hoffmann arranges matters for my own education. She takes me to the local school, which in this case is rather classy, where there's the usual form to fill in with the usual box about my Aryan descent or lack of it. Frau Professor Hoffmann has a whispered word with the secretary and what if anything gets written in that box I never see.

Lo and behold, I'm registered in the school, and Frau Professor Hoffmann says no one knows my mother's Jewish. "And don't you tell anyone she is," she adds. I wonder if there are any more crypto-half-Jews like me in the school. "Never you mind," Frau Professor Hoffmann replies on the way back to Tante Maria's home. "Remember you're just the same as everyone else." One thing I do know: if they pull my pants down to find out, they'll certainly think I am. My Christianized mother never considered such a mutilation and as for Willibald—you need every bit of it you've got, is the tenor of his Gentile thinking. It's one of the few things they've always agreed upon. That, and Ilse's slowness.

■

The school is in the Steglitz district, where Tante Maria and her father live, and nearly all the kids are officers' children, or lawyers' or doctors'. And as Maria predicted to Gabi, I find I'm far behind them, except in reciting the morning salute to Adolf, which, depending on the teacher, they often do in a perfunctory manner, and sometimes even miss out altogether. That's a far cry from the well-drilled practice of the loyal village school I'm used to. Although I'm word perfect at it, neither Frau Professor Hoffmann nor Tante Maria seems impressed by my prowess in that department, nor by my ability to recite the soldier's oath, which Willibald has a habit of intoning under his breath when he's feeling nostalgic for the heroic soldier's life: *I swear this holy oath by God to give unconditional obedience to Adolf Hitler, the*

Leader of the German State and People, and Supreme Commander of the Army. I further swear that I am prepared to lay down my life at any time in fulfilment of this oath. In fact they stop me halfway through when I try this out on them one lunchtime and I sense that even a Jägerlein poem might go down better, if only I could remember one.

Soon after that I too start getting private tuition from them, in math and German, where it seems I'm most deficient. They assume that since I'm a pastor's son, I must be well up in the religious department. Lucky they don't put that to the test. I've hardly ever been to church and when I have, I've usually been daydreaming. And Willibald is far too busy writing plays to teach his own children in the home what he's not allowed to teach others' children in the schools. Consequently, I scarcely know Saul from Paul, or John the Baptist from Ditto the Evangelist, although I've got grace as word perfect as the Soldier's Oath, or, come to that, the prayer for Führer, People and Army (*Bless above all our Leader and Supreme Commander in all the tasks he undertakes*), which is another of Willibald's favorites.

Frau Professor Hoffmann appeals to me because she's got one false eyetooth which she sometimes puts in and sometimes leaves out. I can't discover the principle behind these dental epiphanies, but trying to do so certainly sets my brain cells humming. I like Tante Maria too, because she smells of powder and eau de cologne and turns her head aside when she coughs, which she often does, and neither sniffs wads of the stuff back down her throat nor noisily evacuates it in full view onto her handkerchief as Willibald tends to do. She says she hopes I don't believe everything I hear on the wireless at home. When I tell her our wireless went with the dog and the rabbits, she first shakes her head, then shrugs. "Better nothing than lies."

I'm not sure how much I like Tante Maria's father, though. He reeks of nicotine and something indefinable that I associate with age (Martin says it's stale piss), and there are usually egg or coffee stains upon his shaggy white beard. Besides, he's unpredictable. Sometimes he's full of chesty good humor, when he shows me pictures of people he says are Kaiser Willi and Marshal von Hindenburg, whose belly's so enormous I wonder if he'd be taller lying down than standing up (and he's no dwarf when he's upright). At other times Onkel Karl, as I've been told to call him, seems gruff and irritable, and I keep out of his way. But that's nothing to the tantrums and scenes I've been used to in Heimstatt, and all in all I think it's pretty serene here. In fact, a new thought is beginning to dawn in my mind (I'm at that age when thoughts do dawn). It is that life here is more or less normal, whereas life in Heimstatt, which up till now is all I've ever known, is not. That's quite disturbing, like finding out you're on the wrong path when it's too late to turn back. What have I missed? What am I going to miss? The query dawns on me, then gets obscured by all the clouds of daily life. But every now and then the clouds thin and dissipate, and then the query dawns again.

One night I'm woken by a curdling wailing noise I've never heard before, and then the *Crrump! Crrump!* of what at first I think is thunder. But this thunder's louder than even that summer storm on the mountain two years ago, and there's no Heinrich Schmidt here now to make me feel all right. Instead there's Martin, who tells me it's anti-aircraft guns and the Tommies are coming. That doesn't make me feel all right at all. Then Tante Maria appears in her dressing gown and curlers, and down into the shelter we go.

Through the curtained but unlit windows in the hall I see a jazzy lattice of searchlights and blooming fireworks far away. Martin pauses to look despite Tante Maria's urging, and says "Lancasters," which makes no sense to me, and then "Damned Tommies!" in a defiant Aryan voice, which does a bit, but not entirely. I know the Tommies are supposed to be our enemies, but who "we" are is still obscure, since my mother isn't kosher German, although she isn't kosher Jewish either, and it's only kosher Germans that the Tommies are fighting. So I leave to another time the question of who's the enemy and who is not—it's just a philosophical problem, after all. Think of all the trouble Fritzi Wimmer gave me over the selfsame question.

"Get a move on!" Onkel Karl growls suddenly beside me, carrying a torch, candle and for some reason umbrella, and on I move. In the shelter are all sorts of people in all sorts of sleeping clothes, all very quiet and listening. Some have hats on, some carry mugs of coffee and thermos jars as though they're off on a picnic, and some are clasping their heads in their hands as if they expect the roof to fall. Onkel Karl opens his umbrella and holds it up above his head. "Dripping!" he declares, nodding at the roof in answer to my mute inquiry. *"Dripping!"* All that fascinates me until rebellious Martin arrives and announces that an enemy plane is going down in flames. His voice is exultant, but curiously no one else seems pleased at all. Maria even shakes her head and coughing murmurs, "Poor young men."

■

Which is what she murmurs, also coughing—she certainly can cough—when cousin Erwin comes to visit us a week or so later with his fiancée Lerke, and his younger brother Robert, who's just joined the Wehrmacht, none of whom I've ever seen before. Erwin, with his iron cross and oak leaf, looks how Luftwaffe aces are supposed to look, except he isn't quite as Aryan blond as I thought he'd be—light brown you'd call it really. But he's an ace all right, and all heel-clicking courtesy, as well. So is Robert (heel-clicking courtesy, I mean), although he's only a lowly Wehrmacht recruit. Still, you can see your face in his polished boots. As for Lerke, she's a strawberry blonde and smiles sweetly at Martin and me with her deep blue eyes while Erwin asks after all the family, and even mentions Tante Gabi by name as though the Nuremberg laws had never even been thought of, never mind passed. Is it Erwin's charm, or the brownish color of his hair, not so very many shades lighter than his own, that induces Martin to forsake Panzers for aircraft on the spot and set his sights on becoming a Luftwaffe pilot?

"Luftwaffe pilot?" Erwin echoes with a smile when Martin confides this dream to him. His smile is more rueful than ironic, although he surely knows Martin has about as much chance of becoming a Luftwaffe pilot as he has of seeing Hitler's willy. "That's what Robert wanted too, at first. But I told him he was mad."

"Mad? Why?"

"Because as a rule the life of a Luftwaffe pilot on active service is about three months."

Then he turns to Lerke and gives her an exaggerated bow and smile. And this time his smile is ironic. "Permit me to observe that I am a lifetime exception to this rule."

Lerke's eyes had clouded, but now they clear and she smiles back at her betrothed with all the trust and patient courage of a noble German girl.

Tante Maria tentatively mentions there are relatives of Gabi's still here in Berlin. Gabi's Aunt Hedwig, she means, and some second or third cousins. That's the first time I've heard them mentioned since we've been here. As I've never met them, they mean very little to me and I don't mind if I never do meet them—especially as I sense meeting them could be a little risky. "I don't know whether you'd like to see them . . . ?" Tante Maria asks Erwin diffidently.

Erwin doesn't even need to glance at Robert or Lerke before he answers, sleeking one eyebrow down with his little finger. "Perhaps another time," he smoothly and regretfully murmurs.

But there's a spasm of embarrassed silence for a few seconds, as though someone has just farted and nobody can think of what to say to distract us from the smelly indiscretion.

■

It's only a week or two after Erwin and Robert have left—Robert to crush the Bolshies in the East, Erwin to subdue the English in the West—that Tante Maria and Frau Professor Hoffmann suggest a Sunday walk in the Botanical Garden, a park I half-expect to be full of lurking Tommies, since Martin told me some parachuted into it after their plane was shot down by one of our heroic German fighters. Martin isn't keen either (surely *he* isn't scared of the Tommies too?), but Tante Maria is strangely insistent, and so he comes along with manifest impatience and sulky ill grace. We reach the gates, but surprisingly don't go in, for which I'm faintly thankful. I don't like the idea of coming across some Tommies behind a bush, even though I only half believe we might, and don't know if they'd be alive or dead—or, for that matter, which would be worse.

Instead we stroll around outside the park and down an empty little lane until as if by accident we come across three people, a man and two women, who look pale and worn and down-at-heel. Each of them has a yellow star on their coat. They seem to want to make the star as inconspicuous as possible with their scarves, without exposing themselves to any accusation that they're hiding them. So these are Jews, the first I've ever seen if you don't count my mother, which for some reason I don't. Is this how Gabi would have looked if Franzi Wimmer hadn't taken her star back, I wonder. It adds a bit of color to their drab and threadbare clothes, but somehow I can understand why Gabi said she'd never go out wearing it. The man raises his shabby hat and speaks to us as if we ought to know him. As I happen to be nearest, I try to brush past this unsavory and disturbing trio, but

"This is your Onkel Solomon and Tante Lotte," Tante Maria says quietly. "And Tante Hedwig. She's your great-aunt."

Great Aunt Hedwig looks like an old woman whose skin has become two and a half sizes too big for her. You can see she might have been fat and jolly once, but now she's just shrivelled away and her emptied skin hangs round her like the rubbery wrinkles of a punctured balloon. She surveys me earnestly with watery eyes, and I look uneasily away at the other two, who merely seem drab, tired and woebegone. Their eyes are always glancing uneasily somewhere else, over their shoulders, across the lane, or just from side to side. But at least they aren't watery or fixed on me.

After some hesitation Martin does a heel-click that Erwin would have been proud of, and we all stand chatting, or pretending to, for all the world like people who've just met by chance and will soon be getting along on their separate ways. The chatting is mostly with Martin and Tante Maria; Frau Professor Hoffmann and I remain on the edge of the group. But even so I can tell they aren't really talking, they're filling in the time until they say goodbye. Our shoes scrape on the crunchy gravel path and the conversation's one of coughs and silences punctuated by words, rather than the other way round. Every now and then they look at me and smile and ask me questions in the way that grown-ups do, but as I don't know how to answer them I only look down and shuffle my shoes in a kind of sulky shyness.

Martin does better—well, he's older and besides, he's Martin—and occasionally there's a minute or two of unconstipated talk. It seems all they're interested in is how everyone is, and Martin paints a picture of jolly amity and good spirits that takes my breath away. Listening to him you'd think Ilse was on the way to university and Willibald to becoming a bishop. As for himself (naturally *he* doesn't get left out), he's probably going to join the Luftwaffe like cousin Erwin.

"Ach nein!" Great Aunt Hedwig murmurs in tearful shock, and there's a silence just as awkward as the silence that followed Erwin's oblique announcement that he wouldn't be meeting these relatives of Gabi's. Then Gabi's second or third cousin Solomon, who looks as though he's out of razor blades, which admittedly are hard to come by in these wartime years, pitches in with a question about Sara, who's also doing very well according to Martin—for a girl, of course.

After about fifteen minutes two men appear at the top of the lane, and Gabi's relatives hunch their shoulders and leave. And still they aren't really people to me—only shadows of people. But then that's what they seem to be to themselves as well. Martin gives another exemplary heel-click, but turns his eyes up to the sky as they shuffle off, as though *noblesse oblige* is all very well, but this riffraff shouldn't have presumed on it so much. I suspect the trio are as disappointed as we are, like beggars that haven't scored and are shifting to another beat. Then Great Aunt Hedwig suddenly turns back and, as I'm nearest, clutches both my hands in hers. "Remember us!" she implores me in a wobbly voice and with veiny tear-stained eyes that peer straight through mine into some dark and hidden place in my brain that I didn't know existed. And that makes me want to cry too.

"Imagine how they must feel," Tante Maria murmurs to Frau Professor Hoffmann as she watches them down the road and round the corner, "working twelve hours a day making bombs to drop on their own son in England . . ."

Frau Professor Hoffmann sighs.

"Son in England?" I repeat in a voice that's suddenly unsteady.

Martin sighs and rolls his eyes heavenwards again, as if my ignorance really is the last straw and his patience is totally exhausted.

"Wolfgang," Tante Maria answers absently, her eyes on the

two men now approaching us. "Solomon and Lotte's son. He got away before the war. He was going to be a pianist."

I'd like to go further into this despite Martin's obvious annoyance, but the two men are a few feet away now, and each of them is giving each of us a hard inquiring stare, which knocks all the curiosity out of me. Then the nearest one stops, takes out a shiny little bronze badge, flashes it at Tante Maria and mutters the word "Gestapo."

I feel as though I've just stepped into an empty elevator shaft, and shuffle my feet on the curb while Tante Maria and Frau Professor Hoffmann show their papers and answer questions awkwardly, like schoolchildren caught playing truant. It's not going to stop there, I know, and there's a definite anxious hush as the functionaries of state security now turn their scrutinizing orbs on Martin and me. Martin's aplomb is clearly out of true as he hands our papers over, which does nothing at all for my own rocky sense of self-possession. I'm scared that something even worse than Fritzi Wimmer is going to happen to me as our papers are suspiciously examined, first by one secret guardian of the Reich, then by the other. Eventually they put their heads together to make one brain, and grudgingly decide our papers are all right. We're all dismissed with a nod. Tante Maria (*still* hankering for martyrdom?) is then emboldened to inquire with something approaching sarcasm in her voice whether they really are quite satisfied that everything's in order.

"There's no room for you in the cage just yet," is the surly reply, and she turns away with mingled flutters of anxiety and triumph.

These endure until we go on into the Botanical Garden after all, where there are no Tommies lurking anywhere, dead or alive, but lots of proper Aryan people promenading in their smart though wartime clothes, and throwing balls for their proper Aryan children or proper Aryan dogs. "Let's have some coffee," Tante Maria suggests, her voice a little uneven and her cheeks a little flushed. "Maria," Frau Professor Hoffmann says reproachfully, "you really shouldn't go looking for trouble." I'm tempted to ask why having coffee would be looking for trouble, although I know full well that isn't what she meant; but then, glancing at Frau Professor Hoffmann's frown and Tante Maria's tightened lips, I find the temptation very easy to resist.

While drinking the milky and diluted ersatz coffee that was specially ordered for me, I remember that Great Aunt Hedwig wrote about her husband Moritz in her letter to Gabi last year. "Why didn't Onkel Moritz come?" I ask Tante Maria.

Tante Maria hesitates, glancing at Frau Professor Hoffmann, and I sense this is another of those questions which are better left unasked. "I expect Tante Hedwig didn't want to mention it . . ." she begins uneasily.

"What?"

"Well, she must have written to your mother by now . . ." Tante Maria goes on, throwing an imploring glance at Frau Professor Hoffmann. "Er, Onkel Moritz couldn't come. He's, he's . . ."

"He's been evacuated," Frau Professor Hoffmann declares firmly. "To the East."

"Yes, evacuated, that's right," Tante Maria agrees quickly, as though she'd quite forgotten what exactly it was that had happened to him until then. "Evacuated. Now, let's be getting back home, shall we?"

I sense with a little twist in my belly that there's more to this evacuation business than they're letting on, especially when I notice Martin's flickering eyes and knowing, supercilious smile. That's what I felt last year when Aunt Hedwig's letter came. But I'm scared of discovering what it is. Besides, I realize neither Frau Professor Hoffmann nor Tante Maria wants to tell me. So I do not ask. I decide not to think about it either, in the hope that it will just go away, which of course it doesn't.

Onkel Karl only grunts offhandedly when Maria tells him on our return where we've been and who we've met. He's hungry for his supper and doesn't want to hear any more about all that, he mutters peevishly. He's got his nose full of it, he says, which is the pungent if coarse German way of saying he's sick to death of it.

On the wireless an enthusiastic voice declares that the new territories in the East are welcoming more and more Germans every day who are coming to help the Führer build the New Europe. And there's a woman's voice to prove it, proudly announcing she is one of them and has never been so happy in her life.

"Will you switch that damned thing off at last?!" Onkel Karl demands with his mouth full, consequently spraying blobs of food onto his napkin and beard. It's as if he knows the relatives we met today would soon be moving East themselves like Onkel Moritz, and the thought of the contribution *they'd* be making to the New Europe is spoiling his appetite.

It's wurst and potato salad for supper, which reminds me of both Adolf and Brutus, but I eat it all the same, feeling vaguely uncomfortable and ashamed of my clearly poor and inferior relations, and ashamed of myself for feeling ashamed. And so I judge does Martin (only the first kind of shame for him though—he's never going to be ashamed of himself), because he dilates upon the superior tactics of German aerial warfare with more than his usual know-it-all dogmatism whenever Tante Maria or Frau Professor Hoffmann gently and indirectly wonders what would happen next to "those unfortunate people."

But the mood soon passes, or rather I soon push it aside, and by Tuesday or Wednesday I scarcely remember the broken, scared and shabby trio, let alone Great Uncle Moritz, whom I didn't meet and never will. Or if I do remember, it's only in my bed at night, when sleep leaves cellar doors unlocked and anguished haggard shadows steal upstairs to haunt my dreams.

Besides, in another week or two, I'm much more occupied by Martin's first Aryan romance.

■

Which is the first of dozens. Tante Maria has a sister Elsa, who is married to a lawyer. And the lawyer is a Party member. And Elsa has a daughter Eva, who's all a German maiden should be—still more blue-eyed than Erwin's Lerke, and still blonder too, a member of the League of German Girls, of course, and a star gymnast in her school. It won't do for Martin and me to call at a Party member's house, but Elsa can hardly fail to visit her father, and so she does, with Eva in tow. Elsa is somewhat cool to us, as befits a Party member's wife, but political correctness isn't Eva's thing, and she's all laughs and smiles. She's got a mole on her cheek which fascinates me, and when she sees it does, she tells me it's her beauty spot. For some reason that makes me blush all over.

Eva is younger than Martin, but you wouldn't know it, and her hormones are as acrobatic as the rest of her. With cake crumbs still on her well-formed lips she slips behind her mother, tucks her skirt in her knickers and performs handstands, cart-wheels and somersaults on the fresh May lawn, then arches over backwards and walks crabwise to and fro, giving us, but mainly Martin, a saucy upside-down grin, which enhances the charm of her beauty spot. All this impresses me, and I try walking like a crab too, which nearly breaks my back. It impresses Martin as well, but he wisely avoids any perilous athletic display.

It impresses her mother Elsa too when she notices, and she tells Eva sharply to pull her skirt down. Her voice has that shade and her eyes that meaning look which Gabi's have when she urges Willibald to pull his nightshirt down when the girls are about. But Eva, like Willibald, seems unconcerned. "That's how we do it in school," she answers pertly, but then she lazily obliges her mother, which is more than Willibald ever does Gabi. But it's too late, the damage has been done. Martin's hormones have been set jigging too, and he's going to dream of fondling those knickered loins for weeks, with one hand fondling his own.

What does he tell her that charms her up into our shared bedroom on one of her next visits? What does he need to tell her? She probably leads the way. Onkel Karl is dozing in his chair in the garden, his beard lying like a bedraggled fleece laid out to dry over his flabby chest and hilly belly. Tante Maria is deep in earnest talk with Elsa, suppressing her cough with a dainty white handkerchief. I gather, from a few words they drop and a few oblique glances they throw, that they're discussing Onkel Karl's declining health. Then Martin whispers something to Eva and Eva laughs beneath her breath, lowering her eyelids and glancing sideways at me, which I feel I have to pretend I haven't noticed. Then suddenly I'm all alone, sitting in the shade of the elm tree where a moment before there were the three of us. I wait for them to come back, but they don't.

That's boring. After a time I decide to go and find them. I try the rest of the garden first, then the house. Something—an intuition that I don't like, perhaps—warns me to leave our bedroom till last. It warns me to try the door ever so gently, too, as if I knew it would be locked. But there is whispering and giggling going on inside, and then a silence so profound it's pregnant. Metaphorically, I mean. I go halfway up the next flight of stairs, which would lead to the maid's room if there was still a maid to occupy it, sit down, cuddle my knees, and wait. Soon I hear Tante Elsa's voice calling in the garden. Soon I hear it inside the house, growing worried or suspicious. Then the door softly opens and Martin emerges, looking as though his balls have suddenly grown three sizes bigger, which they probably have. I lean closer to the banister, where he doesn't see me. Out comes Eva now, doing up the buttons on her dishevelled white blouse. (It was crisp enough when she arrived.) She calls out "Coming!" which she very well might have been a couple of minutes earlier, straightens her rumpled skirt, flings her pigtails back over her shoulders and skips downstairs. Martin follows slowly, with the smug and stately air of a Roman general at his triumph.

"Oh, just playing Skat," I hear Eva insouciantly answer her mother's irritable and possibly accusing query, as first Martin and then I appear behind her. "We didn't hear you."

Eva and Martin play Skat quite often in the next few weeks, although I never see a pack of cards. But then, just when they must be getting really good at it, Martin's fun with Eva has to end, and—

9

All his hopes of further schooling

It seems the Tommies just don't know when they're beaten. According to Tante Maria, who sometimes listens black (I've dimly got the drift of this expression now), we say we're shooting down more Royal Air Force planes than the Tommies say they're sending over. But somehow despite all those enormous losses, the British bombers keep on coming. Two or three times a week we're down in the shelter now, and occasionally, when there are really heavy *Crrumps!*, the roof shakes and bits of plaster fall on Onkel Karl's umbrella, although I've never noticed any drips. My stomach curdles when that happens and I realize I'm not the stuff that German heroes are made of. Or at least I would do if I didn't know already—ever since I met Fritzi Wimmer, in fact, on my first day of school.

But even superior Nazis are beginning to think discretion is the better part of valor now, and the schools are being evacuated. Martin and Eva play their last game in the bedroom and Martin is stoically desolate in the manner of Tristan bidding farewell to Isolde. But there's still worse to come for him, still more to endure.

On the very day Eva is skipping onto the train bearing its precious freight of German presumed maidenhood into the countryside, Tante Maria slits a letter from Heimstatt open with her ivory paper knife. It's Willibald at his most floridly sentimental. There's even a tear splash on one word, which fortunately isn't wholly washed away—he's a careful weeper. Enclosed is the official reply from the educational authorities to his request to allow Martin to jump a year and sit the examination for the eighth grade. Cutting out the bureaucratic introit and the Heil Adolf coda, the theme of this work is negative. According to the regulations, non-Aryan students are not permitted to jump a class. Only thoroughbred Aryans' athletic minds are up to scholastic leaps like that. So Martin's cramming has all been in vain, and his schooling is now terminated. Between the stodgy lines you can almost hear the phlegmatic and methodical officials allowing themselves a moderate chuckle. "Nice try, Willibald!"

What reproaches Willibald has heaped on Gabi's head, what bitter "I-told-you-so's," what countings and recountings of the futile cost, I am too young to imagine. Not that that stops me.

"And I'm sure you would have passed," Tante Maria ruefully assures Martin.

But Martin takes the news of his final dismissal to the wood-hewing, water-drawing underclass quite calmly. "Never mind, I enjoyed learning it all anyway," he replies with the grace of a downed Luftwaffe pilot emerging dauntless from the wreckage of his plane. (Do I see him stroke his eyebrow with a gesture as coolly elegant as Erwin's?) "It's bound to come in useful in the future." Perhaps he's also thinking of what he's learnt from Eva, in which case he's certainly hit it on the button.

I've got my farewells to say, too, since I'm not going with my new school into Eastern Prussia. The principal suggests to Frau Professor Hoffmann that I should, but I'm destined to return with Martin to Heimstatt, which everyone agrees is even safer.

All those transactions go on as usual above my head or behind my back or both, but on the last day of school Frau Stadler, who's always been slack about the morning Hitler salute, tells the class I'm leaving and wishes me well. The boy that sat unknowingly next to half- or full-Jew me all this time gives me his pencil with his name printed on it along one side, and since I can think of nothing else, I give him mine. "My father's been wounded in Africa," Ulrich says solemnly. "He's a colonel."

I'm impressed by both these distinctions, and vaguely wish I could say that Willibald has achieved at least one of them. I wish I knew the etiquette about his heroic father too—should I express condolence as well as congratulation? I've no idea, so I only nod respectfully by way of answer. And so we part.

In a couple of days I'm back in Heimstatt, sitting in my old seat in the primary school with the unchanged view of the tide mark on Heini Beranek's red and pimply neck. Everything seems exactly as it was, including Fritzi Wimmer's friendly truculence. "Back from Berlin, Jew boy?" he inquires affably, thumping my arm in the playground. "What's it like, then?" Fraülein Meissner repeats this question in more courteous tones after we've all offered Adolf our customary stiff-armed regards. (Her faith seems to have been restored.) I'm inspired to describe an air raid, and give an imaginative eyewitness account of the destruction of a Tommy bomber that in fact I never saw. Respectful silence settles over the class like virgin snow over a field of nettles, and for a few moments I savor what it's like to be accepted and even admired. Then Fritzi puts up his hand and asks if any of my friends were on the plane. And though Fraülein Meissner scolds him for his cheek, I know from the collusive sniggers all around that I've been put firmly back in my half-Jewish place.

So nothing's changed after all, except that now, owing to my Berlin schooling, I'm top of the class. Or would be if the new principal didn't ensure I wasn't. The old principal's been conscripted. It's the Russians he's supposed to be teaching a lesson to now, though I wonder how his racial-science expositions are going down on the Eastern Front. From what I heard in Berlin, the Russians just can't seem to get these theories through their heads. The new principal is well over fifty, and so exempted for the time being at least from military service. He does his bit for final victory though by cooking my grades. The assumption is I must have cheated, or at least got some unfair advantage in Berlin, since half-breeds clearly can't be more than half as good as the real pedigree thing. So my high grades are altered ("adjusted," they called it) and I come out about average.

This is my first experience of positive discrimination, and I don't like it any more than other people do when they're the ones that get the raw side of the deal. But I don't care all that much for grades anyway, so I don't see it as the scandalous catastrophe that Willibald does. Nor does Gabi—she's always known that Jews should never stick out, and she's certainly learnt by now that half-Jews shouldn't either. So while Willibald rages against the pig-ignorant principal who's subverted the holy traditions of German scholarship, and Jägerlein, who has mysteriously returned with Annchen and been reinstated, closes the windows that Ilse's too slow to get to, Gabi sits at the dining-room table and broods on further schemes for undermining the educational policies of the Third Reich. Could it be the Third Reich has met its match? Well, it certainly isn't long before Gabi's schemes are hatched.

In fact some of them crack their shells so fast, you've got to think she's been sitting on them for months already. Ilse, for instance, slow Ilse that everyone has given up on, Ilse's going twice a week to Plinden now, ostensibly on shopping trips—after all, what else could she do, now her schooling's over? (Though what she could possibly buy and how she could possibly pay for it must be a mystery.) But she comes back with no more in her rucksack than when she left, although she's got a bit more in her head. What she's got in her rucksack is schoolbooks, and what she's got in her head is learning. Yes, in reality she's having lessons with two lay teachers from the very school she was thrown out of. The ardent Nazi Frau Professor Forster doesn't know—at least, Ilse hopes she doesn't—but Frau Professor Lambach and Frau Professor Zauner are teaching Ilse in their shared apartment near the lake. They share it because they're lonely widows, both their husbands having given their lives for the Fatherland, or, rather, the Fatherland having taken them for Adolf. "The Thousand Year Reich won't last forever," Frau Professor Zauner says, who teaches Ilse English and French. "And then you'll go back to school again." Well, of course a thousand years isn't forever, but it still seems a long time to slow Ilse. Besides, she'll be eighteen next birthday.

In pauses from composing *King David* or *King Solomon,* not exactly titles likely to lure a wide public in the Third Reich, Willibald alternately praises the two teachers' magnanimity and deplores the pace at which Ilse digests their intellectual nourishment. "She just creeps along," he sometimes sighs, referring to both her physical and mental progress. Then he shakes his head and lets his voice throb in tragic acceptance of what the fates decree. "She'll never go far."

Ilse's teaching was arranged by Fraülein von Adler, the pipe-smoking Catholic who listens black. She it was who declared that Ilse's education mustn't be neglected. The girl was slow all right, but she'd get there in the end. Now, poking her spit-glistening pipe stem nearly into Willibald's recoiling face, she announces with a cheerful cackle audible throughout the house that the Tommies are bashing Rommel in North Africa and the Russkies are bashing von Paulus at Stalingrad, while the

Amis haven't even started yet. At this rate Hitler will soon be done for. And so will she be, if she goes on about it as loudly as that, although Jägerlein closed the windows as soon as she saw the salty old woman coming. All the same, Gabi and Willibald grimace at her, twitching their eyebrows grotesquely and glancing at me with almost the same expression that Tante Elsa wore when Eva went prancing about on the lawn upside down in her knickers. And I realize that's one more thing it isn't proper I should hear. I'm really getting lessons in discretion here. I've picked up a bit of French as well, from Sara who's learning it at school, and at first I think the Amis Fraülein von Adler spoke of are some kind of friend, though whose I couldn't tell. That leaves questions hanging in my mind which my growing discretion warns me I shouldn't put. It's only later that the picture clears, when Sara tells me "Amis" isn't badly pronounced French but abbreviated German for "Americans."

But Fraülein von Adler's not the only one whose help Gabi's drawn upon. Fraülein von Kaminsky, though unwilling to risk a concentration camp for Martin or Willibald—or probably for anyone else either—Fraülein von Kaminsky knows of a retired Jewish high school teacher in Bad Neusee, a Frau Professor Goldberg, who's just the person to do some private coaching for us. After all, helping a Jew can't do her any more harm than being one does.

And then there's Tante Helga, a friend of Fraülein von Adler. Remember her? Tante Helga was a geography teacher in Vienna till she went blind. On Fraülein von Adler's recommendation, she came down to live on her pension here in Heimstatt. Fraülein von Adler apparently told her how beautiful the place was, which seems to me an unusual reason for commending it to a blind person. But apparently Tante Helga agrees, because she goes out every morning with her white stick and turns her face unerringly towards the most appealing view, even when the snow and rain obscure it. Blind or not, she can find London or Paris on a map she can't see faster than I can on a map I can. Tante Helga doesn't mind teaching us. Her brother was a socialist and did time in a concentration camp before the war, but she thinks they wouldn't bother to put her in. Besides, there's no law against coaching half-Jews is there? (It's a moot point. As Willibald has already noticed, if they aren't allowed to go further than the sixth grade, isn't she helping them evade the law? She leaves that to the bureaucrats, and Gabi's happy to let her do so.)

And finally there's Father Schuster, the myopic Catholic priest, and our own church organist. They're going to teach Latin and music respectively, the latter on a violin that's too big for me and too small for Sara (Martin and Ilse are beyond such frivolity).

These are the warriors Gabi recruits against the Nazis. Not all of them are volunteers exactly. Frau Professor Goldberg, for instance, the retired Jewish schoolteacher—she'd rather stay hidden in her little apartment in Bad Neusee like a timid mouse, hoping the ethnic cleansers won't come for her before death in its more natural form does. And the organist is always backsliding and will neither enter our house to give Sara and me his lessons nor allow us to enter his. We have to have them on neutral ground, in the church vestry, which is cold and damp in summer and freezing in winter. No wonder our fingering never gets very nimble. He keeps his mitts on while he teaches us, and hardly ever demonstrates. Sometimes he doesn't even turn up, and we wait half an hour in the vestry while our feet and hands go gradually numb. It's clear to me he's only doing this because he hasn't got the balls to say he won't. And Gabi's ruthless when it comes to what she takes to be her children's interests. She chivvies her little army and wheedles and badgers them to keep them in the field. You have to be tough to resist her. Conscripts and volunteers alike, she keeps them all up to the mark.

Does she ever wonder if she's demanding too much, asking people to put themselves on the line for the sake of her half-Jewish children? Never, as far as I can see. Of course she knows *she's* running a risk, a full-Jew who shouldn't even be speaking to a pure Aryan except on official business. But the thought that the others, Aryans and Jews alike, might be running risks as well never enters her head; or if it does, makes no impression on it. Would she sacrifice them for her children's sake? Yes, she would, without a second thought.

Of course there's one resource she cannot call upon, one civilian she cannot conscript. Willibald was a dead loss for the German army. She never dreams of recruiting him for hers.

Nor does she expect any help from him in finding work for Martin. Despite all her efforts, Martin's education is only part-time now after all, and unlike Ilse, he is strong and active. Money has to come from somewhere, and the candlesticks have all been sold. Why shouldn't he find a job? Besides, that's actually what he wants. Preferably something technical until it's time for him to volunteer for the Luftwaffe. If he shows his mettle now, he thinks, surely they'll gladly take him in the Luftwaffe later. And then he'll prove to be an unparalleled ace and they'll award him a couple of iron crosses like Erwin's. Or a few more. He even imagines the Führer himself pinning them on his swelling breast. Not for him his pusillanimous cousin Robert's route. He isn't going to get his boots dirty plodding through all that Russian mud. He's going to soar above it in the skies, writing his name in vapor trails of glory across the limpid blue. He can imagine Heinrich Schmidt's crestfallen face when at last they meet again, he with the ribbon of the iron cross decorating his tunic, Heinrich a lowly, unbemedalled infantry grunt. Then that superior ironic smile that Martin still recalls with such smarting pain will be wiped off Heinrich's face for good and all. Why, Heinrich Schmidt, who was once his friend and then treacherously assisted at his alpine humiliation—Heinrich Schmidt will probably have to salute him!

Such are Martin's dreams, but who is it that goes trudging round the local towns, trying to realize the first at least and get him work? Not Willibald, of course. He's the one who should be taking the boy round, explaining he's the son of a pedigree Aryan father who did his best for the Fatherland in Poland etc., etc. and can't you please find something for him? But Willibald isn't doing any of that. Not a bit of it. He's sitting snug in his study and it's *King Solomon* or *King David* he's helping along, not young Martin. He does occasionally wring his Aryan hands over the poor boy's fate, but it's Jewish Gabi who's ringing the doorbells, going the rounds with Martin, trying to mitigate it. And the problem is, who wants to employ a sixteen-and-a-half-year-old half-Jew? Particularly when it's his full-Jewish mother taking him round, who legally speaking may be breaking the law, however "privileged" she may be, by even entering those Aryan establishments? Nobody that Gabi can find, until Jägerlein tells her to try the owner of the brick factory in Plinden. "He's a bit of one himself," she says, meaning he's a partial Jew, not a factory fragment. "At least people say he is."

Gabi and Martin board the Plinden train the next morning, bearing Martin's school report and Willibald's discharge letter with them. The first reveals that Martin Brinkmann (mixed race, first degree) has reasonably good grades (for a half-Jew), the other that Willibald is, if not exactly a hero, at least an honorably discharged corporal—as after all the Führer himself was once. And Gabi's identity card declares of course that she, though Jewish, is privileged because married to a kosher Aryan German, although kosher's not the word employed. This is all her weaponry. Against it are arrayed obtuseness, superstition, racism, arrogance, bureaucracy, fear and more obtuseness.

The brick factory is near the station. It has three tall chimneys that remind Gabi of incinerators although because of what Fraülein von Adler's told her she tries not to think of that. She walks steadily towards them. Martin is a step behind, already preparing to be sullen, since this is obviously not a place where his exceptional gifts can be displayed. Arriving at the gates, Gabi asks for Herr Ziegler, the owner and manager. The aged gatekeeper regards her skeptically for some moments, and Gabi feels her heart hesitate. But the man's voice is quite neutral, and he merely tells them to wait in a little brick office that looks and feels like a little brick cell.

A man with hair as grey as old cement comes in and says "Heil Hitler!" in a voice that sounds like an old cement mixer. At least he doesn't stick his arm out, though. Then he notices that Gabi has only answered with a very fragile "Guten Morgen."

Gabi gazes at him uncertainly. He has hard brown eyes that return her gaze unblinkingly, and she feels she's looking at two flat stones. But then the eyes glance away and there's something like a twitch in them, or the shadow of a twitch at least. And instead of telling him the sob story she's prepared about her loyal German son, unfortunately disadvantaged by his guilty mother's racial background, who (Martin, she'd mean) nevertheless only wants to serve the Fatherland, she finds herself silently laying all her puny weapons on the desk and then saying in a small, small voice, "Please, can you give my son a job? Please? Any kind of job?"

Herr Ziegler negligently picks up the papers. "Half-Jew?" he mutters, glancing at Martin again. "Hm!"

Martin intensifies the sullen face he's already put on. "Half-Aryan," he replies. That's true too of course, but hardly serves the purposes in hand.

"Hmph! Bad money drives out good, they say." Herr Ziegler lays the other papers down on his desk and starts reading through Martin's school report with a bulging underlip and furrowed brow. "Why shouldn't it be the same with blood?"

That might not have been politically correct (how could good German blood be weaker than degenerate Jewish?), but Herr Ziegler doesn't really seem to be interested in ideological debate, and as Gabi keeps winking at her son warningly with her good eye, twitching her lips and puckering her cheek, Martin infers he's not to initiate one himself.

After some time, Herr Ziegler lowers the report to inspect Martin's face again, as though to check this half-Jew really isn't going to try a smart-ass answer, raises it again, then puts it down with the others on the desk. "You seem all right at chemistry," he admits grudgingly. "There's a vacancy in the testing section. You can start washing bottles and things at first. Then we'll see if we can use you for anything else. One week's trial. If you're no good to us, you're out. The only reason I'm taking you on is we're very short-handed these days."

Gabi is so thankful she forgets to ask the salary. Martin's more practical. But it's irrelevant. Like it or not, he knows this is his only chance. He doesn't even register the piddling amount Herr Ziegler mentions. Herr Ziegler calls in a plump blonde secretary, who looks through them as if they were just panes of glass, and dictates a note about Martin. Gabi gazes at the smoking chimneys through the barred window, telling herself it isn't certain yet, it isn't certain, something could still go wrong. She hears the secretary's chair scrape back, but keeps her eyes on those chimneys as if they hold some magic power, and she must watch them till the door has closed.

"Like crematoria, aren't they, eh?" Herr Ziegler's voice grates behind her as the secretary leaves. "Our bricks go into them as well."

"Into crematoria?" Gabi repeats in surprise, imagining a coffin full of bricks sliding into a furnace to the sound of soothing hymns.

Herr Ziegler can spot naivety a mile away. "Into *making* them," he grates impatiently. "For the East," he adds with a grim little smile that Gabi tries not to interpret.

Martin starts work the very next week. He leaves at five and returns at eight. He's smart with test tubes, mixing this chemical with that, and soon he's helping with experiments to improve the bricks' heat-resistant quality. He's good at that, too. Some of the other workers call him Herr Mixture, which neatly captures both his official racial status and his factory function. Others, like the plump secretary, merely look blankly through him. Twice a week, before he returns home, he's off to Frau Professor Goldberg's little apartment in Bad Neusee to learn more math and physics. Then on Sundays he's climbing the steps of Tante Helga's chalet for a dose of geography from the blind map-reader. And after that a session with Father Schuster, deciphering the compressed enigmas of Tacitean Latin. Ilse goes separately to those teachers because, although she's older, she can't keep up with Martin.

That's how Gabi pushes her two eldest children through the curriculum the Nazis have decreed they should not follow. But what about the others? Sara and I need help too, although it isn't exactly academic help we are in want of yet. No, apparently we need polish. I thought I was mixing with the elite in my Berlin school stuffed with officers' and lawyers' progeny, and I still have that parting gift of a pencil from Ulrich, the wounded colonel's son, to prove it. But that's nothing to what Fraülein von Kaminsky has in mind for us two youngest. We're going to rub shoulders with the distant scions of the Royal Habsburgs.

Rolf and Elisabeth, they're called, and they live in a grand and ancient villa in acres of grounds outside Bad Neusee, far removed in class, if not in distance, from Frau Professor Goldberg's modest apartment. Their father's a count and about twenty-ninth-and-a-half in line for the Austrian throne, a distinction which, since there's neither Austria nor a throne, is about as significant as being the thirteenth grandson of a Turkish pasha. However, it's enough to render the whole family suspect to the parvenus Nazis, whom they in their turn look down upon with patrician scorn. So we have something in common, Fraülein von Kaminsky remarks to Gabi, and she counsels her to take Sara and me to pay court to the noble brood. "They'll be pleased to meet you," she assures the diffident Gabi.

"Meet a Jew?" Gabi asks dubiously, considering the penalties they could incur and the still worse ones that she could. She doesn't mind risking her own and other people's necks to get her children some further education or a job. But just for a social visit and perhaps a lesson in good breeding?

Fraülein von Kaminsky waves her doubts disdainfully away. "They are Habsburgs on the mother's side," she majestically declares. "And it will do the children good." Gabi's children, she means of course. You can't do Habsburg children good unless you're a Habsburg yourself. Or a von Kaminsky perhaps.

Unfortunately I'm as usual not privy to these preliminaries, so all I know just now is that we've got to look our best because we're going to visit the nobility. It's the middle of August and half a sweating mile from the big wrought-iron gates to the villa itself when, togged in our best Berlin hand-me-downs, we make our first call. (At our final call the wrought-iron gates will be gone, commandeered like Willibald's church bells, to be melted into cannon.) His Excellency Graf von Haltenstein isn't there, but his Countess is, the unimposing mother of six other royal Haltensteins.

She receives us with casual dignity and three bowls of sour milk topped with sugar and cinnamon, which are proffered to us by one of the half-dozen servants or so that seem to be floating about. I taste mine and nearly puke. So, I note, does Sara. Gabi though sends urgent messages to drink the vile stuff down, through a code of strenuous winks and grimaces, which the Countess, along with practically everyone else in the mansion except the chauffeur in the distant garage, notices, decodes and politely disregards. We manage to do as we're bidden. If that's what the imperial Habsburgs fed on, I surmise, it's no wonder that they lost their throne.

All the other Haltenstein progeny are either too old or too young for us, but Rolf is more or less Sara's age and Elisabeth more or less mine (in each case it's more less than more). Summoned to join us, they bow or curtsey to Gabi as gender dictates, shake hands graciously with us (my palm's all sweaty, but Elisabeth doesn't even flinch) and then tuck in to their very own bowls of sour milk, sugar and cinnamon, which they appear to swallow without the slightest repugnance, and even with a certain relish. I'm now inclined to revise my dietary explanation of the Habsburg decline—if they can take that, they can take anything. On the other hand, Rolf appears thin and drained when I take a second look, a bit like a pressed flower. They both have level pale blue eyes and the finest of fair hair, which makes me think they must be the intimidating quintessence of the Aryan race.

While their sour milk goes delicately down, I listen to my mother making cultivated conversation with the Countess in tones she must have learnt years ago from the days of her youth when she had a governess. Tones I've never heard in all my life before, light and empty as the top notes of a piano. It's astonishing how long these two adults can keep tinkling on about the weather, the local topography, the flora and fauna, with the utmost aplomb and manifest lack of interest. It isn't till Rolf and Elisabeth are told to take us out into the grounds that I hear a natural sound from my mother and indeed actually catch a natural and unusual smile on her stretched face. The countess has added a quiet remark to her in French, which Sara tells me afterwards means something like "We can talk more freely when the children are out of the way." I don't know much French, but that certainly seems about right for the countess's inflection and sidelong glance at us as she spoke. I know *that* language all right.

We stroll through the manicured grounds in the persistently attentive sunlight, first as an awkward quartet, then as two duos. Elisabeth is eleven and a half while I'm only nine and three-quarters, which gives her an even greater advantage than being a von Haltenstein does, and I curl my sweaty fingers up into nervous little fists as I try to play the conversational game her mother played with mine before she sent us out.

"Where do you live?" Elisabeth asks in a voice as clear as glacial water running over pebbles.

"Heimstatt," I truthfully reply.

"Oh."

"It's not like here," I assure her as the silence lengthens.

"Isn't it?"

I'm afraid I might have given her the wrong idea, so "I mean it's nicer here," I explain.

At first Elisabeth doesn't answer this bit of exegesis, and for a moment I wonder if she's taking a dose of the Kaminsky cure for intolerable conversations and carrying a gobful of unswallowed water in her mouth. After all, she *is* a sort of Habsburg, and. that's where the practice comes from. But then "Yes, I expect it is," she agrees coolly without the slightest sign of a sudden gulp.

As, after glancing round the grounds as though to assure

herself her endorsement was correct, she lets that topic drop, I try one of my own. "Where do you go to school?"

"In Plinden. They're mostly Nazis."

I'm not too sure how she regards the political affiliations of her schoolmates, so I keep quiet about that while my fingernails dig into my palms and I wish we could catch up with Sara and Rolf, who seem to be sauntering along in gawky but easy commerce, their heads leaning towards each other like a pair of tulips in love.

Well, he's sixteen, and she's nearly fifteen. Of course it's easy for them.

"Your mother's Jewish, isn't she?" Elisabeth asks, or rather declares, now, in a tone that I would classify as frigidly intimidating if I had the words to do so.

I'm too ashamed to admit my mother's Jewish and too timid to deny it. Just like Martin amongst the Hitler Youth. So, like him, I don't say anything.

"She shouldn't be here, really, should she?" Elisabeth continues severely, taking silence for assent. "With Aryans like us?"

Not to speak of royalty. As if I didn't know. Am I about to be ground through the same mincer that Martin was by the Hitler Youth?

"Because of the Nazis," she needlessly explains. Then, while I'm thinking this politely chilling interrogation is worse than mixing it with ten of Fritzi Wimmer, and I'm sure my gouging fingernails must be drawing blood from my palms, "We don't like them either," she delivers calmly.

Like *who*? I wildly wonder. Jews or Nazis?

After a few more delicately crunching steps along the level gravel path, she adds, "My father says they're frightful. But they wouldn't dare touch *us*."

This is getting frightful too. *Who* is frightful in her father's book? *Who* wouldn't dare touch them? Everyone else says it's the

Jews. I shrink away a bit, to show her that a half-Jew wouldn't either. Or could she possibly mean the Nazis? When will this agony end?

"So you needn't worry, we won't tell anyone," she says at last with condescending grace. "Can you speak English?"

No, I can't speak English, I admit. And a good thing too. It's bad enough trying to follow her in German. But at least I think I know how things stand now, and I feel as relieved as I would in school if Fritzi Wimmer had just turned a threatening scowl into a wintry grin.

"We've got a private tutor for English. He comes twice a week. I don't like him much." Then she says an English sentence, which she tells me means "The pilot has shot down the enemy plane." She might not like her tutor, but he clearly knows his stuff.

Is Sara having an equally difficult time with Rolf? It doesn't look like it, judging by the inclined proximity of those two tulip heads. And in fact she isn't. Quite the contrary. She thinks she's found a soulmate, and so perhaps does he. "I'm anemic," is the first thing he tells her, which sounds a lot more interesting than "Where d'you live?" All the royal families of Europe are anemic, he declares. "It's because we're all inbred. See how pale I am? I shan't live long." He holds his blanched and bony hand out in front of her eyes as if it was transparent, which it very nearly is. "There's a medicine in America, but of course we can't get it here, so . . ." He seems to contemplate his ineluctably approaching mortality with the same steady resigned fortitude with which I myself anticipate returning to school after the holidays. Disagreeable, but can't be helped. And in any case it might not be so bad. "You probably won't live long either, because you're half-Jewish," he adds. "Nor will your mother, of course. The Nazis want to kill you all."

These observations, however candid and veracious, were not

perhaps likely to enamor Sara all at once, but then they're only ranging shots. The heavy salvoes fall all round her later, when Rolf tells her he's an author too. Yes, he's also writing stories. "What about?" she asks. "Oh, you know," he responds offhandedly. "Love and death, that kind of thing." Then Sara timidly confides she's an apprentice in that trade as well, and before long they've agreed to show each other what they've written. "I might be able to help you," Rolf remarks with lordly condescension. "Give you some hints."

At my age, I'm not interested in that kind of stuff, so I never bother with either Rolf's or Sara's literary efforts. But I do see her slip one of her notebooks into her bag the next time we go calling. She does it secretly of course, as she does everything, but I notice. And in any case I know where she hides all her stories. It used to be in the bottom of her wardrobe, but now they're spread out under the mattress. I suppose she thinks that's safer.

Sara can't bear to watch Rolf read her story, so she gives it shyly to him just as we're leaving, and it isn't till a week or two later that she gets his response, which consists of a slow but definite shake of the head as he hands it back to her. "Undisciplined," he comments. "Exaggerated. Overdone." You can tell his literature teacher is a purist.

Rolf goes to the same gymnasium in Plinden that Martin attended till he got the boot, and he confides to Sara that he always thought her brother was a creep, although he's sorry for him now. Well, Sara can take criticism of her brother, she probably agrees with it in fact. But literary criticism's something else—that really cuts her to the bone. She feels like Douanier Rousseau being savaged by an academician in the Sunday paper, although since she's never heard of Douanier Rousseau she's no idea that's how she feels.

"See how I do it," Rolf offers with lofty generosity as he

hands her his latest story. "That might give you some ideas."

I never discover what she thinks of Rolf's stories about love and death and that kind of thing. She's never going to say. I know she reads them in his presence—he isn't one for false modesty and he never doubts they'll knock her silly. He watches her with a calmly smiling and expectant face, as an emperor might regard a courtier summoned to give an opinion on his taste—but what she tells him about them afterwards she never says. I suspect she finds them as anemic as their author, but I could be wrong. Not that it matters; Rolf is immune to criticism anyway. He's not a Habsburg scion for nothing.

Whatever she thinks of his stories though, she certainly takes his criticism of hers to heart. She's silent all the way home, in the manner we thought that only Ilse could be silent. And though it's high summer, she retreats behind the green-tiled oven in the kitchen, which is usually our refuge when Willibald's throwing things, and doesn't come out until Gabi has one of her gallbladder attacks.

A week or two later she shows Rolf another story. This elicits the same patronizing response that the first one did, and she never shows him any more. Or anyone else for that matter. But she goes on writing them all the same—she can't help herself. Her stories, she believes, aren't fit for public consumption, and quite possibly she doesn't really want the public to consume them anyway. Perhaps they're like a private diary that ought to stay unread.

And unread is what Rolf is going to stay, although that's certainly not at all what *he* intends. His anemia turns out to be leukemia, and by the end of the year he's going to be dead. Rolf is probably Sara's first friend, and in a sense her platonic lover, if you can say that about a boy-girl relationship. She's going to wear a tiny bit of black mourning ribbon for him after he dies, but secretly, like every other expression of her feelings, so that you scarcely notice it. I'll glimpse it though, on her worn black overcoat, just peeking out beneath the lapel.

But Rolf is not the only one that's sick. Ilse's come down with tuberculosis now, and it's thought better for his delicate patrician health if we interrupt our visits for a time. It's going to be quite a time as it turns out, but that's neither their fault nor ours. It's autumn already and—

10

Death is in the air

Dr. Koch, whom racial hygiene does not permit to treat my Jewish mother, does however visit the Pfarrhaus to sound the half-Jew Ilse's chest, although he's never to my knowledge been before. While he's there, Gabi persuades him to give us all the once-over. All, that is, except Gabi herself—and he hesitantly pronounces us all clear, except for Ilse of course, who has a persistent fever and lassitude that Gabi doesn't tell him has already been diagnosed by a specialist in Plinden who didn't know, or didn't want to know, her mother was Jewish. Dr. Koch considers Ilse may indeed have got TB and recommends sending her to the hospital in Bad Neusee where young Rolf von Haltenstein is shortly to expire, although he concedes there is some doubt whether they'll accept half-Jews and what sort of treatment they'll give her if they do. But Gabi means to nurse her daughter at home, and assures Dr. Koch she can deliver treatment as well as any hospital. That way, moreover, though this she does not tell him, Ilse can continue with her private tuition—her teachers, or some of them at least, can be prevailed upon to come to the house.

Ilse's case seems mild, and Dr. Koch acquiesces. He does a

lot of acquiescing. His principal function as a doctor seems to be that of acquiescing—in his patients' self-diagnoses, or, in the case of childbirth, in the midwife Frau Kogler's. Jägerlein says that's because when he first arrived in Heimstatt thirty years before, he misdiagnosed a mortal case of diphtheria as a trivial case of tonsillitis, the patient dying two days later. Since then he's had as little confidence as the villagers in his diagnostic powers. They prefer to use him only as a pharmacist and sounding board for their own opinions.

When it comes to us, not only does he acquiesce in Gabi's home-nursing proposal, he even consults her about which medicines to prescribe for Ilse. She assures him she nursed worse cases during her premarital nursing career and has no doubt of how to handle this one. Ilse, she declares, will be better in no time. Dr. Koch is relieved to hear her prognosis. He doesn't like his patients dying on him and would rather ship them off to the hospital, never mind what state they're in, where they can die on someone else. In fact one of the few Heimstatter deaths he ever personally manages will be his own.

Ilse likes being ill. It suits her temperament. But she doesn't like being nursed by her mother, however much she needs her care. Gabi institutes a bracing regime: up, fresh air on the veranda; bed, up, out on the veranda again; back to bed and up and out again. Morning and evening, every change punctual to the minute, medicines and temperature-takings on the dot, and lots of good food (relatively speaking), which means that Gabi eats still less of her own diminished Jewish rations.

This discipline is all too much for Ilse. She'd rather just stay in the hospital, assuming they'd have her, put her hands together and leave it to the Lord, which last two things are certainly all that Willibald is doing for her. But a Jewish curse is venomous and she's heard her mother curse her father. Or she thinks she has at least, late at night in their bedroom next to hers, when in the rising storm of one of their quarrels he suddenly blurted out he'd had enough of looking after her Jewish bastards and she shrieked something incomprehensible in return that Ilse took to be a Yiddish curse. She'd pulled the pillow over her ears, but there was a sullen silence after that anyway, as if her father had been struck dumb. Or even dead. Which Ilse believes is well within the compass of a Jewish curse's power.

No, however much she'd rather lie peacefully in a hospital, she knows her mother would never accept it. There would be persuasion and cajolery, then recrimination and bitterness. And in the end a Jewish curse—and nothing could be worse than that! So Ilse like her doctor acquiesces in Gabi's prescription and submits to her iron discipline.

Love it or loathe it, though, Gabi's regime works, and after a couple of months Dr. Koch pronounces her much improved, or rather Gabi does and Dr. Koch acquiesces. There's been no let-up on the educational front either, and timid Frau Professor Goldberg, blind Tante Helga and the two widowed teachers from Plinden have been calling to continue Ilse's schooling. What Ortsgruppenleiter Franzi Wimmer thinks of a woman like Frau Professor Goldberg, who wears the Jew's yellow star, calling on a half-Aryan house I do not know. Perhaps he reckons it's the Jewish half she's calling on.

Or perhaps that's why Lisl Wimmer has been calling too. She's the fifteen-year-old daughter of Ortsgruppenleiter Franz. In fact she calls whenever Ilse's teachers do and asks, with an artless smile that deceives no one (not even Gabi by now), "Could we just borrow a box of matches?" or "Have you got a candle? We've run out at home." Willibald knows she's been sent to spy on us, but he always puts on his ingratiating parsonical smile and makes sure she gets a whole box of matches or a couple of candles, which, considering how hard both are to come by and how hard it is for him to part with anything, reveals the depth of his respect for Franzi Wimmer's authority. Yet his feelings of humiliation and, still worse, desolation at the loss of his property have to be vented, and hardly is Lisl out of the door than Jägerlein's closing the windows in preparation for the squall of furious and vulgar imprecations that Willibald delivers to the four walls and sometimes to the startled Frau Professor Goldberg.

Personally I like Lisl, who fills out her League of German Girls uniform like a plump and shapely pigeon does its feathered skin. So does Martin. (Like her, I mean.) I know he does, because I've come upon them in the back lane by the Wildbach stream. Martin was returning from work with brick dust in his clothes, and Lisl, in her freshly starched blouse, was on her way to a League of German Girls meeting, or at least that's what she told me. (Martin didn't tell me anything; he only scowled.) But she had brick dust in her hair and all down the front of her uniform, the top two buttons of which had come surprisingly undone, and Martin was hastily brushing her down. He wouldn't do that for Ilse or Sara. And when she's sent into the Pfarrhaus on her espionage visits, Lisl's bluebell eyes, round as little saucers, glisten more at Martin than at the unusual and suspicious guests (the Aryans among whom have in any case been primed to say they're only there to visit Willibald in his dual capacity of Aryan and Pfarrer).

Yes, Ilse's recovering. But Maria Müllendorf is not. From Berlin comes a letter in Maria's hand two days before Christmas, franked with the urgent exhortation *German Women and Girls! Join the Postal Service! Connecting Front and Home! Information at every Post Office!* Gabi ignores this appeal, which after all ignores her too, and opens the letter eagerly, looking rather for comfort and the season's greetings from her best and almost only friend. A gasped "Ach nein!" confirms to the ever-watchful Sara what past experience has already suggested, that Christmas won't be very merry this year either.

Dearest Gabi,

When you have these lines in your hands, you will be very sad. But you shouldn't be—I've only gone on before you, and as we know for certain that Jesus has overcome death, we know we will see each other again. So don't be sad, Gabi, but try to be happy.

Our friendship has enriched our lives so much. We've got so much to be thankful for—our childhood, our youth, and even these hard times that have bound us still closer together. And your children are bound in with us too.

Gabi, follow the path you have to tread. You will never be alone. The King of Kings, the Lord of Lords, who is yet also our brother, will always protect you.

Bless you all. May your children always be able to distinguish what's important from what isn't. Being able to go on with school and then go to university is actually not so important, although it would be good if it became possible again one day. Then perhaps Ilse could become a missionary doctor or nurse—but first she must get healthy again. I only hope that Martin will choose a different career from one that brings death and terror to people. It's too soon to make any wishes for the other two, except that I hope they will find something good and satisfying to do in life.

Gabi, if ever you need any help, ask my father or Gerda. They will always be there for you. But most of all ask Our Lord. It would be nice if the two boys would drop a line to Gerda, it would make her so happy.

With my love to all of you,

And so Maria died secure in that faith that she perhaps suspected—why else would she have preached so at her?—Gabi was losing or even had already lost. She'd gone to the hospital for a surgery on her lung which she knew could well prove fatal, and left a pile of farewell letters behind with Frau Professor Gerda Hoffmann.

The suggestion that Ilse might become a missionary doctor is news to me. In fact, I'm not quite sure what a missionary doctor is. Perhaps it's news to Ilse too. Nevertheless she takes it up. Sickly slow Ilse, scarcely recovered from a bout with the malicious microbes that have just downed Maria, decides to carry the torch that Maria was prevented from bearing and has now passed on to her. Yes, Ilse declares she's going to study medicine if she survives her illness and the war, which admittedly are two big ifs, and bring light and pills to darkest Africa. That she says anything at all is what's astonishing, so silent has she become, not what it is she says—nobody takes much notice of that. But Ilse's ambition nevertheless sustains her recovery just as Maria's faith consoled her death.

A shame if both prove just to be delusions.

Hardly have Martin and I composed the obligatory lines to Frau Professor Hoffmann (Martin tosses them off in a couple of careless minutes; it takes me all afternoon, but mine are twice as many), hardly has Gabi overcome the first shock of Maria's death, which feels to her as though a fire's gone out inside her, than the postman delivers another obituary. This time it comes in a neatly black-bordered envelope addressed to Willibald in a ceremonious hand which he instantly recognizes. Death really is in the air these days. Literally, as it turns out.

"It's Harald," Willibald mutters as he slits the envelope open, thinking perhaps that since Maria sent her own death notice, it must have become fashionable and Harald's simply following the trend. "It's my brother."

Wrong again. It's Harald's son Erwin, the Luftwaffe hero. A British Hurricane caught his Dornier over the Channel and now he's buried in his cockpit at the bottom of the sea, his light brown hair wafted to and fro like gentle seaweed by the chilly ebb and flow of English tides. If life was a novel it would have been Wolf-gang that got him, to provide the proper Sohrab and Rustum touch: Wolfgang, Gabi's cousin Lotte's and Solomon's pianistic son, whom they sent away to England before the war. But it isn't and it wasn't. Wolfgang as it happens was learning how to jump out of planes just then, not how to shoot them down. No, it was a very English fox-hunting voice that was heard shout-ing a jubilant "Tally Ho!" over the sputtering radio traffic, and then another equally fox-hunting though older voice comment-ing "Wizard shooting!" Which last led the German Intelligence officer who monitored it to consider whether the British had de-veloped a secret weapon.

I stoop to read the postmark on this envelope too, which Wil-libald has let fall from his trembling hands. *The Führer Knows Only Struggle, Work and Care,* it declares. *We Want to Lighten His Burden in Whatever Way We Can.*

Once again I am suffering from pronominal puzzlement as well as from a dull and anxious sense of loss. Who are the "we" who want to lighten the Führer's burden? I assume that Erwin was one of them, but what about us? Where do we stand? It isn't easy to work out. But anyway the facts are that Willibald has started grieving loudly over Erwin and that Erwin, who's certainly done his bit to lighten Adolf's burden, won't be do-ing any more. Willibald's voice is trembling like his hands as he slides the letter back into the envelope he's retrieved from me. "The English have taken our gallant Erwin at last," he throbs, making it sound as though every English fighter pilot had *"Get Erwin!"* printed on his goggles. "Our Fatherland has been dealt a heavy blow."

My puzzlement increases. For one thing, I didn't realize the Fatherland depended so heavily on Erwin's survival; for another I'm not so clear it *is* ours. It's this second but long-standing per-plexity that's really bothering me now. *Our* Fatherland? Aren't we supposed to be secretly glad when Hitler gets one on the nose? At least that's what Fraülein von Adler suggests when she shares the black news with us that I'm not supposed to hear. But I know better by now than to ask anyone who I should be rooting for in this war, especially at this moment, when Willibald's subsiding into mournful sighs and groans as he rests his grieving head upon his grieving hands and his grieving elbows on his grieving desk. He seems to take Erwin's death harder than Maria's, although Maria was certainly on *our* side, whatever that is, while Erwin was . . . well, what?

But perhaps the explanation's as much Willibald's love of uniforms as ideological confusion. I know he sometimes takes his old Wehrmacht togs out of the wardrobe, removes the dust cover and brushes them lovingly down. And I remember Erwin's uniform was quite a bit smarter than his, while Maria didn't have one at all. So naturally Willibald would be sad that Erwin's uniform is done for as well as Erwin himself. I know that can't be all of it, but realizing it would be too taxing for my nearly ten-year-old brain, I wisely refrain from further speculation.

And Willibald soon puts aside his grief. A couple of hours later, he's penned a condolence letter that Schiller would be proud of—and *he* certainly is, because he reads it to us all, pulling out every stop. And by evening chuckles from the study suggest that sorrow has not distracted him from his labors on *King David*, which is really getting going now. For all I know, Erwin's death may even have spurred him on.

In the next day's post a letter from Erwin himself arrives. No, not his own obituary after all, but a Christmas letter written on the day of his death, and somehow posted several days after it. They really ought to sort these things out at the field post offices.

Dear Onkel Willibald,
Many thanks for your letter of 24th November. I'm

keeping well, and have lots of work to do. I've been acting squadron leader since the beginning of November, which isn't easy for an officer as young as I am, as you can probably imagine. But it's going all right, I've worked myself in pretty well by now. I'll be spending the Christmas holiday with the men here.

How are things at the Heimstatt Pfarrhaus? Have the two packets of flour I sent arrived? I hope so. Happy Christmas to you and the whole family, and best wishes for the New Year.

Yours,
Ervin

Somehow this posthumously arriving letter affects me more than the news of Erwin's death itself did. I know I'm going to miss Erwin. (I'm going to miss his flour too, because that never does arrive, which means we won't have any Christmas cake this year. Not that we'd enjoy it with all this grief around, but still.) Yes, I'm going to miss my elegant cousin. In fact I'm missing him already. All the same it isn't as though he was Sara or my mother. After all, I only met him once. I miss Tante Maria more, and I keep thinking of her scented handkerchiefs and quiet dainty little cough. That stops me looking forward to Christmas more than Erwin's death alone would have done.

And it stops Gabi too. The dwarf Christmas tree cut from the stony hill behind the house stands undecorated still on Christmas Eve, and our only celebration is a single candle at its foot. It's more like Good Friday than Christmas Eve, and the tree might just as well be a naked cross. No one feels much like singing Christmas carols, and the cheap little presents Gabi has secretly managed to assemble lie bare and unwrapped in forlorn forgotten heaps upon the floor.

It's not surprising really, when you think that Maria was Gabi's best friend and their lives have been so tangled up together. Gabi wouldn't even have become a Christian if it weren't for Maria, and then she'd never have met and married Willibald (although that can't mean as much to her now as once it must have done). She couldn't be expected, despite Maria's exhortation, just to shrug her death off and carry on as usual. Her silent and withdrawn mourning persists for two more days, and the house is like a gloomy cave, which even Jägerlein's poetic bustle (she recites a lot these days) and Annchen's vacant cheerfulness can't warm. But then suddenly one morning there's a change in the emotional weather, a crackle of fresh energy. It feels warmer inside although it's just as cold outside. Yes, Gabi's formed another plan.

■

She isn't going to let Maria's passing pass without her. That would be a kind of treachery, a blanking out of half her life. No, she's been looking up timetables once more and consulting her credit (there's still some crystal left to sell). She's decided to go to Maria's funeral, and take Martin and me along as well. After all, we lived with Maria for half a year, we owe it to her. Is this breathtaking chutzpah again or stunning naivety?

At nearly ten years old I can hardly say. She puts the plan to Willibald the next day, which fortunately is a Sunday when he's tired out from a day's preaching, and she takes care to keep a gob-stopping mouthful of water handy in a tumbler beside her, expecting him to voice all kinds of vehement objections. But strangely enough he has no objections to voice. All he does is remind her sternly that Jews need permission from the district Authority for travel outside their place of residence. Perhaps he's calculating that the district Authority, in the person of Ortsgruppenleiter Franzi Wimmer, will of course deny permission. But if so, he's wrong again. He ought to know by now that he usually is. Everyone else does.

For reasons we shall never know, Ortsgruppenleiter Franzi Wimmer sees no objection to the Jewess Gabriella Sara Brinkmann, wife of the Aryan Pfarrer Willibald Brinkmann (that's how her permit describes her) attending a funeral in Berlin, provided she doesn't stay in an Aryan home—which is something the Berlin people can worry about, he can't look after everything. Is Franzi turning religious in his middle age, or has Lisl dropped a pleading word in his ear—as Martin has surely dropped some honeyed ones in hers? More likely he's been listening black like Fraülein von Adler, and is paying premiums to insure his future. After all, things aren't looking at all good on the Eastern Front at present, North Africa's already gone in the south, and now Italy is wobbling too.

When Willibald hears a permit has already been issued and that Gabi has already phoned Frau Professor Gerda Hoffmann from the box outside the post office (which, strictly speaking, Jews are not allowed to do—is it just the Christmas season, or are the post office people listening black as well?), he discovers a pile of reasons after all why Gabi shouldn't go, all of them financial, and Gabi has need of two doses of the Kaminsky cure (she swallows one, is about to let fly, but restrains herself and quickly takes another). Yet somehow the battle is half-hearted on Willibald's side. Not a single book gets thrown on the floor, not a single picture torn from the wall, and neither I nor Sara feels any urge to take refuge behind the kitchen stove. There's one last lachrymose appeal to the state of Ilse's health, but Ilse's actually better than she's been for years and besides she'd like a break from Gabi. Even Willibald's histrionic talents aren't up to pretending she's hovering at death's door, and the appeal goes as unfinished as it is unheeded. Yes, Ilse would like a break from Gabi, and so in fact would Willibald. So he surrenders and the battle's over. It's only a token battle anyway. The dreary Christmastide is past, and we're going to Berlin for a week.

Willibald's concession is as puzzling as Franzi Wimmer's. Can it be that Willibald is mellowing? Does he too feel Maria's passing shouldn't go without a Brinkmann presence at the rites? Does he even want perhaps to show a little (just a little, mark you) defiance of the Nazis?

Not a bit of it. No, none of that. Willibald is indeed quite happy for us to go, but his reasons are more personal. Pfarrer Willibald Brinkmann, upstanding Lutheran minister and fervent moral preacher, Pfarrer Willibald Brinkmann has got an Aryan lady-friend, a sympathetic feminine Aryan ear to pour his troubles into, a cushiony feminine Aryan breast on which to lay his weary or for all we know lascivious head. (She'd better like dead cats in that case, or anyway dead cats' pelts.) And she's a Nazi, too, a Leader in the League of German Girls. His mind is naturally occupied with other things than Maria's obsequies, and quite frankly, as far as he's concerned, the further Gabi goes and the longer she's away, the better.

But I don't know this yet, and nor do any of us except Willibald. What I do know is that it's the fag-end of the year, we haven't seen the sun for months, the lake is frozen, the windows are iced over, the snow's piled heavy on us like a solemn shroud—and Gabi, Martin and I are setting off towards the Jew-free city of Berlin once more. At least that's what little Dr. Goebbels thinks it is, strutting proud as a crowing if limping bantam before his Führer at a Nazi bigwigs' meeting. But he's wrong, he can't even get that right. No wonder Adolf's magnetic glower is beginning to look glum.

■

Which, to my surprise, is not at all how Frau Professor Gerda Hoffmann looks as, quite illegally, she settles Gabi as well as us all in with her in that comfortable Steglitz district I know so well. On the contrary, except for her black dress, she behaves like someone preparing for a wedding, not a funeral. And the other mourners behave in the same way when we join them next morning at Onkel Karl's house. There they are, all members of the Confessing Church, smiling and laughing, recounting episodes from Maria's life and leading Onkel Karl about by the hand. He seems happy too, carrying his furled umbrella everywhere with him, ready for the next air raid.

"Where's Maria?" I hear him ask his remaining daughter, Elsa, who alone appears a bit down in the mouth—almost, in fact, as if she wishes she weren't there. His query causes me to look apprehensively around. I haven't seen a dead person yet and didn't expect to meet one in the form of Maria today. But Martin tells me in an impatient mutter not to shit myself, the old boy's simply lost his marbles. He's had a stroke and doesn't know what's going on anymore.

Does Gabi reflect that Maria's letter enjoined her to ask Our Lord as well as Onkel Karl if ever she needed anything? Obviously Onkel Karl is too absent now to pay her any heed, assuming he might once have done so. Does she wonder, despite the presence of all those Confessing Church ladies, if Our Lord is absent too?

To Elsa, whose Nazi husband is "too busy" to appear, Martin is the soul of courtesy, bowing and heel-clicking like a von Haltenstein, or like dead Erwin. "And how is Eva?" he politely inquires, and learns that she is well. Is there a touch of frost in Elsa's reply? At any rate, she turns away and Martin looks a little chilled. After a swift embarrassed greeting she turns away from Gabi too, and goes to sit stiff and awkward beside her docile father.

Gabi asks to see the bedroom we shared during our educational sojourn a few months ago. It's tidy and spacious; the wintry sun peers wanly into a room more comfortable and elegant than any in Heimstatt. "You must have enjoyed it here," she remarks a trifle wistfully to both of us, but it's Martin who vigorously nods his head.

Sometime later we go into Maria's room, which remains just as she left it. There too it's all smiles and happy reminiscences, and several ladies smelling of scent and good breeding say they remember me although I don't know them from Adam or I suppose I should say Eve. Gabi whispers to me that they all belong to the Confessing Church, and—don't I remember?—they used to visit us in Heimstatt while Willibald was away subduing the treacherous Poles, though that's more his way of putting it than hers. I falsely nod my head and turn awkwardly to read the contradiction Maria had embroidered on a little cloth hung on the wall above her bed. I've read it before, and it's always puzzled me:

We dead aren't dead, we're by your side.
Unseen, unheard, we have not died.

For some reason quite apart from my respect for logic, all that trusting faith makes me certain Maria isn't really by my side at all. And when I later see the flower-covered coffin in the nearby church being serenaded by a choir of Maria's coreligionists (*Joy, oh Joy! Eternal Joy! Jesus takes our cares away*) and then being borne out and lowered into the grave, I feel certain that's where she is now and where she'll always be until she's rotted away and isn't anywhere at all anymore. That's the day I discover Death is real and full of maggots, and nothing will ever be quite the same again for me. The second of January, 1944, to be exact.

Gabi discovers something too, today. When the sirens start moaning soon after we return to Onkel Karl's and the wireless reports large enemy bomber formations heading towards Berlin, she finds out that air raids really happen. Down into the cellar we go, where Frau Professor Hoffmann whispers composedly to Gabi while Onkel Karl opens and shuts his umbrella, flapping it irritably as the ground trembles with gunfire and the thump of distant bombs, and whitish plaster dust drifts down over us like Erwin's missing flour packets being sifted through a sieve. "Where's Maria?" he unconcernedly asks Gabi. "When's she coming?"

She doesn't tell him. Nor does she tell him she's thinking of attending another—

11

Celebration for the dead

Yes, the very next day she announces we're going to Erwin's memorial service at his home in Lüneburg. Having seen Maria off, she feels obliged to see Erwin off as well. You have to say she's even-handed. You could say crazy too.

Frau Professor Hoffmann looks amazed and anxious, and wonders aloud whether that would be wise. I wonder too, but Martin thinks it's just the ticket. Attending heroes' obsequies and—who knows?—rubbing shoulders with another Luftwaffe ace or two? That certainly beats burying Tante Maria and humoring anemic Confessional Church ladies in Steglitz.

"But Gabi, your racial background!" Frau Professor Hoffmann protests openly at last. "What about the laws . . . ?"

All to no purpose. Surely "privileged" Gabi can attend her brother-in-law's son's memorial service, can't she? If Gabi needs any encouragement, Martin's given it, and now she's not to be deflected. This certainly wasn't mentioned to Ortsgruppenleiter Franzi Wimmer when she asked permission to attend a funeral in Berlin. She's got no permit, she's taking us near Hamburg, a city the Amis and the Tommies regularly sow with their quick-blossoming bombs, she can't exactly expect to be welcome (she doesn't ask, she simply phones the night before and tells them she's coming) and she's actually running Onkel Harald's family as well as the rest of us into danger. But she's taken it into her stubborn head and she's determined to go. So there we are the following day at the commemoration of a German hero.

Where I meet Onkel Harald for the first time in my life. He's the fat nervous-looking one with a black armband on his sleeve, and a Nazi badge in his lapel. And there's Robert, on compassionate leave from the East. Willibald would have enjoyed that smart Wehrmacht uniform, without a speck of Russian mud on his gleaming boots. I wonder if Robert's glad he took Erwin's advice and let the Luftwaffe get on with things without him—or is he any better off slogging it out on the Russian steppes? And that shrinking face is Tante Erika's, whom I've never met before either, the mother who proudly sacrificed her son for Fatherland and Führer. At least that's what it says in the death notice in the paper, a big black-bordered affair beginning *In deepest grief and pride* . . . For myself, I think I see the grief all right, but where's the pride? She reminds me of Fraülein Meissner on that morning in school when she forgot to say the morning prayer to Adolf. However, both proud and grieved in the true Aryan tradition is what blonde fiancée Lerke looks. See how high her head is held, how deep the sadness in her long-lashed eyes? You can tell she learnt her lessons well in the League of German Girls.

It's a private afternoon send-off in Onkel Harald's luxurious home, Erwin being unfortunately prevented from attending even in a coffin by thirty fathoms of the English Channel, which I know from my science lessons is quite a load to bear. And fortunately for us the Allies have considerately decided not to target Lüneburg today, though it's unlikely their forbearance has anything to do with Erwin's final send-off. But although it's a private do, there are quite a few swastikas around (with people wearing them, I mean) and enough arm-flapping Heil Hitlering going on to make you think you're at a puppet show, which is not of course to say you aren't. These people make me want to hide, but Martin mutters to me again that I needn't shit myself, they're only tame officials from Onkel Harald's office. But as I've no idea how he knows that, I'm only mildly reassured. There's an enormous swastika hanging down the whole length of the wall from where the eulogies are delivered. In front of it stands a little table, also swastika-decorated, on which Erwin's Luftwaffe cap and his iron cross symbolically rest even if he doesn't. I don't know what all these people make of Gabi, but I suppose Onkel Harald must have put the word out that she's his brother's wife fresh from another funeral, and she gets a few bows and hand-kisses and muttered condolences from people who'd give themselves a hasty mouthwash if only they knew what they were doing. No wonder Onkel Harald's looking nervous.

What Gabi herself makes of it, I can't imagine. She looks pretty uncomfortable, I know that. In fact she looks petrified, like a hare that's wandered into a pack of greyhounds resting from the hunt, except that a hare wouldn't shake paws with the greyhounds and ask them how they were. Why's she *doing* this, I wonder as I shrink back in the corner. Is it really just to pay her last respects to Erwin? Or does she perhaps want Martin and me to feel that we're proper Germans after all and can hold our heads up anywhere? If so, her prescription doesn't work for me, nor, to go by appearances, for her, and Martin hardly needs it— he's always known he is a proper German. So while she makes agonized polite conversation with a Luftwaffe ace and two tame Nazi officials (at least I hope they're tame), I cower in my corner and pray that no one will speak to me, which fortunately no one does. Martin though is in his element. When someone Heil Hitlers him, he gives it back as though he's been doing it all his life, and I even overhear him telling one of the swastikas that he's going to join the Luftwaffe as soon as he's old enough, earning thereby a congratulatory little punch on the shoulder, which really makes his day. Has he reflected that most Luftwaffe heroes end up like Erwin, and so probably would he? Of course not—he's Martin!

Unlike Maria's, this party's a solemn one. Gravity's the keynote here. We sit on chairs from the living room, dining room and for all I know the town hall, while gravity, patriotism, Führer-loyalty and faith in final victory are intoned by one solemn speaker after another, each revealing in his own way (no woman speaks, of course) how Erwin excelled in all these qualities. I've been told by Gabi in a hasty pre-memoriam briefing that Onkel Harald is an Anthroposophist, but we shouldn't mention it because the Party doesn't like it. When she explains that this freaky sect believes people don't really die, but just pop in and out of the spirit world, I think I don't like it either. It strikes me as about as ridiculous as the contradiction embroidered over Maria's bed. I saw worms wriggling in the muddy earth of Maria's grave and I know that baby herrings are probably swimming in and out of Erwin's eye-sockets by now too. That's enough for me.

Now Onkel Harald reads a letter out from Erwin's commanding officer in France. It brings manly tears to portly Onkel Harald's eyes. Well, to tell the truth, it brings them to mine too, except that mine aren't manly.

I was fond of your Erwin (it goes), *and was very conscious that he did everything that he could to make himself the virtuous officer and gentleman that only Germans can be. I soon came to realize that your son exemplified all those values that characterize a German officer, and that he fully illustrated Bismarck's observation "Other countries can copy everything else about us perhaps, but not the German Lieutenant." It is so very sad that Erwin, who though so young was already a Squadron Leader, was not spared to show his remarkable qualities in the higher ranks to which he would undoubtedly have risen. His career was cut short, but it must count for something that he made so many successful sorties in so short a period against enemies as determined as the English are. Erwin always had Walter Flex's book with him* The Wanderer Between Two Worlds. *But on his last flight, he left it behind. While assembling his possessions, which I trust you have now received, I found he had underlined the following passages in it.*

Here Onkel Harald pauses in his reading and holds up the worn leather-bound volume itself, which he evidently has received, and reads from it now, instead of from the letter:

It is an officer's duty to put his men first. Dying first is sometimes part of that.

He takes a steadying breath, turns over several pages, then reads again into the reverent hush:

Do not mourn for us dead. Do you want to make ghosts of us, or do you want to bring us home? We want to sit at your hearth without disturbing your laughter. Please don't cry for us, you'll only make our friends afraid to talk about us. Give them rather the courage to speak of us with laughter and smiles. Bring us home, home as it was when we were alive!

These sentiments, which it occurs to me Tante Maria would approve, seem nevertheless to produce the opposite of their intended effect. Onkel Harald's voice breaks off with a throb, and Erika and Lerke are quietly choking. So are quite a lot of other people—even Gabi, who might be thought to have a different take on German officers, dead or alive. And Martin too—for all he's trying to make himself seem stern and proud, his eyes look quite dewy to me. And I'm sniffing myself as I recall debonair young Erwin suavely sleeking his eyebrow down with his elegantly curled little finger. As for Onkel Harald's undisclosed Anthroposophical beliefs—he certainly isn't behaving just then like someone who thinks Erwin's just ducked out of his body and popped up in the spirit world. He's behaving like someone who sensibly believes his son is gone for good.

No, despite the injunction in his final text, there doesn't seem to be much laughter in Erwin's commemoration. It was merrier by far at Maria's, who wasn't even a German officer, let alone a hero—although, come to think of it, she might well have been a heroine.

That same evening, we're back on the train to Berlin. Onkel Harald and Tante Erika kiss Gabi on both cheeks before we leave. Tante Erika kissed her when we arrived as well, but Onkel Harald only gave a formal handshake. Perhaps Erwin's commemoration has unhinged his mind—or at least the Nazi part of it.

Lerke kisses Gabi too. And Martin. And me. She smells nice—a heady blend of damp girlish skin (the room is overheated), mint toothpaste, lily scent and tears. I see that Martin presses her arm as she kisses him, but my hands hang limply down by my sides. I'm not up to that stuff yet. She tells Gabi, who tells us, she's going to keep a copy of everything that's been read out this afternoon, as well as all the letters Erwin ever wrote her, and place a different one next to her heart every day for the rest of her life. Gabi blushes when she says "next to her heart." I'm just able to remember Erwin's mentioning a French mademoiselle in one of his notes to us a few years ago, and wonder if *she's* going to be wearing some of his letters next to her heart too.

In any case, I get a nice feeling imagining those folded papers nestling on Lerke's warm and generous breast. And if I get one, you can bet your life Martin does too.

Our train is very late. While we've been visiting Onkel Harald, the Tommies and the Amis who've given Hamburg a miss have been visiting Berlin instead, and they've been having their own kind of celebration, with lots and lots of fireworks. It takes us hours to get into the station because there isn't much of the station left to get into. As we're in one of the rear carriages, we have to get down onto the track in the end and finish our journey on foot, stumbling over heaps of bricks and glass in the cold and dismal light of dawn. As we reach the station, I see the roof has gone except for a few twisted girders and there's a lot of broken glass and piles of rubble everywhere, and iron pillars tortured into crazy shapes.

But that's not all. There are neat long rows of people lying peacefully asleep along a cleared space on the platform, with a couple of policemen watching over them to make sure they're not disturbed. Gabi tugs my arm and hurries us past them, and that's when I realize they aren't asleep at all. "Don't look," Gabi says, but I've looked already and can't stop looking now. Some of those people don't have arms or legs anymore, and some of them don't even have faces. Most of them, if they're still wearing any, are wearing different clothes, advertising the different status they attained in life. Some are, or were, men, some women, a few children. Some are, or were, officers, others ordinary rankers, some well-dressed well-foddered gentlemen like Onkel Harald, others lanky workers in their overalls. One without a head has at least preserved a pair of handcuffs on his wrists—or are they hers? I've not yet heard Death called The Leveller, but if I had, I would understand it now. As it is, all I'm capable of thinking is that I'll be glad to get back to Heimstatt, and I'm thinking that pretty hard. Martin's looking at these leftovers from the Allies' party with the same repelled fascination that I am, but what he's thinking I don't know. Perhaps he's working out how many kilos of high explosive he'd need to do the same job on a London station.

Yes, we're really getting the feel of death here in Berlin. And there's more of it to come. "Come on!" Gabi says urgently as she tugs me away. "We've got to see if they're all right in Steglitz!"

But in Steglitz they're perfectly all right. They don't even know what's happened to the station, although they certainly heard it happening. Onkel Karl looks like a veteran miller from all the plaster dust that's fallen in the cellar during the night, which his strenuous umbrella flapping doesn't seem to have prevented. And he's still occasionally asking where Maria is, though apparently uninterested in any answer. But the bombs that shook the plaster down have left the house intact. Frau Professor Hoffmann has prepared a breakfast for us, which has the double advantage of being preceded by a shorter grace and lasting a bit longer, because there seems to be more of it, than is usually the case in Heimstatt.

∎

In the afternoon Gabi makes another announcement to Frau Professor Hoffmann. Now she means to go and see Cousin Lotte and Solomon, and sloppy, once-jolly Aunt Hedwig "while we still have the chance."

Frau Professor Hoffmann blanches. "I don't think . . . I mean, I don't know where they are now," she hints, glancing askance at me and then hard at Gabi.

"I've got their address here," Gabi says obliviously, rummaging in her large black handbag. For someone who sends out her own ocular signals like a mastful of flags on the battle cruiser *Bismarck*, she really is slow to spot the signals others hoist. Frau Professor Hoffmann regards her with an incredulous and pityingly anxious look as Gabi unfolds Great Aunt Hedwig's address. *You don't know?* it says. *My God, how am I going to tell you?*

"But they've moved," Frau Professor Hoffmann repeats, glancing askance at me again, and then appealingly at Martin. "They've . . . they've gone away . . ."

"Gone away? Where?" Gabi considers Frau Professor Hoffmann wide-eyed with amazement, but then comprehension begins to gleam at last like winter sunlight in a leaden sky.

"Didn't anyone tell you?" (Of course not—Maria was too busy preparing to die and no one else thought of writing to Heimstatt.) "They were . . . evacuated last month."

"Evacuated?" Gabi repeats in a voice that has somehow suddenly been hollowed out, lost all its marrow. Since she heard of Onkel Moritz's evacuation she understands at last that evacuation means deportation. Before, she might have visualized some pastoral retreat, complete with log chalets, fir trees and gallons of free milk. Stranger thoughts did sometimes use to wander through her head in the early morning hours, when the world was remade according to the blueprint of her naive optimism. But not any longer. "So it's too late, then?" she asks, sitting heavily down and gripping the table edge as though she felt unsteady. "Evacuated."

"Concentration camp," Martin growls with his customary brutal accuracy. And Frau Professor Hoffmann, who took Maria's death so calmly, now has tears starting in the corners of her eyes.

As usual that makes me want to cry too, cry for that shabby trio we met outside the Botanical Garden last spring. I dream that night of Great Aunt Hedwig turning back towards me in her threadbare clothes with her yellow star, her face two sizes too small for its haggard envelope of skin. I see her hands reaching out towards mine, see her fixing me with her teary eyes, imploring me in her teary voice. *"Remember us!"* I hear her calling. *"Remember us!"*

And I do.

◼

Next morning, the day of our return to Heimstatt, Gabi takes it into her obstinate head at least to go and see Great Aunt Hedwig's and her cousins' place before we leave. Does she somehow hope to find them still there after all, although she knows full well they won't be, and ought to know they probably aren't anywhere by now? Or is it rather that she wants to see with her own eyes if there's some scrap or remnant of her cousins or her favorite aunt lingering somewhere in the Jews' house where they were removed to from their middle-class home in its prosperous and fashionable district? A letter perhaps? An old hat? A worn and empty purse? Or is there some still deeper longing?

Frau Professor Hoffmann clasps her hands as though in prayer, or perhaps indeed in prayer, and protests to no avail again. "The Gestapo may be hanging about there," she warns Gabi. "What will you do if they stop you? It isn't safe." But Gabi, who's blessed or cursed with an optimistic as well as a stubborn and naive cast of mind, answers that she's got a permit to be in Berlin and she's "privileged" as well. She still trusts in the rule-following orderliness of the Germans, and believes that the same punctiliousness which keeps the cattle trucks rolling to the East on time will also keep her from being on one herself without out a properly issued and duly validated ticket. And in a way she's right. The liquidation of the Jews is a massacre all right, but it isn't a riot.

Martin thinks no better of this scheme than Frau Professor Hoffmann does. The last thing he wants after his posturing at Erwin's memorial service is to be caught hanging round a Jew's house and be taken for a Jew. So he's left behind to keep Frau Professor Hoffmann company, which he doesn't seem to think much more of. Well, she's certainly no substitute for the lissom Eva, the last female he was alone with in Berlin.

Gabi used to know the city, and I thought I knew my way round a bit too, but somehow everything is different, now that so much has been bombed since each of us was last here, and it's an hour and a half before we locate Great Aunt Hedwig's final Berlin address out in Prenzlauer Berg. But that's not the only reason it takes us so long. It seems that Gabi has other and much grander addresses she wants to see first, if only for a moment. "That's where your grandfather used to live," she tells me on a wide but scarred boulevard, pointing to a narrow plot of rubble where only weeds live now. And a little later, "That's where Josef had his clinic."

I glance at her in surprise. That's the first time I've ever heard her call the mysterious Dr. Stern simply Josef. It's always been Dr. Stern or Onkel Josef before. If I was old enough to think such thoughts, perhaps I'd think she's got some special reason for wanting me to see his clinic now and hear him called Josef in that mellowed melancholic tone. But all I do is gaze unimpressed at a large bomb-damaged building with boarded-up windows like an old blind bandaged face.

And then, quite far away, we do find Great Aunt Hedwig's final address at last. It's down a dreary sidestreet off the main road, along which we hear a solitary tram forlornly clanking. This house is undamaged, but so run-down you'd think the best thing that could happen to it now would be a direct hit from another Allied bomb. As we're walking towards it on the other side of the street, a humpish and noisy black car draws up. Two men get out, wearing long shiny raincoats and brown trilby hats. They ring a bell impatiently several times, then, as we approach, start hammering on the door.

Suddenly I'm feeling scared, more scared than in any air raid and more scared even than when Fritzi Wimmer accosted me in the playground. And I know Gabi's feeling scared too, because she's grabbed my arm as if she wants to crush it. The two men step back and look up, craning their necks, then go back to ringing and hammering on the door. At last the door is opened by a shabby middle-aged man, who begins apologizing for the delay, and has his face slapped as he does so. "Ach nein!" Gabi gasps and I feel her hand trembling as it crushes my arm still more. The two men shove the man inside, and the door swings lazily shut behind them as though it's seen all this a hundred times before and is quite frankly bored with the whole business.

Why is it that Gabi can't move? Why does she have to stand there gripping my arm and watching that blank closed door, when all she ought to do is run away? Has she recognized the middle-aged man? Can this be someone else she knows? Or is it just the need to find out beforehand, to see how one day it may be with her? I'll never know, I'll never ask.

Then the driver of the car, who's been gazing vacantly down the street like a horse waiting for its master to return, winds down his window, leans his head out and calls quietly but urgently across the road, "Get out of here! Get out!"

I'm not sure if that's an order or a recommendation, but it certainly galvanizes me and I turn away, only to find that Gabi still will not move. She stands there as though paralyzed, gazing at that paint-peeling door without so much as a nod towards the driver, whose head is now back where it belongs, lolling patiently inside the car. "Mutti," I plead, tugging at her sleeve with the hand that isn't imprisoned in her vise of a grip. She doesn't even hear me. "Mutti!"

But then the door opens and the two men come out in their shiny raincoats with the middle-aged man between them, who is now wearing a black Homburg hat. The door swings lazily shut again as they all three walk down to the hump-backed car, where the driver is now sitting upright and alert. "Ach nein!" I hear Gabi moan. The middle-aged man removes his hat as he steps submissively into the car.

There's no slapping or shoving now, no violence or abuse. There isn't any need. You'd almost think he was going of his own accord, it's all so quiet and calm. As though they're just taking him out to lunch. The man's empty-eyed glance strays towards us before he ducks his head under the low roof and for a moment his eyes seem petrified in a wide startled stare. Then he is gone. One of the men gets in beside him, the other in the front beside the driver. The doors clunk shut, and away rolls the car with a peculiar clattery growl that will prevent me from ever buying a Volkswagen Beetle in the whole of my later life. And I realize that my mother is crying. Crying and shuddering. "Ach nein!" she keeps unsteadily sobbing. "Ach nein!" while I watch the wheeled beetle scuttle away up the dreary empty street until it has safely disappeared. Then my eyes, as empty as that cowed middle-aged man's were, wander to the blank indifferent door and absently absorb the faded number above it—11. A number I will never forget.

And the strangest thing about all this is that I don't ask Gabi what was going on and she doesn't tell me. In fact we don't even mention it to Frau Professsor Hoffmann or Martin when at last we get back. We never mention it to anyone, ever. We just each know what we've seen, and know, when we sometimes catch each other's eye, that the other knows as well.

We keep our secrets, even from ourselves.

■

Martin is waiting in the hall with the suitcases when we reach Frau Professor Hoffmann's and we're only just in time to catch our train. It's a silent journey for the first few hours. Martin munches more than his share of the sandwiches Frau Professor Hoffmann has thoughtfully provided, but I'm not hungry, and nor is Gabi—although she never is in any case when Martin's around. She gazes at the blacked out window without moving or speaking, her eyes still and unfocussed, as if the train was Charon's ferry and she was crossing to the other side. I keep wondering what will happen if we're asked to produce our papers. So far on this trip we haven't been, but that only makes it all the more likely that we will be now. And lacking Gabi's trust in Teutonic orderliness or Franzi Wimmer's rustic authority, I keep imagining us being booted off the train and stuffed into a sinisterly humped black car like that one in Berlin.

But the train gets shunted into sidings several times during the night, to let some SS boys go through to get at the Russkies—or so the harassed ticket inspector says when he appears to punch our tickets—and nobody is interested in checking who we are. "They need every able-bodied soldier they can get on the Eastern Front," he brusquely tells Gabi when she respectfully asks him if she should keep our papers handy for inspection or put them safely away. "They've got no time for any of that now." And he slides the door shut with the irritated air of one who's being bothered while he's doing his significant bit to get those able-bodied soldiers where they ought to be while they're still able-bodied.

After that at last I fall asleep, and dream of Tante Maria and Erwin whom we'll never see again. And of Great Aunt Hedwig and Gabi's Cousin Lotte with her husband Solomon, and the middle-aged man from that house in Prenzlauer Berg as well. All of whom we'll—

12

Never see again

But it isn't only our relations that are disappearing. Millions of other people's are too, although we won't know about them till later. But I do know our boys on the Eastern and Italian Fronts are disappearing. They've been giving ground and blood then disappearing for months now, though, according to the papers which Willibald still sometimes brings home into our semi-Jewish household, every city lost is in fact a battle won. Fraülein von Adler pulls on her stubby black-stemmed pipe, which she fills with tea leaves when she can't get tobacco, and declares sardonically that in that case they ought to lose Berlin tomorrow and win the war at once. I've got a feeling she'll be disappearing too if she doesn't watch out. That episode outside that shabby house in Berlin has really brought things home to me.

And to Gabi too I judge, because she's been subdued and withdrawn ever since we came back. As though she realizes her own time may soon be coming and she'd better be prepared. I come across her in the kitchen with Sara one afternoon, when Willibald's away on one of his longer pastoral visits. At least that's what he calls them, but it's a plump and sympathetic Aryan lady in Plinden that he's mainly doing furtive good to, and she perhaps to him. Gabi is reading aged and discolored letters to herself, then dropping them one by one into the stove, while Sara watches her like some acolyte at a sacrificial rite, which is probably just what she is. Gabi is shaking her head and wiping her drooping eye on the corner of her apron as she watches the sheets of paper blacken at the edges, curl up and burn like ancient fragile bodies in a crematorium. "What do you want?" she demands, slamming the grate irritably shut when she sees me. I wanted to get warm by the stove, but I'm not so sure about that now, so I merely shrug my shoulders guiltily, although what I'm guilty of I'm also not so sure. But then she seems to forget me altogether and sits down by Sara, gazing at the oven with far-focused eyes. It's as if she's still reading all those letters whose ashes were now eddying like delicate black butterflies up the chimney.

It's not the best time for Ortsgruppenleiter Franzi Wimmer to come calling at the Pfarrhaus, but that's exactly what he does, disturbing Gabi's melancholic reverie. He's doing the rounds collecting money to buy warm clothes for our boys on the Eastern Front who are saving Europe from the International JewishCapitalist-Bolshevik hordes. He'd like a contribution from the Herr Pfarrer, he tells her meaningfully—that is, not from her—and holds his position on the second step as steadfastly as our boys are holding theirs on the Russian steppe—those that haven't disappeared yet. Or are they already back in Poland now?

Gabi's eyes are still abstracted. "He's out."

"Every house makes a contribution," he insists, peering blearily but warily past her for some half-Aryan he can dun. Or perhaps he's doing a bit of counter-intelligence himself instead of Lisl, whose heart may well not be in it anymore, if it ever was. Does he expect to find a stack of yellow anti-Nazi leaflets full of plutocratic communistic poisonous Jewish lies?

Gabi opens the door wider, silently if coolly inviting him

in. He shakes his head in embarrassment, either at the suggestion that an Ortsgruppenleiter might accept an invitation to a semi-Jewish house, or at the imputation that he'd stoop to snooping on the Pfarrer's wife. Or perhaps at both, since his mind's already such a generous host to contradiction and confusion. But then his stertorous exhalations even at that distance are definitely beery and he's swaying a bit too. Perhaps it's just he doesn't want to risk tripping on the next step or the doormat.

Now Gabi deliberately takes a Reichsmark out of her purse and before you can say "Heil Adolf" has dropped it smack into the Ortsgruppenleiter's swastika-decorated collection box.

Jewish aid to fight the international Jewish conspiracy? You can see the quandary poor Franzi's in. "Sign here," he mutters after a moment's brow-furrowed cogitation, pointing to the list he's holding out. "Brinkmann will do."

But after entering the amount, Gabi writes *Gabriella Sara Brinkmann* in her largest and most distinct handwriting, fixing the paradox securely in Franzi's official records with a neat underlining of the *Sara*. "I'm legally obliged to sign like that," she politely explains.

Who should know that but Franzi? "Yes, well," he mutters uneasily and trudges off unsteadily across the crunchy glittering snow, remembering just in time not to say "Heil Hitler!" It's probably one of those days he wishes he hadn't taken on the job of Ortsgruppenleiter. If so, it won't be the last.

We have no more photos in our album now, as we have no more entries in our Visitors' Book. That's because Franzi Wimmer confiscated our old Leica some time ago, as he would have our typewriter if Willibald hadn't claimed he needed it for his official pastoral duties. The Leica wasn't needed for the war effort as Willibald's church bells were, gone about the same time from the steeple, and the von Haltensteins' iron gates, gone from their villa. The bells and gates went into cannons for our boys on the front, but the camera went because you cannot trust a Jew—Gabi might have used it to take secret photos of our military installations, for instance, and sent them off to the enemy.

Willibald meekly protested that the camera was his, not his wife's, but that cut no ice with Ortsgruppenleiter Franzi Wimmer. If Willibald could let a Jew get her hands on his prick, the official thinking seemed to be, wouldn't he let her get them on his camera as well? As Gabi hadn't handled either instrument for years, and never fathomed how to operate the photographic one anyway—she usually closed the eye she should be aiming with and cut off people's feet or heads—those fears were groundless. Besides there are no military installations anywhere near us, unless you count the Ortsgruppenleiter's office, which contains three World War One rifles and one tin box of ammunition. But rules are rules in Germany, even in the Third Reich, and the Leica's gone. Mark you, there's an official receipt for it. You can't say Franzi Wimmer's slack about the regulations.

It's not just the gates that have gone from the von Haltensteins' villa in Bad Neusee, by the way, it's the von Haltensteins as well—Rolf the leukemic budding author gone to heaven, and the rest we don't know where. Fraülein von Kaminsky sent a letter from Vienna not long ago, saying they wouldn't be back for some time. The death of young Rolf was hard for the Count and Countess to bear, she explained (as it was for Sara—she's still wearing that scrap of black ribbon on her coat). And besides, she opaquely hinted, they might be having "some difficulties." What sort of difficulties? Gabi wondered. Surely not the same as ours? As for myself—*"But they wouldn't dare touch us,"* I recalled Elisabeth saying, with that scornful tilt of her regal little chin. I couldn't help wondering if she was right. It's amazing the effect two men and a sinister beetle of a car can have on your views. Not to speak of all those disappearances, Tante Hedwig's and the others'.

But all those disappearances, bad as they were, are nothing to me, compared with those that are about to happen.

■

It's April again, and the sun is quite definitely over the mountaintops for spring. The last snow has melted in the village, the days are chilly bright and the alarms of war and disappearances are lulled to sleep by the plash of oars on the placid vernal lake. It's the Führer's birthday once more and we've celebrated it as usual in school with arms outstretched like symbolic phalli to the Great Prick on the wall. I'm in the top class now, and missing Fraülein Meissner, whose frustrated motherly instincts are finding surrogates in the children of and from the lower classes, who I'm sure do not appreciate them half as much as I would. She hardly ever smiles at me anymore either. Perhaps it's because I've taken my turn like Sara before me as a paradigm of the half-Jew in the elementary racial-science lesson, and she realizes more clearly now that I am quite beyond the pale. Or is it that she's distracted, having become engaged to another soldier, this time on the Russian Front—which sounds to me like throwing good money after bad?

After that Racial Science lesson, by the way, Fritzi Wimmer asked me with a mischievous grin when my mother was going to be picked up by the Gestapo. But I said she was privileged and anyway I'd seen the Gestapo picking someone up in Berlin, which was more than he had. That flummoxed him for a while. I even got a bit of credit in the class. None of them have seen what I have. They haven't even seen an air raid. But in any case Fritzi's malice is merely habitual now and almost good-humored, a piece of routine badinage. I've become like the Fat Boy or the Swot, the familiar and uncomplaining butt of genial banter, not the target of deep-seated racial hate.

Nor is Annchen the target of deep-seated racial hate, but

she's the victim of it all the same. Where there's hate there's love, which in this case means that Aryans love the Aryan race as much as they detest the Jewish. And the quality of the Aryan race has to be protected from its own mistakes as well as from the malice of The Jew.

As in the case of little Annchen. It's the morning after the Führer's birthday. Tiny puffs of cloud are playing hide-and-seek with the sun, and clumsy Annchen with her skirt above her fat white knees is sitting cross-legged in the garden, intently pulling petals off a dandelion that has struggled to survive upon that barren stony earth. Behold her stubby nose and open mouth, the light of simple pleasure in her small blue eyes, as she tears the little flower gradually apart. But don't feel sorry for the flower. It's nothing but a weed after all, fit only to be rooted out and thrown away. Which, it soon turns out, is what Annchen is as well.

Behold next Dr. Koch, unwanted visitor to the Pfarrhaus now that Ilse's on the mend, entering the garden with a hangdog air, my mother in surprised attendance. Behold Jägerlein following, wiping her rough peasant hands down her spotless apron, a baffled, proud yet suspicious smile upon her rough peasant face. The doctor's come to see her Annchen—that makes her proud—although she hasn't asked him to—that makes her suspicious. No wonder she looks baffled as well. This morning Jägerlein has regaled Sara and me and drop-mouthed Annchen with an extemporary poem on white clouds, blue skies and towering mountaintops, recited by the kitchen window as she waited for the iron to heat up.

There will be no recital tomorrow morning. "Come here, Anni," Dr. Koch says in a voice so heavy it makes you wonder how he manages to drag it up out of his chest. But Annchen is busy with a smaller murder and has no time to pay attention to the prelude to her own.

Then, since Annchen won't come to him, Dr. Koch follows

the Mahomet principle and comes to her. He asks her questions like "What are ten times twelve?" and "Can you spell Berlin?" Since everyone in the village knows that nine-year-old Annchen can't count, read or write, these questions seem otiose. Annchen apparently thinks so too, because she doesn't bother to respond. But Dr. Koch has his duty to do, and what German fails to do his duty, even if he is an Austrian German? He takes out an official form now, unfolds it and places it awkwardly upon his case. Next it's his rimless glasses he takes out; he unfolds them too and places them awkwardly on his nose. Then out come first his pen and then his instruments, and he's ready for action.

He peers, awkwardly again, into Annchen's eyes and ears with a little flashlight as though he expects to find the answers to his sum and spelling quiz inscribed somewhere in there. He's even got a pair of calipers like those that measured my supposedly half-Jewish head in school not long ago, but it's Annchen's degenerate Aryan skull that gets the treatment now. Down on the form go the damning details while Annchen patiently allows herself to be inspected and measured, turned this way and that, prodded and sounded. During all these operations her eyes remain fixed on the petal-less dandelion she clutches in her pudgy fingers; it still seems to fascinate her despite its devastated state.

"I'm afraid, er, it appears," Dr. Koch says uneasily to a space between Gabi and Jägerlein, "it appears that Annchen ought to be placed in an, er, in an institution."

"Institution?" Jägerlein repeats as vacantly as Annchen might have done, while Annchen herself now obliviously twists the sappy dandelion stem into a ring around her chubby finger.

"She'd be better off," Dr. Koch says, addressing the same innocent space. "They'll look after her there, I mean. They'll be coming for her next week, I expect. As soon as, that is, I mean when the arrangements have been made . . ."

"How long will she be there?" asks Gabi, who naively believes that even in the Third Reich medical institutions are there only to cure people and send them home again.

"Take her away?" Jägerlein says, on whom the light is beginning to dawn, or in another sense to fade.

"Er, I can't exactly say," Dr. Koch says—to Gabi, not Jägerlein. "They'll, er, they'll have to assess her there."

"But *I'm* looking after her!" Jägerlein declares to Dr. Koch.

"Yes, well," Dr. Koch says, in the voice of a schoolboy caught beside a broken window. "But I'm afraid you're not the legal guardian at law."

At law? That sounds bad. Dr. Koch might be easy to bully, but the law's another matter, and Gabi has gone pensive. But the law doesn't deter Jägerlein. She wouldn't be working for us if it did. "Well I won't let her go!" she says defiantly.

Now Dr. Koch has folded his form and is packing his instruments away. "I'm afraid it can't be helped, Frau Jäger," he apologizes, still with the air of a schoolboy standing by a broken window. "You see, you've only as it were unofficially adopted her. And her parents can't look after her, so . . ." His voice wanders off, or rather fails to wander out, and he seems exceptionally interested in the catch on his case now, bending over to examine it with a professional eye as though it's displaying symptoms requiring still more of his expert attention than poor Annchen does. Then he straightens up. "Some people from the, er, from the institution will come to take her next week, or . . . Well, anyway, when they're ready for her. It will be better for her there," he adds as much to himself as to Jägerlein. But neither of them appears convinced.

"Which institution?" Gabi asks. "Where?"

"In Gallneukirchen," Dr. Koch mutters vaguely. "Or Hartheim, I think. I don't know exactly . . ." And then he's gone with his sheepish smile and his hangdog look. He has other calls to make, he explains as he lays his case in his sidecar, though whether they're of the same nature he doesn't divulge. But there are plenty more like Annchen in Heimstatt and its neighboring villages. We listen to the explosive clatter of his motorcycle engine echoing and dying as he drives away, and somehow it doesn't seem like April anymore, but rather like November.

Jägerlein takes Annchen wordlessly by the hand and leads her unresistingly back into the kitchen. It's no surprise to anyone except Willibald that the ironing doesn't get done today, the dinner doesn't get properly cooked, and the dishes don't get washed. Annchen gets *her* grub on time though, and licks her plate clean with her usual snuffling relish.

■

"Of course she'd be better off in an institution," Willibald declares when he's stopped complaining about his wretched dinner. "And there'll be one less thief to steal our rations." Jägerlein and Annchen might have come back, but Willibald's suspicions have never gone away.

"Ach, Willibald," Gabi begins protestingly with a glance at the open door. But when she sees the veins in her husband's throat start bulging, his cheeks flushing and his eyes flashing with righteous anger, she takes a mouthful of watery tea and holds it steadfastly in her mouth although it scalds her tongue until Willibald has finished a long minatory diatribe accompanied by heavy pounding of the table. Is it that I'm growing up, or that Willibald is growing tired? His scenes no longer seem to possess that vivid lightning and thunder which they used to have. Or could it be that the plump Aryan lady we don't yet know about is having a soothing as well as a distracting influence on his racked and anguished soul?

Willibald wouldn't complain so much in the evening if he knew what morning had in store. Jägerlein is gone, and so is Annchen. On the table where stale bread and ersatz coffee should be standing there lies a scrappy pencilled note which in Willibald's eyes by no means compensates for the absence of his breakfast.

> *Dear Frau Pfarrer,*
> *Sorry I have not done brekfast. I am taking Annchen away. I hope you will excuse not being here for a while.*
> *Yours fathfully,*
> *M Jäger*

Her little room behind the kitchen has been swept clean and the two beds stripped bare. The old blankets which belong to us are neatly folded on the bottom of each naked mattress.

It's another sunny spring day, but Jägerlein and Annchen are gone again and I feel it's cold and rainy.

Willibald, who usually sleeps late, has risen with the lark today—he's got an early funeral and a wedding to perform, and breakfast was just what he needed to see him through all that. "They'll think we helped her to escape!" he cries out in alarm when he's overcome his disappointment. "Aiding and abetting!"

"They'll have gone to her sister's farm," Martin declares knowingly, while Gabi boils the coffee water in the kitchen, and Ilse, released from the rigors of her tubercular cure into the hardly less exacting demands of everyday life, silently saws at the stale loaf she's brought to the table.

"I'll tell the Authorities!" Willibald declares, stuffing the note into his clerical pocket. "She won't get away with this, trying to get us into trouble! As if we haven't got enough as it is!"

"You know what they'd do to Annchen in that institution?" Martin unconcernedly inquires as he takes a slice of bread and sniffs at it with wrinkled nose. He's been learning things in the brickworks, picking up the gossip.

"Whatever they'd do, it's where she belongs! Why are *you* late?" This to Sara, who's been scribbling in her corner by the

stove. "Where have *you* been?" And then back to Jägerlein's abs-
scondence. "How dare she just run off like that without even
making breakfast?"

"I thought you'd be glad she was gone," I sullenly suggest.
"Seeing she's such a thief." My sense of desolation has momen-
tarily overridden my dominant instinct for survival.

"Impertinence!" Willibald roars, swinging his hand. "Into
the cellar!" Perhaps his lightning and thunder are still there after
all. He certainly clips my ear pretty sharply, and it's still sting-
ing as I'm shoved breakfastless into the cellar, where there's no
light at all and my only companions are the decreasing supply of
coal and the increasing supply of rats, which, unless it's just the
ringing in my ear, I hear scuttling and squeaking in the dark.
Oh God, don't let one run over my feet! I pray in that access of religious fervor that misfortune generally engenders, while overhead
I also hear Gabi's tearful protestations and Willibald's crescendo
yells. These are accompanied by several dull thumps, which I
correctly infer are caused by heavy books being thrown. Soon,
if the battle continues, I'll be hearing the sharper crash of picture frames smashing and the tinkling of broken glass. But no,
Willibald's ranting is in the rallentando and diminuendo phase
by now; an unaccompanied coda, which tells me Gabi must be
applying the Kaminsky cure once more, and I know the opera
will soon be over.

I've been here before, and I'll be here again, not that that
makes it any pleasanter, especially when a thick moist cobweb
brushes like a bat's wing across my face and clings to my eyebrows. But at least I know what to expect, and I settle down to
wait anxiously for the slamming of the front door that by announcing Willibald's departure to his Christian duties will her-
ald my release from prison. Once he's out of the way, Gabi will
softly turn the key. There really must be something to religion, I
vaguely realize, and quietly thank God for it. If it wasn't for the

summons of Willibald's Christian duties, he might have stayed in all day, and then I might have too.

Willibald doesn't tell the Authorities about Jägerlein's defection after all—any contact with Authority turns his knees to jelly—but the Authorities soon find out anyway. No longer than it takes a letter to go there and back, an ambulance with opaque windows draws up outside the Pfarrhaus and a man in a neat dark suit with a Party badge in his lapel gets out, followed by a pleasantly blonde if starchy-looking nurse, one of the three village policemen and a reluctant Dr. Koch who looks as though he's being taken to be shot. But it isn't him they're after, it's harmless Annchen, the weed in the Aryan garden.

"Where is Keller, Anna?" the man demands, flourishing an official-looking form and viewing Gabi with cold racial disdain. The nurse is already trotting briskly and inquiringly into the hall, like an eager terrier after a hare. If she had a tail it would be wagging stiffly.

"I don't know," Gabi says. "She went away." By now the man is examining the warrant or whatever they call it more carefully. "When? Where to?" Gabi shrugs, perversely reversing the question sequence in her answers. "They didn't say. Last Friday."

"They?"

"Jäger, Mitzi," the policeman quietly remarks, glancing at Dr. Koch, who miserably nods. The policeman is Constable Bolzner, one of whose five children is in my class at school.

Now Willibald emerges from the study where *King Solomon*—or is it *King David*?—is back on the blocks after several false starts.

The man eyes Willibald almost as unfavorably as he's just eyed Gabi.

"Heil Hitler!" Willibald salutes him with ingratiating rectitude, flapping his arm as he simultaneously bows his head and clicks his heels like a mechanical toy. "Brinkmann."

The man's arm rises in return with languid disdain as he mutely interrogates Dr. Koch and Constable Bolzner. Meanwhile the nurse has started coursing to and fro across the living room and dining room. Soon she'll be picking the scent up in the kitchen.

"The Herr Pfarrer," Constable Bolzner respectfully explains to the suit. Dr. Koch nods miserably again. It seems he's only got a walk-on part in this act of the drama. Soon it will be a walk-off one, if you can apply that term to someone driving a motorbike.

"Yes indeed," Willibald agrees with both of them, as well he might, and with a certain meek pride. "I am the Lutheran Pfarrer. At your service."

The man steps forward a pace. Now he's only half a meter away from Willibald. As he's rather short, he barely reaches Willibald's chin. But what he loses in height he makes up for in pugnacity. He consults his form again and then addresses Willibald's puny chest. "Where are Keller, Anna, and Jäger, Mitzi?" he demands, grinding the words out like a rusty sausage-slicer. Before Willibald can answer, he turns to the policeman and inquires in the same menacing tone, "And what were a German woman and a young German girl, however defective, doing in a half-Jewish household?"

Constable Bolzner shifts his feet and mutters something about the Ortsgruppenleiter, which Fritzi Wimmer isn't going to thank him for, but the man waves his hand impatiently, turning back to Willibald. By now the nurse is in the kitchen, but the scent must have gone cold because she doesn't bark or yelp.

"I have reason to believe they have gone to Frau Jäger's sister's farm," Willibald announces to the top of the man's head, standing to attention in the manner of a soldier having the honor to report the whereabouts of the enemy to his commanding officer.

The man examines Willibald's Adam's apple for a moment, which certainly is prominent enough to merit some attention, then jerks his head alertly round towards Constable Bolzner once more, like a bright-eyed hawk that's spotted a lonely sparrow.

Again Constable Bolzner mutters something respectful, which I pick out to be the farm's address. The dark-suited sparrow hawk jerks its predatory head back to Willibald's distinctive Adam's apple, and his curled index finger's talon taps him twice upon the chest. "They'd better be there," he says. "They had better be there, my friend."

And then they're gone. The nurse smiles quite amiably as she lollops down the steps, and I imagine her tail threshing happily from side to side. She's so nice you could almost pat her rump.

"Willibald," Gabi begins reproachfully as the door closes, "why did you tell him that?" But she too has been cowed and her tone isn't what it has been or will one day become again.

"Didn't you hear him?" Willibald interrupts fearfully. "*They'd better be there.* Didn't you hear it? *'They'd better be there, my friend.'* He threatened me, and you expect—? Besides, they'd have gone there in any case, wouldn't they? Where else d'you think they'd have looked?" But this mixture of guilt, rationalization and fear is all too much for him, and his voice gives way to throbbing moans. Back into the study he wanders, looking as much condemned, or self-condemned, as unhappy Dr. Koch looked re-entering the ambulance. I don't know if he's able to get back to work on *King David* or *King Solomon,* but the way things have been going lately, you could hardly blame him if he doesn't.

At least his hypothesis was right, as was Martin's before him. Jägerlein has indeed taken Annchen to her sister's farm. They're discovered that very day hiding in the barn, covered by the remnants of last year's hay that the French prisoner François has complaisantly scattered over them. Kicking and howling like a dog, Annchen is dragged off to the ambulance while Jägerlein is charged by the unhappy Constable Bolzner with abducting a minor. Somehow the starchy smiling nurse is able to hold Annchen still enough for the sparrow hawk to jab a needle into her arm, and the ambulance cruises off as quiet as a hearse.

■

Jägerlein gets a sympathetic judge who reduces the charge and she only does a month in the jug. But a month is long enough for Annchen's ashes to come back to the village with an official note declaring that she died of blood poisoning from warts on her lip and had been cremated to avoid infection. The urn is delivered to her parents, but they say Jägerlein can have it. *It's a hard thing that we do,* the Führer has resolutely said of this aspect of his racial policy, *but future generations will thank us for it.* And perhaps some will, who knows? But Jägerlein won't thank him for it. She keeps Annchen's ashes in an urn in her bedroom in the farmhouse, where she's been assigned to work now that François has been hauled off. Apparently the economy has other plans for him as well, and Jägerlein never sees her Frenchman again.

Nor does she ever see Dr. Koch again, to whom, if she did, she'd have given a salty piece of her mind. *You could have saved her,* she would have told him. *You could have filled that form out differently. You could have said Annchen could spell Berlin. You could have said she knew the answer to that sum, which by the way I didn't know myself* . . . But Dr. Koch is now as far beyond her reach in another element as Annchen is in hers. Soon after Annchen's ashes are returned we hear the doctor's motorbike racing late at night along the lakeside road as though he's hastening to a terrible accident. Which in a sense he is, but it hasn't happened yet. It doesn't happen till he reaches the hairpin corner halfway round, where, instead of slowing, he unaccountably accelerates still more and soars off the edge sidecar and all, into the deepest part of the lake.

The lake does not give up its dead, the villagers say, and

certainly it doesn't give up Dr. Koch. Neither he nor his three-wheeled vehicle is ever seen again.

Jägerlein sees Willibald again, though. But no word of reproach ever passes her lips. Not surprisingly, because she'll never know his part in Annchen's death. No one ever tells her what Pfarrer Brinkmann told the man in the dark suit. Least of all, of course, does Pfarrer Brinkmann himself.

Yes, this is the year of disappearances all right. But there's one more disappearance that's been planned and rehearsed as carefully as any in these months, and yet does not take place. That's a pity, because it's—

13

Just the one we needed

May has passed and summer's definitely come. So have the Tommies and the Amis—they've come to Normandy and seem to be advancing into Fortress Europe despite our boys' fanatical resistance. One of the Tommies is Lotte and Solomon's son Wolfgang, although we don't know that yet and they never will. He's dropped out of the sky near Caen, in a special Jewish Commando Company. That's where some really fanatical Aryan resistance is going on, but he must be up to that because our boys are giving more blood and ground than the Tommies are.

The Führer resolutely assures the world however that this is just the chance he's been waiting for, the decisive battle where he's going to administer their ultimately crushing comeuppance to the Allies. If that's the case, Fraülein von Adler cackles, composedly stuffing tea leaves as fine as dust into her pipe bowl with her blackened thumb, why did he try to stop them coming? But of course she doesn't have the Führer's head for strategy. Nor does she know about his new secret weapon, the Vengeance One (not to speak of Vengeance Two—there's a lot of vengeance going round), that will soon be pulverizing the Tommies' cities.

As if to make up for two of the people that have disappeared—Annchen and Jägerlein—another two have popped up in their place: Fräulein Hofer the seamstress, and her niece Resi. Fräulein Hofer comes once a week to darn our worn-out clothes and sew buttons on our frayed shirts and trousers. Fräulein Hofer's a Catholic, but that doesn't stop her coming to a Protestant house, even a minister's. Maybe she's an early ecumenist, not that she would recognize the term. Nor does she mind entering a semi-Jewish household, although her mother, who scares me rigid because she's got one finger missing, is a zealous Party member.

No, what Fräulein Hofer balks at is the laundry. Gabi asked her to help with that too, but the idea of Aryans washing Jewish clothes is too much for her mother—just think of the contamination in a pair of Jewish socks or knickers—so Fräulein Hofer, in deference to the old woman, who sometimes scowls and shakes her mutilated hand at me as I come home from school, draws the line there. But sewing is all right, or at least it's not so bad. So now our dirty washing gets sent by train to Pels, eighty kilometers away, where it's known simply as Pfarrer Brinkmann's, and comes back neatly washed and ironed by innocent Aryan hands about two months later, by which time we're all looking pretty scruffy. It costs, and Willibald objects. But he also objects if his shirts aren't starched and ironed, and Gabi's efforts in that department, even when she manages to get round to it, just can't match Jägerlein's. So the last of dead Aunt Frieda's unused dowry, which for eleven years has lain along with her nurse's uniform in a trunk in the attic, is getting sold piecemeal in the village. In ten years' time tourists here will be eating off tablecloths embroidered by Frieda's hand with Frieda's initials. If Willibald complains bitterly to his plump Aryan lady-friend about his wife's reckless extravagance, he does so in floppy woollen underpants and starched shirts (if he's still got them on) that have been laundered in Pels.

But as for darning—well, despite the official proscription against performing any kind of "personal service" for Jews, it's Fraülein Hofer who plies her Aryan needle on our washed but mixed-breed clothes, accompanied by her niece Resi, who's ten years old now and mainly sits and watches, although her eyes and lips still offer me that tentative smile I first noticed three years ago in school. How Fraülein Hofer reconciles this with her mother's attitude to racial hygiene and indeed with the official decrees is a mystery, but there are many mysteries in the Third Reich, and this is not the greatest. After all, Ortsgruppenleiter Franzi Wimmer allowed Jägerlein to work in our half-Jewish household all those years, so perhaps she too considers it's the Aryan half she's working for. And she certainly does need the money.

Resi is a kind of orphan. Her mother inconsiderately died in childbirth and her soldier father was so incensed by his wife's desertion that he gave the baby to his unmarried sister before he went back to his artillery regiment. "Here, you take her," he said, as if it was all her fault. "You'll never get married, but at least you can bring a kid up." And he was right on both counts. Fraülein Hofer, plain and sexless as a nun, never has got married, but she's bringing Resi up all right. When her father comes home on leave, they all have dinner together, but he doesn't stay long because he's got a girlfriend in Bad Neusee.

Fraülein Hofer and Resi come every Saturday morning, at nine on the dot. She sits at the sewing machine and Resi sits swinging her legs beside her. Fraülein Hofer never utters a word except to say "Grüss Gott" and ask for instructions, which she rarely needs. Into the basket goes her hand, out comes a shirt or sheet, her foot presses the treadle and the machine whirs away for an hour and a half. She often has a thread of cotton hanging down from her lips, and sometimes I wonder if she's got the whole spool inside her mouth and what would happen if I pulled the end. Maybe she's swallowed it, I sometimes think. Maybe she's got a dozen spools inside her.

At half past ten the treadle stops and they both take a cup of ersatz milk coffee (which Gabi provides) and a thick slice of buttered bread (which they provide). When twelve o'clock strikes on the grandfather clock in Willibald's study, the treadle stops again, Fraülein Hofer packs away the basket and they silently leave.

This is no compensation for the loss of Jägerlein's chanted poems and Annchen's simple grunts of pleasure, but it's peaceful all the same, and I start to like the days they come. Gabi says I should play with Resi, which naturally makes me want to do anything but. Besides, although she's in my class at school and offers me her fleeting smiles, she's still an Aryan and a girl while I am neither, and on both counts we've never spoken to each other, so why should we start now? It's going to take more than Gabi's encouragement to get Resi and me any closer. All the same, something draws me to the living room when they are here.

■

It's on one of those Saturdays in July, when the school holidays have just begun, that Fraülein Hofer breaks her vow of silence an hour or so after she's arrived and casually mentions there's been an attempt on the Führer's life. Her mother heard it on the wireless that morning, she says as she threads the needle. Some army officers, she thinks it was. She imparts this information quite neutrally, in the way she sometimes says she'll darn that tablecloth next time, there won't be time today; so it's impossible to tell what she thinks about the news. After a tantalizing pause to remove the white thread dangling from her mouth, she continues in the same inexpressive tone, "Apparently they failed."

Perhaps it's the unexcited manner of her delivery that conceals the full importance of her news from me, but all the same I sense this is a weighty moment. As for Gabi and Willibald—there's no doubting the effect it has on them. Gabi looks like someone who's just been told her death sentence has been commuted and in the next breath told that no, it hasn't after all. Which is just about the fact of the matter. "Ach nein!" she exclaims in that tone of anguished disappointment that I've so often heard before.

The effect on Willibald is more electric. He's still in his shorty nightshirt, which at least is newly washed from Pels, and which Resi has grown quite used to and contemplates with only passing interest now. Perhaps she thinks, not having a proper father herself, that every proper father dresses like that at home. Perhaps she even thinks that every proper father wears a cat's pelt on his chest as well, since Tabby's floppy paw sometimes waves to her from round Willibald's throat. But now, as Willibald gasps and dashes off upstairs, his nightshirt's minimal tails flap like flustered chickens' wings, disclosing unappealing vistas of flabby and etiolated nether parts. Resi's interest is only mildly quickened by this display, but Gabi hastens up after him, trying ineffectually to block the innocent child's view with her own body. There are tense but hushed interchanges in their bedroom and then Gabi comes down looking flushed, and mechanically bids me yet again to play with Resi, an injunction both of us smile self-consciously at and ignore. She is soon followed by Willibald, who appears now in respectable clerical garb and hurries excitedly off to the marketplace to glean the latest news.

It isn't until after twelve, when Fraülein Hofer and Resi have quietly gone home, that Willibald returns. Yes, it's true, he declares in the kitchen. There's been a plot to kill the Führer. A bomb in his bunker, and it's only the hand of Providence that's preserved his life. Most of the plotters have been arrested, some have been put against a wall and shot, the rest will soon be tried and hanged.

It seems *The People's Observer,* from whose pages Willibald has gleaned his information, consider the Reich has won a great victory just because Adolf is, like God, still with us.

Willibald curses the plotters, and at first I suppose he's mad at them because they bungled the job. That must be what Sara and Ilse think too, because they're going round shutting the windows although it's one of those sultry summer days when even Heimstatt is too hot. But no, he means they're traitors, violating their soldiers' oath (the oath that both he and I still know by heart), and they deserve everything that's come or coming to them, which I later hear from Fritzi Wimmer includes being hanged by piano wire attached to butchers' hooks. "*What?*" Gabi almost screams. "*What?* D'you know what you're saying?"

It seems he does, because he repeats it with flashing military eyes. "An oath's an oath!" he declares. "A sacred promise! A soldier's honor!"

Is that a line from *King Solomon*, I wonder? Or *King David*? I wouldn't know. I'm completely ignorant about the Bible as a whole and the Old Testament in particular, which the Third Reich in any case holds to be a crazy web of degenerate Jewish confabulation. "Any soldier who breaks his oath is a traitor and a villain!" Willibald rushes on in full rhetorical spate. Well, if that isn't *King Solomon* it must be *King David*. I do at least know David was handy with a sling and did a lot of fighting. "*Fiat iustitia,*" Willibald is declaiming now in mystifying exercise of his classical learning, "*ruat caelum!*"

Gabi doesn't know more than two words of Latin, and neither is among those four, but she gets the drift anyway. She's getting a glass of water from the jug on the dresser too, but fires a broadside as she passes. "Have you forgotten your children?" she demands. "Of course you forgot *me* long ago, I know that!" Then her cheeks bulge with a belated mouthful of the Kaminsky cure.

"You wouldn't understand! What could honor mean to you?" Sara and I are edging closer to the oven now. This looks like a big one. So Willibald's powers have not diminished after all.

It looks still more like a big one when Gabi suddenly gulps down the water she's just got into her mouth and splutters out "*Honor?! Honor?!* What about your family's *lives,* for God's sake?"

"Yes, honor means nothing to you, I know that! That's why we're always in debt! And why you take the Lord's name in vain—"

"You typical German blockhead!" Gabi's screaming now, and already clutching her side with an incipient gallbladder attack. "Sticking to that . . . that . . . *murderer?* You call *that* honor?!"

"Can't you get it into your Jewish head that a German officer does not break his oath?" Willibald really looks the part now—the part, that is, of a poor weak former corporal aping a blockhead Prussian general.

"Yes, at last you've let it out!" screams Gabi. "Jewish! You hate me for it, don't you? Just like all the others!"

"Haven't I stood by you all this time?" Willibald demands, which, though pertinent, does not exactly answer Gabi's question.

"Stood by me? You don't have the nerve to throw me out, that's all! All you want is to be rid of me, isn't it?"

"And that's all the thanks I get?" Which, though pertinent again, does not exactly answer her second question either. He's got a plate in both hands now and is holding it above his head for all to see and tremble.

"Well, leave, then!" shouts Gabi. "If that's how you feel! Leave! Send me to a concentration camp like all my relatives! It'll come to that in the end anyway!"

"May I remind you that one of your relatives, so far from being in a concentration camp, has deserted his country?" he inquires with frigid ferocity. Pianistic Wolfgang, he means, whose parents were deported last year to the East. "And for all we know he may even be aiding and abetting the enemy at this very moment!" Smash goes the plate on the floor and out stalks Willibald. As he doesn't threaten suicide, it's probably his plump Aryan lady-friend he's going to, not the lake, though how are we to know that?

The smash of plate and slam of door brings on one of Gabi's acutest gallbladder attacks, and Sara goes to boil some water for a poultice while Ilse silently retreats to her room, taking the stairs slowly one foot at a time like a weary nun returning to her cell. Sara's left her notebook by the stove, but I don't sneak a look inside. For one thing I don't feel like it then. But for another I know the kind of stuff that's in it, and it really doesn't interest me. Not now, anyway. Besides, I've known for a long time that she keeps her notebooks under the mattress in her room, as Martin keeps material of a different nature under the mattress in his. I could look at it anytime. I've sneaked a look at Martin's already.

I found it odd. Why were all those ladies half-undressed? How ridiculous they looked! Still, something about them did capture my attention. I thought I might look at them again one day, which I don't think about Sara's notebooks for quite a time to come.

As soon as Martin arrives home (who knows where he's been? It's his day off and he certainly isn't telling. Wherever it was, though, it's a safe bet Lisl Wimmer's been there with him)—as soon as Martin arrives home, Frau Wimmer comes knocking at the door, a thing she hasn't done for several years and never in my limited memory. "Have you heard the shocking news about the Führer?" she asks Gabi in a hushed and cloying voice. Has she taken over the counter-intelligence duties that Lisl doesn't seem to have the heart for now and Franzi not the stomach?

"Yes," Gabi replies. She's hobbling about with a hot-water bottle pressed to her side now. "Shocking," she agrees, though what's shocked her about it might not be what's shocked Frau Wimmer.

"I suppose you don't happen to have a box of matches to spare?" Frau Wimmer continues artlessly. She can't be very inventive if that worn-out cover is the best she can think up.

"I do have a match or two," Gabi answers guardedly, mindful of the Nazi allegations that The Jew, or what is left of him, is hoarding all the goodies that are in short supply. "But I don't have a spare box. We're down to our last one. They haven't had any for weeks, my husband says."

"All right then," Frau Wimmer says, peering past Gabi into the hall. "Of course it's not so bad for you, is it? I mean *you* wouldn't mind as much as we would, would you?"

Gabi grimaces, pushing the hot-water bottle hard against her aching side. "We need matches too," she protests mildly.

"No, about the Führer," Frau Wimmer says, smiling archly now. "I mean it stands to reason, doesn't it? *You* wouldn't miss him like we would, would you? If anything happened to him, I mean . . . ?"

Gabi hesitates. Has this afternoon's big one left her reckless? I sense she's on the edge and there's a long drop down if she steps over. Sara's filling another hot-water bottle in the kitchen, Martin's gone upstairs like Ilse (though he won't be praying as she probably is, unless it is to Venus) and I know I'm not the kind that can pull my mother back from the brink. All I can do is wish Gabi had another dash of water in her mouth. But it's all right, she pulls herself together and steps back of her own accord. "Where would the Fatherland be without the Führer?" she asks Frau Wimmer blandly at last.

Frau Wimmer, who has small glinty eyes and a sharp nose set in a face that's always pushing inquisitively forward, looks as disappointed as a weasel emerging from an empty rabbit burrow. She gives a baffled smile and starts to retreat.

"Didn't you want some matches?" Gabi reminds her. For someone naturally deficient in the art of irony, she's beginning to make real progress.

Not that she can hold a candle to Fraülein von Adler, who declares on her next visit, when the papers and wireless are still full of Adolf's providential escape, that all Germany stands mourning by Hitler's empty grave. She assumes a tone of such solemn piety when she says it that Gabi is at first as puzzled as I am, but Willibald's no sloth when it comes to ironic uptake, and he rises at once and walks silently and with great dignity out of the room like the officer and gentleman he wishes he was, pursued by Fraülein von Adler's relentless and sarcastic cackle.

"If only we can last out the war," Gabi mutters to Fraülein von Adler, but I've hardly any notion what she means. What else is there but war? I don't know what peace is. Does it mean we can go to school like everyone else and not sit by ourselves or get dumped when we reach sixteen? But I know what war means all right. Apart from those air raids in Berlin, it means people disappearing. And now the disappearances are as many as the falling leaves in autumn, although we've only just reached August. What will it be like in October and November, I wonder. The answer is it will get worse and worse.

■

The bomb plot was planned by aristocratic army officers, and that meant lots of them are on the skids now that Providence has preserved the Führer to continue his fanatical struggle against The Jew. But of course The Jew must have been behind the plot, since The Jew's behind everything bad, and so the few of them that are left will soon be on the skids as well, never mind if they've been "privileged" up till now. Then there are all the trade unionists and social democrats, the members of the Confessional Church and anyone in short who's got a conscience. They'll be skidding soon too if they don't watch out. Or if they do, for that matter.

And so the leaves keep falling in the gentle heat of summer.

First there's Ulrich, my school friend in Berlin, if someone can be called your friend whose only social contact with you was to give you a wooden pencil with his name on it. Not that *he* disappears—at least, not as far as I know. But his father does, and so does his pencil. His father's name is on the list of traitors that Willibald brings back in *The People's Observer* one day, and there's a blotchy picture of him in civvies at his trial (no uniform for treacherous serpents like him). He looks frail and beaten, which he probably is, and has to hold his beltless trousers up with his hands while standing rather bowed to hear his death sentence pronounced in the kangaroo People's Court. "That must be Ulrich's father," I tell Willibald with a mixture of pride and dismay, and go to fetch my pencil with Ulrich's name printed on it. "Look, he gave me his pencil and I gave him mine."

"With your name on it?" Willibald demands in consternation. "Suppose it's traced? Why didn't you think? Giving traitors your pencil! Why didn't you *think?*" Into the kitchen stove with my one and only treasured souvenir, and into the cellar with me, as punishment for thoughtless swapping. I think of Ulrich while I'm there, and wonder what it's like to have your father's picture in the paper, being sentenced to be hanged. It certainly takes my mind off the rats.

Nearer home (forty kilometers to be exact), it's Ilse's Plinden teachers that disappear next, those military widows whose husbands were offered to, or rather taken by, the Fatherland for omnivorous Adolf. Ilse's well enough to go back to visit them for her lessons now, but one Monday morning at the end of August, as she labors up the stairs to their shared apartment with her rucksack half full of books, she sees a policeman standing there outside their locked, sealed door.

She's never been grateful before that she's become so slow, but this time she is, because it gives her time to think. At which admittedly she's also slow, but fear lends wings to flagging thought. She climbs laboriously on past the policeman, who watches her impassively, and rings the bell on the next landing.

When a plump but severe-looking woman answers, Ilse asks if Frau Schmidt lives there, choosing the name at random and hoping it is not this woman's. "No," the woman answers, pointing to the nameplate on the door. She has the presence of a Leader of the League of German Girls, which isn't surprising considering that's exactly what she is. Ilse mutters that she must have got the wrong address, while the woman stands silently surveying her from top to toe and back again as if she knows full well what's going on. She looks as if she's half-inclined to interrogate Ilse and yet half-inclined not to. Fortunately it's the second half that wins. She glances downstairs towards the policeman a moment, then closes the door.

Ilse turns and slowly, tremblingly, descends. Past the policeman, beside whose arm she glimpses *Deutsches Reich* stamped on the imposing seal upon the door. Along the landing, feeling the policeman's gaze rest thoughtfully upon her rucksack. Down the stairs once more, telling herself she mustn't run, and then recalling that she hasn't run in years and couldn't if she tried. Out into the bright and balmy August air, where skiffs are being rowed across the lake and yachts are being sailed, as though it has always been summer and always will be.

She never returns to Frau Professor Lambach's and Frau Professor Zauner's apartment. They've been being a little more socially disruptive than teaching half-Jewish Ilse. In fact they've been in imprudent correspondence with one of the minor plotters, and their letters have been found among his things. As "Politicals" they spend some time in jail, where they do at least get fed, before being sent to Belsen concentration camp, where they don't.

Willibald and Gabi spend a suspenseful week, during which they keep a truce with each other, waiting for the knock on the door which will signify that the net from Plinden has been cast over them as well. Perhaps Willibald has a few secret conversations with his Aryan lady-friend too, but if so he naturally doesn't tell Gabi. Then, as nothing happens, they gradually relax, which allows their marriage truce to grow ragged and the sniping war to recommence.

Ilse grows still quieter and slower, and starts dragging her foot still more. Is her TB coming back, or is it something else and worse? Gabi's sure it's something else, but won't say what. Whatever it is, her education has to continue, and now that Frau Professor Zauner and Frau Professor Lambach have gone, it's timid Frau Professor Goldberg that must—

14

Take up the slack

At least until it's time for her to disappear as well. She starts coming twice a week, on Wednesdays and Saturdays, and coaches Sara into the bargain as well, since by now they're at the same level, which means that Ilse's level can't be what it should be. Frau Professor Goldberg would prefer it if they came to her, as Martin still does come, but Ilse's health is clearly on the downward path again, and so she bravely comes to us. She enters with the air of a small brown mouse with glistening wide brown eyes, peering anxiously about her for the slightest hint of cat. But there's no cat here—we're not allowed to have one—and Fraülein Hofer and Resi bid her "Grüss Gott" on Saturday mornings quite as if she was a normal person, not a vicious and degenerate Jew with the yellow badge of shame emblazoned on her breast.

But vicious and degenerate Jew she is, and her name is on the list. Yes, although the Führer's great counter-offensive is running out of steam in the West and his Vengeance One and Vengeance Two secret weapons haven't pulverized the British cities after all; although the Russkies are grinding our boys down to bone dust in the East (not to mention the treacherous Italians swapping sides down in the south); although, that is, things are looking distinctly bleak for him, it's the final extirpation of the European Jew that Adolf's planning with his cronies now, not a repair job on the bleeding armies or a quick strategic fix. And it stands to methodical reason that it's the remaining Jews who aren't "privileged" like Gabi that have to be deracinated first. There are about a hundred thousand of them still in Hungary alone, not to speak of those still in the occupied West.

And there's Frau Professor Goldberg in Bad Neusee.

The Hungarian Jews will have to be rounded up by the local police and the SS under the indefatigable Eichmann, because they're undisciplined Hungarians who might try to escape, but the Jews of the Reich have been trained in the habits of obedience, so all it takes to get Frau Professor Goldberg where they want her is a notice instructing her to present herself at Gestapo Headquarters in Linz with one suitcase and a packed lunch for the journey. Journey to where? The notice doesn't say, but Frau Professor Goldberg doesn't expect to be coming back. She arrives at the Pfarrhaus on a November Wednesday as usual, but a little more subdued, and gives her lesson quite normally to Ilse and Sara. Then she shows Gabi and Willibald the summons she has just received. "I would like Ilse to have my gold brooch," she says detachedly. "Why should *they* get it? And Sara can have my diamond engagement ring." She doesn't mention Martin.

"Engagement ring?" Gabi echoes in that irritating way she has of repeating in amazement what she's understood but can't believe. She glances down at Frau Professor Goldberg's naked ring finger.

"Oh, I never wear it now. My fiancé was killed in the last war." Frau Professor Goldberg gives a wry little smile. "Fighting for Germany." And suddenly it's Gabi whose eyes are moist, not timid Frau Professor Goldberg's. "I wasn't *meant* to be a spinster, you know," she adds.

"Terrible, terrible," Willibald is murmuring, while Gabi wraps the jewelry in her handkerchief and slips it into her apron pocket. "But perhaps it won't be too bad in Linz? Perhaps they just want to . . ." But he has no idea what they might just want to, or rather he has only too good an idea, and his words straggle off like a bunch of deserters who've just glimpsed the battlefield and feel they don't belong there. Really he's only glad it isn't him that's got to go to Linz. He might even be glad it's not Gabi, though that's not quite so clear. Above all though, he's got that wonderful relieved *It's not me, I'm all right* feeling. But that's just where he's partly wrong. Frau Professor Goldberg, timid yet courageous Frau Professor Goldberg, is about to put him on the spot.

"Herr Pfarrer," she addresses him, "would you mind going with me on the train? Only as far as Linz station," she quickly adds, seeing shock and terror transfiguring Willibald's unhappy face. "Not to the Gestapo. It would be such a comfort if I didn't have to go all the way alone, if someone was with me, I mean. Even only part of the way. I've always had to do everything alone, you see, and now this last time . . ." She glances sideways at me.

"Of course, Frau Professor," Gabi answers for Willibald. "I'll come along too." She doesn't see any danger in that. She still believes they do things by the book in Germany, so if her name's not on the list yet, no one's going to touch her. Perhaps she's right, but Frau Professor Goldberg isn't taking any chances.

"No, no, no!" She holds up her frail little hand, hardly bigger than a mouse's claw. "It wouldn't be safe for you, Frau Pfarrer. And if something happened to you, how could I . . . ? I couldn't have that on my conscience. But an Aryan and a minister of religion . . ." And she looks appealingly at Willibald again.

And though Willibald doesn't have much courage, he numbly nods his head and instantly becomes a minor hero. Perhaps, as he said, it won't be too bad. Not for him, anyway. And he certainly won't go a step further than Platform Three in Linz Station.

Frau Professor Goldberg thinks she'd like to say goodbye to Ilse and Sara, but they're working on their exercises in their separate rooms, and on second thought she decides that after all she'd rather not. The strain, she thinks, might be too much. So she says goodbye to me instead, and says I should say goodbye to them. I nod numbly too, and like Willibald tell myself it won't be too bad in Linz. But I've seen that sinister black beetle of a car in Berlin, and something tells me that it will be.

Gabi and Willibald accompany Frau Professor Goldberg a few yards down the street, Willibald keeping a little distance from the two women as though he isn't really promenading with a second Jewess. No sooner have they left than Sara comes downstairs.

"She isn't coming back, is she?" she asks.

It's warm today but I feel cold and I've crept beside the stove. "She said goodbye," I mutter. And pretend to be intently drawing invisible pictures with my finger on the oven tiles. "How did you know? She gave Mutti something for you."

Sara doesn't tell me how she knew. But it certainly wasn't a flash in the pan. She's going to know the next time too.

And Willibald plays his part to the very end. He sits in the train two days later beside yellow-starred Frau Professor Goldberg, who has to show the official warrant in order to be allowed onto it, and because she wears the yellow star, they have the whole compartment to themselves. Frau Professor Goldberg isn't talkative on the journey, he tells us later, and it seems unlikely he'd have had a lot to say himself. But he does his job, he sees it through and even hands her suitcase down to her when the train arrives at Platform Three in Linz.

Frau Professor Goldberg thanks him dry-eyed for it and shakes his hand. Her fragile hand is trembling, Willibald thinks, but then it's hard to tell because his bony one is too—he shouldn't even have been travelling with Jews, let alone shaking Jewish hands. Then she picks up her correctly packed and labelled suitcase with her correctly packaged lunch, and walks slowly and lopsidedly, leaning away from it, down towards the station exit. There are people who look at her yellow star with sympathy and people who don't notice it or don't want to, and people who do and turn their heads away. Willibald watches nervously from behind an iron stanchion as she pauses undecidedly at the end of the platform, then turns to ask a tall SS officer of all people which way to go—but then presumably she reckons he certainly ought to know. She holds out her warrant. He takes and scrutinizes it. He points out the way and hands the warrant back. She appears to thank him and he appears to curtly nod his head. And then she's gone without a backward glance. For all the world just like a little old lady going on an autumn vacation.

"Perhaps it'll be all right," Willibald tells Gabi when he returns. "Perhaps it's only . . ." But again his words desert him, and like Frau Professor Goldberg they do not come back.

■

Nor do other people who disappear for other reasons. Most of my teachers, for instance, called up for labor in the factories or for the decisive battle, which is always the one after the one we've just lost—except that our boys never lose battles, they just make strategic withdrawals and regroup. The principal who replaced the principal has himself been replaced and sent off to the Eastern Front, although he's so shortsighted he could scarcely see the back of the class. He won't be shooting many Ivans, but the reverse may well be the case. His successor's a seventy-year-old spinster just like Frau Professor Goldberg except that she isn't a degenerate Jew. She's been dragged out of retirement and clearly wishes she hadn't. She never remembers to say "Heil Hitler!"

and forgets most of her pupils' names. And maternal Fraülein Meissner has gone as well, to do something with munitions, or possibly to get herself married and pregnant before she loses her present fiancé. (Fritzi Wimmer says she's got a bun in her oven already, but Fritzi Wimmer would—he's at that age.) Fraülein Meissner doesn't say goodbye and I think I'll never forgive her. Other teachers disappear from one day to the next, their places taken by refugees from Vienna who feel the Ivans are coming a mite too close and they'd be better off cozying up to the Amis. A retired opera singer called Frau Trifallner is teaching us arithmetic, and Tante Helga is teaching every class geography despite her suspect political background and total blindness.

I half-expect operatic Frau Trifallner to sing her lessons, but apparently arithmetic's not a musical subject and the only sign she was an opera singer is her enormous bosom, on which Fritzi says a piece of chalk could rest without rolling off, and a tireless voice that seems to shape each word with loving care before she launches it into the receptive air. It seems that opera singing's no preparation for arithmetic, however, because she often gets her sums wrong on the board and has to wipe them out and start again.

Tante Helga's voice isn't tireless, it often wheezes and squeaks. But she never makes mistakes. "Open your atlases," she commands, bulging over her chair like a chesty eiderdown as she rubs her forefinger and thumb together in anticipatory relish. "Open it at Great Britain. Now." She feels the edges of her own atlas with her fingertips, running them round and across the page in a sort of tactile triangulation. Her face is turned upwards in inward concentration, but she can hear the softest whisper at the back of the classroom and identify the whisperer. Her sightless eyes are almost sealed. How small they look, sunk, shrunken and petrified beneath their wrinkled lids. "How far north of London is Coventry?" she demands. Perhaps she should have said "was"—I know Erwin helped turn them both into rubble nearly four years ago. "How far east is Cardiff? How far south is Portsmouth?" Perhaps Cardiff and Portsmouth should have been "was" as well. I believe our boys have given them a pasting too. She knows all the answers, she could even draw a faultless map of the English Channel on the board. Erwin might still be alive if he'd taken her along as navigator. She never says "Heil Hitler!" either, anymore than Frau Trifallner does. In fact hardly any teacher does any more, and those that do don't give the sacred words that solemn ring Fraülein Meissner used to give them before the perfidious Gaul mowed down her first heroic Aryan fiancé. On the contrary, their voices sound a little tired and hollow. I sense that things are breaking down.

And so does Gabi. Every week our rations are cut a little more, she says. Especially hers, because her coupons are stamped with the shameful *J*. "The Jew should not be eating German food at all," the bantam Goebbels is reported recently to have declared. (He was looking a bit scrawny himself in the greyish paper of *The People's Observer,* which Willibald still occasionally smuggles home from his pastoral visits—or is it from his Aryan lady-friend?) "He"—The Jew, that is—"should count himself lucky to get even half a German's rations."

Yes, Gabi sees that things are really breaking down. But she wonders if they'll break down fast enough for us. I come across her one evening in the kitchen debating with Sara, or rather with herself in Sara's presence, whether the war will end before we do, and what she'll do if *they* come for her. I don't know what that does to Sara, but it makes my stomach churn a little till I think of something else to do.

And suddenly Christmas is upon us. The leaves have all fallen and gone like the disappearing people, the sun has disappeared too behind the mountains (but at least that will probably be coming back), the lake has frozen and snow has fallen a meter deep. The Ivans have nearly come too—they're almost at the Danube. And the Amis and the Tommies as well—they're nearly at the Rhine. At this rate, Fraülein von Adler says, rubbing her blue and chilblained hands together gleefully by the stove—at this rate final victory must be near. But whose victory does she mean? Theirs or ours? And I'm still puzzled as to which is which. Besides, "Will we live to see it?" Gabi asks anxiously in one of those quiet asides that I'm not meant to hear but nowadays listen to intently. Our rations have been cut again, and having an extra cube of meat now counts as hoarding. You could be put up against a wall and shot for that, Fritzi Wimmer tells me, especially if you've got a *J* on your coupons, which means you shouldn't be having any meat at all—as indeed Gabi isn't. No wonder she's doubtful whether she'll last out.

Even Fraülein von Adler, who can lay her hands on anything, says she hasn't had any tobacco for weeks, not to speak of coffee, and if she smokes her tea, what's she going to drink? But she still listens black and tells us what she hears. The black news doesn't please Willibald, while Gabi dares not believe it. "Our beautiful German cities destroyed by that barbarian Churchill!" Willibald exclaims, shaking his fists at the skies from which—or rather from their neighbors north and west—the Tommies' bombers rain destruction down. And in church he still faithfully recites the prayer for Fatherland and Führer—I've seen it in his hymn book—*Bless our German people in Your goodness and strength, and keep the love of our Fatherland deep in our hearts. Bless especially our Führer and Commander-in-chief in all the tasks he undertakes* . . . Does he pause to think what tasks the Führer's undertaking now? If he does, it doesn't stop him asking for God's blessing on them. But then Willibald's still such a patriot. He keeps his uniform lovingly pressed and brushed in the wardrobe as a bride might keep her bridal gown. And sometimes, I'm soon going to discover, he takes it out and puts it on, like a woman reliving the most wonderful day of her life.

We sit down hungry to our meals and get up from them hungry. But Willibald still murmurs grace and thanks God for the reduced rations He allows us, which seems pretty generous of him (Willibald, I mean). Gabi asks us what we'd like for Christmas, but the question's as perfunctory as the teacher's "Heil Hitler!" in school. I'd just like more to eat, but I know I won't get that. Sometimes I think we're starving, which only shows I don't know what starving is. Yet. Only Martin seems to get enough, but he's got Lisl Wimmer to thank for that. Her uncle's the butcher and the Wimmers don't go short—well, nothing like as short as we do anyway. She often meets Martin as he's coming home from the brickworks, and as there's no Frau Professor Goldberg to teach him physics now, he's got more time to pursue anatomy with her. Her father doesn't seem to mind. He really must be listening black as well and thinking it's time to put peace feelers out. And Lisl does that excellently. I've seen her at it in the lanes. She may not be as lithe as Eva, but she's every bit as willing. It's her mother who's the unbending ideologue. She's taken to snooping round at mealtimes now, to check if we're eating on the black market as she is, though how she thinks we'd pay for it, Gabi declares, is beyond all comprehension.

Whatever we might like for Christmas, what we get is refugees. Nature really does abhor a vacuum, at least it does in Heimstatt—for every person that disappears another seems to turn up. And many of them turn up in the rambling old Pfarrhaus, people who used to know Gabi and Willibald in the days before the Nazis and find it expedient to know them again now. Willibald gets a letter from one or two of them almost every week, asking if there's room in Heimstatt because their own place has been flattened by the Amis or the Tommies or is getting within range of the approaching Ivans' guns. And a week or two after the letters, or sometimes before them, the letter-writers come themselves, with packed and labelled suitcases just like Frau Professor Goldberg's. But for them this really is a holiday, a holiday from war. No bombs, no guns, no barbarian hordes. Not yet, anyway. The fact that ours is a half-Jewish household doesn't seem to faze them now, however much it may have in the past. Very generous of them. Onkel Karl and Frau Professor Gerda Hoffmann do not appear though, the only ones who might deserve a place. Onkel Karl doesn't because he's died without taking in that Maria's died before him, and Frau Professor Hoffmann doesn't because she's been evacuated to Bavaria with her school.

Yes, after so many years of emptiness the pages of Willibald's Visitors' Book could all be filled up by now, if he bothered to put it out and the visitors bothered to write in it. Which of course he doesn't and they wouldn't anyway, in case by some strange chance our boys really do turn the war around as the Führer keeps promising, and the Thousand Year Reich does somehow survive another year or two.

But I'm feeling crowded, even if the Visitors' Book's pages aren't. The Pfarrhaus may be large, but we're retreating like our boys in the east and west, consolidating our forces. First one room's given up to a refugee, and then another. Sara's had to move in with Ilse, and I've had to move in with Martin. It's like being back in Berlin again, except that Martin hasn't found a way of getting Lisl inside our room yet and locking the door with me outside. Then we give up the living and dining rooms, withdrawing into the kitchen for our meals. Willibald has to fight a politely desperate battle with Herr Professor Schumacher, his retired high school mathematics teacher from Berlin, to preserve his unimpeded right to his own study. Ortsgruppenleiter Franzi Wimmer, who's getting more and more affable the nearer the Ivans come, says between beery belches that he'll procure us some beds for all these refugees, and anyway they won't be here long, it's only a temporary measure until the front gets stabilized. Not a word about the laws concerning Aryans and Jews. He's even abandoned his old stand on the second doorstep now, and advances quite amiably if cautiously inside, which for him of course is an ideological retreat. And true to his word, ten beds do appear on the back of a truck on Christmas Eve, which we celebrate on our own in the kitchen with a two-foot-tall fir branch stuck in a bucket of sand. There's nothing special to eat, in fact there's nothing much to eat at all, and we give and get no presents.

Yes, things really are breaking down. "Perhaps next year," Gabi says wistfully, as if next year was a century away. Sara's given up her little black ribbon in memory of Rolf, the von Haltenstein would-be author. She took it off her lapel on the anniversary of his death. But she might as well have kept it on; it would have saved her trouble later.

The refugees have all brought their ration coupons with them (they'd rather leave their clothes behind than leave their coupons) and get what food they can in the village, guarding it jealously and casting suspicious glances at what the others manage to bring back, whether openly in their string bags or concealed in their rucksacks. All except Herr Professor Schumacher, who has a mouthful of gold-filled teeth and, having once been Willibald's teacher, now undertakes to teach Martin in return for Gabi's cooking his dinner.

He goes out to the marketplace each morning and returns without a glance at the others, handing his provisions directly to Gabi.

It's she who set up the deal. She may no longer expect to get through the war herself, but she does hope her children will, and she isn't giving up on their education. That at least is where she means to beat the Nazis, whatever victories they score elsewhere. And Herr Professor Schumacher is persuaded to help her by the offer of coffee and baked potatoes served in the dining room while he instructs Martin in the subtleties of calculus. I don't know how things are going on the calculus front, but they certainly aren't running smoothly in the kitchen. Herr Professor Schumacher hands over a few half-frozen potatoes and some coffee beans each day, with the request to use them for his dinner. Being a mathematician, he counts them out, the same number each time, and requests Gabi to bake the potatoes for his dinner and make two cups of coffee with the beans. I get the job of holding the coffee mill between my knees and grinding the beans with the crank. It's like grinding little pebbles. The dust that comes out just about fills a medium-sized teaspoon. Herr Professor Schumacher complains that the anemic liquid he's later served is too thin, and hints that it doesn't represent full value for his beans (he always counts the number of potatoes on his plate as well, and at least is satisfied on that point). There's even talk of discontinuing Martin's lessons. But Gabi takes to secretly grinding his baked-potato skins with the coffee powder, and Herr Professor Schumacher is mollified.

Martin isn't the only one to get some education out of the refugees. There's another musician from Vienna, Frau Schneider, a singing-teacher friend of our Nazi friend Doktor Saur-that-was, who professes to know nothing of Frau Trifallner, our opera-singing teacher at school. She practices her tonic sol-fa to Herr Professor Schumacher's intense irritation every evening in the living room. Down Frau Schneider sits at the untuned piano and out pour her penetrating scales, regardless of who else is there or what they're trying to do. If Herr Professor Schumacher objects, she merely tosses her head, mutters something not quite under her breath about Philistine German mathematicians, and resumes her thrilling, ringing notes. Gabi has persuaded her to continue the violin lessons for Sara and me which lapsed after our return from Berlin and the reluctant organist's conscription. (He'll be returned wounded from the Eastern Front, although five frostbitten toes won't come with him. But his fingers will all be there, saved by the mitts he used to wear when teaching us in the church vestry.) Frau Schneider isn't much of a violinist, and she doesn't find either of us apt pupils, but in return for her vesperal possession of the piano and her tonic sol-fa, she perseveres.

And then suddenly in the New Year the refugees are all going, moving further west as though by magnetic polar repulsion as the Ivans do the same a hundred miles to the east. Apparently we aren't so safe here after all, the war might roll over us, and there are even rumors that an SS regiment is coming to set up its headquarters in Heimstatt. That would certainly bring the bloodthirsty Bolshies down on us—there's nothing they like more than killing our Teutonic racial knights. Unless, according to separate warnings from both Herr Professor Schumacher and Frau Schneider, it's ravaging our women. I think ravaging means knocking them about and wonder why it's only women the Bolshies knock about until Fritzi Wimmer enlightens me.

Herr Professor Schumacher and Frau Schneider are the last of our refugees to leave. They haven't been on speaking terms because of their musical differences, but they are of one voice when it comes to the dangers to Ilse and Sara from the Russian barbarians our boys are so fanatically resisting for the sake of world civilization in general and Europe in particular. They think of nothing but plunder and rapine, Herr Professor Schumacher mutters through the splendors of his gilded dentition (meaning the Russian barbarians, not our magnificent boys), and he glances so significantly at Sara and Ilse that they have to lower their eyes. Frau Schneider's voice is deeply thrilling as she whispers tales she's heard on every side of streets littered with the bodies of ravaged girls, and urges Gabi to take her own daughters to the safety of the heartland of the Reich, where she herself is going and where she's sure she'll always be protected. And then they both are separately gone, with their rucksacks, their cases and their ration coupons. Why don't we go as well, I begin to wonder. It doesn't sound as though we'll get along with the Ivans. Perhaps Willibald wonders too, but not Gabi. What would a Jew be doing heading into the heartland of the Reich? Or a half-Jew, for that matter? Others may find someone to protect them there, but not a Jewish woman, even a privileged one, or her half-Jew brood.

Nor does she give much credit to all those scary tales. She thinks her girls, not to mention herself, whom Herr Professor Schumacher and Frau Schneider seem to have overlooked in all their warnings, haven't done so well by the Germans that they can't afford to take their chances with the Russkies. But Willibald seems more receptive. Perhaps he's been softened up already by the stories his Aryan lady-friend's been feeding him—as a leader of the League of German Girls, she's bound to be an authority. Is that the reason I come across Willibald dressed up in his corporal's uniform a few nights later, when Gabi's already gone to bed and I'm on my way to pee in the freezing outside toilet? Does he fancy himself heroically defending his hearth and home to the death, alone against the raging Cossacks, or does he mean to leave us in the lurch instead and join our boys in the decisive battle for the German heartland, which evidently isn't going to take place here in Heimstatt? Or is it just nostalgia for his glory days in Poland? Whatever it is, there he stands fully uniformed in front of the mirror in his study, sucking in his belly and pushing out his chest. But push and pull how he will, neither of those organs seems quite the right shape for a military hero.

"Are you going to join the army again?" I ask as he turns and sees me sleepily regarding him.

He seems caught between anger and embarrassment, demands why I'm spying on him like that and warns me not to tell Mutti as it would only upset her. My question hasn't been answered, but I sense it would be unwise to put it again, so I go and pee, and the thought of Willibald in his uniform distracts me from the fears that still occasionally beset me in that cold dark outhouse with its bottomless pit. On my return I see the study door is firmly closed.

The next day all the hospital beds are removed and sent to a military hospital in Bad Neusee, where they'll bear the weight and blood of our wounded heroes now, and we're entirely on our own again. Half the schoolteachers have gone with the refugees and school is closed. "For the duration of the emergency," Orts-gruppenleiter Franzi Wimmer announces, looking as though he suspects the emergency might last as long as he will.

Martin is still working at the brick factory, which is still turn-ing out fireproof bricks, Gabi's wearily trying to make frayed ends meet and Willibald, his uniform neglected if not forgotten, spends hours on what he calls his pastoral visits. But the rest of us have nothing to do. Which is just as well because we have al-most nothing to eat either. Ilse moves slowly about the house like the wraith of a drag-footed nun, Sara spends long hours staring into space with her notebook open in front of her, and I myself decline into listlessness and apathy.

Things really must be breaking down indeed—Frau Wim-mer's given up spying on us now, and, because there are hardly any trains, Fräulein von Adler's given up visiting from Graunau. Doktor Saur-that-was has written a letter from Vienna (it took two weeks to arrive), saying she thinks everything will be all right in the spring, but what she means by everything nobody knows—is she talking about the war, Gabi's racial categoriza-tion, or her own unhappy marriage? The snow keeps falling dense and wet, as though it too is tired of everything, and just wants to flop down and sleep. Fräulein Hofer and Resi still call on us every Saturday, but Gabi has to tell them apologetically she can no longer give them their milk-coffee as we've neither milk nor coffee. Not even powdered milk or ersatz coffee. I watch them uncomplainingly eat their stale unbuttered bread, which Fritzi Wimmer tells me is mixed with sawdust now, and drink a glass of warm water. Fraülein Hofer looks pale and sometimes winces, but when Gabi asks what the matter is, she merely shakes her head. Everyone's just waiting for the war to be over. Or nearly everyone. The Gestapo in Linz are—

15

More interested in Gabi

Whose teeth are killing her. So she decides that despite the expense she just has to go to the dentist in Plinden, who long ago has fathomed she's Jewish but treats her anyway after his receptionist has gone home. Of course there's an extra fee—danger money, he calls it, and he's right. He could go to prison for that, and Gabi to Auschwitz, which it turns out is just where the Gestapo mean to send her anyway.

So she's out of the Pfarrhaus and out of the village when Constable Bolzner, the policeman who had to arrest Jägerlein for abducting her own Annchen, comes sheepishly along in the snow to arrest Gabi now for being a Jew. Yes, for some zealots the only thing that matters now is the total extinction of the European Jew. Never mind if despite all their fanatical courage our boys aren't winning the war, never mind if the walls are crumbling and the Ivans are battering at one gate and the Amis and the Tommies at the other—that's ultimately not the point. Purify the race, eliminate the vicious Jew, and write our glorious page in history! Victory may not be ours, but the lasting honor will! And so the methodical bureaucrats who make up the lists have at last selected Gabi to follow Frau Professor Goldberg to oblivion. It's time to complete the sacred task and get rid of the privileged Jews, now that all the others have been dealt with.

Willibald's at home. He never goes to Plinden when Gabi does. To be so near and yet so far from his plump lady-friend would be too painful. Besides, what if they all met in the street? How could he hide his confusion? So Willibald it is who comes from the study where *Samson and Delilah* have just got their four feet on the blocks, to receive Constable Bolzner after I've opened the door and nervously backed off as he considerately shakes the snow off his coat and stamps his boots on the mat. I don't like policemen, even Constable Bolzner, who's never done me any harm except by being the reluctant accessory to Jägerlein's and Annchen's disappearance. Willibald doesn't like policemen now either, but he performs a stern "Heil Hitler!" and simultaneously an ingratiating smile, of which salutations each tends to neutralize the other.

Constable Bolzner returns the first salute, if somewhat perfunctorily, but the second not at all. In fact he looks quite glum, which, as things develop, he has every reason to. Glancing over Willibald's shoulder, he awkwardly inquires if the Frau Pfarrer is at home. "I'm afraid," he announces on hearing that she isn't, "I'm afraid I have a warrant for her arrest. It's not a police matter," he continues hastily, disclaiming both responsibility and inclination. "She's not being charged with any crime, I mean. Except that, well, it's only that, er, well, it's the Gestapo in Linz."

I feel something like a cold wind rushing through my insides, which have plenty of room for it because they're so empty. And Willibald must feel the same, because he totters back a pace. *Samson and Delilah* are certainly going to be blown off course by this today. Constable Bolzner considerately takes the Herr Pfarrer's arm and guides him to a chair. "Of course they may only want to question her," he says in that same unconvinced and therefore unconvincing tone that Willibald used to Frau Professor Goldberg.

And then to duty. "Er, when will the Frau Pfarrer be back?"

Willibald must know the warrant in Constable Bolzner's hand is Gabi's death sentence, but all the same he doesn't want to divulge her crime of going to an Aryan dentist in Plinden—as if that somehow might make her serve two death sentences consecutively, instead of only one. Or else he's afraid it would put him on the spot as well. Not to speak of the dentist. "Not till late," is all he can say. And it's four o'clock already, and the light is almost gone.

Constable Bolzner looks as though he's going to settle and wait for Gabi's return. He takes off his cap and examines the other chairs in the living room with the air of someone who doesn't quite know whether to ask permission or just plonk himself officiously down.

"Very late," Willibald says. Then, recalling there's a curfew for Jews and they must be in by eight o'clock, "About half-past seven, I mean."

Constable Bolzner glances at his watch. Three and a half hours to wait, and he likes to have his supper early. You can see he's thinking perhaps he'll come back for her after he's had his grub. He stands irresolutely for a few moments, regarding the faded print of a dramatic Caspar David Friedrich painting over the mantelpiece and evidently wondering how to form a tactful compliment upon it without seeming insensitive to the other drama now proceeding just outside its frame.

"Nice," he says at last. "Very nice. Pretty."

But art appreciation is the last thing on Willibald's mind just now, and his response is a practical inquiry. "Will you be taking her to Linz tonight?" he asks in a quavering voice.

Constable Bolzner turns from the painting and shakes his head. "No train, is there?" he reminds Willibald almost reproachfully, as if Willibald's question revealed a somewhat unfeeling desire to get the whole thing over and done with at once. "She'll have to be, er, detained overnight until the six thirty-five tomorrow." He unfolds the warrant and frowns down at it again, pushing out his underlip as he gives it the thorough hermeneutic attention that German bureaucratic documents generally demand. "She's got to be there in Linz by two o'clock," he concludes from this examination.

Willibald is thinking of Frau Professor Goldberg getting down at Linz station, politely asking that tall SS officer the way to the gates of hell. "Couldn't she go by herself?" he asks tentatively. "Without anyone knowing? Frau Professor Goldberg did."

"'Fraid not," Constable Bolzner replies regretfully. "Our instructions are to accompany her to Gestapo headquarters."

"They didn't say that about Frau Professor Goldberg," Willibald protests feebly.

"Goldberg?" Constable Bolzner answers. "When would that have been? Ah, well, they've tightened the rules up since then. Probably some Yids—some *people*," he delicately amends his phrasing—"didn't show up, that'll be the reason." He takes a step towards the door. "Not that the Frau Pfarrer wouldn't show up, of course," he adds hastily, anxious not to impute any blemish to her law-abiding character. "But, you know how it is, Herr Pfarrer, rules are rules, aren't they? Rules are rules." That's a tautology he's going to hear quite often in the future, and one that Willibald in principle approves of. But on this occasion Willibald doesn't endorse it despite being given the chance to do so, and after a moment's disappointed and embarrassed silence Constable Bolzner takes another step towards the door. "Anyway, think I'll come back for her later on. Half-past seven, did you say? She'll need to take a small suitcase, tell her. Spare clothes and soap and that. And a packed lunch." Now he's got it off his chest, he seems to be growing less sheepish. Officialdom has spread its soothing balm all over his discomfort. *Come on,* you can almost hear him telling himself. *It's just another job, after all.*

And that's where Willibald shows what he's made of. "Constable Bolzner," he asks in a wheedling yet sepulchral tone from the chair where the policeman has deposited him, "Constable Bolzner, couldn't you make an exception and let her meet you at the train tomorrow morning? Or at the ferry pier, at least?"

Constable Bolzner pauses, hesitating. "The ferry pier?" he repeats dubiously. The train is clearly out of the question.

"Think how I'll feel if she's put in prison tonight and paraded through the village under arrest tomorrow like a common criminal! The wife of the Lutheran pastor! How will I be able to face my congregation in church?"

Is that what really worries Willibald? I gape at him. But Constable Bolzner sees his point. He's a Catholic and he wouldn't like to see the Catholic priest's wife paraded under arrest through the village either. Not that Father Schuster has a wife, of course, although he does have a housekeeper who has a daughter who looks just like Father Schuster.

"And then you needn't come back for her tonight," Willibald cunningly adds. "You must have so many things to do, what with all your duties and everything . . ."

"You wouldn't believe how many," Constable Bolzner says with feeling and a nod. "And some of them aren't pleasant, either." He raises the warrant in his hand to indicate that Gabi's little business is one of them.

"And she could pack her things in peace and say goodbye to her children," Willibald continues insidiously with a sob in his voice that's both theatrical and genuine. You can tell he's an effective preacher all right.

That decides Constable Bolzner. He replaces the warrant in his breast pocket, and the cap on his head. "Got kids myself," he mutters. "She can meet me at the pier at six tomorrow. Tell her not to be late, though, all right? Otherwise I'll have to come and get her." And he leaves with the relieved and complacent air of a man who, while doing himself a favor, hasn't made a bad thing worse, but just a little better.

I don't know what Willibald does next. I suppose he goes upstairs and tells Ilse and Sara (Martin isn't back yet from his experiments in the brickworks and maybe subsequently in Lisl Wimmer). Myself, I go and sit beside the kitchen stove, hugging my knees and staring blankly at it and simultaneously at something inside me that's as dark and empty as a cave. And though, there being no more coal, the stove is burning all the wood we can find, I feel as cold and numb there as I would outside in the snow. After I don't know how long Sara comes and sits beside me, looks at me, then goes and doesn't sit beside me. Ilse passes slowly to and fro and I know she's getting the supper ready, although I can't imagine who she thinks will eat it. Martin returns and sounds sulky at first—has he quarrelled with Lisl or is it just post-coital tristesse? Then he's as silent as Ilse and Sara. Willibald with moist and red-rimmed eyes has got the yellow suitcase out for Gabi and laid it on the kitchen table with its lid gaping open like a little corpseless coffin. Ilse removes the case with a frown and places it on a chair, as if to say "Untidiness won't help."

None of this is real, I keep thinking. *It can't really be happening.* But the trouble is, I keep remembering that humped car in Berlin and the two men impatiently ringing the bell and then that stooping man with his Homburg hat walking out onto the pavement between them, meekly getting into the car. And I know only too well how real this is, I know it really is happening. I wish that Gabi would come back, and at the same time wish she wouldn't. I want to see her, but I don't want to see her go away. The customary access of religion takes place and I start praying to God to make it not happen, or at least to make it all have happened already so that I don't have to go through it, because I don't think I can.

◼

And then Gabi does return, with a swollen jaw. One glance at us and she doesn't need to ask, but of course she does ask anyway. And then she sits down on the nearest chair and nurses her jaw in her hand, for all the world as if that's the only thing that's bothering her. "Tomorrow morning?" is all she says. And then she repeats it slowly, with a thoughtful, not an interrogative, inflection.

"Tomorrow morning, then." As if this was a summons she has long expected, and now at last it's come. Willibald says in his hopeless voice, "Perhaps they only want to ask you some questions? Perhaps it won't be so bad, after all?"

"Like Frau Professor Goldberg, you mean?" Gabi asks in a weary tone that shrivels Willibald into silence.

After several minutes of nursing her jaw and gazing into her own dark cave, Gabi shakes her head and turns to Sara, her confidante. "Take your brother to the nuns' house," she says quite calmly. "Father will ask them if you can both stay there tonight."

The nuns' house? She means the retired Protestant nuns—*Diakonissen*—who've been living in a hamlet at the end of the lake ever since they were bombed out of their home in Silesia. What are we going to do there? And what's she going to do while we're there? Actually, I think I know the answer to the second question, but that's knowledge I can neither name nor face.

"Just until tomorrow," Gabi says, looking at me as though she's read my mind.

"Are you going to go to Linz?" I ask, knowing that if she does she won't come back. And probably if she doesn't. But I try not to think of that.

She shakes her head again. "Don't worry, it'll be all right."

"You're not going to Linz?" I insist. I have to get this straight. Linz, I somehow know, is worse than anything else.

"No, don't worry, I'm not going to go to Linz. Now you'd better get your things ready."

I do as I'm told. The fact is, I'm glad to be out of it. Whatever's going to happen, I'm not going to have to live through it, it will happen out of sight. I'm grateful to God for answering my prayer. I even promise Him silently I'll talk to Him at other times too, not just when things are bad.

"I don't want to go there," Sara suddenly and even truculently declares. "I want to stay." She's got more guts than I have, but then she's older too. I just want to play at ostriches and keep my head in the sand until tomorrow morning, when everything that has to happen will have happened already. But Sara wants to face the music now, and hear it to the end.

"No, Sara," Gabi says, glancing first at me, then at her. And something in her look persuades Sara to acquiesce. It's as if they've been planning this all along, rehearsing every detail, and Gabi has just reminded her what part she has to play.

I don't know how or when, but at some time Willibald goes out to the phone box by the post office wrapped up in coat, hat and scarf, to phone the nuns' house and arrange for us to stay. And sometime later Sara and I are walking silently towards the nuns' house similarly dressed, with our night things in a rucksack, which Sara shoulders although she is a girl. Gabi doesn't even make much of kissing us goodbye, as though to prove it isn't really a proper parting. Just a peck on the cheek, like an ordinary goodnight. Or perhaps there's an extra pat on the shoulder as well, a sort of gentle rub. I don't know, I'm too mixed up to tell. It's a clear moonlit sky above us, glittering with stars, although down here on earth the snow is turning slushy, and I try to persuade myself that nothing bad can happen on a peaceful night like this, that Gabi will come for us in the morning and everything will somehow be all right.

Of course I don't succeed.

■

The nuns' house smells. It smells of many things, of cleanliness and carbolic, of dried-out virginity like dead leaves, of soured dreams and long frustration, of narrow penny-pinching sanctity. Except in the toilet, which smells of something rotten overlaid with the scent of dried lavender, and in the bare and gloomy dining hall, which smells of boiled cabbage and ham. (They can still get both.) Not that I recognize all these smells till long afterwards. But they hang around my memory, waiting to be known. And every now and then for years to come, whenever I catch a whiff of one of them, the rest of the sickening bouquet is wafted back.

The round-shouldered nun with grey-whiskery lips who receives us doesn't seem to like us very much. *I'm only doing this for the Herr Pfarrer's sake,* she seems to be saying when she opens the door, although what she actually says is "Wipe your shoes," in a high nasal bloodless voice. Dressed in something between a nurse's uniform and a Catholic nun's habit, she leads us silently down a dimly lit corridor, and I listen to the shuffle of her steps and the sniff of her nose. Every now and then that cold wind which Constable Bolzner brought with him howls through my insides and I think with a wrench of Gabi packing or not packing her yellow case. And I feel just as sick and numb whether she's packing it or not, and ask God again to get it over with or make me fall asleep at least, so that I don't have to think about it anymore, because otherwise I'm probably going to scream. What Sara thinks I do not know. Sara is as silent in her own way as Ilse is in hers. But Sara's silence is a brooding one, while Ilse's is just passive and resigned. I listen to her steps beside my own and the shuffling nun's. I'm not going to ask Sara anything when we're alone again. I know she knows something I don't know, but I don't want to find out what. All I want is to be unconscious.

We come to a bare room with two beds in it and a wooden cross upon the whitewashed wall. The aged nun leaves us, sniffing a dewdrop up her broken-veined and beaky nose. Sara places the rucksack on one of the beds and starts unpacking it. I lie down on the other bed fully clothed and turn towards the wall. The wall is cold, the room is cold. Sara pulls some blankets over me. I listen to her still unpacking the rucksack. I'm getting ready to be sleepy. In a few moments if I'm lucky, I *will* be sleepy, and then soon after that I'll be asleep. So long as I don't think about Gabi and her yellow suitcase.

Somewhere behind me sounds the swish of a long dress and the step of quick and lively feet. "I've brought some food for you," a young woman's voice says cheerfully, but not too cheerfully. "Oh, is your brother asleep?" I make sure my eyes are closed as someone leans over me, and gently pulls the blankets higher round my shoulders. "I'm Sister Maria Luther," the cheerful voice murmurs now to Sara. "You just let him sleep, and try to eat something yourself. I'll be back in a minute."

There's a smell of steaming cabbage in the room, but I don't hear any sound of knife or fork, and judge that Sara isn't eating.

I know the nun comes back, because I hear her whispering to Sara. Later I hear Sara's bed creaking as she climbs onto it. Then I really am asleep until I wake up much later knowing that I have to pee. Sara is sitting on her bed, the blanket round her shoulders, staring at the window opposite, which would give a view of the lake if it wasn't covered by a blackout blind.

"I've got to pee," I say.

She points me silently down the corridor to where a yellowish gleam slants across the floor. The blackout blind there, I notice, is leaking light out to the enemy, whoever that might be, and automatically I conscientiously press the loose edge back against the window frame. I wouldn't have made it to an outside toilet like ours, I'd have simply gone outside the door. But this is a real flushing toilet with tiles and everything, and I'd enjoy myself despite the smell of rot and dried-up lavender, if it was any other night but this. All the same, it must have made me a shade optimistic, because when I come back I'm telling myself everything will be all right tomorrow, we'll find out it has all been a mistake and the Gestapo didn't want Gabi after all, they wanted someone else of the same name who wasn't privileged like her. Yes, she's privileged, I keep telling myself, she's privileged—that makes a difference. In any case, it's still pitch dark and that means tomorrow won't be here for hours and hours yet and I can go on hiding in the soft cocoon of night.

Sara watches me climb still fully clothed back into bed.

"She's gone," she says flatly.

Sister Maria Luther, I think she means. "What time is it?" I ask.

Sara peers at the alarm clock she's brought with us from the Pfarrhaus, and the sight of it makes me want to cry. "Ten past twelve. Mutti's gone."

That cold wind immediately blows a full gale inside me, and I resent Sara for bringing it on. "How can she be?" I mutter peevishly. "The train doesn't go till six thirty-five."

"She's gone," Sara repeats with finality. "I heard her." And then at last she lies down, as if that's what she'd been waiting for all those long cold hours.

I won't listen to that. It makes me shiver. I refuse to let it in. I cover my head with the pillow. But the damage has been done. I don't go back to sleep, I listen to my pulse thudding in my ears for the rest of the endless night, while images of trains leaving stations and men with Homburg hats getting meekly into humped black cars whirl round and round on the restless carousel inside my brain. I ply God with lots more messages about making all this not happen or putting time forward until it's all already in the past, or at least sending me to merciful sleep until it's passed, but He doesn't seem to be listening now. Perhaps He's gone to sleep Himself. Or perhaps He's angry with me. Anyway, I don't get an answer.

Before it's light, Sara is up and packing our things. I pretend to be asleep, so that I won't have to hear her say "She's gone" again, although everything about her slow and heavy movements delivers the same message. She's started mourning already. In fact I sense she started on the way here, before we'd even arrived.

"You'd better wash yourself," she says.

No sooner had I come back from the bathroom than Sister Maria Luther enters the room again—I know it's her because of the quick rustle of her skirt and the cheerful sound of her voice. "Breakfast!" she announces as though that's all we've been waiting for. She's much younger than the nun who let us in last night, and she's younger than any of the other nuns too. That's because she hasn't retired yet, I suppose, as she leads us to the dining hall. And I indistinctly infer from that a conclusion which I've never doubted since, that retiring is a kind of chronic ailment.

Nothing in the dining hall at least leads me to change my mind. Once someone has muttered grace in an ancient reedy voice, the nuns sit silently nibbling and mumbling their food, working their jaws without pleasure and shooting suspicious little glances this way and that to see who's got more than her share of food or not enough of piety. But Sister Maria Luther hasn't been soured yet—perhaps she never will be—and she sets us down at the end of one long table where a couple of withered nuns move silently away a bit as though we're lepers, which in a sense of course, being Gabi's kids, we are. I discover that I can eat after all, and the unstale bread and real milk-coffee go down quite fast. Where do they get them from, I wonder. Why can't we at home? Then I recall with a thump—although I've never really forgotten it—that there's something else we may not have at home just now. Namely, a mother.

Sara has lost her appetite, and despite Sister Maria Luther's urging doesn't touch a thing. She nudges her bread across to me, and after a brief struggle with my better self, which I know it's going to lose, I eat it. Then there's no reason not to drink her coffee too, of course, so down that goes as well. It doesn't make me feel much better. In fact it makes me feel quite sick. But I drink it all the same. And all the time I'm feeding my face, my mind is contemplating images of Gabi packing her yellow case, of Gabi lying dead in bed, of Gabi walking through the village with Willibald, or without him, going to her destiny with the ferry and Constable Bolzner.

It's half-past seven by the clock on the wall when the nuns all rise and leave like a flock of wretched crows. The train will have gone an hour ago already, I think. Was Gabi on it or not? Sister Maria Luther leads us back to our room. "I know," she says brightly. "We'll go for a walk in the garden. It's not too cold. I'll just get my things on and then we can go." But while we sit silent on our beds, numbly waiting for her to reappear, and the chill wind still finds room to blow through my insides despite my double breakfast, it's Willibald who opens the door.

His face looks about ten years older than it looked yesterday and his eyes are so full of liquid meaning that my own eyes start to prick at the mere sight of them. He looks at each of us in turn, opens his mouth and closes it again, taking out his handkerchief to mop his leaking orbs instead.

"She's gone," Sara declares in that same flat tone she used in the middle of the night. It reminds me of the tolling of the church bell when someone dies.

Willibald nods. "Your mother fell, went, threw . . ." He

stammers, gulps, continues, "She, er, she fell into the lake."

He goes on mopping his eyes, but mine are completely dry now, not even pricking. There's just a heavy hammer covered with cloth that's beating inside my chest with muffled thuds, reverberating right through my body. It takes me some time to realize it's my heart. Does he mean she fell or went or threw herself?

"When?" Sara asks.

"During the night." His voice is sobbing now and his whole face covered with the handkerchief, which I notice has not been ironed very well. That one couldn't have come from Pels. "She couldn't face . . ."

"I knew," Sara says. "Ten past twelve."

Willibald blows his nose, wipes his eyes, stands up.

I understand that means we're going back to the Pfarrhaus now, where I will see Gabi's body laid out in her wet clothes on the bed. For some reason that comforts me.

"We'll go back in the boat," Willibald murmurs, which explains something that's been quietly bothering me ever since he came in—the wet cuffs of his overcoat sleeves. So he's rowed there along the icy lake and he's going to row us back, and we'll sit watching his spindly arms dragging on the dripping oars. Does that mean he's been searching for Gabi's body? That she's not upstairs in bed after all, but still drifting somewhere among the lumbering chunks of ice? I can't believe that. She *must* have been pulled out! She *must* be lying in bed waiting for us to say goodbye! No, I decide, the reason Willibald rowed here instead of walking through the village is that he couldn't face the villagers in his grief. Yet something whispers to me that that can't be quite right either—Willibald loves an audience for all his emotions, whether they're acted or real. Or, as so often, both. It must be he's ashamed, then. Ashamed of the humiliation his Jewish wife has brought upon him.

Sister Maria Luther reappears. She hasn't put her coat on, but she helps me put on mine, although I'd rather do it myself. Still, there's something comforting about the way she smoothes it over my shoulders that reminds me of how Gabi rubbed and patted them yesterday as she said goodbye. She goes silently with us to the boat and embraces us both. She's no longer cheerful, but calm and consoling, and as she watches us leave, the oars splashing and thumping against the wallowing ice, she looks in her long black dress like the figure of a gentle kind of Death. As we gradually draw away and I keep my eyes on her for fear I might otherwise see Gabi's body sliding about under the ice, I imagine Sister Maria Luther embracing Gabi in the same way, putting her arm round her shoulder and leading her quietly away. But she hasn't led her away, and nor has the real Death. Nor will Gabi be floating like a dead fish in the freezing water. She'll be lying on the bed at home as if she's just fallen asleep and I'll be able to see her and say goodbye, now that it's all over. I feel a kind of wounded gratitude to God after all for making the best of a bad business, although there's also a nagging suspicion that He could just as easily have made it a much better business instead, so why didn't He?

■

But I'd forgotten the lake does not give up its dead. As soon as we arrive I go upstairs, grief mastering fear, to the bedroom where I expect to find Gabi reclining in a peaceful state like sleep. But she isn't there. The bed is bare and freshly made, as if no one's ever slept in it, and suddenly I know I'll never say goodbye to her. *She isn't there,* I keep thinking as I go slowly down again from the empty, empty room. *She isn't there.*

Constable Bolzner is there though, and he's looking almost as unhappy as Willibald. So are Martin and Ilse there, pale and silent. And a note on the table that Constable Bolzner now takes up and reads, probably for the tenth time.

It's a hurried but pithy one-sentence note. *I have decided to kill myself rather than be killed in a concentration camp. Gabriella Brinkmann*. She missed out the obligatory *Sara* in her signature. She could have been in trouble for that.

"What do you know about this?" Constable Bolzner asks Sara and me, in a tone that's heavy with both condolence and suspicion.

Sara shrugs. "She told me she was going to drown herself if they came for her," she says in that same unnervingly inexpressive tone she's been using since last night.

Constable Bolzner sighs. "When was that, then?"

Sara shrugs again. Her eyes are quite dry and she seems so composed that I think for a moment she's unaffected by Gabi's death. But of course I'm wrong. Still waters do run deep. "Many times," she tells Constable Bolzner simply. "She said if they came for her she'd just walk into the lake." So it's walking, I tell myself, not falling or throwing. As though that made any difference.

Constable Bolzner seems to be considering whether Sara's statement if true could amount to aiding and abetting a suicide. But he's more interested in saving his own skin now than in getting someone else's, so he lets that drop. Besides, he's sorry for us too. "And what about you?" he demands of me, who's now imagining Gabi walking out over the cracking ice, which I see suddenly opening and tilting, tipping her smoothly in and closing like a coffin lid over her head. "Where's your mother really gone? Did she tell you what she was going to do?" That he appears to doubt that Gabi's really dead upsets me. As though she'd deceive me like that, letting me believe she was dead when she wasn't! I shake my head and at last begin to cry. *She isn't there* is still all that I can think of. *She isn't there.*

Nothing touches Constable Bolzner's heart more than a child's tears. He turns away awkwardly and pretends to scrutinize Gabi's note once more. But it's having a heart that's got him in this shit and soon he's probably considering how deep in he is—and realizing it's pretty deep indeed. He's followed Gabi's footsteps down to the lake, he's seen her coat lying on the shore, he's inspected the melting ice floes tilting and heaving against each other like clumsy seals gambolling in the slowly changing currents. Willibald is sobbing, and I'm sniffing. Martin and Ilse are pale as ghosts, and Sara's a statue of inward grief. To cap it all, he's got that suicide note in his hands. It looks as if the Frau Pfarrer's gone and killed herself all right, and it's all his fault. He should have put her in the lock-up last night. He can kiss his chances of promotion goodbye now. Rules are rules and duty's duty, they're going to tell him. A view, he's probably uncomfortably recalling, he put to Willibald last night. A view which Willibald, considering his stern views on the Officers' Plot against the Führer, ought himself to approve.

But Willibald's got other things to think about just now. So do Martin and Ilse. While I'm standing on the balcony of the Pfarrhaus turning blue with cold and forlornly gazing out over the ice-grey lake after all for some sign of my mother's body, while Sara's sitting dark-eyed in the kitchen with her hands clasped in her lap, while Constable Bolzner's going unhappily off to make his report—while all this is going on, the other three are wondering silently, each with their own style and degree of fear, where Gabi is by now, whether she's dead or alive, and whether they can carry their deception through.

Yes, deception. Because Gabi isn't really dead at all. She's only playing dead, except that what she's doing's—

16

Definitely not a game

While Sara and I are visualizing her being dragged by her waterlogged lungs deeper and deeper into the black tomb of the lake, she's actually chugging along aboveground on a local train towards Graunau and Fraülein von Adler, and, if not hale, and certainly not hearty, at least so far she's whole. She's become a U-boat, though not the kind that goes to sea. She's disappeared from view, that is, and surfaced as another person, her long-dead older sister Frieda.

Nothing of that was in her mind when she sent Sara and me off to the nuns' house. She meant to kill herself as she'd often told Sara she would. But she wanted Sara to take me out of the way. I was too young, she thought, to witness her mortal preparations. And Sara—well, Sara had known about this for months, whereas the others had to be prepared from scratch. Besides, who else could take me to the nuns' house and stay with me? Not Ilse, despite her affinity to nuns of any order, Catholic or Protestant, because she couldn't go trudging through the snow with her just-healed TB and her present unknown illness and halting gait. And not Martin either, because—well, Martin just didn't do that kind of thing. No, the responsibility fell on Sara as it so often did. She was Gabi's confidante and assistant, and that would be her final task. No wonder Sara's later years are spent forlornly searching for the childhood that she never had.

But Willibald and Martin each had different plans for Gabi. Willibald's was that she should go to Linz as tamely as Frau Professor Goldberg. "After all, they can't do anything bad to you, because you're privileged, you're married to an Aryan."

Whether or not Willibald really believed that, Gabi certainly didn't. Nor did Martin. That would-be Hitler Youth member, would-be Panzer commander and would-be Luftwaffe ace could read the Nazi mind better than his father. Or perhaps he merely had less of a motive for self-deception. Anyway, he shot his father's feeble suggestion down like the latest Messerschmitt engaging an antique Russian biplane. "You can't go," he told Gabi. "Privileged or not. You'd never come back."

"I'm not going," Gabi assured him. She was still nursing her jaw, and at the same time thinking, *So it was all a waste of money, then, going to the dentist.* "I decided months ago."

"You must run away," Martin said. Hide somewhere."

"And I'm not running away either." She was speaking as matter-of-factly as Sara would later, but deep below all that calm the waters churned and seethed.

Willibald understood perfectly what she meant, but offered no objection. Suicide was bad, but running away might be worse. First of all she'd almost certainly get caught. And secondly he'd be interrogated by the Gestapo. And what about the children? And his Aryan lady-friend in Plinden? Every one of them might be interrogated! And the Gestapo wouldn't be as considerate as Constable Bolzner, you could be sure of that. Of course the prospect of Gabi killing herself terrified him. But it didn't terrify him half as much as the Gestapo did. He'd prefer her to simply take her chance, go to Linz and get quietly processed by the system, decently and out of sight, since that was what the Authorities required. And after all she was "privileged." But at least if she did kill herself as her sister had done, there'd be no trouble from the Gestapo, no trouble for him, the children or anyone. (And he might eventually be free for his plump Aryan lady-friend—did he also think of that?)

"Of course you must run away!" Martin insisted. "Go somewhere where nobody knows you!" His strategic thinking was bold, but had it outrun his sense of the practical?

"And what if she's caught?" Willibald almost shrieked. "What will happen to *us*?" The question was rhetorical. He knew what would happen: Concentration Camp. And he was right. Martin's scheme was rash, and certainly the safest course was Gabi's or his own. If she went to Linz or killed herself, the rest might survive. If she tried to escape, she'd probably be caught and then they'd all go down together. From the point of view of accountancy and cost-benefit analysis, Martin's scheme was faulty and Willibald's was right. But some people just aren't born to be accountants.

"We'll simply say we don't know anything about it!" Martin retorted. "And she can pretend she's killed herself." You can see what the Nazis were missing, keeping him out of their ranks. That's just the kind of quick contrarian thinking they needed just then. But how did Martin come to be employing it against the very State he longed to serve? Well, there are limits to anyone's loyalty, and Martin had just bumped into his. Fatherland and Führer, yes. But Mother came in somewhere too. And as for the Gestapo, nobody liked them.

And what was sad Ilse doing while all this was going on? She'd closed her eyes and was as usual praying. There's no doubt who she was praying to, but what she was praying for is harder to determine. Peace at the last, perhaps, though where and what the last would be, nobody could tell. On the other hand, perhaps she was praying for guidance. Because guidance is what she very soon gave, and where else could she have got it from?

As the minutes passed, Gabi was growing less and less inclined to take the icy plunge. Yes, Martin was right. If she could get away before tomorrow and pretend to be another refugee bombed out of Silesia or somewhere, she might after all last out the final months of the war—which surely couldn't be so many now? Germany was a nut in a nutcracker, being squeezed between the Russians on one side and the Amis and the Tommies on the other. Surely the Third Reich was going to be crushed soon like a walnut with a rotten kernel? And then she'd be there for her children when the war was over. Could she afford to throw away that chance?

Against that weighed Willibald's objection that they'd all be killed if she was caught—but against that weighed her sudden lust for life. Or rather her horror of a watery death. If like her sister Frieda all those years ago she'd had some tablets and a syringe handy, she might have gone upstairs later that night and quietly lain down on the bed. It's easy to swallow tablets and quite easy—for a nurse at least—to stick a needle in your vein. After all, that's what Frieda did when the Nazis dismissed her from her post at her hospital in Berlin. But Gabi had no tablets, Gabi had no syringe. Jews weren't allowed them, even if they'd been there to have. So short of something more violent, her way out of life would have to be through the lake. And that would mean forcing herself not to swim, letting herself sink under the broken ice, sucking water down into her lungs in place of air—and such black and freezing water too, full of fish and weeds! She saw herself thrashing about, splashing and heaving, her body frantically trying to save her while her mind tried to kill. The dread that she might do it badly, that at the last moment her nerve might crack, began to unman her, if that term can be applied to a woman who had more courage than most men. Yes, if only she could just pretend to kill herself and get away with it . . .

"And what would happen the first time she was asked for her papers?" Willibald demanded. "Everything she has is stamped with a *J*. She'd be picked up at once! And then they'd come for *us*." He never lost sight for a moment of accountancy's perspective.

"She could use Tante Frieda's passport," a voice said quietly from the kitchen. The voice was Ilse's. She was still slowly making something to eat, but her thoughts were not exclusively on the Last Supper. "Tante Frieda's passport doesn't have a *J* on it. It's from before." Before the Nazis, she meant. "And Mutti looks quite like her too." Ilse was afraid of her mother, of her unquiet hurricane energy, of her tainted blood and her supposedly maleficent Jewish curse. But she drew the line both at sending her off to the slaughterhouse and at watching her walk into the lake. Besides, whatever her mother thought about her illness (not the TB, that was cured—the one that slowed her down and made her drag her foot), Ilse herself believed she was going to die soon anyway. So it wasn't a life-or-death matter for her if Gabi was caught. It was only death or death—death now or death a little later. "Tante Frieda's things are still in that case in the attic," she said now, bringing a saucepan of reheated soup into the room, and a basket of hard stale bread. She hadn't said so much for weeks.

"Well . . . ," said Gabi hesitantly, "I suppose we could have a look at them . . ." She was discovering how hard it is to just blow out life's flickering candle.

And so, without anyone actually making an explicit decision, it was accepted that she was going to impersonate her dead sister. Ilse uncomplainingly took the food back into the kitchen and got Tante Frieda's clothes out of the suitcase where they'd lain for nearly twelve years. Martin worked out his mother's escape plan. Willibald accepted what he couldn't prevent, and began composing a suicide note for Gabi in the style of Schiller—some things never change.

"What shall we tell the other two?" he glanced up to ask in fretful fear.

"Let them believe she's really killed herself," Martin said. "They're too young, and anyway the fewer the people who know about it, the better . . ." He really should have been on the general staff. He'd got a mind for these things. All those years in which he dreamt of Panzer tactics and Luftwaffe sorties really paid off now. His plan was a masterpiece of impromptu strategy, although it did have the essential benefit of slow Ilse's passing comment.

Gabi would leave a suicide note of her own (Willibald's was soon discarded as too literary to be anyone's but his). She would walk over the intact snow of the garden down to the lake. She would drop her coat there and return to the house, walking backwards in her own tracks. She would wear Frieda's clothes, take Frieda's old passport and adopt Frieda's identity. She would pretend she'd been bombed out of Dresden, and had rescued only the things she carried with her. Nobody could check with the Dresden authorities now, because there weren't any authorities to check with. The city had just been completely destroyed by the Amis and the Tommies. (That was some post-coital news Martin had had from Lisl Wimmer that very day. Yes, her father *must* have been listening black.) Martin would then lead her through the slush of the lanes, where her footprints couldn't be traced, over the mountain to Habersdorf, the next station on the railway line, where there was less chance of her being recognized. There she would take the first train to Graunau and Fraülein von Adler. In Graunau she would look for work in a hospital—that was his daring masterstroke. They were bound to be short-staffed in a hospital so near the front, and nobody would suspect her of being an escaping Jew. She'd be as safe as in the Führer's bunker—who'd look for a Jew there?

"What about if someone sees her in the village?" Willibald asked, broken-voiced and broken-hoped. "What about Frieda's papers? They're twelve years old at least. Suppose they check them?"

"They'll be too busy with the war. The Amis are only sixty kilometers away." (More post-coital news from Lisl Wimmer. At least they'd had something to talk about afterwards.)

Ilse sewed Frieda's clothes to make them more or less fit Gabi's smaller figure. She emptied Gabi's bag of everything that could associate her with Heimstatt—addresses, receipts, train tickets. She even cut the labels off Gabi's sensible but worn underwear and rubbed the old Plinden optician's name off her glasses case. Gabi wrote her pithy suicide note, and was amazed to see how steady her hand was. Willibald wrung his hands and was not at all amazed to see how unsteady they were. Then Gabi was ready to go. It was ten twenty when she set out for the lake, eleven fifteen when she returned from it backwards like a courtier leaving the Emperor's presence—and certainly she owed it some respect; where would she be without it?

"Did anyone see you?" Martin asked.

How could she tell? She'd been too frightened to look, and anyway was so nervous that she'd almost stumbled into the lake by accident. Perhaps, she thought, it would have been better if she had. But she hadn't, so she carried on, because that seemed now the only thing to do.

It would take them three hours to get over the mountain, and two and a half for Martin to get back before anyone in Heimstatt was up to see him. They set off at once, barely muttering good-bye. On their way they passed four graveyards, the Lutheran, the Catholic, the Catholic children's and the suicides', where the remains of Frau Dr. Kraus lay in their roughly reassembled bits. Would they have put *her* there if she'd killed herself, Gabi wondered, or would even that be forbidden to a Jew?

From a saddle five hundred meters above the village, Gabi could look down, panting for breath, on the lake and the moonlit roof of the nuns' house below. It was just past midnight. Every window was dark, but a crack of yellow light gleamed at the imperfect edge of the blackout blind on one. She imagined she was looking at the room where Sara and I lay peacefully sleeping. Why she thought we'd be sleeping peacefully is difficult to conceive, but in any case she was wrong. It was not our room, but the bathroom, into whose toilet bowl I was then about to pee.

How could she go on and leave us?

How could she not?

"Keep going!" Martin muttered urgently. "We haven't got much time!" The dim gleam vanished and Gabi turned away. Along paths covered with thawed and refreezing snow they clambered and slithered on towards the village of Habersdorf. And all the time Gabi was breathlessly rehearsing the details of the new life she'd taken on, while minor avalanches grumbled menacingly in the mountains above them. *I am Frieda Brandt,* she whispered to herself. *Nurse in Dresden Central Hospital. My age is fifty-four, I am unmarried, I lived in Hauptstrasse 45, Apartment Three, Second Floor. The place has been completely destroyed. My name is Frieda Brandt . . .*

But what if she met someone from Dresden Central Hospital?

The Habersdorf station lay then, as it lies now, outside the village, and they could approach it without being seen. The ticket office was closed, the platform empty. So far, so good. But here was a challenge for Martin's tactical thinking. Several people in Habersdorf knew Gabi and she might well be recognized if she entered the waiting room or bought a ticket when the office opened. She'd better skulk at the end of the platform, then, behind the furthest name-board, and slip onto the train when it arrived.

"Without a ticket?" The idea in itself disturbed Gabi, quite apart from the danger of being caught by the inspector. Good citizens just didn't travel without a valid ticket, even when they were escaping from the Gestapo.

"There won't be an inspector on the first train of the day," Martin retorted in an impatient whisper. He was usually impatient with women once he was sure of them, and there was none he could be more sure of than his mother. Besides, there's no denying, master tactician though he was, his own nerves were stretched as taut as Gabi's were just then. "Buy one at Pauchen, when you change trains."

"From Pauchen to Graunau?" Gabi asked anxiously, still wondering about that stretch from Habersdorf to Pauchen that she would have traversed illegally.

"Yes, from Pauchen to Graunau, for God's sake!" came the hissed response. "Where d'you think?"

Gabi fumbled for her purse in her bag, to make sure once again she'd brought enough money with her.

"Don't stay long at Fraülein von Adler's. They might be watching her. Get away as soon as you can."

And then Martin was getting away himself, and she would be alone. She was not a hugging mother, but now she clung to Martin until he pulled himself free with a muttered and, it must be conceded, choking "I must go." And she watched him fade into the dark. For a time she thought she could still hear his boots crunching and slithering in the snow. Then there was nothing except the occasional whining of the telephone wires beside the empty gleaming rails.

She waited and waited, her feet and hands growing numb with cold. *My name is Frieda Brandt, nurse in Dresden Central*

Hospital. I am fifty-four years old. I am unmarried. I lived in Hauptstrasse 45 . . .

At seven o'clock the first train arrived. Gabi boarded it like a guilty ghost, slipping into the last carriage while the sleepy under-stationmaster was chatting to the sleepy engine driver. As she did so, she realized with a shock that this was the train she should have been on anyway in the company of Constable Bolzner, the six thirty-five from Heimstatt. So in a sense it was Constable Bolzner who'd failed to keep their appointment, not she. Not that Constable Bolzner would look at it in that light.

The train drew away from the station and Gabi drew herself into the darkest corner of the last carriage. All the time the train was jolting along, she listened in dread for the unhurried sound of an inspector's voice approaching with routine inexorability down the corridor. Whenever the train stopped, she listened in greater dread for the orderly sound of policemen's voices and the measured scrape of boots on the carriage steps. She thought of jumping out of the train at every noise, and several times had her hand on the door handle. But Martin had been right; no inspector came. And as to the police, why should they search for her on the very train they knew she hadn't boarded at Heimstatt?

The sun dragged itself up and surveyed the world with its bleary and indifferent eye. When its cold anemic light seeped into the carriage, Gabi gingerly lifted the blackout blind and gazed out at a desolation of snow-covered fields and black, leafless trees.

At Pauchen she got down. An elderly inspector, who might have asked her for her ticket, helped her with her case instead and called her "Sister." She thanked him in a voice croaky with fear and waited till he'd turned away before she went to the ticket office.

Now, she thought, nobody would recognize her. But there she was wrong. Seppi Kammersberg, a Heimstatt lad who'd avoided conscription by getting an "essential" job as an engine driver on the railways, was leaning out of his warm cab and complacently contemplating first the steam puffing serenely from his engine's boiler, then the early morning passengers stamping their feet and panting their own kind of steam from theirs. He noticed Gabi on the next platform and briefly wondered, before relapsing into his habitual vacancy, what she was doing there so early in the day, and dressed so queerly too.

■

Meanwhile, after many delays and tremulously having her ticket punched without comment by a blowzy woman ticket inspector with greying hair, Gabi arrives late in the afternoon at Graunau, where two troop trains are also just arriving, one from the east, one from the west. The train from the east is full of bloodied soldiers, the train from the west full of soldiers going to be bloodied. There ought to be plenty of work at the hospital. Another train arrives while Gabi walks slowly with her suitcase down the platform. This train discharges a slew of refugees from the east, who look as bewildered and bedraggled as the bloodied soldiers now being loaded onto stretchers. She mingles with them as they flow along the platform. The two soldiers standing guard at the station entrance slide their eyes unconcernedly over her face. Only men of military age interest them. They're looking for deserters, not middle-aged Jewesses. For the first time since she left Heimstatt, Gabi begins to feel she might really escape, but that only transfers her fear from herself to her children and (less intensely, it must be admitted) to her husband. Has her escape meant their arrest? The safer she becomes, the guiltier she feels and the more fearful for them. Perhaps Willibald's accountancy perspective was the right one after all?

The city's streets are clogged with army trucks, guns and ambulances, and as she lugs her case through the wheel-

churned slush towards Fraülein von Adler's apartment, she realizes she'll be living with that anguish and fear until either
she no longer lives herself or she sees them all again. She'd
give herself up then and there, stop the first policeman she sees
and humbly confess "I'm one of them, I'm a Jew who's trying
to escape," if she didn't see it was too late for that now. Giving
herself up would be exposing them—Martin, Ilse, Willibald
and even the other two who knew nothing about it. And then
they'd all be done for.

Yes, Willibald was right, but it's too late to turn back now.

But it isn't too late to turn back from Fraülein von Adler's
apartment building when she sees it swarming with soldiers. In
and out they march, carrying in equipment and boxes of supplies
from an open truck past an armed sentry posted at the door.
Gabi turns away with a quaking stomach. As she walks trembling off, she glances back over her shoulder at the large window
on the first floor, where a bare-headed grey-haired officer stands
gazing idly out as he speaks on Fraülein von Adler's phone.

Three quarters of an hour and many apologetically polite requests later she has entered the matron's office in one of
Graunau's hospitals and sits at the desk of a large Mother Superior cradling a crucified Christ on her generous bosom. The
Mother Superior places a pince-nez on her nose and reads Frieda's references of twenty years before.

"I'm afraid everything else was lost in the air raid," Gabi says
timidly. She gestures at her case. "This is all I have left." Which
she suddenly realizes might indeed be true by now.

The Mother Superior studies first Frieda's passport, then,
removing her pince-nez, Gabi's face. Gabi's stomach is empty,
but if it wasn't, it would have emptied then. "Yes," the matron
says, glancing down again. "We heard it was terrible in Dresden.
Of course we can use you, with your qualifications. We're very
shorthanded. Do you speak any foreign languages—French or

English? Or Russian, even? We have a ward full of prisoners of war here."

"French and a little English," Gabi says breathlessly.

The Mother Superior nods. "We've just lost a nurse in that ward, I'll start you off there. You'll be working with Sister Brigitte. She's . . ." She doesn't say what Sister Brigitte is, and Gabi guesses that the missing predicate is *nice* or *friendly,* or even *non-political.* "But you must be tired, after all you've been through."

"I didn't sleep at all last night," Gabi replies. It feels good to say something true at last, as though that makes the lies all true as well.

"Have some rest first, then. You can start work tomorrow. I see it doesn't say what your religion is here?"

"Aryan," Gabi blurts out too quickly.

The Mother Superior glances up at her quizzically, her eyebrows arching towards her spotless wimple. "It was your religion I asked about, Sister Frieda."

Gabi blushes. "I, I'm afraid I'm a Lutheran," she stammers, as uneasily as if she was confessing her actual race rather than her professed religion.

"Lutheran," Mother Superior repeats in a flat tone that expresses neither doubt nor belief. "We're nearly all Catholics here, but it doesn't matter. All except Sister Brigitte. She's . . ." But again the Mother Superior leaves Gabi to guess what Sister Brigitte is as she folds Frieda's references inside her passport and slips them into the top drawer of her desk. "We'll keep these safe in here for now," she says as she turns the key. "I'll just show you your room . . ."

Why did she keep them? Gabi wonders in a new surge of fear as she follows the Mother Superior down the corridor. *Why? Is she going to check when she goes back? To show them to the police?*

Mother Superior leaves Gabi in a little room with two beds

in it, separated by a thick grey curtain. "You'll be sharing here with Sister Brigitte," she says. "The prisoners' ward is at the end of the corridor. Sister Brigitte will explain everything to you when she comes off duty tomorrow morning."

As she swishes away, Gabi imagines her going to the desk again, unlocking the drawer, taking out Frieda's passport, poring suspiciously over it, then picking up the phone . . . She feels like a prisoner at her trial waiting anxiously but fatalistically for the verdict. If it happens, it happens. There's nothing she can do about it now. One of the beds is made. That must be Sister Brigitte's. She shuts the door, sits down on the unmade bed, pulls a blanket round her shoulders and waits.

And as she sits there, her eyelids sliding irresistibly down over her glazing eyes, she sees Constable Bolzner opening the door and leading Willibald, Ilse, Martin, Sara and me into the room, each holding the next one's hand, as though in a funereal dance. "Now you're all under arrest," Constable Bolzner says reproachfully. "D'you think I enjoy doing this? Why didn't you kill yourself like you said?"

"No, don't take them!" she screams out in a strangled voice. "I'm the guilty one! Not them! Not them!"

Her scream wakes her. The room is empty, the door still closed. The blanket has slipped off her shoulders onto the bed. *I must rest*, she thinks, shivering in the dusk. *Otherwise I'll only give myself away.* She makes the bed and lies down between the sheets without undressing. But now she can't sleep. *I'm Frieda Brandt*, the words keep going through her head. *Nursing Sister from Dresden. Gabi Brinkmann? Who's she? I'm Frieda Brandt, unmarried, I lived in Hauptstrasse 45. I've been bombed out and come to work in Graunau* . . . She gets up and goes to the window to remind herself where she is, to ram her new identity into her brain.

In the courtyard below are armed sentries, two ambulances,

a black staff car with a pennant flying from its hood. Two orderlies are carrying a patient on a stretcher across the courtyard. The patient's arm hangs stiffly down from the stretcher and Gabi wonders detachedly why the orderlies don't place it more comfortably by the man's side. Then she realizes his face is covered. He's dead, then. She feels in her detachment a strange sense of relief that it's not a living person they're treating so negligently. As though that's a good omen for her own fate. She watches the orderlies carry the stretcher past the sentries and through some swing doors.

A lamp comes on behind the doors, and a subdued light seeps out into the courtyard like a yellowish fog. One of the sentries mutters something to the other. *I'm Frieda Brandt*, the ribbon of words unreels in Gabi's head. *Fifty-four years old, unmarried. I lived in Hauptstrasse* . . . And all the time that never-ending fear, stirring quietly in her stomach like a faintly seething swamp.

She eats the last of the sandwiches quiet Ilse made in Heimstatt, and drinks some water from a carafe on the scratched wooden bedside table. When she lies down again at last, she stuffs a handkerchief into her mouth in a variation of the Kaminsky cure, so that she won't betray herself by blurting something out as she did before in her sleep.

She is awake, washed and dressed long before Sister Brigitte appears at six the next morning.

Sister Brigitte is healthy and young, with thick bouncy blonde hair beneath the starched white cap that perches like a jaunty seagull on its waves. "How glad I am to see you, Sister Frieda!" she declares. "Did Matron tell you how short-staffed we are here? The reason is I had to report the last nurse for defeatist remarks. You should have heard what she was saying, you wouldn't believe it! And now the prisoners are really uncooperative. I'm almost scared of them. No, not really, don't worry. That's an exaggeration, I'm always overdoing things, people say.

Besides, we've got an army unit next door. They'll take care of them if they get nasty. That's the first thing you'll notice about me, by the way—always exaggerating. Mark you, what that nurse was saying—Astrid, her name was, Sister Astrid—you'd hardly believe she was German if you'd heard her. In spite of her name. Absolute disgrace! Come along, I'll show you round, then I must get my beauty sleep. I'm completely smashed!"

Gabi follows her, her heart congealing in her chest. So that's what Sister Brigitte is—a zealous Nazi who reports defeatist talk. And their beds are scarcely four feet apart! She follows Sister Brigitte numbly to the dying room, nearest theirs, to the large and shabby main ward, where prisoners lie so close together that you can hardly get between the beds, to the primitive latrines and the treatment room, where there are almost no medicines or syringes. "There are all sorts here," Sister Brigitte says with a sort of indulgent contempt for her patients. "Russians, Poles, English, French . . . We can't do much for them. Either they get better of their own accord or they die."

"We're the only two nurses?" Gabi asks, glancing round at the forty or so men whose dazed or feverish eyes are silently interrogating hers.

Sister Brigitte nods. "And we take it in turns to do the night watch, so then there's only one of us. That's when they tend to die, of course. Another one went last night. With a bit of luck we get an orderly to hand the food round, but half of them are too sick to eat it anyway. Frankly I wouldn't touch it myself even if I was starving, but there's a war on, isn't there? *We* get military rations," she assures Gabi with the smile of a happy warrior. "The same as our soldiers. Real pumpernickel and wurst. Even real coffee sometimes."

Today is one of those times. They breakfast on food such as Gabi hasn't eaten for years and drink real steaming coffee. "Where'd you say you come from?" Sister Brigitte asks. "Dresden? Wasn't that barbaric? It must have been awful for you. They say our men are shooting any airmen they take prisoner now; you can't blame them, can you? Imagine if you were a soldier who came from there. I come from Munich, myself. You can hear it in my accent, can't you? Now I must get some rest. See you later, all right?"

When Sister Brigitte has turned in, Gabi is left alone in the ward. Two men are dying of gangrene in the dying room, several more outside it look ready to take their places. Others mutter to her in Russian, French, English. A few in broken German. "Vous êtes aussi Nazi, comme l'autre?" one of them asks, a young Frenchman with an uneven pulse and high fever. She doesn't answer. And yet she feels better, as though she's found some friends at last.

■

Just before noon, an SS doctor enters with a loud "Heil Hitler!"

"Major Friedländer," he announces himself, surveying Gabi up and down as if she was a new recruit on parade. "And you are Sister Frieda? Sister Frieda Brandt?"

Gabi nods and murmurs, "Yes, Herr Major." She's used to military doctors from the first war, and her attitude seems to satisfy this one. "Most of these prisoners are either too sick to be worth treating, Sister Frieda," he goes on, "or not sick enough. Let the really sick ones die. The ones that are lightly sick should be returned to the camp as soon as possible, instead of fattening themselves on hospital food. I don't know why they were sent here in the first place. This isn't a rest home for malingerers. The few that are in between have a certain scientific interest for me. They're the only ones I want taken care of. Sister Brigitte will tell you who they are. But don't bother too much with them. They're all expendable in the end. They're still our enemies, remember. Well, I hope we shall work well together. The last nurse we had here was a disaster." His eyes, not Aryan blue, but as brown as Gabi's, hold hers for a moment, then he nods dismissal. "Heil Hitler!"

Gabi half-raises her hand in the forbidden salute, but the words just won't come out. Yes, she thinks as the door closes on Major Friedländer, she should have killed herself. And now it's too late. This reflection takes her to the dying room, where there is no morphine (reserved for German heroes) but a smell of pain that's even stronger than the smell of blood and putridity. She mechanically does what she can with what she's got and is surprised how easy it is to slip back into hospital ways. And all the time she wonders anguishedly—

17

What's going on in Heimstatt

Where the Gestapo have just been to sort us out. Two bully-boys from Linz, to be exact, who banged rather than knocked on the door just as those others did in Berlin, and barged their way in past shrinking Ilse, shoved Willibald up against the wall and started turning out his desk drawers. Constable Bolzner was a sheepish witness and occasionally caught Willibald's frightened eyes with a look that said *Now see what you've brought on yourself. You can't blame me, you know.* Nor did Willibald blame him. He didn't blame anyone unless perhaps Gabi for not doing the decent thing. He was just scared rigid he was going to be taken away in the black Mercedes outside, which had already attracted the attention of half the village. And even if he wasn't taken away, how would he be able to face his congregation now? Not to speak of his plump Aryan lady-friend.

After the meatheads had finished with the study, it was the whole house that got the treatment. Every cupboard ransacked, every bookcase emptied, every desk drawer yanked out and upturned. The place looked as if Willibald and Gabi had just had one of their major marital disagreements, except that

Gabi wasn't here to have one and the pictures didn't get torn off the walls. It was lucky Martin wasn't here either, but off at the factory when they searched his room. He might have said something when they pulled the drawers out of his desk, and got a slap across the mouth for his pains. Lucky they didn't look under his mattress too, where as far as I knew the semi-naked ladies were still awaiting his thrilled nocturnal peeping—unless Lisl Wimmer had taken on that role. But perhaps that wasn't quite the kind of material the Gestapo were looking for, or would object to if they found it.

Or perhaps they weren't really looking for anything at all and only wanted to mess us around a bit? Not that Sara or I cared much what they wanted. We were still aching with the loss of Gabi, still numb and dumb, still gazing out over the lake every hour or so as if she was going to arise like Aphrodite from the ice floes, except she wouldn't be either naked or beautiful and I'd never heard of Aphrodite anyway. So we didn't care about these two heavies—why should we? The worst had happened already—and we couldn't comprehend the fear they inspired in Willibald and Ilse, especially after they left us alone and wandered down to the shore accompanied by harassed Constable Bolzner to the place where Gabi's coat was found. They examined the spot carefully, apparently unaware it had already been covered by a new snowfall, and looked about them as though they expected to see her pop up from behind the nearest tree and light out over the ice to give them a bit of target practice. But it was freezing again, so they soon tired of that. Then, flapping their arms and stamping their feet, which weren't suitably shod for meter-deep alpine snow, they got back in their car and drove away. Not, however, before they'd given Constable Bolzner a noisy piece of their mind.

It was my birthday, by the way. I was eleven, but I didn't feel like celebrating.

Now unhappy Constable Bolzner catches a cold and wastes precious police time rowing up and down the unfrozen passages in the lake, peering hopelessly under lumbering half-meter-thick slabs of ice for a sight of Gabi's wallowing body. And Willibald is surprised by a visit from Ortsgruppenleiter Franzi Wimmer, who offers ale-hazed condolences on Gabi's decease and lets it be known he had nothing to do with the Gestapo visitation of the day before. The black news he's been listening to must be really black. Willibald would be even more surprised, and scared as well, if he knew of the visit young engine driver Seppi Kammersberg paid to Franzi himself the day after Gabi disappeared.

"I saw her in Pauchen!" Seppi began their conversation. "On platform five! Eleven twenty exactly."

Franzi knew full well whom he meant, but he affected chummy hebetude. "Saw who?" he asked. "'Lots of people in Pauchen, aren't there, Seppi?'"

"The Frau Pfarrer! Dressed up in nurse's clothes. Eleven twenty, it was. I was just taking the Salzburg regular out."

"Frau Pfarrer Brinkmann? You can't have done."

"But I did, I tell you! Plain as I'm seeing you now."

"How could you have, Seppi? She's been in the lake since yesterday morning."

When Seppi persisted, Franzi grew more avuncular. "Now listen Seppi, you can't have seen her because the woman's dead, all right? And what would she be wearing a nurse's uniform for anyway?"

"Well, it looked like her, anyway," Seppi said doggedly.

"Dare say it did. But it can't have been her, can it? Look, I'd forget about this, if I was you. You go round spreading stories like that, you could get into trouble, know what I mean? Wasting police time, they call it. Don't want that to happen, do you?"

Seppi Kammersberg certainly didn't. He'd imagined he'd simply get some credit for being a patriotic sleuth, but now that he saw himself getting tangled up in a net of complications, he swiftly reassessed his memory and found it might perhaps have been mistaken. "Well, I can't be sure it was her, I suppose," he admitted with a face-saving show of grudging reluctance.

Least said, soonest mended is not a German proverb, nor an Austrian one either, but there's something nearly twice as long that's rather similar and Seppi silently applied it then. Later, when the war is over, he's going to subscribe to a different principle, and will often be heard declaring how he saved the Herr Pfarrer's family by refusing to answer the Gestapo's questions about his train-spotting at Pauchen at eleven twenty on a February day in 1945. Well, Franzi Wimmer won't be disposed to put the record straight. Did Franzi dissuade Seppi from reporting his Gabi-sighting out of humanity, or merely to further hedge his bets? He won't be disposed to tell us that either, if ever he knew himself. He won't be disposed to tell anyone anything.

Soon after the Gestapo visitation Martin announces on his return from his efforts in the factory and subsequently Lisl Wimmer that it's the crisis now. The final desperate and decisive battle is really approaching at last: the battle at which the Führer will deploy his latest and most devastating weapon, although just what that is he's not too clear. He announces all this exultantly, as though he'd just left a staff meeting in Adolf's bunker, rather than a groping tryst with Lisl Wimmer.

Sara and I are shocked by his apparent callousness. He doesn't mention Gabi once, doesn't seem to care that his mother has just killed herself—he scarcely seems to notice it even, despite the black armbands he, Willibald and I have on our sleeves, and the black dresses Ilse and Sara are wearing, all of which silent melancholic Ilse has run up or altered on her sewing machine with the help of Fraülein Hofer, who came specially to sew although it wasn't her day.

Resi came with her, carrying a worn pack of cards, and spoke to me for the first time in all these years. She asked me if I wanted to play Skat. I said no. Not that I thought she was offering me the kind of cardless Skat that Eva played with Martin in Berlin. Though I appreciated her gesture, it made me want to cry again, and I went off to the balcony to have another look for Gabi and let my tears fall unobserved. But I couldn't keep on crying, because Resi followed me and asked if I'd rather play Black Peter instead. I shook my head dumbly and she stood behind me sending waves of silent compassion into the middle of my hunched shoulders. Then she murmured in a low voice, "My dad's gone too. At Stalingrad." I didn't move—or perhaps I hunched my shoulders a bit higher. "Missing believed killed, they said," she went on. And then went quietly away. That was my first experience of a girl's tenderness and it made me feel sorry for her as well as for myself. But I still felt more sorry for me than for her because her father couldn't have meant much to her since he'd given her away to Fraülein Hofer when she was a baby. And anyway he was only missing believed killed, whereas Gabi was definitely and irrevocably dead.

I've been crying a lot these past few weeks, and I've spent more time than Sara standing on the balcony gazing out over the lake for a sight of my mother. I even hoped that Constable Bolzner would find her as he poked about in the ice, although the thought of him trawling her frozen body in behind his little boat did give me nightmares.

But Sara's different. She's as silent as Ilse and hasn't cried once that I know of. Every scene in the drama of her life plays on that inner stage of hers, and no one gets invited to the show. She sits behind the kitchen stove, which doesn't give much heat out now because there's so little wood to burn in it, never mind coal, and stares at the tiles as if they were speaking to her, whispering some profound message. But what it is I'll never know. Her notebooks lie almost untouched beneath her mattress.

And as for Ilse—I've never seen her cry in the whole of my life. She's so sad at all times that tears are redundant at any of them. Besides, I know she's got a different take on Gabi; she can't miss her as Sara and I do.

After another week, when the snow's beginning to thaw, a chief inspector from Plinden appears in Heimstatt and orders the lake to be thoroughly trawled, which turns up nothing worth eating or keeping. Then there's an inquiry into Constable Bolzner's conduct regarding the disappearance of the Jewess Gabriella Sara Brinkmann, in consequence of which Constable Bolzner is dismissed from the police and simultaneously inducted into the army. That's bad news for Frau Bolzner and her five children, who are evicted from their comfortable police lodgings, and they look at Willibald as though they hold him responsible for their predicament, which in a sense he is. However there's bad news everywhere just now and Willibald merely smiles blandly to hide his discomfort and speedily averts his eyes. After all, there's no point singling out the Bolzners for special sympathy when the news is worse for everyone than anyone supposed. Unless you're on the Allies' side, that is, which nobody in Heimstatt is—until, that is, it turns out afterwards that everyone was all along. In fact you could say the Bolzners are lucky; the Eastern Front has dissolved by the time the ex-Constable gets to it and all he does is spend the next six months finding his way home again. Admittedly he doesn't get his police job back. Orders are orders, they remind him—doesn't he know it!—and rules are rules, never mind if they're the wrong ones.

The first material differences that Gabi's disappearance makes to us are that the house gets tidier and colder and there's even less to eat. I notice that within a week. Ilse spends hour after weary hour cleaning and dusting the unheated rooms, but they're as lifeless now as they used to be messy and full of life, even unhappy life. And as for food, somehow it just isn't there, even in the minimal amount it was before. "They don't have any bread," Ilse says resignedly when she drags herself back from the few shops that will serve us. Or "They say they're out of potatoes." The truth is, Gabi wheedled and coaxed and begged at those shops to let her run up large debts against the security of Frieda's dwindling dowry and her own furniture. But now that Gabi's gone they're even more worried about repayment than they were before, and they won't extend our credit. Besides, supplies really are scarcely coming through anymore—our boys at the front must get the best—and the shopkeepers think they'd better keep what they do get for themselves or those who can pay black-market prices. All that's a mystery to unworldly Ilse and she settles submissively down to live or die in grinding hunger.

Willibald, who used to mutter peevishly about his meager rations, now eats without a word of complaint what little's set in front of him. He even forgets to say grace sometimes, and Ilse even forgets to remind him. Well, there isn't much to be thankful for. After our meals he wanders off to the study, where we hear no more of those little barks and yelps of delight which I've come to associate with dramatic composition. And when I go in, I find him sitting with a closed book on his desk, staring at the window as blankly as the window stares back at him. Something tells me this isn't mourning for Gabi, but nothing tells me it's quiet terror that she'll be caught and so will he. He's so scared in fact he's even stopped making those pastoral visits to Plinden where unbeknown to us his Aryan lady-friend resides. In any case, if her situation's at all like ours, by now she won't be quite so comfortingly plump as she used to be.

In a month or so there's even less grub. Supplies have dried up completely, and that decisive battle still hasn't happened yet, though Martin maintains it's only a matter of weeks now. The war will be over by the summer, he declares. I don't ask who will win; in fact I can't imagine what winning will be like, whoever does the winning. Will it mean the schools will open again? Will there be more food, or any? Or will there be nothing but victory parades and further exclusions? War was all I could remember a year ago, and it's all I can remember now. The peace I was born in, uneasy as it was, lies well below my memory's horizon. No, war is all I've ever known, and I'm beginning to think that win or lose, it's all I ever will. Not that I care much anyway, now that Gabi's gone.

And if the war isn't going well for the Führer, it certainly isn't going any better for us. Sara's been in a decline since my mother's disappearance and so has just about everyone else except Martin. Ilse laboriously cleans and washes and Sara and I slowly help her. She also cooks what there is to cook, which isn't much. Warplanes drone overhead quite often, but unchallenged and so high we scarcely see them, and all we do is listlessly glance up then look away. Sometimes their wings make long cottony vapor trails like ethereal railway lines, sometimes they glint a moment in the sun. And speaking of the sun, though that's just reappeared above the mountains and the last snow is beginning to melt and it's definitely spring again, no one's making daisy chains or gathering early flowers.

Not that we aren't gathering something. We're gathering nettles from the lakeshore in fact, whole armfuls of them—Ilse, who can scarcely walk now, Sara and me, who are almost as slow as she is. Nettles have become our meat and drink, our daily sustenance. A large saucepan full of them boils down to a few spoons of greenish soup, which tastes like . . . well, nettles. And it goes through your gut like prefabricated diarrhea. We also get the odd kilo of frozen potatoes and an occasional loaf of stale bread, which, if it isn't mixed with sawdust, certainly tastes as if it is. Ilse religiously cuts the bread up into as many little cubes as she can and distributes some to us at every meal. Each of us guards his own cube and sizes up his neighbor's with apathetic yet greedy eyes. Cubes with a crust on are at a premium. We think they contain more nourishment. At any rate they need a bit more chewing, and that keeps the digestive juices running a bit longer.

I don't realize I'm withering away, but the others realize they are. We lie around a lot, because we haven't got the energy to do anything else. Sara's latest exercise book sometimes lies around too, but she scarcely ever writes in it. She just keeps it there with her for comfort, I imagine.

It's a strange thing to starve. You don't realize it's more than just being very hungry until it's too late, you've given up and become an aching, hollow-eyed, lethargic spectator of life, no longer interested or participating in the show. I think our eyes are getting larger, but actually it's our faces that are getting smaller.

Yes, we're starving by now, Willibald, Ilse, Sara and I. But not Martin. As his brick factory has no more supplies, it's stopped working and so has he. However, Herr Ziegler, his gruff employer, has become quite friendly as the war runs down, and finds him other work on a farm ten kilometers away with an old friend of his. Farms mean food, and Martin stays there all week and most weekends, feasting on meat, milk, butter, eggs and cheese, or so it seems to us. On the few Sundays that he visits us, he doesn't seem to notice we are starving, though he does once bring a bit of cheese with him. Yes, the farmer gives him enough to eat, and he's got a daughter who's probably giving him something as well. He's all right, and he'll stay all right till the Fatherland's final call to arms and glory goes out even for him.

Ilse notices he's stopped wearing his black armband. He says he lost it somewhere on the farm, but when she offers to make him another, he doesn't answer and she doesn't insist. Insistence never was one of her stronger qualities, and starvation certainly hasn't nourished it. But I wear my armband all the time, and so does Willibald, although you'd scarcely notice it since he wears clerical black anyway, just like an undertaker. We're going to wear black for a year, and so are Ilse and Sara. At least, that's my understanding, although a year seems an immeasurable time to me and I can't imagine it ever ending.

All the same I can't deny we're getting used to Gabi's death. I've stopped gazing out over the lake for a glimpse of her body, and I don't think I'd want to see it now anyway, since I know it wouldn't look very nice after two months in the water. Sara stopped gazing before I did—after all, she's older. We seem to feel nothing anymore, in fact, and do nothing either, except drag ourselves down to the lake to gather nettles and mumble the bits of bread we get with the consequent watery soup. Sara tells me we're all going to die soon and asks me to burn her notebooks if she dies first, but I'm not sure I'll have the strength to light a match. As for myself, I don't think I'm going to die—but only because I've just about stopped thinking altogether.

Sometimes Ilse gazes at Sara and me with her luminously sad brown eyes as though she's got something on her mind and is about to tell us what, but then she turns away. Once, though, when we're pulling nettles up by the lake, she does ask, "Do you really think Mutti's gone to heaven?" Her voice seems to express some doubt as to her eligibility for that distinction. Both Sara and I bridle at that and we snap back, insofar as we're capable of snapping, "Of course!" Although I don't believe in heaven at all, and haven't since Tante Maria's funeral, I'm quite sure that if there is one, Gabi's earned her place in it. I don't know whether Sara believes in heaven, but anyway she's just as snappy as I am towards Ilse's imputation. Ilse seems unaffected by our unusually energetic acerbity and only murmurs "Yes," absently, and then a moment later sighs "Yes" again, as she looks down at the bundle of nettles in her arms. As though we're welcome to believe that if it makes us happy, but as for herself . . .

She has very drawn cheeks now, and her olive complexion has gone sallow, as though the blood beneath her skin has drained away. And yet she seems more peaceful than she was before. Is that what makes me guess she doesn't really miss Gabi? It's not just her question; it's the sense that she feels relieved even though she's starving. Relieved of the strain of all that nervous energy, that bustle and push, that anxious concern, those perpetual swings between hope and despair which constantly and obliviously battered at the walls of her introverted quietude. Not to speak of course of a Jewish curse.

In the village Franzi Wimmer has stopped wearing his Ortsgruppenleiter's uniform except on important official occasions, and there aren't many of them happening now. He's trying to revert to the role of genial innkeeper, although there's nothing to be genial about and not much more to keep in his inn. Even his zealous wife, whose features have grown still more sharp and edgy, and soon will grow yet more so, has stopped spying on us and mutters "Grüss Gott" when she meets people in the lanes, instead of barking out "Heil Hitler!" In fact "Heil Hitler!" seems to be going out of fashion. You hardly ever hear it these days. And Lisl sometimes leaves us half a loaf of bread when she drops by of an afternoon, looking forlorn and wan and hoping to glean a bit of news about Martin, who doesn't seem as keen as he used to be, now that he's off working on the farm.

But she'll soon have more to think about than that. The final battle really is about to be joined and it's time for the inauguration of Martin's glorious military career.

■

The Führer's birthday's fast approaching and so are the Allies from east and west, although they haven't exactly been invited to the party (which will be the last occasion by the way that Franzi Wimmer wears his Ortsgruppenleiter's uniform, although he isn't going to be invited either). It's time for Adolf to do something to stem the tide at last and so the rallying call goes out for every German who can carry a pitchfork to fight fanatically in the last, ultimate, final, truly decisive battle of the war. Though not fully Aryan, Martin ranks high enough to serve as cannon fodder in this "People's Army," so he gets his summons too. A soldier in the German army! Throwing the barbarian hordes back, side by side with his resolute Aryan comrades! What could life offer to compare with that?

Nothing, Martin thinks, and neither apparently does Willibald when he hears the news. Martin doesn't mind that it's not the Luftwaffe or the Panzer regiments after all whose colors he's been called to. The point is, he'll prove himself a hero and get accepted at last in the Aryan Reich. And then even his runaway mother will be tolerated as well (acceptance is too much to hope for, even he recognizes that). The Holy Grail hovers before him and he reaches out for its flickering gleam through romantic mists of self-delusion.

As does Willibald. On the morning of Martin's departure, he delivers a throbbing speech on the German soldier's sacred duty to defend hearth and home, as he in his time has done and others in their time before. If it weren't for his present infirmity he'd be marching along beside his son. Hindenburg gets a mention after himself, and so does Frederick the Great. Martin's in good company all right (and so of course are they). Then Willibald embraces Martin theatrically on the doorstep for Ortsgruppenleiter Wimmer to see what patriots we are and wipes away a manly tear, though unluckily Franzi isn't there to enjoy the show. It's all too much for Willibald though, and he totters backwards, waving feebly as Martin strides away to death or glory. Resolute Martin doesn't look round at the hearth and home he's off to defend, and so fails to observe his father nearly collapsing in Ilse's arms, which are in no state at all to support his gangling frame, however emaciated it may be.

This People's Army has no weapons yet and no uniforms, not to speak of training, but they've got some food and they're going to inflict a decisive defeat on the International-Jewish-financed Mongol-Slavic-Bolshevik hordes by means of sheer German (or half-German) determination and valor. Now that things are running down, nobody seems to bother about keeping half-Jews in their place, which just lately has been outside the Third Reich's armed forces. But then half-Jews always were a tricky category at the best of times, since they were also half-Aryan. At the worst of times they're trickier still. So the policy now is: let them in.

Some weeks ago in the Plinden cinema Martin saw a newsreel of the Führer inspecting blond young lads about Martin's own age or even younger and clapping them on the back with a paternal smile as he sent them off to fight the Russian tanks with their pitchforks and shovels. How Martin had longed to be one of them, receiving the ultimate accolade from the Führer's own hand! Now he can thank imminent defeat for getting his chance at last. Never mind that there was something forlorn about the Führer's expression, as if he knew the game was up. It's true his cheeks were drooping, one arm seemed to hang listlessly as if it had grown tired of the whole business, and his face sagged between bidding farewell to one young hero and greeting the next, as though his mind kept wandering off to something else altogether and it wasn't Eva Braun. But still he was the Führer, the Fatherland's Guide and Protector, the Man of Destiny, the Defender of Europe, the Savior of the World and quite possibly the Universe.

The young heroes do a bit of drilling under NCOs brought out of long retirement who are chiefly wondering where they're going to throw their uniforms and rank badges away when the Russians come. They give their orders in a world-weary and cynical tone unless a young officer happens along (and there aren't many of them left now), when they sharpen up their act a bit. After that the recruits are loaded onto trucks and taken somewhere near the front. They know it's the front because they hear the *Crrump!* of artillery all the time and see columns of victorious German troops hastily and unaccountably heading in the opposite direction. Surely our boys haven't lost their way? No, they're making a strategic withdrawal of course, after inflicting untold casualties on the Ivans, who have nevertheless managed to make a slight and temporary advance. The Ivans will doubtless all be wiped out in no time, but the haggard faces of the triumphantly withdrawing troops don't quite fit our young heroes' picture of a strategic withdrawal and some of them feel queasy in their valiant stomachs. If our boys on the Western Front are making strategic withdrawals with the same rapidity as they are here, they'll be bumping into each other's asses before long.

Soon the young heroes are issued rifles and a few rounds of ammunition and given a bit of instruction how to use them. The world-weary NCOs have become resigned and hopeless now, like trainers who know their fighter can't win but push him into the ring regardless and place their bets upon the other man.

The bold confidence with which Martin joined this ragtag army is beginning to ooze away. It leaks out altogether when they come to a devastated town five miles from the front where soldiers from an SS regiment are digging in and have hanged a couple of deserters about Martin's own age on the nearest convenient lampposts. One of the corpses looks familiar although he's beginning to go off by now—he's been there three days, an awed voice mutters. Martin feels compelled to look more closely despite a not quite equal compulsion to look away.

The blond-haired corpse swings gently to and fro in the

balmy spring breeze like a sack fastened at the neck or a cloth puppet—except that what he looks like most of all is a very dead young human being. The last time Martin saw such light blue eyes, such fair hair flapping languidly upon its broad Aryan brow, was on a mountain at sunset. But then the owner's eyes weren't popping like that and his head wasn't lolling all the way to one side. He wasn't sticking his tongue out either.

■

For two days Martin's subdued unit is moved forwards, backwards and sometimes sideways like a pawn in a sloppy chess game while some general tries to make up his mind which gap in the porous front it might be used to plug. At one place in the dusk their trucks pass a straggly line of skeletal figures in filthy striped uniforms and wooden clogs. They're marching, or rather stumbling, towards the rear, marshalled by SS guards. When one of the walking cadavers falls and does not rise, a guard shoots him once in the back of the head.

By now Martin feels he's learnt more than enough about being an Aryan hero, and to go by the crushed silence in which they plod, on foot now, past the charred and ruined witnesses of war, so have the rest of them. They all know full well they're going to melt away when the chance comes, but Martin keeps getting a feeling like a rough hemp rope tightening round his throat whenever he thinks of that dangling corpse, whose owner must have melted away too soon or not quite fast enough. He tries surreptitiously pressing his fingers and thumb against his windpipe and finds it even more painful than he'd feared. Which is it worse to face, Russian tanks or SS nooses? His stomach cringes. War wasn't meant to be like this, it was supposed to be all painless victories in which only the other side got hurt—*Bang bang! You're dead!*—then thumping drums and waving flags.

But he doesn't have to make an anguished choice between the horns of this dilemma. The solution comes of its own accord. Before they've gone much further forward, or it might be sideways for all that Martin knows, they are confronted by the flooding sludgy tide of a whole army in retreat—battalion after battalion of exhausted, glum, torn, wounded and defeated men with dark eyes haunted by what they've seen or done. The untested tyros view their broken but experienced comrades with despair instead of lordly scorn, and as if by common consent falter, halt, turn and join the throng. It's like a disappointed and unruly football crowd pouring out of the stadium where their team's just lost, except they're desperate, not just disappointed, and what they've lost is not a game.

Soon the soldiers are joined by fleeing civilians, humping rucksacks, lugging cases, pushing prams. And the world-weary NCOs are themselves transmuted into rankless, badgeless and sometimes toothless old men in civvies, merging with the widening flood of refugees. Shellfire is close behind them and the curdling whine of the Ivans' rockets. Sometimes there's the distant rattle of small-arms fire as well, at which the pace of the rising flood first hesitates, then increases. Martin has never heard the whirr and clank of Russian tank tracks, but he's listening for them all the same and thinks with gasps of panic that he hears them every other second.

But it isn't tanks that come to pay them a visit, it's strafing fighters, at first far-off harmless humming ladybugs, but then suddenly close and furiously angry wasps. Down they swoop, sending bullets and cannon shells crashing into the ground, and then they've soared away before you even know if you've been hit or not. But that's only to swing round and swoop down again. Martin's stomach's in revolt, and so are his watery legs as the earth shakes with explosions and people all around him scream out in pain or terror. He throws himself on the earth like everyone else and moans to God to save him, a personage he's previously invoked still less frequently than I.

This experience convinces him he's not cut out to be an Aryan hero after all, and he soon decides to be a Nazi victim instead, which at least is what he really is. Yet the heroic role still tempts from time to time.

■

But that is not the only battle being waged.

There is the siege of Graunau, for instance, still to come. And before that even sleepy lethargic Heimstatt is due for its brief flurry of excitement.

Yes, it looks as though an SS battalion really is going to defend Heimstatt heroically and of course fanatically till their last breath and probably ours. First a couple of motorcycles appear in the village, then a column of armored cars and trucks. These people are the right stuff all right, they have death's heads on their helmets, and Fritzi Wimmer assures me as I weakly watch some of them drawing up outside the Pfarrhaus that each one of them has killed a hundred Ivans with his bare hands. I'm not entirely reassured by that. If it's true, I imagine the surviving Ivans will want to get their own back when they come, and I don't have the strength to run away.

Some of the soldiers tramp into our house, and a colonel says "Heil Hitler!" and he's making his headquarters here so where's the kitchen? Willibald, to whom these brief remarks are addressed, attempts a weak "Heil Hitler!" in return, gives a feeble smile of welcome and mentions both Martin's absence at the front and his own part in the glorious Polish campaign. But the colonel doesn't seem to be too interested and brusquely tells his orderly to get some coffee going. Willibald withdraws meekly back towards the study, but is curtly informed that's been requisitioned and he can use the maid's room instead wherever that is. Soldiers come rolling in phone cables, setting up a wireless receiver near the piano in the living room and arranging map boards on Willibald's desk. The colonel's orderly brings him real coffee in next to no time, which leaves the scent of paradise all over the house and even brings a gleam into Ilse's and Sara's lackluster eyes. The colonel shouts down the phone with his mug in his hand, sits at Willibald's desk, pores over the maps, goes to speak in a high-pitched singsong tone on the wireless microphone, then idly runs the backs of his fingers up and down the keys of the piano. Unaware of her ambiguous status, he addressed Ilse as "Madam" when he sees her, but doesn't seem to notice the rest of us.

Willibald's so weak now, he can scarcely manage the stairs down to the kitchen and Jägerlein's empty room, where he sits, then lies on the bare mattress, folds his hands together on his chest and closes his eyes. However this is not death or resignation, but conservation of his strength, and when it's time for nettle soup and a cube of bread, he struggles into a sitting posture with a sort of weary alacrity that turns out to be well-founded since the colonel's orderly has given Ilse half a sausage, which she's laboriously cut into slices you can see through. The sausage lasts three days, which is about half what the SS battalion does, but only makes the pangs of hunger worse. There's a kind of headache we have now which Sara later christens the starving headache. Each of us feels as though there's a tiny place three inches behind the eyes, which someone's slowly splitting open with a hammer and wedge. And whenever we move we're dizzy, so we scarcely move at all.

Meanwhile the resolute and relatively well-fed soldiers are busy felling trees across the roads into the village and setting up machine-gun nests at every corner. The armored cars snarl up and down the single passable road, chewing up the surface and spitting stones and mud out behind their heavy wheels. Inside the

Pfarrhaus, the colonel shouts down his phone and the wireless receiver crackles in the corner of the living room. Late every night when work is done he lets his fingers idly brush across the piano keys, sending tinkling sounds drifting through the somber rooms, sounds we haven't heard since Gabi left off playing years ago.

One evening when I return with a late-cropped bunch of nettles in my arms, I see Franzi Wimmer, who's been keeping a low profile since the SS moved in, approaching the colonel as he smokes his evening cigarette outside in the market place. Franzi isn't wearing his Ortsgruppenleiter's uniform, nor is he carrying the drink very well that he's clearly been imbibing. "Vienna's fallen, Colonel," he says companionably if thickly.

The colonel turns slowly to survey Franzi with an up-and-down look that should have knocked him cold sober, but unfortunately doesn't. "And who are you?" he inquires in a level tone, which reminds me of a bayonet being slid out of its scabbard, a sound I've grown quite familiar with in the last few days.

"The Russkies've occupie' Vienn', I said," Franzi answers blurrily. He takes great care not to sway on his feet, but does so anyway, and speaks now with labored distinctness. "'s all over, isn't it? 's all over."

"I asked you who you are," the colonel says with a distinctness of his own that isn't labored at all, but definitely menacing.

"Wimmer. Or'shgruppenleider Wimmer. Ad your shervice." And Franzi makes a slurry bow, which he compounds with a slack-lipped leer. "For wha' tha's worth now."

The colonel examines the glowing tip of his cigarette and apparently decides that *that* at least is not worth much. He drops the cigarette on the ground, grinds it with the heel of his polished boot, turns his head a fraction and raps out "Sergeant Major!" Then he turns back to Franzi and addresses him in tones of icy amiability. "So you've been listening to enemy lies, my friend? And spreading them abroad?"

"Nod ad all," Franzi answers airily, waving the charge away with a floppy hand. "Vienna's gone, know for a fac'. So why don' you jus' give up? By the way, know whose house you're shtaying in?"

The sergeant major now appears running, and crashes to a bone-jarring halt before the colonel. "Sir!" he snaps out in a whiplash voice.

I think I've heard enough of this conversation, and hurry with my nettles through the back door into the Pfarrhaus. Which makes me dizzy, but I'm used to it.

It seems hours later that a volley of rifle shots echoes across the lake and back again. But it isn't long after that that the colonel quietly closes the front door behind him and we hear the slow reflective tinkle of the piano keys in the living room once more, up and down, up and down, above the frantic splutter and crackle of the wireless receiver. Guessing from this that Franzi didn't get the chance to tell the colonel he was staying in a racially tainted house, I feel that now it's safe to fall asleep.

The colonel might not have heeded Franzi's counsel to give up, but at dawn the very next morning he's making one more of those heroic strategic withdrawals. The phone cables are wound onto their little drums again, the wireless set loaded onto a truck, the map boards all packed away. The colonel clicks his heels and bows to Ilse as he departs and apologizes for the inconvenience. "Necessities of war, Madam," he murmurs regretfully. "Heil Hitler!" The orderly leaves two slices of stale pumpernickel behind on the kitchen table.

The tree barriers are shoved aside, the machine-gun nests dismantled, and soon the motorbikes, the trucks and armored cars are gone. So in one sense is Franzi Wimmer. But in another he's still there, lying crumpled against the bullet-pocked back wall of the Ortsgruppenleiter's office.

Why is it that I can think *That's taught you one, hasn't it?* at the same time that I'm feeling truly sorry for Fritzi and Lisl, and even for Frau Wimmer, all three sobbing and wailing as neighbors carry their dead father and husband away? Perhaps it's because I think that Gabi's dead as well and they deserve what's come to them, whereas we definitely don't. But in fact Gabi isn't dead at all, she's—

18

Hanging on in Graunau

And if she felt like a hare among the hounds at Erwin's memorial service, here she feels more like a sheep in wolf's clothing, surrounded by a pack of rangy wolves. Every night she stuffs a handkerchief into her mouth to prevent herself from screaming in her sleep. And every night she dreams the same dream of Constable Bolzner entering the room and leading us all away to prison and death. *Why didn't you kill yourself?* Constable Bolzner asks her reproachfully every night, and every night her stifled scream awakes her, gurgling in her parched gagged throat.

It's better in the daytime. She's more in control. And there are the prisoners to keep her occupied, sheep in sheep's clothing, among the wolves like her. Do some of them realize she's kin to them? Do they scent the hunted sheep beneath the lupine clothing? She doesn't know. But some of them may have sensed she's not a Nazi: John, the English chaplain who's lost an arm somewhere or other, Alain, the Frenchman dying of gangrene, and Roger, his older friend. They were in the Free French forces and Major Friedländer refuses to treat them—he thinks they should be shot. Then there are the few Russians, whom Major Friedländer refuses not so much to treat as to notice. Some of them catch Gabi's sleeve when Sister Brigitte isn't there and whisper words she can't understand, nodding fearfully at the door as if they expect Hitler himself to walk in—or is it Stalin? Another, a one-legged man with shoulders humped round the pads of his crutches, whispers "Deutschland kaput!" and nods vigorously as though he's crazy, before swinging swiftly away.

It's the English chaplain John who gives Gabi her first lesson in hospital air-raid precautions when a lone American plane strafes the whole place, military barracks and hospital together (you can't expect them to be too picky). Another doctor has taken over while Major Friedländer's on leave, a young man just out of medical school, and he has prescribed morphine for Alain, who's muttered hoarsely to her that he is a poet. At least, that's what she thinks he said. Or could it be pilot? The warning siren is just beginning to wail as Gabi hurries to the dispensary to get the drug before someone countermands the order. *Sister Frieda Brandt* she signs for it at the little window as distant anti-aircraft guns begin to hammer at the sky. And she wonders at the ease which practice has given her in masquerading as an Aryan nurse. Carrying the precious vials back, she reaches the middle of the courtyard at the very moment the American pilot two hundred feet above her arrives at his superior view of the place and presses the trigger regardless of the red cross painted on the roof. She clutches the morphine protectively to her breast and stands transfixed as the ground kicks up all round her, chips fly off the bullet-spattered walls and an empty ambulance has a row of jagged holes punched through its roof. At the same time a dark shadow swoops across the courtyard with a whoosh of air, and a split second later she hears the clatter and roar of the departing Mustang's engine.

The English chaplain hurries out from the wall he's been

crouching against and pulls her into its safety with his single hand. "No need to give them target practice!" he exclaims, words whose tendency she understands even though she doesn't fully get their meaning. "Watch out, he might be coming back!" Her fingers are curled tightly round the morphine vials and suddenly her whole body is shuddering, her heart bounding in her chest like a springbok hunted by a pride of lions.

The morphine will last as long as Alain does, she later thinks (but is mistaken), the other patient having died already. Unless Major Friedländer notices the prescription and cancels it when he returns. But he always passes the dying room by without a glance at the patients, never mind their records. The ones he's interested in are those he gives his experimental drugs to. They seem to do no better than the rest. In fact, they get worse, but that doesn't stop him giving them the drugs. "Science learns from failures as well as successes," he tells Sister Brigitte, who looks puzzled and even uneasy, but continues doling out the drugs. Doctor knows best, especially SS Doctor.

It's strange how, as the weeks pass and she's not discovered, Gabi begins to feel, not just more secure, but as if she actually is the person she's impersonating. There's no pause before she answers when "Sister Frieda!" is called, no sudden lurch of panic when Mother Superior makes her rounds, the crucified Jesus lulled on her expansive bosom, a sheaf of forms rustling in her hand, the pince-nez firmly clipped upon her nose. It's almost as though Gabi has sloughed her past like a snake its skin, and now this new one will be all she has. Sometimes she imagines herself living like that for years, for all her life perhaps, and being buried in some Lutheran cemetery, a second Frieda Brandt. And yet she knows her security is fragile and temporary, sooner or later the truth will out, and the safer she feels, the greater the risk she'll let down her guard, make some chance remark and suddenly betray herself. So she still sleeps with a handkerchief stuffed in her mouth, which makes her throat as rough and dry as sandpaper.

And the dream still visits her three nights out of four. But now it's changed. Now Constable Bolzner marches straight past her because he doesn't see she's there. No accusation, no reproach. Just the four of them following him hand in hand, disappearing behind an iron door that clangs shut and awakens her as her scream used to before. It's not discovery she fears now, she realizes, but the fate of her family. Did the police and the Gestapo believe she killed herself? Did they interrogate Willibald and the children? Torture them, even? Send them to a concentration camp? Suppose she survives and they do not? Every time those thoughts occur to her, as they do at least ten times a day, her stomach curdles and she knows she should have taken her sister Frieda's path, or like Fraülein Goldberg tamely gone to Linz.

If only she could get news of them! If only she could unburden herself to someone! If only, she sometimes madly thinks, her confidante Sara was there! She's been past Fraülein von Adler's on every one of her half days off duty, but the sentries still stand there and there's not a civilian in sight. And she dares not inquire in case Fraülein von Adler has been arrested and they're watching the house. Besides, the growing confidence with which she's Sister Frieda Brandt in the hospital evaporates outside, where there's always the chance some casual visitor from Heimstatt or thereabouts might chance along and recognize her. She keeps her head lowered and hurries back to the hospital.

Where on her seventh day off she's met by Mother Superior, who still has her papers and passport (that is, Frieda's) locked up in her desk drawer. *Oh God, this is it!* Gabi thinks as Mother Superior asks her into her room. *They've found out.* She feels she's gulping for air as though she's suffocating. But Mother Superior is alone—that's reassuring—and she closes the door before she speaks. "Sister Frieda, you look so sad, and you must be very lonely. You have no friends here in Graunau? No? Perhaps—you lost everything in Dresden, after all—perhaps, you'd like to talk to Father Johannes?"

"Father Johannes?"

"It sometimes helps to talk when things are on your mind," she says with the placidity of one who knows that clichés only become so because they're true. "Yes, Father Johannes, our confessor. Of course he'd never divulge whatever you told him," she adds, holding Gabi's gaze. "That is between you and God."

"But I'm not a Catholic."

"I know," Mother Superior says, looking as if that isn't all she knows. "That doesn't matter. It's just if you want to talk to someone, that's all. Only if you want . . . You could say whatever was on your mind to him, I mean. If anything is on your mind? Father Johannes is a German from Latvia, you see. He talks to the Russians as well. He's not . . ." She hesitates for several seconds, not as though she's lost for a word, more as though she's wondering whether to risk saying it. "He's not like Sister Brigitte," she says at last, looking Gabi straight in the eye again. "He doesn't share her . . . interests."

Gabi promises to think about it, and she does. By now she knows what one of Sister Brigitte's interests is, but surely that can't be the one Mother Superior was alluding to. On her afternoons off, Brigitte, as she asks Gabi to call her now (and she calls Gabi Frieda), paints her lips a brilliant red and powders her face and even puts bright red varnish on her nails. It's the same on her alternate Sundays off—Sabbatarianism's certainly not her thing. And when she returns late at night, her face looks different, with rosy cheeks and a glistening light in her slate-blue eyes.

Presumably that's an interest Father Johannes doesn't share with Sister Brigitte. But Gabi's sure it's not his chastity Mother Superior was getting at. It must be his political views she had in mind. And so, after two nights in which Gabi repeatedly dreams of that iron door clanging shut behind the four of us, she forces her trembling body to Father Johannes' door in the German soldiers' wing of the hospital. The German soldiers, she notes as she passes the wards, get rather better treatment than their captive foes. But that, she supposes, is what it's all about.

She has to wait. After five minutes or so, a young soldier with a bandage round one eye comes out. He's sniffing his nose and rubbing the other eye with his wrist exactly as though he's been crying, except that German soldiers never cry. He walks past her with hunched shoulders. Already another two young soldiers are waiting beside her on the bench, keeping a shy, respectful distance from the nursing sister. "You're next, Sister," one of them politely says, nodding at the open door.

Father Johannes has a samovar in his room, as did Gabi's father in the palmy pre–Great War days of old Berlin. Somehow that gives her the confidence to speak. She never could keep her own counsel for long, and now Father Johannes becomes to her here what Sara used to be in Heimstatt. Out her pent-up story floods with scarcely a pause for breath. As she rushes not very coherently on, Father Johannes, who'd be no balder if he was tonsured, but has a compensating thick grey beard, leaves his desk and comes to sit beside her, tufty eyebrows raised like perfect prickly Roman arches. She ends in tears, sobbing that she must have caused the death of her own husband and children.

The old priest takes her hand, pats it, then hastily lays it down as if recalling his vows. "It may not be so bad," he says, huffing and wheezing. "They may all be all right."

This doesn't reassure her. "Couldn't you write to them in Heimstatt and find out what's happened?"

Father Johannes fingers his beard with a bemused look as

though wondering what this hairy excrescence is up to growing out of his chin like that. "Their mail might be opened," he says, glancing up to heaven, or possibly just the ceiling.

"I could go and ask a Lutheran minister here?" Gabi suggests doubtfully. "They might have heard something."

"No, no! Some of them are *German* Christians," Father Johannes replies hastily, with an emphasis on "German" that makes it sound like blasphemy. "Besides, you might be recognized. No, you must stay here in the hospital. In fact, you must come to mass every Sunday."

For a moment Gabi wonders if this is a subtle play for her conversion to popery, and considers telling Father Johannes she no longer believes in any god, Catholic or Protestant. After all, she plausibly reasons, if God existed, Hitler wouldn't.

"It's for your own good," he goes on. "God will forgive you. You mustn't stick out, you know. You must be like all the others. Then they won't suspect you. Who would expect to find a Jew taking Holy Communion?"

"But my family!" she starts sobbing again. "I must know what's happened to them!"

"Shh! Shh!" Father Johannes murmurs, glancing towards the door. "We must find another way."

"And I've already told Mother Superior I'm a Lutheran!"

"Mother Superior will understand. In fact I think she understands already."

And so next Sunday Gabi takes her first communion with nurses and soldiers in the makeshift Catholic chapel of the military wing in the hospital, which, incidentally, the Americans are now only ten miles away from (they can hear the guns). Lucky for her, she can follow the others and doesn't bungle the rituals. And the wafer doesn't taste too bad, although she wonders why only the priest gets to taste the wine. She even makes a decent show of crossing herself.

But Catholic rituals are not the only things she's got to learn that day. She must also find out when the singing has to stop.

■

Returning to the prisoners' ward, she finds the English chaplain John holding his own customary service, to which today for some reason a few of the atheistic communist Russians are peripherally drawn. Those who can still walk, that is. They stand on the edge of the group watching the peculiar rites of their capitalist allies with dark attentive eyes. And at the ragged and fairly tuneless rendering of "Abide with Me" which concludes the service, a couple of them start humming the melody in voices that suggest they could be members of the Russian army choir.

Somehow one thing leads to another and before long a regular allied concert gets going, each nation singing its national folk songs. "Frère Jacques," which everyone seems to know, is followed by a monotonous English dirge about a bachelor and the foggy foggy dew, which Chaplain John ostentatiously does not join in and Gabi finds incomprehensible as she goes about her nursing duties. She assumes it concerns the notoriously rheumy English weather. What the French or Russians make of it she cannot guess, but they certainly seem as mystified as she is. Then the Russians start on a predictably melancholic song in which the two possibly army choir singers let themselves go like tragic opera stars.

Suddenly the door crashes open and Major Friedländer makes an entrance in full voice himself, although it's not a very tuneful one. The other voices die away like guns on Armistice Day, except that peace is the last thing on Major Friedländer's mind. "Sister Frieda! This is scandalous! Why are you permitting these prisoners to sing their national anthems? Don't you know the Führer has expressly forbidden it?"

"But they're not their national anthems, Herr Major," Gabi timidly answers. "They're only folk songs."

"How do you know what they are? Besides whatever they are, they're not to sing them, is that understood? It's a kind of resistance! If they're well enough to sing, they're well enough to go back to work."

Gabi nods submissively. "I'm sorry, Herr Major."

Major Friedländer approaches her now and addresses her in a low gritty tone. "I shall be watching your conduct very closely from now on, Sister Frieda. This is not what I expect from a German nurse. It's not what I expect at all." He nods twice to drive the point home, turns and leaves the ward. He's so angry, he forgets to say "Heil Hitler!"

And Gabi realizes her guard has slipped, she's nearly given herself away. Major Friedländer has only to start asking questions about her papers and she'll be done for. She continues her work mechanically, her head reading temperatures and registering pulses while in her stomach the sickening drums of fear pursue their soft insistent beat. And the silent glances of the prisoners express a kind of guilty sympathy, as if they're thinking of the previous nurse, Sister Astrid, who's now a prisoner herself, but in a concentration camp.

The national singing stops, but the vernacular groaning of the dying carries on. The Führer hasn't forbidden that—quite the contrary, he's all in favor. And it's Alain the poet or pilot whose groans are worst, awakened as he is from morphined dreams to find there's no more morphine to be had, and consequently no more dreams.

"Let me hear a French poem," he begs in a pain-thickened voice—or that's what Gabi thinks he begs, and subsequent events bear out her hypothesis. "If I'm not going to see France again, at least let me hear a French poem." There are tears rimming his eyes, which slowly overflow and trickle down onto his grubby pillow (the laundry gets done once a fortnight now, if that). He tries to sit up. Roger, his older friend, assists him. Others gather round the bed and help. Then Roger recites a poem, which he says is called "L'automne," in a low voice that sometimes wobbles but never quite breaks down.

Before the last verse, Alain's eyes have closed, and so have his tear ducts. So, in fact, has everything else except his bowels, which last a little longer. But Roger continues as though Alain is still listening, down to the last line: *And summer passes as a friend departs.*

They lay Alain gently down and Gabi closes his eyes, holding her breath with professional detachment against the putrefaction of his gangrene and the stench of his shit. Then she notes the time of death on his record and summons the orderlies to take him away. Roger goes with him until the sentry bars his way at the courtyard door. No one knows where Alain's buried, or if he's buried at all, but that's not surprising—the gravediggers can't keep up as the air raids begin in earnest and the rumble of artillery fire grows steadily louder like an approaching thunderstorm, except the skies are clear. Clear, that is, of everything except American planes which strafe and bomb the city every day and almost every night.

The prisoners are locked in, but those that can walk stagger into the basement when the bombs start falling closer. The bedridden have to take their chance upstairs. "They haven't got much chance anyway," Brigitte says with a resigned shrug. Her half-day outings have ended, but she's almost as happy as before. When they're both down in the basement, she leans her head close to Gabi's and whispers that her boyfriend's been sent to the front, "But when he comes back, we're going to . . ." The rest is lost in a shattering explosion that makes the walls shudder, and she covers her head with her hands.

Gabi's frightened in the air raids, which are far worse than anything she went through in Berlin. She tries to soothe her thumping heart by telling herself they mean the war will soon be over. But what use will that be if they kill her first? She wants the bombs to fall, but not on her. She's caught between begging God—yes, she too invokes that great myth again now—to end the raids and begging Him to make them worse so that it will all be over before Major Friedländer can catch her out.

After the next raid the roof is on fire. It's the prisoners who put out the flames. The guards are too busy looking after their own damage to bother with the prisoners unless they're trying to escape. The one-legged Russian almost dances on his crutches when he sees the sooty hole in the ceiling of the main ward. Two bedridden prisoners are cut and burnt, but they're past caring now anyway, and past caring for.

The thunder of the guns creeps nearer and so do the refugees—endless harassed columns of them straggling through Graunau before the advancing Americans. The men are old and round-shouldered, the women gaunt and anxious, the children puling and scared. All of them are shabby. They don't look much like the master race now. "Deutschland kaput!" the one-legged Russian keeps whispering to Gabi, thumping his crutch gleefully on the floor, nodding and winking manically before swinging away. "Deutschland kaput!"

Flu breaks out among the refugee children, and their distraught mothers have to leave six of them behind in the hospital while they themselves are chivvied on by officials who don't want them in the place when the siege begins—there isn't enough food as it is for those who are needed there to throw the enemy back from the Thousand Year Reich's proud three-rivered city. But the children aren't admitted to the German soldiers' wing—the last thing the commanders want is a flu epidemic among the convalescent cannon fodder needed for the coming battle. So into the prisoners' ward come the sickly children. It doesn't matter if they spread their bugs round there. In fact it might be an advantage.

The children are kept in the far end of the ward, away from the contamination of the prisoners and the broken ceiling, but some of the prisoners haven't seen a child for four years and the walking wounded cluster round them like iron filings round a collection of pretty magnets. Sister Brigitte and Gabi try to shush them away, but it's hopeless, they are always drawn back, and eventually the two nurses realize they can use the prisoners to do the simple work they have no time to do themselves. Chaplain John empties a chamber pot, Roger makes a bed, one of the Russian singers sponges the children's faces and hands.

One by one the children fade away from malnutrition and the flu's pneumonic complications. And in the dying room another prisoner gives up the ghost to untreated gangrene.

As the children grow weaker and more feverish, the prisoners devise ways to amuse them. They make shadow animals on the walls with their hands and tell them stories they don't understand. The Russians clown about, the English try cat's cradle with a piece of string. Roger the Frenchman recites French nursery rhymes. Some of the children smile, others regard them forlornly with frightened hopeless eyes. When all else fails, the prisoners hold the children's hands and stroke their hair. Only when Major Friedländer appears do they grudgingly retreat, but they advance again as soon as he is gone. And even Sister Brigitte connives at their strategy. She can't deny they're good for the children. As for Major Friedländer, his stony face shows pity and dismay as he bends over the dying boys and girls, and Gabi thinks she detects doubt in his veiled eyes at last. Providence shouldn't be letting this happen to Aryan children, she can see him thinking. Especially when racially inferior specimens manage to survive.

So Nazis too suffer crises of faith.

The children's lungs clog up, their fever rises and they struggle for breath. Roger is the most adept of the prisoners and soon Gabi and Brigitte gratefully allow him to make the hot poultices and lay them on the children's fragile chests. All to no avail. Their breathing becomes faster and shallower, their cheeks more flushed, their eyes more glassy. Major Friedländer comes round twice a day now and the prisoners know when to make their strategic withdrawals.

"Herr Major," Gabi tentatively suggests, thinking of her own children and what she's brought them through before, "if oxygen was possible?"

"D'you think I haven't thought of that, Sister Frieda?" Major Friedländer snaps. His temper's getting tauter by the day. "All the oxygen here is reserved for military use." And yet he breaks or bends the rules to order a couple of cylinders in from the stores where they are being preserved for the revival of adult Aryan cannon fodder. Saving the children has become his mission, as though the future of the Aryan race depended on their survival, and his mission improbably unites him not only with his two nurses, but with his despised prisoners as well. He scarcely glances at the progress of the patients on his experimental drugs now, most of whom in any case are dying faster than the ones that aren't.

Sister Brigitte loses her habitual casual indifference and works herself almost to death nursing the children all the way to theirs. But it's Sister Frieda who Major Friedländer notices has the surer touch. "You seem better with children than with prisoners," he says abruptly to Gabi. "Did you work in the children's ward in Dresden? Was Professor Braun still there when it was bombed?"

"Er, I'm not sure," Gabi murmurs, flustered. "I . . . I don't remember, I mean."

"Not sure?" Major Friedländer's tired eyes harden slightly.

"You don't remember?" He views her coldly a moment, then turns away. Gabi's stomach churns. She thinks of Frieda's papers in Mother Superior's desk drawer. She sees the outdated passport with its not very resembling photo. She sees Major Friedländer half-sitting on Mother Superior's desk, studying the photo with an interrogative frown, his high peaked cap thrown arrogantly on her empty chair. She sees him picking up the phone . . .

But other things preoccupy the Major's mind just now. Even with oxygen the children keep dying. First the young ones go, then one after another the older ones as well. They are too thin, too weak, too frightened perhaps, to cling on for long. Even Hansi, the oldest at six, is slipping painfully away. Roger has become his special friend. Scared of the oxygen mask, Hansi won't wear it unless Roger holds his hand. When Major Friedländer finds the Frenchman by Hansi's bed, he orders him curtly and even suspiciously away. What could a treacherous Frenchman want with an Aryan child? But Hansi struggles to pull off the mask and whimpers feebly when the Frenchman's gone. "That's the denial of life you see there," Major Friedländer observes grimly. "Tie him down." But instead Sister Brigitte marches Roger firmly back under Major Friedländer's nose and places Hansi's wasted burning hand in his. Now Hansi accepts the oxygen, but life itself is just too much for him. Major Friedländer *humphs!* and turns away, his face itself a mask behind which who knows what is going on. And who knows what is going on for that matter behind Sister Brigitte's narrowed eyes?

The oxygen hisses peacefully into Hansi's nose, but Hansi's lungs have had enough and so has Hansi. He dies a couple of hours later, his frail hand still clasped in Roger's, oblivious of the continual window-rattling *Crrump-crrump!* of shellfire, at which the prisoners, those that are conscious, cock their ears to estimate how near the Amis are by now.

While the oxygen cylinders are rolled back into the storeroom, the children are laid out in white (well, nearly white) hospital gowns, awaiting transport to the graveyard, or wherever they'll be put. In each one's stiffening clasped hands a makeshift wooden cross is placed, made by the atheistic Russians of all people, out of laths that fell from the damaged roof. And Chaplain John holds his single arm out over them and commends their souls to the Lord, who certainly hasn't done much for their bodies.

This is a funny old war, Gabi might think if she was given to the English style of humor and didn't have more serious things to think about. One of which is how we all are—

19

Back in Heimstatt

If indeed we all still are there, or, come to that, are anywhere at all. She visits Father Johannes after the next Sunday mass, at which she almost feels she now belongs. So much so that she wonders as she receives her wafer why in her youth she'd agonized with Maria about becoming a Christian. These faiths are all the same, she thinks as she chews and swallows. A bit of ritual, a bit of prayer, a bit of hymn singing and some obscure and sacred book. Choosing which one to follow is no different from choosing which dress to wear, and she never cared much about that anyway. In fact, if she had time or interest enough to pursue the analogy, she'd probably say she was a nudist now as far as all that went.

Father Johannes's samovar is bubbling and he offers her tea, but nothing in the way of news. All he can do in that direction is pluck at the strands of his beard as if at a hairy harp and murmur that it's too dangerous to ask, and anyway he'd heard that whole area was now a battle zone. That's hardly comforting, and she's still got Major Friedländer's suspicions to deal with here in Graunau.

A few days later, Mother Superior calls her into her office

again, and as usual on such occasions Gabi's stomach flips over. She half expects to see Major Friedländer there, examining her passport with a supercilious and cruelly knowing smile. But Mother Superior is alone again, her placidity unruffled. "If anyone asks for your papers, Sister Frieda, just say that you left them with me. I have unfortunately mislaid them." She raises her hand. "Yes, I know. Major Friedländer. He has been asking certain questions, but I think I've set his mind at rest for the present. The war, you know, is not going well. Even the children . . ."

"We did what we could for them," Gabi apologizes uneasily, as if Mother Superior is blaming her for all their deaths. She knows she should be thanking her for her subtly coded message and the protection it implies, but she senses indirectness is the order here, words that don't incriminate, that leave no evidential trace.

"Yes, I know," Mother Superior answers, gazing away out of the window as she absently touches the crucifix on her breast. "Perhaps—I sometimes think—you even did too much. In such a world as this, I mean, perhaps it's better if they go to heaven sooner."

Does she really believe in heaven? Gabi finds herself wondering. *What does she think it's like?* She examines the dimples Mother Superior's pince-nez has left on her nose but finds no answer in those shallow pip-shaped indentations.

Mother Superior sighs and shifts her chair back to get at a key hanging from a ring at her ample waist. "I'm storing some basic medicines in that cupboard in the corner," she says more briskly now. "I want you to have a spare key in case something happens to me. We must think of such things now. Hide it somewhere and tell the English chaplain where it is, in case something happens to you. But don't tell him anything more than that. The less everyone knows, the better."

When she leaves Mother Superior's office Gabi doesn't know at first whether her fears have been lessened or increased. Major Friedländer's been asking questions, but Mother Superior's put him off. He might ask further questions, but the war isn't going well. She's been entrusted with a key to the medicines in case something happens to Mother Superior, but she must tell Chaplain John in case something happens to herself—so perhaps something will. No, she finds as she walks across the courtyard, her fears have not been lessened. Her quietly churning stomach tells her they've been boundlessly increased. It can only be a matter of time now before she's discovered, and then—she glances at the currently indifferent sentries at the door, who give her a familiar nod. Unless the Amis capture Graunau first. She prays to the God she no longer believes in to let the Amis get there soon.

And how is she going to translate what Mother Superior wants her say to Chaplain John, she wonders anxiously as she enters the prisoners' ward. Her English isn't up to it. "There are many medicines in the box in the room of the Mother," is the best she can manage. "The key stands in my yellow case. The yellow case is in the room of the nurses."

But Chaplain John seems to understand. At least, he nods his head several times and murmurs, "Oh yes, very good."

But seeming's not enough. She's got to make sure. So she leads him to the room and points to the yellow case under her bed. Chaplain John murmurs, "Very good," again, but there's a puzzled and even mildly apprehensive look in his eyes, as though he's wondering what she's really up to. Can it be the bed he's contemplating, not the case beneath it? There's no time to resolve this matter in her lame and halting English because the sirens have started and they can already hear the drone of Ami bombers.

Down to the basement they scurry, leaving the bedridden

patients to gaze up at the shuddering ceiling with anxious eyes and wait for it to fall.

Mother Superior must have a line to God, or perhaps she's been listening black, because this raid is the beginning of the battle for Graunau, and the raids are almost continuous now.

Soon the Amis' artillery starts ranging on the city's walls as well.

Only in brief lulls can Gabi and Sister Brigitte go up to check the bedridden prisoners and give what little care they can. The walls tremble, the ceiling snows grey plaster over the patients and their beds, food is irregular and meager, but deaths are not. Yet the hospital somehow stands intact. Are the Amis considerately leaving it alone? Or is it just haphazard marksmanship?

Outside in the city, buildings collapse and the dead pile up. No time now for individual burials, one of the sentries says; paraffin-soaked corpses are burned in rubbish dumps en masse. The Russian crutch-dancer seems to have gone right off his head, screaming "Deutschland kaput! Deutschland kaput!" all the time now, and his comrade choristers have to hide his crutches to prevent him from hopping with his war cry out into the courtyard, where the sentries might well shoot him.

Sister Brigitte's pretty face grows every day more tense and haggard under the constant bombardment, her clear complexion grey and smudged. Her Aryan confidence leaches clean away, and she sits with her head in her hands in the darkened basement while the ground shakes beneath her, addressing muttered prayers to God now, not the Führer. And Gabi? Gabi has retreated into a cave deep inside herself, where she lives alone with the dank cold smell of fear. She listens to the thudding of her heart, which mimics the thumping of the shells and bombs, licks her lips and swallows, waiting trembling for the end.

And all the time the hospital loudspeakers keep up a flow of patriotic hymns, punctuated by stirring announcements of new

German victorious withdrawals and pledges of ever-firmer German resolve. The last of these comes one evening a week later, when the loudspeakers play "Deutschland Über Alles" and Major Friedländer's solemn voice declares:

> *In spite of our forces' glorious resistance, the enemy has made a temporary advance. Without doubt the enormous losses inflicted on him will weaken his strength and the coming counter-attack will throw him back in disorder, but in the meantime Graunau must be prepared for a siege. Bridges and roads leading to the city will be destroyed, to halt the enemy's progress. Our forces will fight with fanatical resolve to defend the city. Please go into your shelters at once and await further announcements. Graunau will remain German forever! Heil Hitler!*

But Sister Brigitte does not proudly raise her resolute Aryan head at this brave talk. It droops still more, in fact, like a flag of surrender. Is she thinking of her boyfriend fighting and possibly dying fanatically at the front, or remembering Sister Astrid, the nurse she shopped for defeatist talk?

For two days there's no more food and not much water, but there's still plenty of gunfire and bombing. Two more of the bed patients die and have to be carted down to the courtyard in the dark by the four men who can still lift them. What happens to them after that nobody knows, but next morning they're gone. Then Father Johannes, emerging in a brief lull like a dusty badger from his lair in the other wing, announces Major Friedländer has gone too.

"Where to?" Gabi asks with a sudden small hope flickering in her chest.

Father Johannes shrugs, "Disappeared," and returns to his lair as the sirens start their wrenching wail again.

Yet another disappearance.

But the very next morning there comes a silence that goes on and on, almost more menacing than the barrage they've grown used to. No one can say when it began, but after dawn everyone is listening to it with raised heads, waiting for it to be broken by another barrage still worse than all that they've endured so far, or perhaps by the rattle of rifle and machine-gun fire and the shouts of the attacking Amis. But the silence holds and holds. And holds.

Eventually the Frenchman Roger clambers upstairs, out into the dazzling light of the courtyard. The sentries are gone. He walks cautiously and with weak unsteady steps to the hospital entrance, and sees white flags floating over the ruined buildings of the city, and not a soldier in sight.

"C'est fini! C'est fini!" he croaks down into the basement. And one by one they come out blinking into the bright May morning sunlight to view the ravaged countenance of peace.

■

They stand about in the courtyard, uncertain and uneasy.

"Where are the Amis?"

"Why don't they come?"

"Are they going to leave us here till we starve to death?"

"All they think of is themselves."

Some talk of going out into the city to look for food, but they've been locked up so long they've lost the habit of freedom, and besides they're too feeble to wander far and might get lost or even shot by some idiot on one side or the other. Chaplain John cautiously enters the German soldiers' ward and finds it full of hungry wounded men who wear the subdued look of prisoners already, although they are not yet. A nurse rises from her desk at the end of the ward, and then sits down again. Unsure of the etiquette now, she continues counting out tablets into symmetrical little heaps on a metal tray as though nothing has changed. "Very good, very good," Chaplain John murmurs reassuringly and leaves, as uncertain as she is.

Meanwhile his services are required for another patient dying in the prisoners' ward. It's an English airman with a broken back who's never spoken since he's been there and now departs with wildly gleaming eyes and an incoherent flutter in his throat. Chaplain John murmurs a prayer so generalized it will do for any creed or none, and Gabi notices that Sister Brigitte is sniffing back tears as she closes the Englishman's eyes. Tears for the Englishman, the Fatherland's defeat, her past behavior, the likely fate of her German lover, or just the damned perverseness of the world? All five, perhaps. It's a lot for her to deal with.

As for Gabi, she suddenly gives up. She sits outside on the courtyard steps, her leg shaking uncontrollably as if she's got Parkinson's. And some muscle in her paralyzed cheek keeps flickering uselessly in unison with her leg. She's eaten nothing for two and a half days, but feels as heavy as a corpse. *They'll all be dead,* she's thinking. *I'll go there and open the door and walk in and they'll all be dead.* And every time the words sound through her head, she sees a different picture of our deaths. She sees us shot, she sees us hanged, she sees our emaciated corpses lying on bare boards, she sees us laid out on our separate beds in the Pfarrhaus. She screws her eyes shut to squeeze the pictures out of her mind. But it's like closing your fist on water. They slip away and immediately come flowing back. She almost wishes the guns were still firing, so that she could suffer the endurable fear for herself instead of this unendurable fear for us which has taken its place.

And then at last the Amis come.

The first American she ever sees is a giant black soldier driving a camouflaged Jeep at eleven minutes past twelve that morning (she glances at the watch she keeps pinned to her uniform). Next to him sits a white officer who would appear a giant as well but for the black soldier beside him. As the officer climbs out of the Jeep, unfolding himself and stretching, another Jeep follows, from which four more giant Ami soldiers casually remove themselves, carrying carbines as if they were golf clubs and they were off to play a round somewhere. They hitch their weapons onto their shoulders, lean back against the Jeep, adjust their helmets to a rakish angle and, feeding wafers of chewing gum from colored wrappers into their mouths, survey the silent prisoners, who cautiously survey them back. The officer drags a cigar out of his tunic pocket, inspects it, rolls it between his fingers, sniffs it, bites off the tip and spits it to the ground, then finally lights it with a heavy metal lighter. He draws several deep breaths on it, examines the glowing end to make sure it's really going, then exhales a long blue funnel of fragrant smoke. "Any you guys speak English?" he drawls at last.

Chaplain John nods, clears his throat and confesses that he does.

"You a Brit?" the officer inquires, narrowing his eyes behind the haze of blue smoke that's drifting up over his face. His tone suggests he might be harking back to the War of Independence.

Chaplain John admits he is. As the Ami doesn't answer, John further confides that he's a chaplain. "Chaplin?" the Ami says, "That your name? Like Charlie?"

"My profession," Chaplain John corrects him mildly, and then corrects himself. "My vocation."

"Profession, huh?" the Ami repeats, ignoring Chaplain John's more refined job description. He considers Chaplain John for some seconds, then shoves himself away from the Jeep with a sigh. "OK, Mr. Chaplain, d'you wanna show us around?"

Despite its syntax, John correctly interprets this sentence as more of a command than an inquiry, and the tour begins. "So what happened to your arm?" the Ami asks as they head into the prisoners' ward. "Krauts cut it off?"

It's not until the following day that the Amis' medical team arrives to take over the hospital. In the meantime the Russian crutch-dancer has died, toppling backwards down the stairs and fracturing his skull. "Deutschland kaput!" he'd been crowing triumphantly as he hoisted himself precariously up on his crutches. "Deutschland kaput!" He'd reached the top stair when his crutch skidded on a wet patch from the rain that had leaked through the Ami-damaged roof.

The medical team swiftly asserts victors' rights and the German patients are transferred to the prisoners' ward, while the prisoners are transferred to the more commodious Germans'. Nobody objects to this arrangement; but Sister Brigitte and the few surviving capable prisoners, who by now have eaten three square Ami meals, spend half the day cleaning the floors and making the beds before the Germans arrive. This generosity is too much for Gabi, who has more to forgive than the prisoners, and she takes no part in it. Besides, she's thinking of Heimstatt.

"You could help, Frieda," Brigitte remonstrates. "It's for our boys, after all."

"They're not my boys," Gabi coldly replies.

"What d'you mean, they're not your boys?" Brigitte starts indignantly.

"I mean I'm Jewish. And as a matter of fact my name's not Frieda, either."

Poor Brigitte. She's just got too much to deal with now and can only stand and gape.

A Captain Morris appears the next day. Father Johannes and Mother Superior have spoken to the Amis' Catholic padre, who studied in Heidelberg before the war and speaks German like an American. The padre has spoken to Captain Morris. "As a polidically purrsecuded purrson, you have top prioridy," Captain Morris, who speaks English like an American from the Bronx, tells Gabi.

Gabi doesn't understand his swift delivery or nasal accent, let alone the words they decorate, and merely smiles and shrugs. "We'll take you back to Heimsdad tomorrow," Captain Morris continues.

"Heimsdad tomorrow" she does after some effort understand, and at once she feels the returning traveller's panic sink its claws into her heart. What will she find when she arrives? She almost asks Captain Morris for a week's delay to prepare herself, but she doesn't know how, and besides she knows she can't prepare herself however long she waits.

The next morning Father Johannes shakes her hand with one of his and plucks his beard with the other, while Mother Superior clasps both her hands in both of hers and tells her to come back and see them all when she can. Chaplain John, having only one hand, extends that to her formally and remarks he always thought there was something funny going on, which bemused Gabi ascribes to the eccentric English sense of humor. Captain Morris drops her battered yellow case into the back of the jeep, and Gabi suddenly finds she's crying as they drive out of the courtyard and she waves a jerky goodbye, bouncing over the holes and displaced cobblestones. Can it be she's actually sad to leave them all, even Brigitte, who half waves back among the ex-prisoners and blinks her still bewildered eyes but hasn't dared shake her hand and perhaps still doesn't want to? Or is it just the agony of anticipation, dread of the looming unknown? They're already passing the gutted railway station when she remembers

Mother Superior's key still tucked into the little pocket inside her case. Now she has a reason to return, and that is strangely comforting, Or perhaps not so strangely, she reflects. By now that might indeed be all she's got left in the world.

The road back to Heimstatt leads through scenes of desolation or summery peace, depending how the war has cut its swath. One village a grimly smoking ruin, the next smiling in the fragrant May sunshine, with placid women leading placid cows home from their placid fields. Children stare or wave or sometimes jeer. Only the men are missing. In the towns the roads are clogged with trucks from different armies, the Russians mainly heading east, the Amis mainly west. But here and there trucks push wildly against the national direction, like frantic ants that have lost their way. The opposing allies view each other warily, like bear and buffalo lowering their heads at the same watering hole.

It's in those towns and cities that Gabi sees the true harvest of the battle. Their homes destroyed, people sit apathetically on rubble at the street corners, hunched over their salvaged belongings, watching the conquerors' procession with numbed and hungry eyes. Some of the older ones are begging, but shamefacedly and by fits and starts. They're new to this trade and haven't learnt it yet. Perhaps they never will. Those that learn it best are the young girls in flimsy frocks who cluster round the Amis' trucks whenever they halt, giggling and begging for cigarettes and chocolate. Some are getting a stern cold brush-off. Others are getting everything, even nylons, and perhaps giving something as well. But hardly any of them beg from the Russians.

They reach Linz in the evening. Captain Morris drives up to the fanciest hotel, which a few short weeks ago would have thrown her out if she'd dared so much as show her Jewish face inside the door, leans over the reception desk, blows a funnel of blue cigar smoke into the aged clerk's face and orders the best room for Gabi. In the long soft twilight she stands on the balcony and looks out over the city where the former Gestapo Headquarters' once racially pure portals are being contaminated by young black soldiers chuckling in their slow honeyed voices as they swing in and out, dumping boxes of Gestapo files onto a waiting truck. There goes Gabi's file, which is still open, did she but know it, and there goes Frau Professor Goldberg's, which is closed. There goes Fraülein von Adler's, who's just been found alive in Mauthausen Concentration Camp; there goes blind Tante Helga's, who will never know how close she came—a few more weeks and she'd have gone there too. And there go Ilse's war-widowed-teachers' files, Frau Professor Zauner's and Frau Professor Lambach's, whom the Tommies have just found alive in Belsen, but only just alive. Naive though Gabi is, the irony might not be lost on her, did she but know what was going on. But she merely gazes out over the city in abstracted ignorance thinking fearfully of Heimstatt, which she's bound to reach tomorrow.

■

Where we awoke a week before to see Austrian flags flapping in the balmy breeze and my first thought was *Does that mean I can go to school again?* And just about my only thought, because I was too weak to think much more. As were all the others—even Martin now, who'd just walked forty miles without sleep or food to put his glorious military career behind him. He's lying in bed resting his blistered feet and blistered soul while Ilse, Sara and I are dragging ourselves to and from the lake gathering armfuls of nettles for our daily soup. Peace has not changed that. In fact we scarcely know what it has changed. I don't think of Gabi anymore, and nor does Sara. As far as we're concerned, she's gone. I don't know about the others.

As we're struggling slowly back with our daily nettle ration, I lethargically notice an Ami Jeep (I've seen a few of them already), jolting along the road. It stops outside the Pfarrhaus. An Ami officer gets out (I've seen a few of them already too) together with a nurse. *Father's ill,* I think. Or rather, since I know he's ill, *Father's dying.* Something prevents me from telling Sara and Ilse, who are trailing laboriously behind me. Some fear perhaps of being the messenger of bad tidings. Or else the thought that saying it would make it true. We plod on, and I let myself fall back behind them. I don't want to be the first to see my father dead or dying. Or perhaps it's only Martin, I now more hopefully think. He'd like a nurse for his blisters. By now Ilse and Sara have noticed the Jeep too, in which the officer is leaning back smoking a cigarette. But they haven't noticed the nurse, because she isn't there to be noticed.

She's inside the house, walking from living room to dining room, from dining room to kitchen. Everywhere she finds is empty and still. As still as the tomb, she apprehensively thinks. At last she pushes the study door open and sees an aged ghost of Willibald sitting at the desk, his heavy head propped on his spindly arms. "Ilse?" the ghost feebly asks, then slowly turns his head. "You!" he now exclaims, startled into not entirely joyful life.

"Are you all alive?" is Gabi's tense but practical response. Only when he weakly nods does her body start to tremble and let go. She could almost love the man again for that one nod. In fact she does try to embrace him, but it's so long since they've touched each other that it feels like two bare branches clashing in the wind, and she's as relieved as he is when they hear the noise outside and separate. A crowd has begun to gather, through which Ilse, Sara and I are now threading our slow and anxious way. Fritzi Wimmer, wearing a black armband as I do, says "It's your mum," which makes no sense at all to me. Then the nurse appears at the door. "I'm back," she says, holding out her arms.

I'm terrified. I'm scared of ghosts. I don't know what Sara feels, but I do know neither of us moves. We aren't prepared for this, we don't know what to do. It's quiet Ilse who saves the day. She walks forward, dragging her foot, and in her low flat voice says, "We've been picking nettles." What she doesn't say is that she's just gone blind in her left eye, the moment she saw her mother.

Gabi embraces her awkwardly—after all, there's quite a crowd watching now—and comes down the steps to Sara and me. I still don't know about Sara, but myself, I'm no less scared now than I was ten seconds ago. I let myself be held and hugged, but then I mutter "Mind the nettles," and follow Ilse with them into the kitchen. Soon Sara joins us, and we take longer than we need to lay them on the table. Neither Sara nor I seem eager to go back to face the resurrection, and neither of us speaks of it. Are we shy, or just incredulous? Both, of course. We're going through what the disciples went through in the Bible, and believe me, that's not easy.

"I'll make the soup," Ilse says, and starts washing the nettles. That lets her off the hook, but we're still wriggling. We know we ought to go back and show some emotion, but the fact is all we feel is shock. I'm not even sure whether I should take my black armband off or not. How do I know this is the real Gabi that's suddenly appeared, and not some look-alike impostor? How will I ever know?

Meanwhile Gabi is bidding goodbye to Captain Morris in a mixture of sign language, German and English. "Pleasure to be of surrvice," he says as he starts the Jeep engine. "Hope we'll meed again someday." And who knows, perhaps they will.

■

This ought to be the end of the story. And in a novel I suppose it would be. Life however's not so tidy. The guns have stopped firing, yes, and the dead have been buried (or in at least ten million cases not). But among the survivors are the walking wounded, those whose—

20

Scars will never heal

True, we've all survived the war, but first of all we're starving now, except Gabi, who's had solid German soldier's food for months. And secondly she may have just come back from the dead, but we're all stunned and disbelieving. She was dead and now she's not. That takes some getting used to.

At least Martin takes it all in his stride, if that can be said of someone who can scarcely stand for blisters. Not unnaturally he attributes Gabi's safe return to his own strategic planning, which is more or less true. And not uncharacteristically he assumes that now she's back she'll look after all his needs again, except those that only blonde Aryan girls can satisfy, which is also more or less true. Yes, he's pleased to see her back in his sulky sort of way, but Ilse's not so sure. She doesn't really want—as opposed to need—her, nor does Willibald. Neither of them wants the tornado back in the house, that tempest of energy that exhausts while it saves. Willibald has of course another reason besides peace and quiet why he'd prefer her not to be there, his now not-so-plump Aryan lady-friend in Plinden, with whom in his famished dreams he daily communes. But that's a reason we don't know of yet.

As for Sara and me, we're just numb. We're the only ones who never doubted she was dead, and initially we can't believe she isn't. *Is this really her?* is my question for a day or two. And when that's settled, *Is she going to disappear again?* After about a week I've been persuaded she won't, except in the usual way that people do by getting ill and dying, and I don't think she's going to do that just yet. So she isn't going to simply not be there again one morning when I wake up. Sara, being older, has another and more refined dimension to her doubts. It isn't physical disappearance that bothers her, but psychological. In fact for Sara Gabi hasn't really come back at all. She lost her in that nuns' house at the end of the lake, grieved for her throughout those last long months of war and eventually accepted her loss. What was there is gone and cannot be replaced, and Gabi's return doesn't alter that one bit. Because things just aren't the same. Nothing ever can be quite the same again. Jesus may have been resurrected, but the world's gone on, and there's no place in it for Jesus anymore. She's concluded in some deep part of her that nothing good lasts, life is a succession of losses. Heraclitus without the bullshit. Yes, Sara carries loss around with her as Ilse carries her own patent physical disorder, like a wasting disease, a shadow on the lung of life.

So one way or another Gabi must feel disappointed by her reception. But she's soon got things to do that take her mind off that, because everyone is nearly dying. It's as though she's merely exchanged one hospital for another. The worst is still the hunger. The shooting's over all right, but the starving still goes on. We don't have relatives on farms, we certainly don't have money, and the rest of us don't have energy either. But hunger isn't all. Willibald's heart's so irregular it sometimes doesn't beat at all for five or six seconds before it switches on again, when it gallops along as though it's desperately trying to catch up with itself. And Ilse's gone blind in one eye and drags her foot still more as though she's had a stroke. People say proper food and medical supplies won't get through until the autumn or the winter; but the question is, will we? Not that we're alone. There are thousands of refugees from the camps, from the East, or just from the devastated cities, looking for food and shelter all over Europe, and a lot of them will never find it.

Did that long diet of nettles dull my memory, by the way, or is it some need to forget that makes me unable to remember how or when it was that Gabi told us of her escape and life in Graunau? I'll always remember the story, mind. Just not remember how I learned it. Did she sit down and tell us one day? I don't know, but I suspect she didn't have the time. Did she let it out in dribs and drabs? I'll never recall. Nor will I ever hear it from her lips again in later life. She's going to pull the shutter down and never look inside that room again. Somehow I absorbed the tale without absorbing how.

■

Well anyway we lie about listlessly while Gabi surveys the last of our furniture, glass and plate and considers how and where to sell it. And then off she goes at four in the morning, still wearing Frieda's uniform, which has become a talisman for her, hiking to the farms and villages for miles around, bartering plates and saucers for butter, offering crystal wineglasses for cheese and eggs. At first she only goes to places she can reach on foot, because there isn't any transport. But as the trains start clanking along again, she travels further afield. Soon our sideboard's empty, and she's taking bids for the sideboard itself, and the grandfather clock and the piano from the living room. As she can't imagine how she'd get them out of the house without Willibald's having a heart attack, she takes down payments on them for later delivery. She's even considered nabbing a few books from Willibald's library, but something warns her there's no market in farmhouses for leather-bound volumes of Schiller and Hegel. Besides, Willibald would be sure to miss them.

By the time the autumn chill sets in, so does some sort of food supply, and the worst is over. But Gabi's still selling what she can for the extra vitamins that Willibald and Ilse in particular need. I go with her one day before school starts again—yes, peace does mean we can go back to school—because she simply can't carry all our wares herself. Martin's stronger than me and could carry more of course, but he's far too busy looking after number one to start looking after anyone else. We find ourselves offering sheets and blankets to the very farmer whose fields Martin worked before he embarked on his short-lived military career in the ragtag People's Army—which, incidentally (the career, I mean; he no longer cares about the People's Army), his reminiscences ornament with various acts of selfless heroism, just like his father.

The farmer's daughter's eyes do a little jig when she hears Martin's name, but her father shakes his head at what Gabi has to offer before she's even had a chance to get it out of the bag. "No thanks, the only thing we haven't got is gold earrings for the cows." But he gives us six eggs and a slab of cheese anyway. Gabi's a useful person to know—now. His daughter asks me to tell Martin he should come by and see them sometime. By now I'm of an age to sense that "them" meant "me," and to deliver the message when Martin is alone. But this delicacy did not move Martin to reciprocate. He treats girls he's had like worn-out penis gourds and merely tosses his head and gives a sniggering little laugh.

Willibald's a useful person to know now, too. In fact there are about two hundred people who've suddenly discovered how useful. They all want to know him these days, although none of them wanted to a few short months ago. Nearly every day they come, from Plinden, Salzburg and Vienna, and even from what's left of Berlin and Leipzig. All of them want testimonials, and many of them have written them themselves, so all that Willibald has to do is sign them. Some even come with typewriters in their rucksacks, carbon copies already inserted, in case he wants to add a word or two of his own. All of them are unctuous smilers, bowing to the Frau Pfarrer, still in her nurse's uniform, as they declare how pleased they are that everything's turned out all right. Even Pfarrer Kretschmann from Vienna, who had our Saint Bernard and our rabbits taken away, and the widow of Ortsgruppenleiter Franzi Wimmer, who used to spy on us—they too expect Willibald to declare what worthy citizens they were and how they did all they could to help us in the war. Pfarrer Kretschmann cunningly contrives to arrive when Gabi's out on one of her trade missions to the local farmers, and to disappear before she returns. Frau Wimmer artfully sends Lisl, becomingly got up in mourning black, to make the plea on her behalf, and Lisl drops a few tears as well to remind Willibald of her martyred father's devotion to our welfare. "And how are you, Martin?" she asks brightly when she's got her testimonial signed. But Martin's got another kind of itchy feet, now his blisters are all gone, and he's anxious to be off to fairer fields where other cherries grow to pop. He answers her in the easy faintly sneering tone of someone turning down used goods.

All this signing tires Willibald out. It also reminds him of that far-off time when he was endorsing copies of baptismal entries for ancestral certificates, those guarantees of Aryan pedigree that many of the current testimonial-hunters needed then to advance their career in the Party whose name today they dare not speak. But, weak as he is, he signs the latter now as readily as he signed the former then. He just likes being fawned on.

Doktor Saur-that-was and her husband come from Vienna too, to get a testimonial for each of them. She's stopped being a Nazi (who hasn't?), but doesn't hide the fact she was one once.

She doesn't know yet whether to believe what the Allies say about the death camps. Might that not just be propaganda? Where did she think the Viennese Jews all went, then, during the war? "To labor camps in the East," she answers blankly. "Didn't you?" Some delusions really do die hard.

Her husband is tall and erect, and Martin envies him his two-inch duelling scar. He's distantly correct, if not courteous, too, and seems to think it's he who's doing us a favor, not the other way round. He does condescend to mention though that his career suffered because he never joined the Party, and because on legal and administrative grounds (he doesn't mention moral) he opposed the orders for the transportation of the Jews. They were, he said, "irregular." Every pedant has his day.

Doktor Saur-that-was is outwardly as good-tempered and genial as ever. But not inwardly. She means to leave her husband at last, she confides when she asks Gabi if she's got any calamine lotion to spare. (Gabi hasn't. She hasn't got anything to spare.) Despite her husband's devilish legal cunning, the injured wife believes the new regime will be more disposed than the old to grant her a divorce and custody of her newborn daughter. Her resolve is fortified by the thought of this child, with and for whom she imagines she'll live till the end of her days. Another delusion taking root.

Herr Ziegler, the owner of the brick factory in Plinden, arrives one morning too, driving his own car, which is a novelty these days. He's had big orders in the past to supply fire-resistant bricks for crematoria in the East. That's a strike against him, but on the other hand he's one-eighth Jewish, which cancels it out. So a testimonial about how he employed Martin in his hour of need would put him in credit—particularly since he's got a contract with the Amis now. They want bricks too, though not, they say, for crematoria.

And then there's Willibald's brother Harald, who hasn't

heard from his son Robert for several months and fears he may have gone the way of gallant Luftwaffe hero Erwin. Onkel Harald can't come to Heimstatt in person for his testimonial, because he's languishing in an internment camp, but he does write and ask his younger brother to declare how nice he's always been to Gabi and the children. Well, it's true, he sent us all birthday and Christmas greetings, and even let Gabi into Erwin's memorial celebration. So Willibald sends him his testimonial too. Not that it gets him off a denazification course and heavy doses of Civics 102, an Ami freshman course in good citizenship hastily adapted for middle-aged Nazis.

All the other supplicants are as obsequious as Willibald would be to a field marshal, which is about as obsequious as you can get. All except Dr. Schmidt, who's been informed his son Heinrich finished the war disgracefully, sticking out his tongue on the wrong end of a rope. Dr. Schmidt doesn't come to us, in fact, although the journey isn't far from Plinden. No, Gabi goes to see him. So he isn't strictly a supplicant at all. It's Martin who urges this course on Gabi. A certain hanged face still swings gently to and fro in Martin's memory, the fair hair flapping blithely in the April breeze as though it doesn't know the head it grows on is stone-cold dead. If Martin's ever hero-worshipped anyone except himself, despite everything it's Heinrich Schmidt, and now the time has come to pay his last respects.

Dr. Schmidt looks cowed, crushed and ashamed when Gabi calls on him at his hospital. (What it feels like to be able to walk into the place without fear and trembling!) She gives him her polite if cool condolences, and offers to write some words in his favor. All lies, but it helps him keep his job, and Gabi wants medicine for Willibald and Ilse. "I was sorry for him in the end," she confesses when she returns with a packet of some new wonder drug called penicillin and the promise of more. "Besides,

Martin wanted me to go." She still can't refuse him anything, as she couldn't in the past and will not in the future.

Willibald doesn't say so, but he also provides a testimonial to his Aryan lady-friend in Plinden. She's not got much to cover up, but still she was a member of the Party and a group leader in the League of German Girls as well. A few kind words from Willibald won't do her any harm. At least he's not exaggerating when he declares she provided comfort to him in the war. There's no one Willibald refuses a testimonial to at all, in fact, and I sometimes think he'd give one to the Führer himself if Adolf only asked him nicely.

■

Then the sun declines behind the mountains for its annual snooze, and winter comes to Heimstatt with its frosty icing. So do hefty cardboard cartons from America with *CARE* stencilled neatly on their sides. The cartons contain tins of powdered milk, dried egg, tinned butter and Spam, all paid for by kind Episcopalian or Presbyterian ladies in strange-sounding places like Oregon and Ohio, Memphis and Minnesota. We're the only people in the village to get them because we're the only Nazi victims and we're Lutherans as well. Every one of these packages requires an effusive letter of thanks, which Sara has to write since she's now by far the best at English. Gabi wants to keep the packets coming—they're what's putting Willibald and Ilse on the road to recovery, and also putting flesh on Sara and me. Every time Gabi slits one of those packets crisply open with the carving knife, she imagines a dozen rich old ladies in a large and cheerful church hall, packing it with the goodies that sustain us in benighted war-ravaged Europe. She multiplies that dozen by a hundred million (demography is not her strongest suit) and concludes that America is a land full of milk and honey and teeming with a billion generous people anxious to share their good fortune with the rest of the world. So begins her American Dream.

For the moment we are the lords of the village. Gabi can buy in any store (or could if she had the money), sit on any bench and enter any inn. That's an exhilarating feeling after the last seven years, even if she thinks she'd better still be careful. After all, how long will this last? She can't believe the leopard's changed its spots. As for me, I sense that if I felt vindictive I could probably kick Fritzi Wimmer full in his Aryan crotch and get away with it, even though he's still wearing a black armband while I am not. But actually I like Fritzi, and he likes me. I've even given him some Spam from one of our *CARE* packets, which he said tasted just as good as wurst. So far from being vindictive, I'm only glad I'm back in school now, in the first class of Gymnasium. And Sara's back in her Catholic school as well. Admittedly, we have to make that daily three-hour railway trip to Plinden. We could stay in lodgings during the week now if we wanted, but it costs too much and anyway Gabi's trust in the new order doesn't reach that far. It's almost as though she thinks some Plinden Nazi might still be lurking there to gas us while her back is turned.

Martin and Ilse aren't back in school though. They're too old for that now, so they're getting special preparation to take the *Maturer* or University Entrance Examination. Ilse's recovered her sight, but her leg's still gammy and she's in the Neurological Institute in Bad Neusee, which contains a hundred or so raving, twitching, shell-shocked soldiers, but welcomes her with open arms as well, as if she was quite the proper Aryan now. Not that she's getting any better. Multiple sclerosis is suspected, but no one quite knows what that is or how to tell you've got it, let alone what to do about it if you have. Gabi visits her every day, bringing her books to study and undertaking half the nursing although there are nurses aplenty and Ilse would rather lie alone in peace. She tries in her meek and mild way to persuade Gabi to stay in Heimstatt, unsuccessfully of course. Nearly everything she does is unsuccessful, and she assumes it always will be. It's a reasonable assumption.

But everything costs money, and there are all the debts that Gabi's run up at the shops. She might seem welcome anywhere (though what they really think she doesn't know), but still they want their money. And now that we're no longer outcasts, they think we must be able to pay our way as well. The bills keep turning up insistently on Willibald's desk, and he keeps shouting she must pay them. (One of the changes peace has wrought is that we no longer close the windows when he shouts. But then his voice is pretty feeble now.)

"How can we pay them on your salary?" Gabi asks.

"That's right, blame me for your extravagance!"

You can tell he's getting better. He's even well enough by now to take an occasional trip to Plinden, where he says he's again got parish business, though Plinden still isn't in our parish.

While worrying over her nagging financial problems, Gabi's glance wanders one day across the *CARE* packages that stand neatly stacked along the kitchen wall. We're getting more of them just now than we can use, and she's storing them against the rainy day when they stop coming, as, despite her trust in the wealthy Episcopalian and Presbyterian ladies' generosity, she fears eventually they will. And then lightning strikes her with a revelation as blinding as St. Paul's. We have what the villagers have not—foreign food. And they have what we have not—money. The conditions of trade are present, and trade must duly flow.

So a shop is set up in the disused outhouse by the kitchen, as far away from Willibald's offended gaze as possible. Prices are fixed, Sara and I become assistants and hey presto we're in business. What a tin of Spam or dried milk fetches in times like these! And as for a tin of butter! Taking the money and giving change does wonders for my mental arithmetic too. Just about everyone in the village has bought something before a week is out, even Dr. Kraus's former mistress, now his present wife, and Father Schuster's housekeeper with the little girl who so resembles Father Schuster. So long as the *CARE* packages keep coming, we'll be raking in the money.

And Gabi's doing her best to make sure they do keep coming. The letters she gets Sara to write are models of ingratiating effusiveness, if that's something you want a model of. Whenever Sara tries to tone them down, Gabi insists on retaining the humble superlatives that she believes rich Episcopalian and Presbyterian ladies (and what's the difference, Sara sometimes wonders) lap up like cats do cream. This may improve Sara's English, but it doesn't help her self-esteem. She feels she'll never be able to say thank you again for the rest of her life without squirming inwardly and curling up her toes. But the *CARE* packages do keep rolling in, and trade is certainly flourishing.

Willibald feels uncomfortable about all this. He knows there's something off-color about selling goods that charity's bestowed on us, but on the other hand he enjoys the medicines and other benefits of Gabi's trade, one of which is that the tradesmen have stopped dunning him. Sometimes he talks darkly about Christ and the moneychangers, but he makes no Christlike move to drive them out of the temple. Generally he sniffs like one who disapproves, but smacks his lips over the occasional schnapps and other goodies which Gabi buys him off with. He's secured his moral position by pretending to be above this sordid commerce, to have nothing to do with it, but he downs the penicillin as fast as he can when bronchitis camps on his weakened lungs a few weeks into winter.

Rudi Fischer, a man I think I've never seen before, is the first prisoner of war to come back to Heimstatt. He's been starving too, because he says the Amis who captured him had neglected to order food for all the prisoners they were going to take (or else they hadn't meant to take any prisoners at all), and they certainly weren't going to give them any of their own. But hunger seems to have sharpened both his lust and his wit, unless he was already endowed in head and loins with something keener than the usual Heimstatt portion. In next to no time he's shot his pent-up seed into his wife's receptive womb (she has twins exactly nine months later) and coined a new name for the Pfarrhaus— *The Good Shepherd Emporium.* I'm not sure I like it when Fritzi Wimmer tells me this, and Willibald certainly doesn't when I tell him. In fact he shrieks imprecations, first against Rudi for his blasphemy, then against Gabi for provoking it. Luckily Rudi's a Catholic, so he won't mind a Protestants' curse. And Gabi's used to all his trade tantrums by now, so she doesn't take much notice either. And later on that evening Willibald sits peacefully drinking schnapps in his study, now that penicillin's cleared up his lungs, barking like an excited puppy as *Samson and Delilah* limber up once more on the literary starting blocks.

■

But prisoners of war and *CARE* packages are not the only things the Amis send us. They also send us soldiers, black and white.

The black soldiers are at one end of the village and the white ones at the other. Considering they're all Amis, they don't seem to mix much with each other. In fact it's a bit like it used to be among us with the Aryans and the half-Jews. Is that perhaps why the Nazi racial theory gets inverted, now it's out of favor, and it's not the white soldiers that the children and the young girls of the village mostly cluster round, but the black? Adolf would be turning in his grave if he knew. Or his remaining teeth would anyway, which I believe is all that's left of him by now.

Sara has succumbed to this polar attraction too, and fallen

in a kind of love with a black sergeant who sometimes takes her about with him in his Jeep. This sergeant is an army photographer and takes pictures of Sara for his paper. He also tells her stories of New Orleans, where he was born, and of New York, where he lives. Sara's interest in this American is not like Lisl's in Martin, nor is his like Martin's in Lisl. Her hair is never mussed, her blouse is not unbuttoned. That's not Sara's way, and it's never going to be so. Apparently she reminds the sergeant of his daughter in Harlem, but what is he to her? Does she tell him in her uncertain English the things she can't or won't tell us? Sara never says, and no one thinks to ask. I do notice he's got melancholy eyes, though that's not the word I use ("He looks down in the dumps" is what I say) and gives her chocolate, which she sometimes passes on to me.

Her letters to the Episcopalian/Presbyterian ladies get neglected, her schoolwork isn't properly done, and her stories, the stay and succor of her life till now, lie untouched like outgrown dolls, except they aren't so bulky, underneath her mattress. I take a look one day. I'm getting a bit more interested in them now, although I'm getting much more interested in the magazines that Martin still keeps beneath his mattress. I tell myself I need to find out about these things, it's part of growing up. But I know I'd still do it even if it wasn't.

But Sara's stories—my God, one of them's in English! She started learning English in earnest with Rolf von Haltenstein, I remember, who told her he was going to America after the war if he was still alive. And I knew she was getting good at it—how else could she write all those thank-you letters for the CARE packages? But I never realized she'd got this far. She's actually composed a *story* in that awkward language where they always put the verb in the wrong place! Why is she making it so hard for herself? I ask her when she catches me trying to read it.

She doesn't seem annoyed. It's as if she's discarded all her stories now she's found this black American, and doesn't care what happens to them anymore. "I decided when Mutti died" (that's how we still speak of Gabi's disappearance), "I decided to learn English properly, so that one day I'd never have to speak German again."

It isn't just the Amis who've arrived in Heimstatt, by the way. There are—

21

Soldiers from the other armies too

First-cousin Robert turns up in civilian clothes he's begged or stolen somewhere on his tortuous odyssey from the Eastern Front. And a day or two later second-cousin Wolfgang arrives in a British paratrooper's uniform. He's got a week's leave from Berlin, where he's interrogating captured Nazis and looking for his parents on the side. He's found some Nazis who've never heard of extermination camps or claim they haven't anyway, but of his parents all he's found so far is their former neighbor, who kept the silver coffeepot for them in case they ever returned, together with the receipts for the jewelry they had to surrender before they surrendered themselves. Rings, wristwatches, necklaces, bracelets and brooches, each piece neatly in its proper category. And in the official files, the date on which they and Great Aunt Hedwig were transported to Theresienstadt: December 14, 1943.

■

The four veterans (Willibald includes himself) sit on the upstairs balcony overlooking the tranquil springtime lake and swap military stories which perhaps only Wolfgang has no need to embellish or distort. I hang about watching the sometimes cloudy windows of their souls. Willibald, performing his hackneyed tale of how he shamed a German officer in Poland, gazes into everybody's panes with a theatrical intensity which makes you glance uncomfortably away. Robert, recounting what he's seen done but never done himself, stares fixedly across the lake as though he doesn't want anyone to look through his panes. Martin, telling some fiction of how he saved a wounded comrade from Russian machine-gun fire and was nearly shot himself, looks hopefully into every pane except Wolfgang's, seeking a glimmer of that admiration which he considers his due and cannot live without. Pianistic paratrooper Wolfgang says only how scary it is to jump out of a plane with a parachute on your back and a rifle strapped useless to your leg while people on the ground are popping away at you as if you were a clay pigeon. But he avoids no one's panes and laughs about it as if after all it's only a joke. And I realize that the windows to his soul are as limpid as the soul itself.

Then the schnapps goes round, which Willibald usually reserves for Willibald alone. I want to know what clay pigeons are, but Wolfgang is telling Robert he's sorry about Erwin, and Robert is telling Wolfgang he's sure his parents will turn up soon. There were lots of people in the camps, he says, it's bound to take some time before the inmates all get home, especially if they're in the Russian zone.

"Yes, yes," Wolfgang agrees hopefully, and there's a little silence, in which I could make my clay pigeon inquiry, except that I've been put in mind now of that shabby wretched trio that Martin and I met outside the Botanical Gardens in Berlin three years earlier. And that makes ornithological research seem somehow inappropriate. *Remember us!* I hear Great Aunt Hedwig's imploring voice again, and suddenly I know that Robert's encouragement is empty and Wolfgang's hope unfounded.

Martin and I, who last saw Wolfgang's parents and Great Aunt Hedwig, have seen the last of them as well.

Another round of schnapps, then Wolfgang plays upon the untuned piano which only Gabi knows is mortgaged to the butcher, and says he'll never be a pianist now, because he hasn't got the technique and it's far too late to get it. Never mind, he might take up composing, and he gives us a piece called "Reverie" that he's been working on in his spare time. I haven't heard the piano played since that SS colonel ran the backs of his fingers up and down the keys just after having Franzi Wimmer shot, and though the piece is quite beyond me, I do recognize that Wolfgang's playing is a cut above his. Wolfgang's piece makes my eyes prick as I remember Lotte and Solomon and Great Aunt Hedwig once more. And perhaps it does Gabi's too, because she comes in from the kitchen with floury hands, sits down a moment in unusual quietness, and then goes out again, brushing her eyes with the unfloured knuckles of her wrists.

∎

Soon Wolfgang has gone back to Berlin in his khaki uniform and ballooning cherry-colored beret, and Robert has started on the next leg of his odyssey, which he completes about the time his father is released from his denazification course at last and the tedium of Civics 102.

It isn't long before the Ami soldiers are on their way as well, off to share Vienna with the Ivans, who apparently are not so friendly now. So Sara's going to lose her black sergeant too, just as she earlier lost Rolf and Gabi. The Amis leave before dawn one chilly April morning, and Sara gets up secretly to make her sad farewell. She stands outside the Pfarrhaus to wave to the sergeant, but for a long time the sergeant doesn't come.

Truck after truck grinds past, first the white troops, then the black, and she's almost given up, rigid with frozen tears when at last the sergeant's Jeep appears. She's afraid he's going to drive past without noticing her, but at the last moment the Jeep stops while the other vehicles growl by. Out steps the sergeant to take a final picture of this teenage Austrian village girl, and then he helps her into the Jeep, drives her slowly through the village and helps her out at the other end. Before he drives away he gives her a last chocolate bar and scrawls his Harlem address on the wrapper. She stands forlornly watching till the Jeep's red tail-light fades like a dying cigarette and disappears.

Another departure, another loss.

She comes back with deeply hollow eyes, and Gabi's furious. So is Willibald when he gets up as usual three hours later. So there are still some things they can agree upon. Sara doesn't speak—she's too full of loss, if emptiness can make you full. And she doesn't eat the chocolate either. But she tells me I can if I peel the wrapper off without tearing it and give it back to her. It's not the first time I've done well out of her poor appetite. She smooths the wrapper out and keeps it in the pages of her stories, which she now takes up again like a disillusioned voyager returning home.

A few weeks later a picture arrives through the post. There she stands by the Pfarrhaus door, small and thin for her age, bereft and sad. Her eyes look startled as well, because the sergeant used a flash, which she'd never seen before. She places the photo next to the wrapper in her exercise book and lays it on the desk beside her whenever she writes in it. As though to remind herself of what she has been and will never be again.

■

And then I hear Jägerlein's voice on the stairs one May morning, a morning which is apparently the anniversary of the Nazi surrender. She's back and she's reciting that poem about the cuckoo calling in the woods that I first heard from her lips in Annchen's company, when I was nine or ten. It almost makes me think that things are normal again, although I'm still not sure what normal is.

Jägerlein moves back into her old room behind the kitchen and tells us how much she still misses fat Annchen and skinny François. She even asks Gabi to describe all the French prisoners she nursed in Graunau, in case one of them might turn out to have been hers. But Gabi isn't good at describing French prisoners and doesn't remember anyone called François.

Jägerlein sets to work, washing, cleaning and cooking. On Sundays she goes to listen to, or at least attend, Willibald's morning sermon. "Who else will, if I don't?" she asks Gabi, who somehow never finds the time to go herself. The answer's eight or nine. I wonder if she'd still go if she knew what we all know about how Annchen was discovered on her sister's farm.

And now Fraülein Hofer's sewing for us once more too, although she's grown so much thinner and frail-looking that Gabi gives her an occasional tin of eggs and Spam to buck her up. Resi doesn't come with her now, she's staying with her seven-fingered grandmother (I'm not counting the thumbs), who's gone dotty because her son—Resi's father—never came back from the war. The old woman's started going to the ferry pier and waiting for him all day long until the last ferry in the evening, a ritual that will last as long as she does. Resi has to cook her meals and coax her back to eat them.

I feel the lottery winner's guilt. Resi's father didn't return from Russia, whereas my mother did return from the grave. Why me? Why her? Whoever's running this show, he isn't very fair. But I'm relieved that Resi doesn't come with Fraülein Hofer, all the same. I wouldn't know what to say to her except "D'you want to play Skat?" But suddenly we're too old for the kind of Skat you play with cards and too young for the kind that Martin played with Eva. Sara's right: things change.

And change in other ways as well. Now that summer's sun's

come flooding through the windows, the *CARE* packages have stopped flowing through the door. The Episcopalian and Presbyterian ladies in Omaha and Idaho have found other causes to support, and God knows there are plenty of them. Our *CARE* cartons come in only a thin erratic trickle now, and for all Gabi's efforts and Sara's improved effusive English, that trickle's slowly drying up. So in consequence is trade. *The Good Shepherd Emporium*'s stocks are running low, its profits dwindling.

But Gabi's expenses are increasing. Martin's passed his examination and is off to Vienna to study engineering, where he expects to lay the foundations of a brilliant career. And with a bit of affirmative action, and to great surprise as well, Ilse's passed her examination too. She took hers as a patient in the Neurological Hospital at Bad Neusee, and Willibald, in the guise of her father and spiritual adviser, was able to supply her surreptitiously with the answers to the Latin test. Apparently without a thorough knowledge of that ancient tongue you can't go far in modern medicine—which, following Maria's posthumous suggestion, it's Ilse's sad ambition to do. She wants to learn to heal herself, and maybe heal the pagans too.

If Willibald ever does anything for any of his children, it's always silent Ilse that he does it for first. They share the same fate, living too long too near a restless fire which scorches when it merely seeks to warm, and that has forged a bond. Besides, she's the only one of his brood who takes religion seriously. She even goes along to church twice a day on Sundays, which sometimes gets the congregation into double figures. Willibald's affirmative action took the form of leaving the answers to the Latin test behind the cistern in the bathroom, which Ilse naturally must drag herself to in the course of her three-hour examination. So Ilse, who can never tell a lie, and her father, who can but isn't supposed to, have managed to cheat, and now she's been accepted to study medicine in Innsbruck, though how she'll get through the course, nobody knows. Least of all her anxious, astonished and probably self-reproaching self.

But all this is going to cost money, piles of it, far more than we have got. Ilse will have to go and live in Innsbruck, Martin in Vienna. They'll need money for travel, food, rent and books. The *CARE* carton stream's drying up and we've scarcely got enough to feed ourselves in Heimstatt as it is. How's it to be done? For herself, Gabi lives only in the present, but when it comes to her children's education, she sees the future clearly, and she sees it will not work.

And that is when the parish in Vienna floats into tantalizing view.

■

A black Mercedes rolls through the whole length of the village one August afternoon, just like the one the Gestapo arrived in last year after Gabi disappeared. The car stops ominously outside the Pfarrhaus, and with a quiet lurch in my stomach I half expect to see the same two thugs get out. But when the chauffeur opens the door, it's a brace of stiff clergymen that emerge, dressed undertaker-like in black trousers and tails; in fact I think they *are* undertakers at first, until I spot their white clerical collars. A reasonable assumption, since Willibald has conducted a funeral early this very morning.

The two ravens stalk companionably towards the front door, which, since I'm there, I open for them. The strains of Bing Crosby's gooey crooning on the US Forces network greet them from our returned wireless, which Martin repaired some time ago with a valve supplied by the obliging black US sergeant that Sara fell in a kind of love with. "Bishop Gutmann," the shorter and plumper raven announces, indicating the longer and thinner, and "Superintendent Schwartz," indicating himself. He concludes with an avuncular smile.

Unused to ecclesiastical visitations, I gape up at them, while behind my back Bing Crosby gets abruptly throttled in mid-croon.

"From Linz," Superintendent Schwartz explains, indicating himself this time. And then, indicating Bishop Gutmann, "From Vienna." As I'm still gaping, he continues, "Are you Pfarrer Brinkmann's son?"

I feel on surer ground here, although perhaps I shouldn't, and nod dumbly.

"We've come to see your father," Superintendent Schwartz remarks, with the air of an archangel dropping manna from heaven upon the children of Israel, which may very well be exactly how he feels. "Can you tell us where he is?"

I can, but do not need to, because Gabi's hand is now placed on my shoulder and I'm firmly steered aside. "Ah, Frau Pfarrer Brinkmann!" the smiley duo now chirp together, and a moment later, "Ah, Brother Brinkmann!" with even greater delight as Willibald appears with an ingratiatingly welcoming bow. He isn't much used to ecclesiastical visitations either, and he gives a rather weak and foolish giggle. It's lucky there was that funeral this morning, otherwise he might have had to greet them in his nightshirt.

The two ravens spend a few moments making courteous and even deferential motions towards Gabi, and say how glad they are to see her and how much they hope she's well. (Considering how pleased they seem to see her now, it's a bit surprising they forwent that pleasure through the long years of the war.) But it's Brother Brinkmann they've really come to see, even though it's only because of Gabi that they've come at all.

Gabi prepares coffee and cakes, courtesy of dwindling *CARE,* and Sara helps her carry them into the study, where the holy trinity are talking small. I drift in with them, and Gabi is about to ease us both out when the Bishop says, "No, no, Frau

Pfarrer," in a resonant voice. "Let them stay. Suffer the little children . . ." although we're hardly little children anymore. He refrains from completing the quotation, either because he recognizes this is so, or else for fear he might appear to be assuming his Master's place as well as His voice, although to judge by the Superintendent's swift lidded glance, that damage has already been done.

Sara and I get a bit of cake and some weak coffee, and after the others have dabbed the crumbs off their lips and said how nice it was, the Bishop gets up, flaps the tails of his frock coat, sits down again and then stands up once more. I judge this means he's about to broach the subject of his visit. The Superintendent meanwhile folds his hands over the gentle mound of his portly stomach and gazes expectantly up at his superior's face.

"Brother Brinkmann," the Bishop begins, "you may have guessed why we've come to see you?" He pauses to give Brother Brinkmann the chance to acknowledge he has, but Brother Brinkmann only smiles bewilderedly as if the Bishop was speaking Serbo-Croat. "You suffered a great deal during the war, because of the er, on account of the policies regarding er, non-Aryans." He looks at Gabi now and nods discreetly. "Particularly you, Frau Pfarrer. Though not of course you alone."

Gabi looks faintly guilty, as if she's been presuming on her victimhood, and drops her eyes.

"But now we can repair the damage," the Bishop continues with an expansive smile. "What would you say to a parish in Vienna, Brother Brinkmann?"

"Vienna?" Brother Brinkmann repeats blankly, as if he's never heard of the place.

"Yes, Vienna." The Bishop rolls the word round his tongue like a tasty morsel. "Vienna, Brother Brinkmann. Vienna." You can tell he likes the sound of his voice. And why not? It's certainly a ringing one. I could imagine it filling a cathedral. Even Willibald at his best would have trouble matching that, and Willibald's no slouch when he gets going either. "The parish has just become vacant owing to the retirement of Brother er, of Brother . . . ?" He glances appealingly at the Superintendent, who mouths a word he can't quite get. "Yes. And the salary there would be three . . . ?" Again he sends a visual SOS to the Superintendent, who now smugly signals back with four outstretched pudgy fingers. "*Four times* your present one here in Heimstatt. Four times, Brother Brinkmann! It's a large parish with a professional congregation—doctors, teachers, lawyers and so on. It needs a good preacher such as yourself And your children's education, which was so sadly, er, interrupted during the war—as were so many others'," he smartly adds with a cautionary glance at Gabi which causes her modestly to drop her eyes again—"that can be very well taken care of there, whereas here in Heimstatt—well, it's really a single man's parish, isn't it? Not for someone with a large family. Now, Brother Brinkmann," he rubs his hands together as though he's about to tuck in to another round of coffee and cakes, "what do you say?"

What does Brother Brinkmann say?

Nothing at first. That present cynosure of every eye still looks bewildered. We see his lips are trembling slightly with emotion, but it's not the emotion we all think it is. The Bishop and the Superintendent are gazing at him like two genial uncles giving a birthday treat to their awkward spindly nephew. Gabi's regarding him almost fondly again. Sara and I are thinking *Vienna! We won't have to get up at four every day to go to school!* At the same time I'm watching the razor nick on Willibald's Adam's apple going up and down as he swallows. It has deposited a little crust of blood on his otherwise immaculate white collar, which, now that Jägerlein is back, no longer goes to Pels for laundering. What a pity Ilse isn't here, I'm thinking. She's still in the hospital in Bad Neusee, but expected to come out next week. And what a pity Martin isn't either. He's probably in another of the village blondes.

No, they aren't here for this historic moment. They'll be sorry when they find out.

The expectant silence stretches out until it seems it's got to snap. "Oh I wouldn't like to profit from a political change," Willibald says tremulously at last, looking anywhere except at Gabi. "I think I'd rather stay here with my Heimstatt people. I couldn't desert them now, after all they've done for us . . ."

Sara and I glance at each other in the ensuing astonished hush and see the same amazed inquiry reflected in each other's irises. "What *they* have done for *us*"? We can't think of more than two or three who've done anything at all, though that precious few have certainly done much. How could we know that Willibald's thinking the political wind might change again, the Nazis might come back, and where would he be then? Or that he's terrified of the Red Peril, the Bolshie Ivans in Vienna? Or that he's worked out in a flash that his duties in Vienna could hardly extend to making parish visits to a once-more plump ex-Nazi lady in Plinden? No, we know none of that. We go back to thinking dismally of that interminable ferry and train journey to school, both ways in the cold and dark.

But our thoughts and the astonished hush are scattered by what sounds and looks like apoplexy from the region where Gabi sits perched on the edge of her chair, a coffee cup at first halfway to her mouth, then halfway to the floor. She's managed to take a mouthful of steaming coffee in an attempt to stifle Kaminsky-wise the outraged scream that's rising up her gorge, but now she's caught between letting the coffee peel the skin off her throat and spitting it back into the cup. She chooses what she conceives to be the politer alternative, which is certainly the warmer one, and is now spluttering like a woman drowning in burning oil.

Willibald is the only person who doesn't notice, or rather affects not to notice, this. His foolish giggly simper has returned, revealing to those like Sara and me who know him well that he's hugely embarrassed in front of the reverend duo and simultaneously both terrified of what he'll have to face when they're gone and indignant that he'll have to face it. To divert attention from his wife's gasping and coughing, he repeats what he's just said.

The Bishop and the Superintendent glance at each other in puzzled dismay. The uncles' birthday treat has gone all wrong.

"But Willibald, the children's education!" Gabi croaks piteously at last in a husky scalded whisper.

Willibald's giggly look grows stubborn now. "We don't want to take advantage of a change in the political wind," he declares sternly to her, but so that all can hear once more. That's the third time he's said it, so presumably he really means it. Perhaps he wasn't quite sure when he first gave his answer, perhaps he'd even have let himself be talked round. But now that Gabi's shown her shock before the reverend duo, he feels humiliated, and digs his heels in with all the obstinacy of a weak man cornered.

The Bishop asks nevertheless if that really is his final answer. Willibald's giggly simper widens slowly to become a stubborn foolish grin, which the Bishop takes to indicate it is.

Eventually the two ravens flap the wings of their frock coats in disappointment and make to leave. Gabi is still speechless, but she won't be once they're gone. Willibald conducts them to the car, where the driver, who's been smoking a furtive cigarette, hides it in the cupped palm of his hand until he's closed the door on them and can drop it safely on the ground. Willibald waves a brotherly goodbye for as long as he can, putting off the dreaded moment when he must face his injured and insulted wife.

"Have you gone mad?!" she demands hoarsely as soon as he's stepped reluctantly back inside the door. "Have you no thought for your children? How are they going to go to university now?"

Willibald gesticulates feebly and declares for the fourth time that he's not going to take advantage of a change in the political wind. He should set that theme to music. They'll manage somehow, he adds as he makes a dignified withdrawal to the study. And Gabi should economize more, he further adds as she follows him in hot pursuit. She's so extravagant, and always has been.

"Extravagant? Me?!"

"And if the worse comes to the worst, Martin and Ilse will just have to work for their living instead of going to university." That comes out a touch self-righteously, as though he's been doing all the hard work so far, while they've been idly wasting his substance.

"Not go to university?! You don't want them to go to university?!"

"I didn't say that."

You can see Willibald's hoping to get angry himself soon, but at the moment shame or guilt is keeping him in mild-protest mode, and it's only when Gabi calls him a heartless selfish mockery of a father that he can begin to work himself up. Then his voice rises and his eyes flash.

"*Heartless?*" he shouts. "*Selfish?*" And then loudest of all, "*Father?!*"

It isn't long before the thud of hurled books and the crash of falling pictures sounds and resounds from the study. Passing with some laundry to the kitchen, Jägerlein tranquilly remarks during a brief lull in the conflict that the Herr Pfarrer always does shout a lot when he gets upset.

The battle ends only when Gabi suddenly screams a different scream, staggers out of the study gasping and clutching her side and collapses on a chair. Another gallbladder attack—the first, I realize, since she returned from the dead. "We can't go on like this, we *can't*," she groans through her agony. "We *can't*!"

Now Willibald emerges too, stares at us with wild and weepy eyes, silently mouths words he can't or maybe daren't speak aloud, then clenches his fists and beats his head like a crazy drummer before retreating back into his sanctum.

Sara and I no longer take cover behind the kitchen stove on these occasions. That's another phase of life that's passed. But as she goes to boil the water for Gabi's steaming poultices, she glances at me with a look of numb and dumb despair that seems to say that Gabi's right, we can't go on like this—but probably we will.

"What about your homework?" Gabi gasps at me now between her agonized and agonizing moans. Even now education's on her mind. "Have you done your Latin?"

As I trudge slowly but obediently upstairs, I come across Sara's exercise book where she must have dropped it when she went to Gabi's aid. The black sergeant's photo of her peeps out of it, and the wrapper I peeled off that chocolate bar she let me eat not long ago. I take the book with me to my bedroom and lay it on the desk beside Livy's tedious *History of Rome*. But I do not open Livy. I open Sara's exercise book instead where it enfolds her photo and begin to read. Have I reached the age when Sara's dark imagination will speak to me at last?

■

Once upon a time there was a mother and her daughter. "Listen," the girl's mother said one day, "I'll tell you a story, a very old story. You are old enough to hear it now. It's a story, and yet it's true. People tell it and then they forget it. And then they remember it again—but only when it's too late."

The girl listened. And while she listened she began braiding her long black hair.

"It started long ago," her mother began. "And yet not so very long ago at all. And it was far away, and yet not so very far. It was

in another village, not like our village, and yet not so very different after all . . ."

Her mother began to sound strange, and the girl felt uneasy. She let her hair fall loose. She stood up and touched her mother's hand. It felt as cold as stone.

Her mother stirred at her touch and went on speaking in a strange hoarse voice. "One day the church bells began pealing loudly, from one end of that village to the other, just as they are now in ours, and there was great excitement in every street. All the people stopped work and gathered in the market square. They had heard there was to be a festival that day, a wonderful festival, a time for renewing all that was good in their village and ridding it of what was bad."

Her mother's eyes widened suddenly and she glanced round in alarm, as if startled by some sudden sound. The girl touched her hand again. "It's only the church bells pealing," she told her mother.

"Yes," her mother went on. "Everyone was excited. They were standing crowded together in the square, all pressed shoulder to shoulder, chattering and impatient, waiting for the festival to begin."

Again her mother hesitated and again the girl looked up. Her mother wasn't smiling at the happiness of the people in the story, but staring about her, staring with fearful eyes, her mouth open, her lips pale and dry.

And then suddenly the girl heard beneath the sound of the church bells pealing something that her mother had already heard. It was the steady tramp of marching feet, the tramp of soldiers, strange men she had never seen before, with shining jackboots and shining guns. Her mother shuddered and uttered a choking wordless sound.

And then the soldiers were all round them. The girl was frightened now, she wanted to run away. But her mother sat there motionless. There was terror in her mother's eyes, and yet she did not try to escape. Some of the soldiers took her mother away and the girl could only watch, because others were holding her still. Then they took her away too, they dragged her to the market square. There was a large crowd there, but a space had been cleared in front of the church, and everyone was silent, watching the space. The great old wooden doors of the church were closed and locked, and the bells had all stopped pealing.

"Look," said one of the soldiers as he pushed the girl to the front of the crowd. And when she looked, she saw her mother standing all alone in the middle of the clearing in front of the church. All alone she stood there, her hands behind her back, staring down at the ground as though she was ashamed. Her lips seemed to be moving, but no one could hear what she was saying. She stood there between the church and the fountain, her head bowed as if she knew she was guilty, yet didn't know what she was guilty of.

"Mother!" the girl cried, but her mother took no notice. Perhaps she did not hear her daughter's voice. The girl tried to go to her mother, but the soldier held her back, his hand gripping her arm. Then another soldier went up to her mother. He was holding a pistol in his hand.

And while all the villagers held their breath and watched, there was suddenly a single loud shot. Her mother's head jerked, she staggered backwards and fell down. She lay there very still, her lips no longer moving. But after a moment blood began trickling out of her mouth. Now the soldier who had been holding the girl let her go. He gave her a shove and she ran over to her mother and knelt down and whispered into her ear.

"Get up!" she whispered. "Get up! Let's go home." But her mother would not get up. She would not look at her either. Her eyes stared fixedly at the cobblestones where her blood was draining away, as though that was all that mattered to her now or ever would again.

Everyone was watching the girl, almost as though they too were stunned, and the hushed silence stretched out longer and longer, as if it would never break. But then the soldiers started cheering, and then someone in the crowd cheered too, and then someone else and *someone else. And before long everyone was shouting and cheering. The cheering flooded back through the crowd like a wave that came and passed and came again. The people leaning out of their windows were the last to cheer, but when they did, they cheered the loudest, as if to prove they were as eager as the rest of them to show how pleased and happy they were.*

After some time—it might have been one hour or many—the crowd began to leave the market square. The villagers all shook hands with each other and wished each other goodnight. Everyone said what a wonderful festival it had been and how much better the village was going to be now. But the girl stayed kneeling by her mother's body.

Then some men came with a cart and took the dead woman away. When the girl tried to go with her, they knocked her to the ground and kicked her. She lay where she had fallen, staring at her mother's blood drying beside her cheek.

Soon it was suppertime in the little village, and behind the shutters there was the smell of steaming soup and dumplings. When they had all eaten their fill, the villagers went to bed and fell sound asleep. But the girl lay there still on the cobblestones outside the church, half asleep and half awake, unable to move.

Hour after hour she lay there, until, when the moon was at its highest and its pale light reached her slumping body, a tall man in a long black cloak with a face serene and dark as night appeared in the marketplace. He went to the girl and raised her in his arms. Wrapping the folds of his cloak round her, he carried her slowly away from the closed church. He walked along the crooked streets, onto the road that led through the peaceful fields, out into the countryside towards the next village. Into that village he carried her, and through that village into the next, and then into the next village and the next after that.

Through one village after another the tall dark figure walked, night after night, month after month, year after year, looking for a place where he could set the girl down safe at last and she could live in peace.

   And he is walking still.

   Fable, Sara's written in her large round hand above this story. But it seems to me she might just as well have called it *History.*